The O. Henry Prize Stories 2005

The O. Henry Prize Stories 2005

Edited and with an Introduction by
Laura Furman

Jurors
Cristina García, Ann Patchett,
Richard Russo

ANCHOR BOOKS
A Division of Random House, Inc.
New York

The Series Editor wishes to thank Sue Batterton, Rebecca Bengal, Peter Short, and Susan Williamson for their help and good company during our long talks about short stories, and the staff of Anchor Books.

To JWB, SCFB, and KS, thank you for your love at home. *LF*

Note to the Reader: As of this collection, *The O. Henry Prize Stories* will be published in January rather than October. The present collection was chosen from stories published in 2003. The next collection, *The O. Henry Prize Stories 2006*, will be selected from stories published in 2004.

AN ANCHOR BOOKS ORIGINAL, JANUARY 2005

Copyright © 2005 by Vintage Anchor Publishing, a division of Random House, Inc.
Introduction copyright © 2005 by Laura Furman

All rights reserved under International and Pan-American Copyright Conventions. Published in the United States by Anchor Books, a division of Random House, Inc., New York, and simultaneously in Canada by Random House of Canada Limited, Toronto.

Anchor Books and colophon are registered trademarks of Random House, Inc.

Permissions appear at the end of the book.

Cataloging-in-Publication Data for *The O. Henry Prize Stories 2005* is on file at the Library of Congress.

ISBN 1-4000-7654-4

Book design by Debbie Glasserman

www.anchorbooks.com

Printed in the United States of America
10 9 8 7 6 5 4 3 2 1

Publisher's Note

MANY READERS have come to love the short story through the simple characters, easy narrative voice and humor, and compelling plotting in the work of William Sydney Porter (1862–1910), best known as O. Henry. His surprise endings entertain readers, even those back for a second, third, or fourth look. One can say "Gift of the Magi" in conversation about a love affair or marriage, and almost any literate person will know what is meant. It's hard to think of many other American writers whose work has been so incorporated into our national shorthand.

O. Henry was a newspaperman, skilled at hiding from his editors at deadline. He wrote to make a living and to make sense of his life. O. Henry spent his childhood in Greensboro, North Carolina, his adolescence and young manhood in Texas, and lived his mature years in New York City. In between Texas and New York, he served out a prison sentence for bank fraud in Columbus, Ohio. Accounts of the origins of his pen name vary; it may have dated from his Austin days, when he was known to call the wandering family cat, "Oh! Henry!" or been inspired by the captain of the guard in the Ohio State Penitentiary, Orrin Henry.

Porter had devoted friends in New York, and it's not hard to see why. He was charming and courteous and had an attractively gallant attitude. He drank too much and neglected his health, which caused his friends concern. He was often short of money; in a letter to a friend asking for a loan of fifteen dollars (his banker was out of town, he wrote), Porter added a postscript: "If it isn't convenient, I'll love you just the same." The banker was unavailable most of Porter's life. His sense of humor was always with him.

Reportedly, Porter's last words were from a popular song, "Turn up the light, for I don't want to go home in the dark."

Eight years after O. Henry's death, in April 1918, the Twilight Club (founded in 1883 and later known as the Society of Arts and Letters) held a dinner in his honor at the Hotel McAlpin in New York City. His friends remembered him so enthusiastically that a group of them met at the Hotel Biltmore in December of that year to establish some kind of memorial to him. They decided to award annual prizes in his name for short-story writers, and formed a Committee of Award to read the short stories published in a year and to pick the winners. In the words of Blanche Colton Williams (1879–1944), the first of the nine series editors, the memorial was intended to "strengthen the art of the short story and to stimulate younger authors."

Doubleday, Page & Company was chosen to publish the first volume, *The O. Henry Memorial Award Prize Stories 1919*. In 1927, the society sold all rights to the annual collection to Doubleday, Doran & Company. Doubleday published *The O. Henry Prize Stories*, as it came to be known, in hardcover, and from 1984–1996 its subsidiary, Anchor Books, published it simultaneously in paperback. Since 1997 *The O. Henry Prize Stories* has been published as an original Anchor Books paperback.

Over the years, the rules and methods of selection have varied. As of 2003, the series editor chooses twenty short stories, each one an O. Henry Prize Story. All stories originally written in the English language and published in an American or Canadian periodical are eligible for consideration.

Three jurors are appointed annually. The jurors receive the twenty prize stories in manuscript form, with no identification of author or publication. Each judge, acting independently, chooses a short story of special interest and merit, and comments on that story.

The goal of *The O. Henry Prize Stories* remains to strengthen the art of the short story.

To Anton Chekhov (1860–1904)

Without Chekhov, many of us wouldn't read or write stories as we do, for he showed us that the precise and subtle evocation of a moment can express a character's whole life. Even those who have not yet read him experience Chekhov through other writers who love him and learned from him. Writers as different from one another as Katherine Mansfield, Raymond Carver, and V. S. Pritchett echo Chekhov's sensibility and timing.

Tolstoy said: "In Chekhov, everything is real to the verge of illusion." "The Black Monk," which Chekhov wrote two years before his death, exemplifies Tolstoy's uncanny remark. Kovrin, a brilliant young scholar who suffers from nerves, retreats to the childhood home where he was raised by Pesotsky, a horticulturist with a remarkable garden. Kovrin soon has a vision of a black-robed monk who pronounces him a genius, set apart from all men. Encouraged by this apparition, Kovrin falls in love with Tanya Pesotskaya, his guardian's daughter, and they marry. All seems well—until Tanya overhears Kovrin talking with the invisible monk and persuades her husband that he's mad. Pesotsky eventually loses his masterpiece of a garden; Tanya loses her father and comes to hate her husband; and Kovrin himself, ceasing to see the monk, becomes an embittered mediocrity. As Kovrin is dying of tuberculosis, the black monk reappears, and Kovrin recalls the summer and the beautiful garden where he first saw the monk and fell in love with Tanya. He "feels a boundless, inexpressible happiness," convinced once more, as the monk whispers, that he is a genius. In that moment of contradiction, of madness and belief, Chekhov reveals Kovrin's plight.

With its hero's grandiose hallucinations, the rise and fall of young love, the loss of a beloved parent, and the destruction of dreams of greatness— Pesotsky's and Kovrin's both—"The Black Monk" has the scope of a novel. No one is blameless and no one can be blamed, but this is not casual relativism; it is a cool-eyed vision of how our entanglements can become a strangulation.

Although symptoms of the tuberculosis that eventually killed Chekhov appeared earlier, his first serious, and public, hemorrhage occurred in 1884, when he was twenty-four. From then on, he could no longer deny that he was ill with a disease for which there was plenty of treatment but no cure. He told Gorky, "Living with the idea that one must die is far from pleasant, but living and knowing that one will die before one's time is utterly ridiculous."

A man who spends half his life dying lives in another country, and must watch the healthy and the ill, wastrels and paragons of virtue, with a certain dispassion. It is his almost unnerving combination of remoteness and intimacy, and a controlled depth of emotion, that makes Chekhov indispensable for readers and writers of the short story. He died on July 2, 1904, at a German resort where he went in a last attempt to relieve his illness. One hundred years later, *The O. Henry Prize Stories* celebrates Anton Chekhov's art.

Contents

Introduction

I N THE work of Anton Chekhov, to whom *The O. Henry Prize Stories 2005* is dedicated, one feels a force as powerful as a hurricane moving toward his characters. His knowledge from a young age that he had a terminal illness may account for some of this, but he was also sensitive to the gathering political storm in Russia. The 1905 revolution broke out within six months of his death. Writers and other artists respond to the same political and societal pressures as everybody else. Some explicitly use a political figure or an overwhelming event such as the Vietnam War in their art. Others are engaged by the public tensions of their time without any direct reference to current events.

The twenty writers of *The O. Henry Prize Stories 2005* live all over our planet—a family farm in Kentucky, the city of Perth in Western Australia, urban Florida. Their stories are set in India, Paris, London, Brazil, and New York, also possibly in heaven. Whatever their origin, whatever their private or public inspiration, our Prize Stories are all preoccupied with notions of community. The relationship between individual and society is usually portrayed as a struggle—think of the destruction of Lily Bart in Edith Wharton's *The House of Mirth*. In these O. Henry stories, community and individual appear most often not in opposition but in some kind of disintegrating relation.

·   ·   ·

Among the New York City characters of "Dues," nothing is forgiven, neither a minor crime of property nor a love affair that won't quite die. Dale Peck sprinkles his story with doubles and dualities from the deuce of the title on, but all the odd couples are joined when an ironic community arises from disaster. Another New Yorker, in Paula Fox's "Grace," is opaque to his fellow office-workers and too obdurate for love. It's not because he's in New York that John Hillman is isolated but because he's himself. In the New York of Caitlin Macy's tale of real estate and social distinction, "Christie," well-being is defined by living at the right address, even having the right doorman. The fun of the story is that we root for the narrator's happiness though we know, and hope she knows, that it's unattainable.

Happiness, almost an ecstasy, radiates from Sherman Alexie's "What You Pawn I Will Redeem," a tall tale of an unnamed Spokane Indian's circular attempts, during a drunken twenty-four-hour odyssey, to repossess his grandmother's regalia. In the course of his hero's haphazard encounters, Alexie creates a community of people who, without expecting much, receive, and sometimes give, great gifts.

Kevin Brockmeier's "The Brief History of the Dead" is set in a heaven-like yet down-to-earth city of the dead where acceptance is the norm, a city whose inhabitants are linked by the beat of a communal heart, the "pulse of those who are still alive." The absence of hostility among the city's dead citizens marks the afterlife as an almost enviable place to live.

Port William, the setting of Wendell Berry's "The Hurt Man," is a river town, unplanned and apparently ungoverned, "the sort of place that pretentious or ambitious people were inclined to leave." Berry's is a story about learning from those we live with, told by five-year-old Mat Feltner, who's still wearing dresses and isn't sure if he'll be a boy or a girl, though he's taken a step toward masculinity by learning to smoke cigars and chew coffee beans. He comes to understand that in the best communities we inherit one another's stories and are sometimes remembered by them.

The love triangle in Timothy Crouse's "Sphinxes" begins with piano lessons and completes itself in tragedy. The reader witnesses lovers wrenching apart, friendships dissolving, and the death of a child. Where once there was a sweet group—a family, three friends—by the end there are only individuals suffering separately. In another love story, Michael Parker's "The Golden Era of Heartbreak," the narrator is a runner pursuing respite from his baroquely relentless misery. He seems like the loneliest man on earth, but when he finds himself with company, his misfortune only increases.

Lillian in Nancy Reisman's "Tea" has an unusual and satisfying life. Single, Jewish, she's made a bold peace with her late-1920s community and with her sensuality by sleeping with the men she wants to and allowing herself no emotional involvements. Then she embarks on a new affair, and what begins with desire grows more treacherous. In Gail Jones's "Desolation," an accidental intimacy in Paris between a desperate man and a distant woman affords little comfort to either of them. The story captures both the loneliness and serendipitous companionship of solitary travel.

Three of the Prize Stories draw on history. In Elizabeth Stuckey-French's "Mudlavia," a community of early twentieth-century health seekers offers an alternative to a boy's unhappy home life; that the alternative has its own flaws makes it no less important to his future. At the center of Ben Fountain's "Fantasy for Eleven Fingers" is a rare piece of music that only a talented pianist born with an eleventh finger can play. It is an emblem for what happens to twentieth-century European Jewish life. In Liza Ward's "Snowbound," the young narrator, trapped in a Midwestern blizzard, lightens her loneliness by imagining a long-ago storm that isolated her frontier ancestors.

Exile creates new forms of community. The narrator of Ruth Prawer Jhabvala's "Refuge in London" grows up in a London boardinghouse full of "European émigrés, all of them . . . carrying a past, a country or countries—a continent." Her involvement with a once-famous artist and his rebellious wife affirms the lifeline that making art can be. In Nell Freudenberger's "The Tutor," set in Bombay, a young Indian man, altered by his student years in America, meets an American girl who has grown up in a series of foreign cities; she needs his help to be admitted to an American college. Rather as a surgeon might explore a wound, Freudenberger considers what belonging to a community means for each character.

In Tessa Hadley's "The Card Trick," Gina is an awkward teenager who's ashamed of herself and her background. She visits a beloved writer's house, now a museum, expecting to find herself as much at home as she is in the writer's work; instead she's alienated by the décor and its bourgeois comfort. Years later, her adolescent awkwardness seemingly behind her, Gina returns to the house, and her new reading of it pulls the story to its moving conclusion.

In Charles D'Ambrosio's "The High Divide," Ignatius Loyola Banner is a loner: his mother is dead, his father mad, and he lives in a Catholic orphanage. He befriends a boy who seems to be his opposite—he has a beautiful mother and a father who "rakes it in"—but a camping trip in the Olympic Mountains reveals that where family trouble is concerned, says Ignatius with wisdom and forgiveness, "there are millions of us everywhere." Too much togetherness and easy community demand a high price in Edward P. Jones's "A Rich Man." A recent widower, Horace Perkins finds a bright life with a new group of friends, until, overcome by locusts in the form of women, drugs, drink, and his own weaknesses, Horace is so alone that he must ask in the end: "How does a man start from scratch?"

The startling beauty of the North Carolinian setting of Ron Rash's "Speckle Trout" distracts the reader at first from the corruption at work in Lanny, the young and bored protagonist, and his rural community. When Lanny steals marijuana plants from an inaccessible plantation, he courts disaster and achieves it. Lanny knows the water and the mountains, the meaning of the sky and the local plants, but he is incapable of using his knowledge for his own good.

When her cousin runs in from the beach with the startling announcement that the body of a drowned woman has washed ashore, the narrator of Frances de Pontes Peebles's "The Drowned Woman" comments: "My father would have never allowed Dorany into the dining room like that under normal circumstances." Yet in her family there are no normal circumstances. None of the relationships are what they appear to be, and the truths that emerge shatter their small community.

Jean Strouse, biographer of diarist Alice James and the industrialist J. Pierpont Morgan, once said of biography that "the assumptions we make and the questions we ask about other people's lives serve as tacit guides to our own." This could as easily be said of fiction. Reading stories can transform our natural nosiness into recognition of another person nothing like ourselves.

After a century of modernist questioning of our ideas and institutions, we still long, as Strouse says, "for models of wholeness . . . for evidence that individual lives and choices matter." Models of wholeness, however different from ourselves, can reassure us that in a world that seems large and impersonal, each individual's choices are worthy of our attention.

The reader of fiction doesn't require that models of wholeness be exemplary, only that they be fascinating. For as long as the story lasts, the reader doesn't question whether or not individual lives and choices matter. We are willing captives, relieved for however long of our own burdens and complications.

There is another gift a story may give its reader. Our experience of the finest fiction changes; over time, we will reread the 2005 O. Henry Prize Stories and find new ways to understand and appreciate them.

—*Laura Furman, Austin, Texas*

The O. Henry Prize Stories 2005

Elizabeth Stuckey-French

Mudlavia

from *The Atlantic Monthly*

T HE SUMMER of 1916 would later be known as the last summer of peace. Within a year the United States would be at war, but that summer we still believed that President Wilson could keep us out of it. As a nation, we were told, we were getting bigger, better, and more stylish. Our population had risen to 100 million. Prohibition laws had been passed in twenty-four states. Every household would soon own an automobile. Ostriches, grackles, blackbirds, orioles, egrets, herons, and doves were slaughtered by the thousands so that their feathers could adorn women's hats. Americans were full of all kinds of foolish hope, and my mother and I were no exception.

On the morning of July 20 Mother and I were riding in a small wooden bus over the rutted back roads of Indiana, heading for magical Mudlavia. Every time the bus jounced, I felt a sharp pain in my knee, a pain that shot through the dull ache that had been my constant companion for three months. I was sweating in my wool knickers and jacket, which my mother had insisted I wear. Whenever she saw pain on my face, she drew me against her. I was too hot to be so close to my mother, smelling her too-strong lavender scent, but I was also afraid, and I felt lucky to have her with me. Six other passengers were on our bus, all adults, all traveling alone. One had a cane, three others hobbled on crutches. A fat man had been carried onto the bus by four farmers in Attica. An elderly woman lay flat on a stretcher at the rear of the bus. She kept making little whimpering sounds that drove me mad.

I closed my eyes to the dust, the cripples, my mother's round face, her dimpled chin, her lips pursed with concern, her eyes searching for every nuance of my feelings, and imagined myself, older and more handsome, soaring over a six-foot crossbar as a stadium crowd roared. I was only ten years old, but I was already determined to become an Olympic track star, setting world records in the high jump and the long jump. That summer, because of my knee, I'd had to give up daily jumping practice in my backyard. I was looking forward to our stay at Mudlavia, because without jumping my life had become a bore. My father was often away on business. I was tired of playing silly games with the Dotties, tired of going calling with Mother on Wednesday afternoons. I was also tired of the ache in my knee, but, I must admit, that was the least of it.

Why hadn't I told my parents as soon as my knee began to hurt? Had I sensed how serious it was? Perhaps I feared being totally smothered by my mother's love and concern—which felt stifling under ordinary circumstances. I'll never know why I didn't tell them, but I still take a peculiar pride in the fact that I managed to hide the pain for so long.

The night they found me out, we were putting on one of our plays—my best friends Dottie B. and Dottie G. and I. Each week Dottie B., who wanted to be a writer, wrote a new play. Every one featured the same two characters—a stupid married couple called Susanette and Losenette Floosenette, who were always having "misunderstandings" with friends, family, and everyone they met.

We put on the plays at my house, because my parents had the biggest house on Ninth Street. That night thirty or so neighbor children and parents were sitting on the new rose-colored carpet in our parlor. My mother's precious Globe Wernicke bookcase and her fumed-oak chairs and couch, with their elaborate carvings and spindles, had been pushed back against the wall. The new carpet was displayed to its best advantage.

I was playing Losenette, in my father's suit coat and bowler hat, and Dottie G., in her sister's red nightgown, was my wife, Susanette. We were visiting the Eiffel Tower on a trip we'd won through a soap-flakes sweepstakes. Dottie B. was the gendarme, telling us we couldn't take our dog, Monique, up to the top with us. I was in love with Dottie B. then, and still am to this day.

"But you don't understand," I said, glaring at the gendarme and tweaking my imaginary moustache. "She's a *French* poodle." I put all my weight on my left leg, accommodating the ache in my right one.

"Oui oui, miss-ouer," Susanette said, patting her hair. She clutched my squirming cat, Flip Flop, who was playing Monique. Susanette went on, "We promised her she could see her native Paris from the Eiffel Tower."

A ripple of laughter emerged from the audience. As always, I listened for my mother's laugh, and I heard it.

The gendarme drew herself up. Her reddish gold hair was tucked up under one of my newsboy hats, and she wore a pair of my knickers. So beautiful, Dottie B. "Sorry, *mes amis*," she said in a deep voice. "But what if she should do her business up there?"

This was the riskiest line in the play. Somebody tittered.

"We've come prepared," I said, whipping one of my father's handkerchiefs from my pocket.

"Oui," my wife said. "We'll take it back to Indiana as a souvenir. They'll display it in the courthouse, and people will line up to see it. Because it's French business, you see."

More laughter—a few nervous chuckles from the adults, snickers from the children. I glanced at my mother, who was shrinking back against the wall. My father got up and left the room. To my surprise, instead of feeling afraid, I felt frustrated and angry. The whole purpose of the plays, I realize now, was to insult an audience that didn't even have the sense to be insulted. The Dotties and I were imitating everything we hated about our stuffy parents, but most people thought we were poking fun at someone else, and some, like my father, took offense at a small impropriety and missed the point. I knew I was in for a spanking, so I decided to step off the plank and say something truly awful. Before I could speak, Flip Flop, for no apparent reason, went berserk. He began to twist and claw at Dottie G., who shrieked and held him out to me. I lunged for him, coming down hard on my right leg, which hurt so much that I collapsed in a ball on the floor. My mother rushed to my side. No spanking after all.

Our family doctor diagnosed my problem as rheumatism and suggested a visit to Mudlavia, which he described as a health spa known for its curative mud baths and mineral waters. It was only forty miles southwest of Lafayette, near the state line. Dr. Heath explained that a Warren County farmer, a Civil War veteran, had been digging a ditch near the spot where they later built the spa, and the mud had cured his rheumatism. People from all over went there to take the cure. Medical doctors were on the premises. It was just the ticket, Dr. Heath said.

"Sounds shady to me," my father said at dinner, the night Mother and I told him about Mudlavia. He helped himself to roast beef, clicked on his stopwatch, and began to eat. That summer he was practicing Frederick Taylor's regime of time management. At first he'd tried to impose it on Mother and me, but we'd rebelled by doing everything as slowly as we could, so he gave up and was now bent on improving only himself. He was thirty years old but looked twenty, so he'd taken to wearing rimless spectacles of plain glass and had grown a sleek blond moustache. I suppose he wanted to look more like a school superintendent and less like the man he'd been before he met my mother, a young rake who'd had a tempestuous, short-lived marriage to a woman named Toots Goodall. I'd stumbled on this information one day when I was poking through a box he kept hidden in the back of his closet. I'd found photos of him and Toots. In one of them he was perched on a large, gaudily painted quarter moon, Toots sitting in his lap. When I asked her about Toots, Mother told me about his failed marriage, and made me promise not to mention it to anyone, including him. I thought then that she didn't want to remind him of his earlier, wilder life, fearing that he might decide to go back to it, but she must have known that part of him already had.

While Father fiercely chewed his roast beef, he stared at Mother and me with accusing eyes, as if *we* were hiding something from *him*, and I guess we were—we were hiding the intensity of our desire to go, to get away. "How do we know the place is safe?" he asked Mother.

"It's out in the middle of nowhere," Mother said. "It must be safe. Dr. Heath wouldn't have recommended it."

"I suppose you're right," Father said, clicking his stopwatch. "Two minutes, thirteen seconds. A new record."

Small-town doctors were gods, and to ignore Dr. Heath's advice would be a social snub. Mother had said the right thing.

Mudlavia was tucked back in the woods, up against a hillside. As our bus rounded the last bend, we passengers strained to get a good look at the place that would cure us. The sprawling building was four stories high, green with white trim, and had a wide wraparound porch. In front was a manicured garden, bordered by hedges, with a bubbling limestone fountain in the center. Despite the heat everything looked fresh, even the pink hollyhocks lining the dusty road.

The bus pulled into a dirt lot beside the hotel, and the engine rattled and died. A feeling of peace, along with the dust, settled over me. It was the quietest place I'd ever been. Ninth Street was one of the busiest streets in Lafayette, and all day long we heard the roar of motorcars and the clatter of trolleys struggling up the hill. At Mudlavia, I heard individual sounds—a crow calling in a tree behind me, the atonal tinkling of wind chimes. A side door of the hotel flew open and a group of men, dressed in white, marched toward the bus. A few of them were pushing wheelchairs.

Mother touched my shoulder. "One of those chairs is for you," she said.

"Why? I don't need it." My crutches were beside me, leaning against the seat.

"The doctor here recommends it. It will put less strain on your knee." She bent over and whispered in my ear. "For you, it's only temporary." Her windblown hair, pulled loose from her egret-feather hat, tickled my cheek.

"Your hair's a mess," I said, sounding like my father.

Flinching, she turned away.

"Welcome to Mudlavia." A deep, southern-sounding voice filled the bus. The speaker was one of the men in white—a tall, strong-looking man with a squarish head. "We're here to make your stay with us as comfortable as possible." He spoke as if reading from a prepared speech, and his eyes were trained on a spot at the back of the bus. "Do not hesitate to ask if you are in need of anything, ladies and gentlemen." His eyes shifted to me. "And young fella." He smiled, two front teeth popping over his lip. Every head turned toward me. My mother had tears in her eyes. I bowed my head, embarrassed and pleased to be the center of attention.

At dinner Mother and I sat at a table for four in the dining room, I in my wheelchair, she in a ladder-back chair. There were white tablecloths and huge chandeliers. We picked at our helpings of glazed ham, mashed potatoes, and steamed vegetables from "Mudlavia's Healthful Garden." In the corner of the large dining room a piano player in a tuxedo played popular tunes that we could barely hear over the rattling of dishes and the diners' chatter, some of which, especially from the table next to ours, was raucous.

At that table sat a thin, almost emaciated man with dark, sleek hair who perched on a red rubber cushion. On his right sat a voluptuous young woman with an elaborate, piled-up hairdo. She wore a low-cut, short-sleeved dress made of shiny silver material. On his left sat a woman who had dark hair cut in the new bobbed style, and wore an equally revealing black dress. A huge green parrot sat on her shoulder. The two women nestled in close to the man with the cushion, and all three were laughing loudly, as was everyone else at their table. Everything about these people was overdone, from the timbre of their voices to the sparkle of their jewelry. I'd never seen a parrot outside a cage before. And except for the man with the cushion, none of them appeared the least bit sick.

I couldn't look Mother in the eye. Somehow I felt embarrassed, as if I were responsible for these "unsuitables," as my father would have called them. I wanted to protect her from them, or felt that I should. And more of these big-city types were scattered throughout the dining room. Only a few people, most of them passengers on our bus, had the same scrubbed demeanor we did. We were outnumbered.

Had Dr. Heath ever been here? I wondered, not able to take my eyes off the threesome at the next table.

"One would think," Mother said, frowning at me, "with all the sick people . . ." She didn't finish her sentence, but I knew she meant that our neighbors ought to be more considerate. "I think this place is more of a resort than a health spa." She took another bite of glazed ham, chewing slowly.

"We could leave," I said, knowing I should offer the option. "We could call Father, and he'd come get us." I drained my glass of milk in one swallow, the way I was forbidden to do at home.

Mother didn't notice. She was staring at the man with the cushion. "No," she said. "We'll be here only three weeks."

"Paul Dresser wrote 'On the Banks of the Wabash' at Mudlavia," I reminded her. This was something else Dr. Heath had told us.

"You say the most intelligent things." Mother smiled, giving us permission to enjoy our dinner.

"Good evening." The cushion man stood beside our table. The woman in the silver dress waited there with him, hugging his cushion to her large bosom.

Mother set her fork beside her plate. "Good evening," she said to the man, but she looked at me.

"Your first night here?" His voice was surprisingly soft.

"Of course it is," the woman in the silver dress said. She also had a big nose. "Isn't this the first time we've seen them?"

The man ignored her. "I'm Harry Jones," he said. "This is Sylvia Smith." He kept smiling at Mother in a way that made me afraid he was going to cause trouble, like the villain, Flip, in the comic strip *Little Nemo in Slumberland.*

Mother said, "Nice to meet you," but didn't tell him our names.

"Come on." Miss Smith gave Mr. Jones a little shove with the cushion. "Let these people eat in peace."

"Enjoy the pecan pie," he said, still smiling at Mother in that peculiar way. "We'll get acquainted later."

Mother nodded. Miss Smith gave Harry another gentle shove, and the two of them left the dining room.

Mother said, "'Mr. Jones' and 'Miss Smith.' Do we look that stupid?"

I wasn't quite sure what she meant, but from then on I thought of them as Harry and Sylvia.

"Let these people eat in peace." I imitated Sylvia's rasping voice.

"Why does he have to sit on a cushion?" Mother said.

I choked on my ham, and she spewed iced tea into her napkin. We couldn't quit laughing. Finally we had to abandon our dinners. Still snickering, Mother pushed my wheelchair out of the dining room while everyone stared at us.

Mother and I shared a room, which embarrassed me, but I was also grateful for her company. We took turns undressing behind a Chinese screen in the corner, and later, as I lay on the hard mattress in my four-poster bed, I listened to Mother's even breathing in the next bed and held my aching knee. I stayed awake for a long time, imagining Harry's eyes watching Mother from the corner of the room.

The next morning I had my first mud treatment. Someone rapped on our door at seven to wake us, and Mother and I had a quiet breakfast of eggs and bacon in the dining room. Only a few other guests were there, and they all seemed to be the sick ones—in wheelchairs or bent over their plates in a twisted way. I looked around for the woman on the stretcher who'd been on our bus, and the fat man, but they were nowhere to be seen. They'd get breakfast in bed, I decided. Being among sick people again brought my condition home, and I felt my heart thump dully in my chest.

"There's our friend Harry Smith," Mother said. "Or is it Jones?" She cut her eyes over to a table next to the wall. Harry was eating alone. He looked even smaller and skinnier than he had the previous evening. He wore an ordinary white shirt, brown trousers, and a linen jacket, but somehow he did not look ordinary. He was again sitting on his rubber cushion.

"Wonder how he managed to get that cushion in here all by himself," Mother said.

I was feeling so nervous that all I could do was shrug. Her efforts to distract me seemed frivolous and coldhearted.

"No need to worry," Mother said. "The treatment is painless."

"How do you know?"

"They assured me."

Harry turned, as if drawn by the sound of my mother's voice. He nodded once and then turned back to his toast and coffee and the *Chicago Tribune*.

"Who assured you?"

But she was watching Harry, studying him, so I went back to my breakfast. I tried to imagine what Dottie B. was doing at that very minute— probably reading L. Frank Baum in bed. If she'd been at Mudlavia, eating breakfast with us, I told myself, she would've ignored Harry and tried to comfort me. But I couldn't imagine Dottie there, couldn't imagine anyone I knew there. That's when I realized how far from home we were.

After breakfast my attendant, who turned out to be the tall man with the squarish head who'd boarded our bus and welcomed us to Mudlavia, wheeled me into a long narrow ward at the end of the first floor. The room was lined with rows of small metal-framed cots. Men lay on the cots, but I could see only their faces and hair—their bodies were covered with mud. Eyes watched me pass. Attendants were bustling up and down the aisles between the cots, pushing carts of steaming mud.

Buster, as he told me to call him, stopped beside an empty cot lined with a few inches of mud and asked me to remove my clothes and give them to him.

I couldn't think how to tell him that I couldn't possibly do either thing.

Buster squeezed my shoulder. "We're used to naked bodies round here. People with clothes on look strange to me!"

His words only made me more self-conscious, but I untied my shoes and took them off, and then slowly took off my socks, pants, shirt, and undershirt, and finally my undershorts. I held the bundle of clothes in front of me, burning with humiliation.

"Lie down there," Buster said. He snatched up my bundle and stuffed it into a wire basket. "Be back directly."

I rolled onto the cot, twisting my knee as I did so. The canvas sagged down inside the frame, so lying there was like being in a shallow tub full of warm mud. I stared up at the beams in the ceiling. Despite the heat in the room, I began to shiver. I listened to flies buzzing and someone breathing beside me.

Finally a voice said, "Hello there, young man." Harry Jones was lying in the next cot.

I'd been so distracted that I hadn't been looking left or right, but now I fixed my eyes on his cadaverous face. I couldn't look at the rest of him. "I'm Matthew," I said. For some reason I didn't tell him my last name.

Harry pointed to a big room adjoining ours. "They dig up the mud out back and heat it up in that room there, over the wood fires. Then they dip it up into buckets and put those buckets on the carts. Here comes my man now." Harry pointed to an attendant and a cart coming toward us up the aisle. "Watch and see how it's done." He winked at me.

"Yes, sir," I said, grateful for his unpatronizing manner. I watched as his attendant, a wiry little man with a narrow red face, pushed the cart up next to Harry. He took a small bucket from the side of the cart and dipped it down into the big bucket of mud, bringing up a steaming heap. He tipped the bucket and, starting at the toes, poured the mud over Harry in a slow, leisurely way, as if he were watering a garden. He refilled the bucket and repeated the process until Harry was covered with a thick layer of mud up to his chin. Then he leveled the mud off with a strip of metal and scraped the extra mud back into an empty bucket. "Relax and get healthy," the attendant said. He wheeled his cart down the aisle toward the mud room.

"Is it hot?" I asked Harry.

"Like a nice warm bath."

I saw Buster starting up the aisle with a cart. I asked Harry, "How long?"

"Not long enough. Hour every day. You'll look forward to it."

I had a squeeze of panic when the first bucket tipped over me and mud began sliding over my feet. I held my breath, waiting to be scorched, but as Harry had said, it was like a warm bath. When Buster had finished, he said, "Relax and get well." I was plastered to the cot. I couldn't move, and didn't want to. The oddly pleasant smell filled my nose, and I realized that I'd always wanted to play in mud, to pick it up and squeeze it, smear it on my body, lie down and roll in it. I remembered the day that Dottie B. and I had come back from playing in the creek behind her house, and how horrified my mother had been. She had sent me straight to the bath. She made me promise never to go near the creek again, and I kept my word. But mud was good. Dirt was good. It was healthful!

My body relaxed under the mud blanket. I was an Indian, hiding from white men. Or a leech, waiting for my next victim. Or a log, buried in a creek bank. This forced passivity was a peculiar feeling. Freeing, somehow.

"You're right, Mr. Jones," I said, turning my head toward him. But his eyes were closed, and he seemed to be asleep.

The time passed too quickly. Buster brought me cool water to drink and wiped my sweaty face. When he pulled me off my cot, breaking me out of my cocoon of drying mud, I had the sensation of landing again on earth after being away for years and years. I felt both younger and older at the same time, and I was no longer self-conscious. Buster escorted me, naked, out of the room and into another room lined with showers. Old men and their attendants were busy scrubbing. I looked for Harry, but didn't see him. I stood on the green-tile floor, and Buster scrubbed my back and legs with a big rag; then he left me to wash the mud off my front as best I could. My knee still ached, but I told myself it felt a little bit better. In a bathrobe Buster gave me, I rested awhile in the cooling room. Later, after I'd dressed, Buster wheeled me along a dirt path toward the front porch. "What will you be when you grow up?" he asked me.

I answered without hesitation. "An Olympic champion in the high jump and the long jump."

"You heard of Ray Ewry?" he asked.

"Of course! The Human Frog!" Ray Ewry, my idol, had gone to college at Purdue, in West Lafayette, and I'd read all about his triumphs in the *Daily Courier*. Ray had won ten Olympic gold medals, in the standing high, standing long, and standing triple jumps—more than any other Olympic athlete has ever won. He might've won more medals if his events had not been discontinued after 1912.

"You know, Ray Ewry was a cripple when he was a boy," Buster said. "Polio."

Yes, I told him, I knew that. The fact that Ewry had had polio was included in every story I'd read about him.

"Doctor told him to take up jumping to strengthen his legs," Buster said.

"And the rest is history!" I said cheerfully, though I felt anything but cheerful. I didn't have polio. I only had a sore knee. Was Buster trying to tell me that I was a cripple too?

Buster wheeled me up a ramp onto the porch, where my mother, in her puffed-sleeve blouse with the pearl buttons, sat in a rocking chair doing needlepoint. She took my hand, and I noticed the mud still caked underneath my fingernails.

"Won't ever get it all off," Buster said, hanging over us. "See you when the cock crows." He ruffled my hair, turned, and lumbered off the porch.

Mother and I smiled at each other.

"So it went well?" Mother dropped her needlepoint in her lap—a picture of three roses, but she'd done only half of one. Our house was full of her framed needlepoint pictures. I hoped she was losing interest in them. "Tell me all about it," she said.

For some reason I didn't describe how pleasurable it had been. I think I felt a bit guilty about how much I'd enjoyed it. I also left out the part about talking to Harry. I wanted to paint a braver picture of myself, or maybe I was wary of letting her know my changed opinion of him. She listened to me, but I could tell she wanted me to hurry up. When I finished, she picked up her needlepoint and began stitching again.

"I've got a scary story to tell you," she said, staring intently at her work. "One of the ladies over there told it to me. Don't look."

I did look, annoyed that her story was usurping mine. All along the ivy-clad porch were groups of white-wicker chairs and tables. Three women sat at one table sipping glasses of lemonade. They were all middle-aged, fat, and dressed in starched shirtwaists and full skirts, their gray hair coiled at the napes of their necks. None of them looked as if she had an interesting bone in her body.

"I said don't look," Mother whispered.

I sighed and stared out at the gardens. It was midmorning, already hot in the sun, but the porch was shady and cooler, and the gladioli and zinnias looked bright and fresh. The air smelled of cut grass and soap from the laundry. The limestone fountain gurgled. A young man and woman strolled down the path toward the woods. He held a pink-and-green-striped parasol over her head. He said something in her ear and she jerked away, but then, a few steps later, she allowed him to take her hand.

"One of those ladies is from Chicago," Mother said, still stitching. "She's here with her husband, a banker. He's taking the cure."

"That's a story?"

"She said that this place is a gambler's paradise. Listen." She lowered her voice. "They have card games in the back parlor, all night sometimes. For high stakes. They drink gin. Most of the people here are from Chicago. Gangsters, or friends of gangsters. That man with the cushion—Harry Jones isn't really his name—is some big mob boss, hiding out from the law. We're in a *nest* of criminals."

"Really?" I sounded more shocked than I was. I'd been to Chicago only twice, to shop for new school clothes, and had found it a dark, claustrophobic place. That one would want to escape if one could seemed only natural. Surely not even gangsters would misbehave here, I thought. I noticed that one of the middle-aged women had a bee crawling down her back. I hoped it would sting her.

"Well?" Mother said, frowning at me. "What should we do? Now that we know?"

I didn't even think to question the woman's claim. It might have been an out-and-out lie, or more likely an exaggeration, but both Mother and I wanted to believe it. "My knee is feeling better," I said, bending it a few times. That was a lie. It felt the same.

Mother nodded and looked relieved. "There's our answer," she said.

"Hello there!" Harry Jones was calling to us from across the porch. He tipped his straw hat in our direction. The woman with bobbed hair stood behind him, clutching his rubber cushion. The parrot teetered on her shoulder.

Mother and I smiled and waved back as though we hadn't just been maligning him, as if he were one of our friends. For a second I was afraid he'd come over and tell Mother about our conversation that morning, but he merely called out, "Off to get some sun!" He and the woman walked arm in arm down the porch steps.

"I suppose," Mother said, rocking too hard in her chair, "that you can tell who his current lady friend is by taking note of who's carrying his cushion." She clucked. "As if he couldn't carry it himself." I heard a fondness in her voice, a fondness for Harry that I also felt.

I said, "He must be very sick. He's much too skinny."

"Poor man."

We watched him and his friend disappear down the garden path.

"A boss?" I asked Mother. "She said 'boss'?"

"Of one of the biggest crime rings."

I grinned.

"We can never tell your father about him," she said, meeting my eyes and clasping both my hands in hers. "Never ever. Promise?"

I promised without a second thought.

We sat awhile in silence, watching the strolling guests, and I marveled at the dishonesty and secrecy that hung so lightly in the sweet-smelling air of Mudlavia, air that had infected not only me but my own dear mother. It was strange, I thought, how much at home we both felt, and how quickly we had come to feel that way. I was suddenly sorry for the Dotties back home, who were no doubt having a very dull summer.

My days at Mudlavia fell into a comfortable pattern. I took my mud treat-ment every morning, always in the cot next to Harry's, and he and I chatted while we waited for our mud. He asked me questions about myself—my last name, where I was from, what my father did, what he was like, and so on. "Goodall," I told him. My mother's first name, I said, was Toots. We'd come from Attica. I told him that my father had once been a gendarme in Paris, but that he'd been fired for shooting a tourist. Now he was a fat farmer who raised cows. Lying became easier as I went along.

Harry nodded as he listened, and I have no idea whether he believed me or not. I think not. He told me he was from LaPorte, Indiana, and had worked as a mailman until he was stricken with crippling arthritis. He came to Mudlavia every summer. He was widowed. "My dear Ida passed five years ago this summer," he said. "Not a one could ever take Ida's place." Ida? Mailman? I fixed a sad, sympathetic look on my face, admiring our ability to pretend. This was much more fun than making up plays.

"I can jump over a fence five feet high," I told him. "World record is six feet."

"No kidding," he said.

"I'd show you," I said, "but, you know." I pointed to my knee.

One morning, as we both lay under our mud compresses, Harry said, "This place is a con game. This mud's just mud. It won't cure me, but I don't care. I love it, but I never let on how much. If people knew how pleasant it was, they'd all be clamoring to get in, and there'd be no room for you and me."

"We won't tell them," I said, and we both nodded our heads, which was as good as a handshake.

Harry always fell asleep as soon as he was covered, but I would lie awake daydreaming, not of high jumping or Olympic glories, as before, but about being all alone, buried up to my neck in the red dirt of Arizona, or the dark earth of a Canadian forest, peering around at the strange and dramatic landscape. For the first time in my life I escaped the prison of my own body, and I found the sensation soothing and exhilarating at the same time.

While I took my treatments, Mother worked on her needlepoint roses and talked to the ladies on the porch, finding out bits of gossip about the guests. Many of them were part of the same Chicago mob family, she told me with a knowledgeable air, of which Harry Jones was the boss. He was wanted for the murder of a South Side butcher. I pictured a mean-faced butcher in a bloody apron. I wondered if Harry had shot him with a pistol or a shotgun. "The butcher probably deserved it," I told Mother, who said, "Matthew!" and then, "Probably so. Maybe they were in rival gangs." I still hadn't told her about my conversations with Harry. Because I'd started out keeping them secret, continuing to do so felt easiest, and so far he hadn't given me away—he'd only waved to us from afar.

After lunch Mother and I would retire to our room. Mother was slogging through a romance novel called *Go Forth and Find*, which she said was tedious. I'd brought along a few Frank Merriwell adventure stories. Heroic Frank was handsome, popular, good, and, most important, athletic. Time and again he won the day in boxing, baseball, football, fencing, lacrosse, crew, shooting, bicycle racing, or, my favorite, track. I loved Frank, but now, for some reason, his feats seemed obvious and pointless and didn't hold my interest, so I took to writing letters. Mother and I had agreed that we wouldn't mention the criminals to anyone we wrote to. We'd write only about the beauty and peace and quiet and the fact that my knee was steadily improving, which it wasn't.

"Should I tell Father I've seen the doctor?" I asked Mother one afternoon. We hadn't seen a doctor around the place since we'd gotten there.

She put down her book. "Good idea," she said. "So he won't worry."

We didn't mention the fact that we'd yet to receive a letter from my father. My mother kept up her correspondence with her older sister, May, a spinster dressmaker who suffered from neurasthenia. Mother wrote enthusiastically to May about Mudlavia, trying, not very sincerely, to persuade her to join us, mentioning the healthful food, lithia water, and musical evenings along with the mud baths, but we both knew we were safe, because May wouldn't set foot outside her house in Cleveland if she could help it.

I also wrote to Dottie B. and Dottie G., telling them I'd met some "interesting guests from Chicago." Dottie G. never wrote back, but I knew I could count on Dottie B., because she liked to write. One day I received a postal with a photo of the Indianapolis Motor Speedway, and on it she said that she missed me "like crazy." I repeated this to myself over and over while Mother took a nap, and I stared out our window at the sky, which seemed always to be blue, listening to wasps buzzing against the screen. Many of the guests went hiking, or swimming in the creek, but Mother stayed with me. Often we would end the afternoon by sitting in the parlor with the other guests, or if it wasn't too hot, she would push me around the garden in my wheelchair. She seemed to be growing younger by the day. She moved in a stronger and more agile way, she laughed more, and her face glowed with sun.

One night, after Mother and I had just sat down in the dining room, Harry Jones and Sylvia Smith approached our table. Sylvia, wearing what looked like a man's suit coat and bow tie, dropped Harry's cushion in a chair and sat down beside him, a sullen expression on her face. Harry said hello to me and then turned to my mother. "Good evening, Mrs. Goodall. May we join you?" My mother gave me a look I've never forgotten. She was not just surprised that I'd ever even spoken to Harry but amazed, as if she'd never imagined I could be so strangely devious. An assessing glint was in her eye, as if she were rethinking everything she'd previously thought about me. But of course she couldn't have done all that, because in just a matter of seconds, during which I held my breath, not knowing what her reaction would be, she turned to Harry. "Certainly," she said. "Everyone calls me Toots."

Sylvia knocked back a glass of iced tea. "Toots," she said, to no one in particular.

Mother gave her a tepid smile.

The piano player launched into his favorite song: "Pack Up Your Troubles in Your Old Kit Bag."

"Matthew tells me you're from Attica," Harry said to Mother. "You and your husband raise cows."

"Herefords," Mother said, nodding.

She knew nothing about cows. I couldn't even believe she'd come up with "Herefords." I knew she couldn't pull it off.

Sylvia must've had this thought too. "Tell us about cows," she said to my mother. "Harry here don't know a thing about cows."

"Surely we can find something else to discuss," Harry said. "Toots is probably sick and tired of cows."

"We both are," I said. "Tired of cows."

"Well, no, actually," Mother said. "I never tire of cows." While the waiter served our drinks, Mother proceeded to describe our life in Attica, our herd of cows, our team of Belgian horses, and our chickens—good layers. It was my turn to marvel. But then I realized she was simply describing her own childhood on a farm in Ohio, a place I'd never seen and she rarely talked about, because her parents had died before I was born.

Sylvia made a few snide comments and then stared across the room as if she were deep in thought. Finally, right in the middle of dinner, she got up and left the table, giving me a sneer. I was the only one who acknowledged her leaving.

The next evening Harry joined us for dinner again, this time carrying his own cushion. His lady friends sat across the room at another table, their backs to us. The parrot, perched on the shoulder of the woman with bobbed hair, turned to face us, his head cocked, as if he were spying on us. That evening I noticed a hint of repressed excitement in the flush of Mother's cheeks, her sputtering laugh, the way she leaned toward Harry when he spoke. He asked her about my father's experience as a gendarme in Paris, and the tourist he shot.

"It was a crazy man, the tourist," Mother said. "A butcher. An Algerian butcher waving a knife. My husband was simply doing his duty."

A butcher! She'd said "butcher"! But Harry's expression didn't change. He asked her about Paris, and she began to talk about Algerian restaurants and the Louvre Museum as if she'd actually seen them. Although they mostly ignored me, I was thrilled by the whole thing, thrilled by my mother's lies and my part in getting them started, thrilled that someone like Harry found us desirable.

I ate my soggy baked Alaska, looking around to see who'd noticed us sitting with Harry. Nobody paid us any attention, but that didn't quell my excitement. My hand, with its mud-caked fingernails, reached for my water glass again and again. I had become a dirty person. Mud had invaded every crevice of my body, and I was always picking off little patches that the shower hadn't washed away. I thought about how I could present this place to Dottie B., how much to tell—the rubber cushion, the parrot, a woman in a man's suit coat?—and how much to leave out, and how impressed she'd be.

After dinner Harry left us with a bow, disappearing into one of the back parlors.

"Sin City," Mother said, cocking one eyebrow.

I asked Mother, "If everybody knows these people are criminals, how come nobody calls the cops?"

"Don't ask 'how come,'" Mother said. "Don't say 'cops.'" Then she rubbed her fingers and thumb together. "Boodle," she whispered, and we both snickered.

On the way out of the dining room she pushed my chair past the parrot, who turned to watch us, his beady eyes blinking. I lurched toward him. He gave a loud squawk, flapped off his perch, and then swooped low over the tables and circled the dining room like a mutant bat, causing the diners to shriek and duck. The bobbed woman leaped up and charged after him. Finally the bird perched at the top of one of the tall windows, and as we left I heard the bobbed woman imploring him to come down. "Tyrone," she was calling. "Come to Mama." Mother called me Tyrone for the rest of the evening.

So Mother and I were having a grand time. The only trouble was that my knee wasn't getting any better. For the first week it didn't feel worse, and I credited the treatment, but now I think the wheelchair might've been the reason. Then it began to hurt worse, with an even sharper pain that kept me awake at night. I didn't say a word about the pain, didn't even acknowledge it to myself. Harry's lady friends had disappeared, and he began sitting with us every night at dinner, and Mother and I were having too much fun thinking of ways to get him to reveal his true identity. We got bolder and bolder.

"So how did you carry your mailbag?" Mother asked him. "Over which shoulder?"

"Right, of course," Harry said. "We're required to."

"What's the most collected stamp ever?" I asked him.

"Pocahontas five-cent." He took a slurp of his cold cucumber soup. He always answered our questions without hesitation, and he could've been telling the truth, of course, though we preferred not to think so.

One morning I got another postal from Dottie B. "We saw your father in downtown Indianapolis," she wrote. "He was walking with your cousin. What a stylish lady! Her skirt was up almost to her knees and she wore a sailor hat. I pestered Mother till she bought me a sailor hat too." Something told me, even at age ten, to rip this postal up before Mother could see it.

"Your mother is a beautiful woman," Harry said to me the next morning when we lay on our cots, covered with mud. "But don't tell her I said that."

"I won't," I said, even though his tone indicated that he wanted me to tell her. Everything said at Mudlavia seemed to mean just the opposite. I didn't like his saying that my mother was beautiful, because it was true, and the whole point of our relationship was to tell lies. Mother doesn't really like you, I wanted to tell him. She's just pretending. But I knew that she and I were only pretending not to like him. It was all too confusing. "Mother likes you," I was surprised to hear myself say. "I do too," I added.

"Really?" he said, grinning at me. He was so thin that he looked like pictures I'd seen of Egyptian mummies. "She does? Really?"

I assured him that she did, but I was surprised to find myself hurt that he cared about Mother more than about me. I'd thought of us as the new threesome, now that his lady friends were out of the picture. "My father has a lady friend," I said to Harry, and told him about the postal I'd received the day before. He listened to me intently, frowning, and without saying a word. I expected him to express shock and outrage, to jump up and do something, or to at least promise to do something. When he continued to lie there, silent and unmoving, I felt a cold anger welling underneath my mud-warmed skin. I'd confided in him because, despite all the games we were playing, I believed that he would want to help us. I'd thought he was our friend.

That night at dinner I watched him joking and talking with Mother, listening to her silly replies. They didn't seem to notice that I wasn't participating in their little charade. I realized, with a sickening feeling, that I had served my purpose and was now expendable. I didn't like the way he stared at Mother, and I didn't like the way she gazed back at him. I'd never seen her look at anyone else that way. It was as if she'd been infected by some strange virus and couldn't help herself. I sulked through dinner, refusing to meet their eyes, grunting and shrugging when I was addressed. Before Mother could finish her cherry Bavarian cream, I told her I was tired and wanted to turn in early. I hoped she would read in bed and keep me company, but she tucked me in and said she was going back down to sit on the porch. It was too hot to read upstairs, she said. Did I mind?

"What happened to the parrot lady?" I asked Mother, who was brushing her hair in front of the mirror. "And Sylvia? Where'd they go? Maybe he rubbed them out."

She rewound her hair in a bun and dug a tortoiseshell comb into it. "Don't be silly," she said.

"Harry says this place is a con game," I said. "He says the mud is just ordinary."

"Go to sleep," she said.

I lay in bed, sweating in my nightshirt, imagining how I was going to get even. I considered calling the cops and ratting on Harry; then I decided to write a letter to Father, not mentioning Harry but asking him to come and get us. I was sorry that I'd ratted on my father, and I asked God for forgiveness. I finally dozed off. When I woke up, a full moon hung outside my window, and Mother's bed was still empty. I clambered out of bed, ignoring the throbbing in my knee, and hopped to the window, where I stuck my head outside, hoping to feel a breeze on my face.

Then I heard Mother and Harry talking on the porch. Their voices were quiet and intimate. I heard no teasing or laughing, no protesting or measured politeness. For the first time since we'd been there, I was hearing the sound of honest speech, and it spooked me. I couldn't see them, and strain as I might, I couldn't make out their words. Were they sitting side by side? Or standing, looking up at the moon? A sharp, stabbing pain went through my knee, and I collapsed on the floor. As I lay there, stinging truths seeped into my conscious mind, drop by drop. Something was very wrong with my knee. I would never be an Olympic champion. I would never jump again. Never use my leg again. Never.

I crawled underneath the bed and curled up in a ball. Mother finally found me there when she came in. "My God!" she said. "What's happened?" She kneeled in front of the bed, sounding satisfyingly terrified.

I rolled out from my hiding place. "My knee's been hurting worse and worse," I said. "It's not getting better." I started to cry then, relieved to be telling the truth, but feeling that I was tricking her all the same, and doing it for her own good. For our own good.

She laid a cool hand on my forehead. "We'll see the doctor first thing in the morning," she said, and I could hear the despair in her voice. "I'm sorry. I'm a terrible mother. I'll never forgive myself."

I closed my eyes and said nothing.

The next morning Mother found the Mudlavia doctor playing poker in Sin City, and he advised her to take me immediately to a hospital. Mother notified my father and made arrangements; we sat in the lobby with our suitcases all morning, waiting to leave. Many people stopped to wish us well, including Buster. He bowed to Mother and shook my hand. "The Human Frog didn't go to the Olympics till he was twenty-six," Buster said. "Remember that." I could give him only a distracted smile. Harry never appeared, and Mother never left my side. That afternoon she and I began a journey to Chicago's Augustana Hospital. The doctor declared that I had a malignant tumor in my knee, and half my leg had to be removed. If we'd waited much longer, the surgeon told us, I might be dead.

We returned to Lafayette, where I was fitted with a wooden prosthesis and began my life as a cripple, learning to hobble around my bedroom with the help of Mother and Dottie B. My mother acted falsely chipper and then wept periodically in her bedroom, muffled, gasping sobs. I assumed she was crying for me and feeling guilty, but the situation was more complicated than that. Three months later, when I could finally manage to get downstairs on my own, using a cane, I told Mother I was going to walk across the street, alone, to Dottie B.'s. I can't remember if she encouraged or discouraged me, but it wouldn't have mattered. I was determined to go.

Since I'd last been outside, the seasons had changed. The world had gone gray and cold. It was only midafternoon, but the lights were already shining in Dottie's house. I left Mother standing on our porch, arms folded, watching me go. When I reached Dottie's front steps and turned to wave, she'd already gone back inside. Did she act different right before I left? I couldn't say, because I'd been preoccupied with making my escape, with getting some relief from her weeping.

A couple of hours later I returned home, sweating with exhaustion. When I called for Mother, she didn't answer. Upstairs, in my parents' bedroom, I saw that her clothes were gone from the wardrobe. I rummaged around the house for a note, all the while knowing I'd never find one. She had taken the sudden opportunity to leave, and she hadn't wanted to linger long enough to write a note, having no idea when I'd return. Maybe she told herself she'd send me a letter when she got to wherever she was going, thinking that a letter would be better than a note anyway. She'd have time to really think about what she wanted to say.

On her bedside table lay *Go Forth and Find*, a leather bookmark near the middle. Later I read the book cover to cover. It was a romance as banal and unbelievable as the stories of Frank Merriwell's athletic prowess, and I assured myself that the book hadn't influenced her in any way. She'd read many such romances, and surely she knew how far-fetched they were. Besides, she'd told me it was tedious. She hadn't finished it, and didn't bother to take it with her, because maybe, at long last, she'd found the real thing. I wanted very much to believe that.

One afternoon, not long after her departure, Father sat on the sofa beside me in the parlor, wearing only his undershirt and pajama pants, his fake glasses and moustache gone, his stopwatch abandoned.

"You sure?" he kept asking me. "She didn't talk to any men?"

I never mentioned Harry Jones to anyone. I told myself that I was keeping our secret, and that Mother wouldn't have wanted me to blab, but that was only part of it. Harry Jones seemed like a fantasy, a figment of our imagination, and I didn't want to expose him to the harsh light of conventional Lafayette. Besides, she could've gone anywhere, with anyone.

"None?" my father said again. "No men at all?"

I recalled her saying good-bye to Buster, thanking him profusely. "Nobody except Buster," I told my father, and he wrote the name in a notebook.

I felt terrible that I might've caused Buster some trouble, so I lashed out. "Dottie told me she saw you in Indianapolis. With your *cousin*."

He flushed but didn't hesitate. "That's preposterous. I haven't gone anywhere near Indianapolis in months." Then he gave me his superintendent's smile. "Dottie's not too bright, son." He patted my good leg, got up, and left the room. He never again pestered me about Mudlavia, and after a while he refused to speak about my mother at all.

For a while I thought about trying to write to Harry, or waiting till I got a little older and looking him up in Chicago, but I did neither of these things, telling myself that Harry Jones couldn't possibly be his real name. I tried to accept my losses, feeling deep down that I was at fault for losing both my leg and my mother. Of course, when I was angry, I also had to ask myself how she could have gone off and left her only son. Especially one who needed her so badly. Perhaps it was *because* I needed her so badly. Or perhaps her flight had nothing to do with me, or with my father, or with Harry Jones, or with anything or anyone we knew about. I kept expecting to turn around and see her, and often thought I heard her calling me on the street. Even now, even though she's long dead, I'm still waiting for her to reveal herself, wearing her egret-feather hat.

After I went away to college in Bloomington, I received a letter from my mother's sister, May, in Cleveland, whom I hadn't seen or heard from in years. Aunt May wondered if my father had told me the truth about what happened to my mother. My mother had written to me many times, the letter said, but May suspected that Father had never shown me her letters. My father, she wrote, had been notified that Mother was hit by a trolley and killed not even a year after she left home. She'd been living alone in San Francisco, working in a hat shop, trying to make a new start. Someone had sent her the money to go out there, set herself up, and hire a lawyer. She'd served my father with divorce papers, which he'd refused to sign. "You must believe," my aunt wrote, "that your mother loved you and didn't want to leave you. She intended to send for you, but she had to escape first." May said that she had no idea who had given my mother the money she needed, but I thought I knew.

I fired off a blistering letter to my father, but he didn't respond. He continued to pay my tuition and expenses, but after I graduated we didn't speak again for seven years, until after the birth of my first child.

I did hate my father for a while, but I never could bring myself to hate my mother. Even now I'd give anything to be with her again, to sit close to her the way I did on the bus to Mudlavia, to laugh with her as we did in the dining room, to hear her breathing quietly in the bed next to mine. I long to go back in time, before everything changed, and in this, I realize, I'm no different from anyone else. Life eventually takes away everything it gives.

Five months after my mother left, America entered World War I. My father began spending more and more time in Indianapolis, and we moved there when he took a position as superintendent of the Indianapolis public schools. Dottie B. and I married young. I worked my way through medical school in Bloomington and became an orthopedic surgeon. Dottie B. wrote a number of popular children's books, including one best seller: *The Floosenettes Go to Mars*. We had five children. Our oldest son, a farmer with young children of his own, suffocated in a grain bin at age thirty-three. Our youngest daughter, when she was twenty-nine, won a medal in kayaking at the 1976 Olympic Games in Montreal. I never returned to Mudlavia, but I read in the newspaper that it burned down, and was rebuilt, and burned down again, and today is a pile of rubble.

In the late summer I always remember Mudlavia, and not with any bad feelings. I remember the gurgling fountain and the hollyhocks, the wide porch, the soggy baked Alaska. Buster saying, in his southern drawl, "Relax and get well." Harry whispering, "This place is a con game." I remember lying beneath the mud, soaking it up, the stillness and the smell and the flies buzzing, forgetting myself, forgetting that I was even a human being with all the worries and vanities and self-deception that go along with it, and I think that if I could've stayed there forever, buried in mud, I might've had a happy life, instead of simply a good one.

Kevin Brockmeier

The Brief History of the Dead

from *The New Yorker*

W HEN THE blind man arrived in the city, he claimed that he had
traveled across a desert of living sand. First he had died, he said,
and then—*snap!*—the desert. He told the story to everyone who would
listen, bobbing his head to follow the sound of their footsteps. Showers of
red grit fell from his beard. He said that the desert was bare and lonesome
and that it had hissed at him like a snake. He had walked for days and
days, until the dunes broke apart beneath his feet, surging up around him
to lash at his face, then everything went still and began to beat like a heart.
The sound was as clear as any he had ever heard. It was only at that
moment, he said, with a million arrow-points of sand striking his skin,
that he had truly realized he was dead.

Jim Singer, who managed the sandwich shop in the monument district, said that he had felt a prickling sensation in his fingers and then
stopped breathing. "It was my heart," he insisted, thumping on his chest.
"Took me in my own bed." He had closed his eyes, and when he opened
them again he was on a train, the kind that trolleys small children around
in circles at amusement parks. The rails were leading him through a thick
forest of gold-brown trees, but the trees were actually giraffes, and their
long necks were reaching like branches into the sky. A wind rose up and
peeled the spots from their backs. The spots floated down around him,
swirling and dipping in the wake of the train. It took him a long time to

understand that the throbbing noise he heard was not the rattling of the wheels along the tracks.

The girl who liked to stand beneath the poplar tree in the park said that she had died into an ocean the color of dried cherries. For a while, the water had carried her weight, she said, and she lay on her back turning in meaningless circles, singing the choruses of the pop songs she remembered. But then there was a drum of thunder, and the clouds split open, and the ball bearings began to pelt down around her—tens of thousands of them. She had swallowed as many as she could, she said, stroking the cracked trunk of the poplar tree. She didn't know why. She filled like a lead sack and sank slowly through the layers of the ocean. Shoals of fish brushed past her, their blue and yellow scales the brightest thing in the water. And all around her she heard that sound, the one that everybody heard, the regular pulsing of a giant heart.

The stories people told about the crossing were as varied and elaborate as their ten billion lives, so much more particular than the other stories, the ones they told about their deaths. After all, there were only so many ways a person could die: either your heart took you, or your head took you, or it was one of the new diseases. But no one followed the same path over the crossing. Lev Paley said that he had watched his atoms break apart like marbles, roll across the universe, then gather themselves together again out of nothing at all. Hanbing Li said that he woke inside the body of an aphid and lived an entire life in the flesh of a single peach. Graciella Cavazos would say only that she began to snow—four words—and smile bashfully whenever anyone pressed her for details.

No two reports were ever the same. And yet always there was the drum-like thumping noise.

Some people insisted that it never went away, that if you concentrated and did not turn your ear from the sound, you could hear it faintly behind everything in the city—the brakes and the horns, the bells on the doors of restaurants, the clicking and slapping of different kinds of shoes on the pavement. Groups of people came together in parks or on rooftops just to listen for it, sitting quietly with their backs turned to each other. *Ba-dum, Ba-dum, Ba-dum.* It was like trying to keep a bird in sight as it lifted, blurred, and faded to a dot in the sky.

Luka Sims had found an old mimeograph machine his very first week in the city and decided to use it to produce a newspaper. He stood outside the River Road Coffee Shop every morning, handing out the circulars he had printed. One particular issue of the *L. Sims News & Speculation Sheet*—the *Sims Sheet*, people called it—addressed the matter of this sound. Fewer than twenty percent of the people Luka interviewed claimed that they could still hear it after the crossing, but almost everyone agreed that it resembled nothing so much as—could be nothing other than—the pounding of a heart. The question, then, was where did it come from? It could not be their own hearts, for their hearts no longer beat. The old man Mahmoud Qassim believed that it was not the actual sound of his heart but the remembered sound, which, because he had both heard and failed to notice it for so long, still resounded in his ears. The woman who sold bracelets by the river thought that it was the heartbeat at the center of the world, that bright, boiling place she had fallen through on her way to the city. "As for this reporter," the article concluded, "I hold with the majority. I have always suspected that the thumping sound we hear is the pulse of those who are still alive. The living carry us inside them like pearls. We survive only so long as they remember us." It was an imperfect metaphor— Luka knew that—since the pearl lasts much longer than the oyster. But rule one in the newspaper business was that you had to meet your deadlines. He had long since given up the quest for perfection.

There were more people in the city every day, and yet the city never failed to accommodate them. You might be walking down a street you had known for years, and all of a sudden you would come upon another building, another whole block. Carson McCaughrean, who drove one of the sleek black taxis that roamed the streets, had to redraw his maps once a week. Twenty, thirty, fifty times a day, he would pick up a fare who had only recently arrived in the city and have to deliver him somewhere he— Carson—had never heard of. They came from Africa, Asia, Europe, and the Americas. They came from churning metropolises and from small islands in the middle of the ocean. That was what the living did: they died. There was an ancient street musician who began playing in the red brick district as soon as he reached the city, making slow, sad breaths with his accordion. There was a jeweler, a young man, who set up shop at the corner of Maple and Christopher streets and sold diamonds that he mounted on silver pendants. Jessica Auffert had operated her own jewelry shop on the same corner for more than thirty years, but she did not seem to resent the man, and in fact brought him a mug of fresh black coffee every morning, exchanging gossip as she drank with him in his front room. What surprised her was how young he was—how young so many of the dead were these days. Great numbers of them were no more than children, who clattered around on skateboards or went racing past her window on their way to the playground. One, a boy with a strawberry discoloration on his cheek, liked to pretend that the rocking horses he tossed himself around on were real horses, the horses he had brushed and fed on his farm before they were killed in the bombing. Another liked to swoop down the slide over and over again, hammering his feet into the gravel as he thought about his parents and his two older brothers, who were still alive. He had watched them lift free of the same illness that had slowly sucked him under. He did not like to talk about it.

This was during a war, though it was difficult for any of them to remember which one.

Occasionally, one of the dead, someone who had just completed the crossing, would mistake the city for Heaven. It was a misunderstanding that never persisted for long. What kind of Heaven had the blasting sound of garbage trucks in the morning, and chewing gum on the pavement, and the smell of fish rotting by the river? What kind of Hell, for that matter, had bakeries and dogwood trees and perfect blue days that made the hairs on the back of your neck rise on end? No, the city was not Heaven, and it was not Hell, and it certainly was not the world. It stood to reason, then, that it had to be something else. More and more people came to adopt the theory that it was an extension of life itself—a sort of outer room—and that they would remain there only so long as they endured in living memory. When the last person who had actually known them died, they would pass over into whatever came next. It was true that most of the city's occupants went away after sixty or seventy years. While this did not prove the theory, it certainly served to nourish it. There were stories of men and women who had been in the city much longer, for centuries and more, but there were always such stories, in every time and place, and who knew whether to believe them?

Every neighborhood had its gathering spot, a place where people could come together to trade news of the other world. There was the colonnade in the monument district, and the One and Only Tavern in the warehouse district, and right next to the greenhouse, in the center of the conservatory district, was Andrei Kalatozov's Russian Tea Room. Kalatozov poured the tea he brewed from a brass-colored samovar into small porcelain cups that he served on polished wooden platters. His wife and daughter had died a few weeks before he did, in an accident involving a land mine they had rooted up out of the family garden. He was watching through the kitchen window when it happened. His wife's spade struck a jagged hunk of metal so cankered with rust from its century underground that he did not realize what it was until it exploded. Two weeks later, when he put the razor to his throat, it was with the hope that he would be reunited with his family in Heaven. And, sure enough, there they were—his wife and daughter— smiling and taking coats at the door of the tearoom. Kalatozov watched them as he sliced a lemon into wedges and arranged the wedges on a saucer. He was the happiest man in the room—the happiest man in any room. The city may not have been Heaven, but it was Heaven enough for him. Morning to evening, he listened to his customers as they shared the latest news about the war. The Americans and the Middle East had resumed hostilities, as had China and Spain and Australia and the Netherlands. Brazil was developing another mutagenic virus, one that would resist the latest antitoxins. Or maybe it was Italy. Or maybe Indonesia. There were so many rumors that it was hard to know for sure.

Now and then, someone who had died only a day or two before would happen into one of the centers of communication—the tavern or the tearoom, the river market or the colonnade—and the legions of the dead would mass around him, shouldering and jostling him for information. It was always the same: "Where did you live?" "Do you know anything about Central America?" "Is it true what they're saying about the ice caps?" "I'm trying to find out about my cousin. He lived in Arizona. His name was Lewis Zeigler, spelled L-E-W-I-S. . . ." "What's happening with the situation along the African coast—do you know, do you know?" "Anything you can tell us, please, anything at all."

Kiran Patel had sold beads to tourists in the Bombay hotel district for most of a century. She said that there were fewer and fewer travelers to her part of the world, but that this hardly mattered, since there was less and less of her part of the world for them to see. The ivory beads she had peddled as a young woman became scarce, then rare, then finally unobtainable. The only remaining elephants were caged away in the zoos of other countries. In the years just before she died, the "genuine ivory beads" she sold were actually a cream-colored plastic made in batches of ten thousand in Korean factories. This, too, hardly mattered. The tourists who stopped at her kiosk could never detect the difference.

Jeffrey Fallon, sixteen and from Park Falls, Wisconsin, said that the fighting hadn't spread in from the coasts yet, but that the germs had, and he was living proof. "Or not living, maybe, but still proof," he corrected himself. The bad guys used to be Pakistan, and then they were Argentina and Turkey, and after that he had lost track. "What do you want me to tell you?" he asked, shrugging his shoulders. "Mostly I just miss my girl-friend." Her name was Tracey Tipton, and she did this thing with his ear-lobes and the notched edge of her front teeth that made his entire body go taut and buzz like a guitar string. He had never given his earlobes a second thought until the day she took them between her lips, but now that he was dead he thought of nothing else. Who would have figured?

The man who spent hours riding up and down the escalators in the Ginza Street Shopping Mall would not give his name. When people asked him what he remembered about the time before he died, he would only nod vigorously, clap his hands together, and say, "Boom!," making a ges-ture like falling confetti with his fingertips.

The great steel-and-polymer buildings at the heart of the city, with their shining glass windows reflecting every gap between every cloud in the sky, gave way after a few hundred blocks to buildings of stone and brick and wood. The change was so gradual, though, and the streets so full of motion, that you could walk for hours before you realized that the archi-tecture had transformed itself around you. The sidewalks were lined with movie theaters, gymnasiums, hardware stores, karaoke bars, basketball courts, and falafel stands. There were libraries and tobacconists. There were lingerie shops and dry cleaners. There were hundreds of churches in the city—hundreds, in fact, in every district—pagodas, mosques, chapels, and synagogues. They stood sandwiched between vegetable markets and video-rental stores, sending their crosses, domes, and minarets high into the air. Some of the dead, it was true, threw aside their old religions, disgusted that the afterlife, this so-called great beyond, was not what their lifetime of worship had promised them. But for every person who lost his faith there was someone else who held fast to it, and someone else again who adopted it. The simple truth was that nobody knew what would happen to them after their time in the city came to an end, and just because you had died without meeting your God was no reason to assume that you wouldn't one day.

This was the philosophy of José Tamayo, who offered himself once a week as a custodian to the Church of the Sacred Heart. Every Sunday, he waited by the west door until the final service was over and the crowd had dissolved back into the city, and then he swept the tile floor, polished the pews and the altar, and vacuumed the cushions by the Communion rail. When he was finished, he climbed carefully down the seventeen steps in front of the building, where the blind man stood talking about his journey through the desert, and made his way across the street to his apartment. He had damaged his knee once during a soccer match, and ever since then he felt a tiny exploding star of pain above the joint whenever he extended his leg. The injury had not gone away, even after the crossing, and he did not like to walk too far on it. This was why he had chosen to work for the Church of the Sacred Heart: it was the closest church he could find. He had, in fact, been raised a Methodist, in the only non-Catholic congregation in Juan Tula. He frequently thought of the time he stole a six-pack of soda from the church storage closet with the boys in his Sunday-school class. They had heard the teacher coming and shut the door, and a thin ray of light had come slanting through the jamb, illuminating the handle of a cart filled with folding chairs—forty or fifty of them, stacked together in a long, tight interdigitation. What José remembered was staring at this cart and listening to his teacher's footsteps as the bubbles of soda played over the surface of his tongue, sparking and collapsing against the roof of his mouth.

The dead were often surprised by such memories. They might go weeks and months without thinking of the houses and neighborhoods they had grown up in, their triumphs of shame and glory, the jobs and routines and hobbies that had slowly eaten away their lives, yet the smallest, most inconsequential episode would leap into their thoughts a hundred times a day, like a fish smacking its tail on the surface of a lake. The old woman who begged for quarters in the subway remembered eating a meal of crab cakes and horseradish on a dock by Chesapeake Bay. The man who lit the gas lamps in the theater district remembered taking a can of beans from the middle of a supermarket display pyramid and feeling a flicker of pride and then a flicker of amusement at his pride when the other cans did not fall. Andreas Andreopoulos, who had written code for computer games all forty years of his adult life, remembered leaping to pluck a leaf from a tree, and opening a fashion magazine to smell the perfume inserts, and writing his name in the condensation on a glass of beer. They preoccupied him— these formless, almost clandestine memories. They seemed so much heavier than they should have been, as if that were where the true burden of his life's meaning lay. He sometimes thought of piecing them together into an autobiography, all the toy-size memories that replaced the details of his work and family, and leaving everything else out. He would write it by hand on sheets of unlined notebook paper. He would never touch a computer again.

There were places in the city where the crowds were so swollen you could not move without pressing into some arm or hip or gut. As the numbers of the dead increased, these areas became more and more common. It was not that the city had no room for its inhabitants but that when they chose to herd together they did so in certain places, and the larger the population grew the more congested these places became. The people who were comfortable in their privacy learned to avoid them. If they wanted to visit the open square in the monument district, or the fountains in the neon district, they would have to wait until the population diminished. This always seemed to happen in times of war or plague or famine.

The park beside the river was the busiest of the city's busy places, with its row of white pavilions and its long strip of living grass. Kite vendors and soft-drink stands filled the sidewalks, and saddles of rock carved the water into dozens of smoothly rounded coves. There came a day when a man with a thick gray beard and a tent of bushy hair stumbled out of one of the pavilions and began to bump into the shoulders of people around him. He was plainly disoriented, and it was obvious to everyone who saw him that he had just passed through the crossing. He said that he was a virologist by profession. He had spent the last five days climbing the branches of an enormous maple tree, and his clothing was tacked to his skin with sap. He seemed to think that everybody who was in the park had also been in the tree with him. When someone asked him how he had died, he drew in his breath and paused for a moment before he answered. "That's right, I died. I have to keep reminding myself. They finally did it, the sons of bitches. They found a way to pull the whole thing down." He twisted a plug of sap from his beard. "Hey, did any of you notice some sort of thumping noise inside the tree?"

It was not long after this that the city began to empty out.

The single-room office of the *L. Sims News & Speculation Sheet* was in one of the city's oldest buildings, constructed of chocolate-colored brick and masses of silver granite. Streamers of pale-yellow moss trailed from the upper floors, hanging as low as the ledge above the front door, and each morning, as Luka Sims stood cranking away at his mimeograph machine, sunlight filtered through the moss outside his window and the room was saturated with a warm, buttery light. Sometimes he could hardly look out at the city without imagining that he was gazing through a dying forest.

By seven o'clock, he would have printed a few thousand copies of his circular and taken them to the River Road Coffee Shop, where he would hand them out to the pedestrians. He liked to believe that each person who took one passed it on to someone else, who read it and passed it on to someone else, who read it and passed it on to someone else, but he knew that this was not the case. He always saw at least a few copies in the trash on his way home, the paper gradually uncrinkling in the sun. Still, it was not unusual for him to look inside the coffee shop and see twenty or thirty heads bent over copies of the latest *Sims Sheet*. He had been writing fewer stories about the city recently and more about the world of the living, stories he assembled from interviews with the recent dead, most of whom were victims of what they called "the epidemic." These people tended to blink a lot—he noticed that. They squinted and rubbed their eyes. He wondered if it had anything to do with the virus that had killed them.

Luka saw the same faces behind the coffee-shop window every day. "HUNDREDS EXPOSED TO VIRUS IN TOKYO. NEW EPICENTERS DISCOVERED IN JOHANNESBURG, COPENHAGEN, PERTH." Ellison Brown, who prepared the baked desserts in the kitchen, always waited for Luka to leave before he glanced at the headlines. His wife had been a poet of the type who liked to loom nearby with a fretful look on her face while he read whatever she had written that day, and there was nothing that bothered him more than feeling that he was being watched. "INCUBATION PERIOD LESS THAN FIVE HOURS. EXPOSURE AT NOON, MORTALITY AT MIDNIGHT." Charlotte Sylvain would sip at her coffee as she scanned the paper for any mention of Paris. She still considered the city her hometown, though she had not been there in fifty years. Once, she saw the word "Seine" printed in the first paragraph of an article and her fingers tightened involuntarily around the page, but it was only a misprint of the word "sienna," and she would never see her home again. "VIRUS BECOMES AIRBORNE, WATERBORNE. TWO BILLION DEAD IN ASIA AND EASTERN EUROPE." Mie Matsuda Ryu was an enthusiast of word games. She liked to read the *Sims Sheet* twice every morning, once for content and once for any hidden patterns she could find—palindromes, anagrams, the letters of her own name scrambled inside other words. She never failed to spot them. "'TWENTY-FOUR-HOUR BUG' CROSSES ATLANTIC. FATALITY RATE NEARING ONE HUNDRED PERCENT."

The people who went knocking on the doors of the city began to notice something unusual. The evangelists and traveling salesmen, the petitioners and census takers, they all said the same thing: the numbers of the dead were shrinking. There were empty rooms in empty buildings that had been churning with bodies just a few weeks before. The streets were not so crowded anymore. It was not that people were no longer dying. In fact, there were more people dying than ever. They arrived by the thousands and the hundreds of thousands, every minute of every hour, whole houses and schools and neighborhoods of them. But, for every person who made it through the crossing, two or three seemed to disappear. Russell Henley, who sold brooms that he lashed together from cedar branches and hanks of plastic fiber, said that the city was like a pan with a hole in it. "No matter how much water you let in, it keeps pouring right through." He ran a stall in the monument district, where he assembled his brooms, marketing them to the passing crowds, which barely numbered in the low hundreds these days. If the only life they had was bestowed upon them by the memories of the living, as Russell was inclined to believe, what would happen when the rest of the living were gathered into the city? What would happen, he wondered, when that other room, the larger world, had been emptied out?

Unquestionably, the city was changing. People who had perished in the epidemic came and went very quickly, sometimes in a matter of hours, like a midspring snow that blankets the ground at night and melts away as soon as the sun comes up. A man arrived in the pine district one morning, found an empty storefront, painted a sign in the window with colored soap ("SHERMAN'S CLOCK REPAIR. FAST AND EASY. OPENING SOON"), then locked the door and shuffled away and never returned. Another man told the woman he had stayed the night with that he was going to the kitchen for a glass of water, and when she called to him a few minutes later he did not answer. She searched the apartment for him—the window beside her dressing table was open, as though he had climbed out onto the balcony—but he was nowhere to be found. The entire population of a small Pacific island appeared in the city on a bright windy afternoon, congregated on the top level of a parking garage, and was gone by the end of the day.

But it was the people who had been in the city the longest who most felt the changes. While none of them knew—or had ever known—how much time they had in the city, or when that time would come to an end, there had usually been a rhythm to their tenure, certain things a person could expect: after finishing the crossing, you found a home and a job and a company of friends, ran out six or seven decades, and while you could not raise a family, for no one aged, you could always assemble one around you.

Mariama Ekwensi, for one, had made her home on the ground floor of a small house in the white clay district for almost thirty years. She was a tall, rangy woman who had never lost the bearing of the adolescent girl she had once been, so dazed and bewildered by her own growth. The batik cotton dresses she wore were the color of the sun in a child's drawing, and her neighbors could always spot her coming from several blocks away. Mariama was a caretaker at one of the city's many orphanages. She thought of herself as a good teacher but a poor disciplinarian, and it was true that she often had to leave her children under the watch of another adult in order to chase after one who had taken off running. She read to the smaller children, books about long voyages, or about animals who changed shape, and she took the older ones to parks and museums and helped them with their homework. Many of them were badly behaved, with vocabularies that truly made her blush, but she found such problems beyond her talents. Even when she pretended to be angry with the children, they were clever enough to see that she still liked them. This was her predicament. There was one boy in particular, Philip Walker, who would light out toward the shopping district every chance he got. He seemed to think it was funny to hear her running along behind him, huffing and pounding away, and she never caught up with him until he had collapsed onto a stoop or a bench somewhere, gasping with laughter. One day, she followed him around a corner and chased him into an alley and did not come out the other end. Philip returned to the orphanage half an hour later. He could not say where she had gone.

Ville Tolvanen shot pool every night at the bar on the corner of Eighth and Vine. The friends he had at the bar were the same friends he had known when he was alive. There was something they used to say to each other when they went out drinking in Oulu, a sort of song they used to sing: "I'll meet you when I die / At that bar on the corner of Eighth and Vine." One by one, then, as they passed away, they found their way to the corner of Eighth and Vine, walked gingerly, skeptically, through the doors of the bar, and caught sight of one another by the pool tables, until gradually they were all reassembled. Ville was the last of the group to die, and finding his friends there at the bar felt almost as sweet to him as it had when he was young. He clutched their arms and they clapped him on the back. He insisted on buying them drinks. "Never again," he told them. And though he could not finish the sentence, they all knew what he meant. He was grinning to keep his eyes from watering over, and someone tossed a peanut shell at him, and he tossed one back, and soon the floor was so covered with the things that it crunched no matter where they put their feet. For months after he died, Ville never missed a single night at the tables—and so when he failed to appear one night his friends went out looking for him. They headed straight for the room he had taken over the hardware store down the street, where they used their fists to bang on the door and then dislodged the lock with the sharp edge of a few playing cards. Ville's shoes were inside, and his wristwatch, and his jacket, but he was not.

Ethan Hass, the virologist, drank not in the bars but from a small metal flask that he carried on his belt like a Boy Scout canteen. He had been watching the developments in his field for thirty years before he died, reading the journals and listening to the gossip at the conventions, and it sometimes seemed to him that every government, every interest group, every faction in the world was casting around for the same thing, a perfect virus, one that followed every imaginable vector, that would spread through the population like the expanding ring of a raindrop in a puddle. It was clear to him now that somebody had finally succeeded in manufacturing it. But how on earth had it been introduced? He couldn't figure it out. The reports from the recently dead were too few, and they were never precise enough. One day, he locked himself in the bathroom of the High Street

Art Museum and began to cry, insistently, sobbing out something about the air and the water and the food supply. A security guard was summoned. "Calm down, guy. There's plenty of air and water for you out here. How about you just open the door for us?" The guard used his slowest, most soothing voice, but Ethan only shouted, "Everybody! Everything!" and turned on the faucets of the sinks, one by one. He would not say anything else, and when the guard forced the door open a few minutes later he was gone.

It was as though a gate had been opened, or a wall thrown down, and the city was finally releasing its dead. They set out from its borders in their multitudes, and soon the parks, the bars, the shopping centers were all but empty.

One day, not long after the last of the restaurants had closed its doors, the blind man was standing on the steps of the church, waiting for someone who would listen to his story. No one had passed him all day long, and he was beginning to wonder if the end had come once and for all. Perhaps it had happened while he was sleeping, or during the half minute early that morning when he had thought he smelled burning honey. He heard a few car horns honking from different quarters of the city, and then, some twenty minutes later, the squealing of a subway train as its brakes gripped the tracks, and then nothing but the wind aspirating between the buildings, lingering, and finally falling still. He listened hard for a voice or a footstep, but he could not make out a single human sound.

He cupped his hands around his mouth. "Hello?" he shouted. "Hello?" But no one answered.

He experienced an unusual misgiving. He brought his hand to his chest. He was afraid that the heartbeat he heard was his own.

Michael Parker

The Golden Era of Heartbreak

from *The Oxford American*

AFTER SHE left, the town where we lived grew flat as an envelope.
Sound carried: the song of a truck driver showering five miles east.
Nothing could block his dirge. Long-distance misery leaking across the
fields while he scrubbed away the road grime. He, too, had come home to
a top drawer cleared of underwear.

I could hear him night and day, asking her forgiveness, beg your pardon, baby, for the times that she'd arrived home to find him gone. I knew
from the rising strings that she'd never come back, that he would never get
clean. Those strings: sweet Nelson Riddle arrangements, country meringue
from the '50s. Pinnacle of lovelorn lament. Fine time for misery.

My house filled to the eaves with this song. Moths waved in the soaring
orchestration. They dusted the lampshades with it, painted the medicine-
cabinet mirror. Up half the night trying not to listen, I reverted to an
opinion I had given up forty years earlier, along about kindergarten:
globes were wobbly lies. The earth was flat as the muted-by-miles-of-not-
much-of-nothing notes of the trucker's song. Nowhere to hide and no
escape, just sleep for the lucky and, for me, punishing runs.

After she left, I ran hundreds of miles along those low-shouldered roads.
It got to where Mexican migrants would stop work to bring me a cucumber when I slashed past in the lethal early afternoon heat. Then the hospital, where they gave me medicine that turned me into a loaf of bread. The

cheerful foreign doc asked me what year it was and I told him pointedly—
I mean to say that I got up in his face so close that his pocked scars from a
wicked case of acne were craters on a magnified moon—that the major
daily of our Nation's capital was contaminated because she had scoured its
ads in want, want, want—I always got stuck on that word. I said to the
doc, Her want spreads spores like anthrax. Say *anthrax* in one of those
places. Is it an irony that registers on anyone but the inmate that you're in
there for behavior interpreted as less than rational, but when you say
something crazy—which in that situation seems to me the norm—they
shoot you full of more breadloaf? Though I confess I ate the ruffled paper
cup that held my pills. I confess I'd have done anything to keep from
returning to an earth leveled by her leaving.

She'd been gone for a year and a half and I had not heard word one. I
knew where she had alighted and with whom, but had no street address,
no lover's last name. Just major metropolitan area with this Rick she met
at a conference. Work-related: how I hate having first scoured the want ads
that brought us here to this town.

"You could just as easily hate the conference where she met him," said
my sister when I complained about having helped Fran find the job. That
was when I was still fool enough to commiserate with family members and
worlds-at-large. Back before, one by one, they all turned on me. Went
from suggesting acupuncture to signing me up for some extended-stay
hospital. People have no sympathy for the brokenhearted because it's what
they fear the most. They pretend it's as minor and obligatory as having
your wisdom teeth pulled, getting your heart ripped from your chest, having feral mutts tug-a-war the bloody organ in your kitchen while you lean
white-veined against the rusty refrigerator, drowning in schmaltzy string
arrangements.

So I had no one—only the Mexican migrants who offered cucumbers
and water from the bossman's cooler and must have recognized in my desperate stride a fellow alien. The only person I got around to trading words
with was the laconic, chain-smoking Deb—or so her name tag read—who
worked at the market where I purchased my few provisions. It was a
sticky-floored, dirty-ceilinged store which Fran had favored over the chain
grocery because after the dogwoods bloomed Deb and her coworkers
would take out the magazines in aisle seven and stock it with chilis and
tortillas and even Spanish videos for the migrants.

One night I drove over to pick up my stock groceries: Band-Aids, ginger ale, Saltines, bulk raisins, chicken broth, and white rice. I could live off this list for weeks at a time. And had been doing so, and the pounds sweated away in the eighteen-mile runs, and there weren't that many to leave puddling the road in the first place and so many times in the days after she left I would not have been able to tell you the correct use for, never even mind the name of, a fork.

"Give me one of those Pick Ten tickets," I said when I had my groceries all lined up on the belt. Deb wasn't there that night. In her place was a high-school boy. His head was chubby and dripping with red-blond lanks. Used to be, in a town like this you got beat up for wearing your hair long. Now the ones doing the beating are the only ones with their ears covered.

"You don't want one of them," said the boy.

So maybe he said *want* when he meant *need*—a mistake so many make. I had never been expert at figuring out what I needed until Fran left. Then I knew: I needed her. I needed her groaning first thing in the morning when I set the alarm to the local gospel station and our day began with a mass choir filling even the shoe-strewn closet bottoms with sonic interpretations of the word *Jesus*. Her tireless interest in the narrative of how we happened to find each other—that miracle recounted, with much attention paid to the extraordinary odds of it happening in this maddeningly flat world—how could I not need that? Each time she asked for it I felt as if I were narrating Genesis. How humans came sweet and innocent up from the earth. I believed I breathed and ate and performed reasonably well at one activity or the other before we met, but in telling that story over and again, in having it received with such lusty anticipation, I came to believe that my life started the moment I met her, the moment we laid waste to those insurmountable odds.

Odds are terrifying if you let yourself obsess over them. In the case of the Pick Ten lottery, I was not interested in the odds. It was a spontaneous thing, asking the cashier for a ticket. I had never once wasted money on such. But I did not care for being refused. I especially disliked being rejected by this boy whose sullen mannerisms implied that the wonder I had known with Fran was nothing more than some sappy song he'd scowl at while scanning radio stations. I believe I did nothing more than push his doughy chest with my fingers. I remember still the squishiness I encountered where I was expecting breastbone. Surely I was as shocked as he was.

"Hole up," he said. Then: "Dude, what the hell?"

I held out a bill—a twenty, for which he made loud change. He was talking all the while, nervous jumble of words, "What the hell man I was just trying to help. . . ."

Out in the parking lot I was afflicted by my own nervous jumble of words. "Oh, help, right, you were trying to help." Now I am squatting beside my car in a dark, rain-steamy parking lot, tapping my forehead against the front quarter panel of the old rusty Nissan we bought together, repeating with the zeal of the clock-radio choir these words: *I cannot do this can't do it don't want to do this without you.*

I don't know for how long: until my nose smashed against the metal and my face went funny-bone numb and I was dropped in a dusty dodge-ball field back of my grade school, lying in the infield inhaling the rubber of the ball that hit me and repeating that strange-to-me-then word I remembered seeing printed across the ball. Voit. Voit.

"What'd he say?" The voice was nasally but curious. Another voice answered, lower but seemingly female and black.

"Boat? Damn if I know."

"He can't do it without his boat," said the nasal-voiced man. "Now what do you think he can't accomplish without his boat?"

"Voit," I said—indignantly—and was answered this time with a rib kick. I hit the pavement then. To feign what? Fear? Death? There was nothing left for me to fake. I knew then that since she left I'd faked everything. Or maybe the opposite was true; maybe I did not know emotion until it up and crawled in bed with me right along the same time she up and crawled in bed with her Rick.

I only know I felt more alive, stretched out on the oil-slick pavement, grimacing against the rib-kicks, than I had since she left. When the kicks would slow or cease I would scream, "Voit!" and soon every bone was numb. My arms and legs stung with pavement scrapes. I smelled that smell—you know the one—the smell of earliest physical pain. Hot rain laced with rust.

"Ain't he about paid?" asked the black woman. Her low, hacking voice concealed a note of sympathy. I wanted to love her for it, but my ribs cried out for more kicks, as if someone had pulled the plug on a song to which I was dancing.

"Not from the sound of him," said the leader. Obviously he knew need from want. But suddenly a new voice spoke up—"Y'all leave off him." The cashier? Strange as it sounds, until then I had not made the connection. I wasn't at all sure this was not something I wasn't doing to myself, or that the weight of my desire had not provoked some miracle posse to torture me.

I opened my eyes—blinked up at the buggy aureole surrounding the yellow streetlight. The cashier stood above me smoking, but he seemed the least of my problems. The nasal-voiced man was dressed in coat and tie, a terrifying outfit for a man choreographing a beating. The black woman was neither: just a skinny shave-headed boy dressed, like me and the cashier, in shorts and T-shirt.

There was talk among them, profane and incomprehensible. I wasn't listening. Fran kneeling beside me, ripping leeches from my skin. I protested hysterically. Fran swathing me in bandages, bedding down beside me in the grocery-store parking lot so slick with squashed lettuce leaves and spilt milk.

And then I passed into very familiar territory: boredom. I was exhausted, as I had often been in those days, by my inability to get over the hurt. I knew what I was going to feel before I felt it and it was stifling, sad, for what is death, finally, but not being able to even bring yourself to anticipate a surprise?

"Can I buy y'all dinner?" I said.

Once I heard a teacher say that a sure way to change things was to honor opposite impulses. See where they take you. At the time—I was an impressionable young student with pen poised and mind open—this advice seemed a simple answer to the most difficult question there is: how to get across the room. I wanted to live my life scathed but not bleeding. This was before Fran came and well before she went, ages before such advice on How to Change would have struck me, before I even heard it, as superficial fluff to sell magazines in a checkout line.

Crouched by my car, I remembered that I had never actually tried this tactic, intentionally at least. I was all the time doing things I didn't want to do, and saying the opposite of what I felt, but that was to me the only possible way to live this life.

In the car the man in the tie introduced himself as Darren. The other one, of the shorn head and confusing voice, went unnamed. The clerk had long ago sighed and disappeared inside the market.

We drove along the river road toward Albemarle Sound. I never named a restaurant, for it did not feel as if we were stepping out for a bite. It felt more like they were driving me to their clubhouse, some cinder-block hut down in the swamp bottom, where they would torture me with country music of the black-hat Vegas variety and perhaps a little later, when the bottles grew light, a stun gun. Out the window I watched Bell Island, where the schoolkids once hijacked the ferry that brought them across the sound to school and rode around the inlet smoking dope until the Coast Guard escorted them back in. Bell Island kept pace with the sunken Olds and I imagined the inside of the clubhouse, the club colors draped over cinder block and flanked with porn centerfolds.

"You going to get along all right without your boat?" Darren said.

"V-O-I-T. Like a dodgeball?"

"What a dodgeball has to do with you breaking bad on my boy Kirk I ain't even going ask."

I started in on a meditation about memory, how we all lived in closets cluttered with primal objects of childhood. Rosebud. Fran, come home. In the middle of a sentence I stopped, for we all had stopped—the driver had coasted still in the middle of the road, Darren was half turned to watch me.

I said, to turn it back on them, "I think maybe what happened was that y'all hurt some part of my brain that stored, you know, old stuff like dodgeballs."

"We ain't hurt shit," said the driver, stepping indignantly on the gas. "You were already fried when we got there."

I fell back into the seat. What could I say? It seemed time to deliver myself to whatever course of action I had set in motion by pushing the cashier in his pliant chest. I thought of a Halloween carnival in grade school, being blindfolded and having my hand plunged into a vat of Jell-O standing in for crushed eyeballs. I believed I laughed a little to myself, a little leak of laughter like air out of a tire which cemented whatever opinion my companions had of me, for they talked in low, brooding voices and I could not even muster up the energy to eavesdrop.

.   .   .

We arrived finally at a restaurant I did not recognize. I knew only that we were headed south, and could feel from the elements, from the song of tree frogs and the lonesome whine of the tires on rough pavement, that we were headed toward the Sound. I spent the last few miles of the trip listening to the road-grimy trucker beg for his baby back. Outside it was deep-country black except for a buzzing streetlight leaning above a pier over the water, casting a thin sheen on the rippling shallows. The establishment—from the low, vinyl-sided looks of it, a modular-unit, short-order grill—was obviously closed for the night. Dry-docked trawlers listed precariously in the parking lot. The scene felt illicit, excitedly so, as if we'd come to score drugs or rob someone. I thought, fleetingly, that I had found something to take the place of my fiercely coddled misery, but was quickly sucked under by those insipid strings, which dragged me to the bottom of the black sound.

The driver had a key to the restaurant. Darren ordered him to bring us beers and fry up some shrimp burgers. He said to me, "What the hell do you eat?"

"Not much from the looks of him," called the driver from a kitchen, lit only by the lights of freezers he was rooting around in.

"I'm on a diet," I said. A diet with its own soundtrack. The heartbreak diet.

"The thing about diets is all these people starving to death and these rich fuckers on a damn diet." This line sputtered out from the darkened kitchen.

"Your point?" Darren said to the shadows.

"Ones that can afford to eat lobster every night going around starving. Bet they ain't sending the money they save over to Africa."

The driver brought us beers. I left mine untouched. Darren said, "His point is a good one, wouldn't you say?"

"I'm not rich."

"You're just skinny and stupid."

It seemed time to protest, to ask why we were here, alone in the south end of the county, where not only corpses but corpses still seat-belted into cars turned up in sullen lagoons. But instead I leaned forward and said, "I'm not real hungry."

"Bring him some coleslaw," said Darren. He squinted my way. "What's your problem?"

I said, "What do you mean?" though I knew exactly what he meant.

"Going off on Kirk for no reason, beating your head upside your car. Calling out for some damn dodgeball."

"I guess I'm lonely," I said. He widened his eyes, as if suddenly I had come into focus for him, and I added, "is all."

"You ever had anyone die on you?" he asked, wincing slightly, as if it took great effort to send his words my way.

"Yes," I lied. Maybe this was the worst lie I'd ever told—out of the dozens Fran knew about, the ones that passed undetected. She wasn't dead; I was dead to her, maybe, but she lived and breathed and was, at that moment, getting on toward bedtime on a Wednesday night in late spring, no doubt moving against some Rick she met at a conference, and the thought of anyone else touching her in the places I'd discovered made me claim now all degrees of suffering as my own.

"You're lying," he said. The driver set a huge bowl of soupy coleslaw in front of me, a fresh beer for Darren. He laid out the place settings, lining up the fork and knife with a prissiness that amused me, given our surroundings.

"He's definitely lying," the driver said, his words lingering as he disappeared back into the kitchen.

From the kitchen came the hiss of frozen meat dropped into a fryer. I tried hard to summon my song, those strings that had driven me out of the house and into the arms of fate; I tried to focus on the trucker's lament, but the tree frogs, the sibilance of fried meat, the buzz of the streetlights kept my song away.

"You think it's all up to you, don't you?" said Darren.

I thought he wasn't who he said he was. I thought Fran had sent him, or maybe the pathetic trucker wailing away the hours as he tried to scrub away his sins. My comrade in want, sending his messenger to set me straight. I thought Darren was not real and I asked him just who he was to the cashier. Friend? I said. Second cousin?

He looked through me and repeated: "Up to you, huh?"

I shrugged, mindful of what my shrug suggested: that the weight of the world was not upon me.

Darren shook his head, burped, pushed his chair back, summoned his driver, who had been eating back in the kitchen, as if he knew his place in the world.

"Get the bag out of the trunk," said Darren. To me he said, "Let's get."

I rose and followed, queasy from the coleslaw. I was thirsty, too, and exhausted, yet I felt oddly settled. Docility was the answer? I could have apprenticed myself to the migrants, their crooked crew boss, had I only known.

I followed Darren along the pier to its rickety end. I looked to the water's edge, the black sucking sand, beach studded with cypress knees and beyond—a stretch of water poised deceptively as earth. I thought that whatever happened to me then had nothing to do with the slow boy filling in for Deb at the market and everything to do with the times that my vanity had come uncaged in some tavern, dancing with some strange thing, maneuvering her around the dance floor by her hipbones while Fran scrubbed kitchen tiles and tried not to think of that person she did not want to acknowledge I was capable of up and becoming.

"Take your clothes off," said Darren. I did so without question because I was gone—off on that flight that took me frequently and far back in time: Yeah, but I always came home alone, I was saying to Fran, I never slept with any of them, just a little lip, some here-and-there tongue. Never once betrayed us like you did with him. She did not get to argue the meaning of the word *betrayal*. I did all the talking, and it took all the energy I would have expended on worrying about what I was being asked to do: take off my clothes for a man dressed like he was about to sell me some insurance.

Darren's driver arrived toting a gym bag from which he pulled a tangle of rope, some handcuffs, and greasy lengths of chain. He uncoiled the rope, surveyed my nakedness with scorn.

"I don't relish getting wet over his bony ass," he said to Darren.

"It doesn't appear to be up to you," I said.

This made Darren smile. But the driver, once he had me in the water and pushed hard against the piling at the end of the pier, wrenched the cuffs tight and lashed the ropes.

Above us Darren had fired up a cigar to ward off mosquitoes, but the smoke didn't appear to be working; I heard him swear and slap himself. The driver bound me tighter to the splintery black piling, which smelled of creosote and rotting shellfish. Sound water lapped black and empty just above my shoulders.

"Wait for me in the car," Darren told the driver, and when he was gone, he said, "You know, you brung this on yourself, chief. We wouldn't be here if you hadn't asked us to have supper with you."

"No, actually it was the lottery ticket," I said.

"Either way, you taking some crazy chances."

I thought that this was a good thing, and almost said so, but I realized just before I spoke that I still did not know who Darren was, or what he planned to do with me. My situation seemed far worse, on the one hand, than it had just hours before, when I had left for the store. Yet there was this other hand. I could not say what it was. Nor was I even sure I wanted to know. Would it cure me, and would being cured mean that I would learn to live my life without loving her, wanting her?

There was a silence, then a puff of smoke arrived from above, seething through the space between the slats, clouding about my head.

"So she fucked you over, whoever she is. And now you get to go around feeling righteous, starving yourself, and beating up on grocery-store clerks?"

I had an answer to this, but he didn't leave enough space.

"You know something about love, chief?" he said through the smoke. "It makes you scared of every damn thing, you all the time worrying about whether she's going to come back from the store or was I good enough and does her daddy like me and on and on. And at the same time it makes you feel free. That's what it does when it's really cooking, right?"

I waited for a puff of cigar smoke, but there was nothing, only mosquitoes feasting on my cheekbones, my bound hands straining against the rope.

"You saying you didn't feel nothing like that?"

"I did." I do, I thought to say, but I didn't want to give Darren any more ammunition than he could divine by looking at me. He was picking up a lot just looking, and it unnerved me, the way he recognized himself in me, the way he described to the letter the way it felt to love Fran. I did feel scared the whole time I was with her, and yet I felt as free as I'd ever felt. But maybe I was loving her all wrong. Maybe what Darren had described was not love but some kind of copycat ailment with the same symptoms.

"Hell, man, why would you want to feel that way?" Darren said. "Far better to be cooped up in your own head than having to go around scared all the time."

"Who the hell are you anyway?"

"Me? I'm that boy you broke bad on's uncle. I came down expecting excitement, I guess. Find you banging your head on a car and I *know* this motherfucker needs to be put out of his misery."

"That's what this is?"

"This is whatever you want it to be."

"I don't think my desire is being considered here," I said. In answer there came a snort, then footsteps tapping away up the pier. I might have called out, but not to Darren or his driver. Fran. Voit. My trucker, oddly quiet now, as if he'd found some end to his suffering, seen through the loneliness and longing to some sweet levitation.

In time I realized the water was creeping up my neck. I thought of what I knew of tides: They were controlled by the moon, and the moon this night was a pasty scythe's blade floating above a line of loblollies, and seemed too sickly to perform such a feat.

Sometime in the night I began the story of How We Met, and it began at the beginning, and wound its way around facts as stock and familiar as the items I purchased weekly from the market, until the moon moved lower toward the water and a hazy light appeared in the sky.

Watching the sky, water lapping at my chin, I remembered hearing how they'd discovered that the earth was round. A boat had sailed out to the horizon, kept on moving, out of sight, over the earth's curve. Inching my way up the barnacled piling, I saw how they could get behind such an idea.

Wendell Berry

The Hurt Man

from *The Hudson Review*

WHEN HE was five, Mat Feltner, like every other five-year-old who had lived in Port William until then, was still wearing dresses. In his own thoughts he was not yet sure whether he would turn out to be a girl or a boy, though instinct by then had prompted him to take his place near the tail end of the procession of Port William boys. His nearest predecessors in that so far immortal straggle had already taught him the small art of smoking cigars, along with the corollary small art of chewing coffee beans to take the smoke smell off his breath. And so in a rudimentary way he was an outlaw, though he did not know it, for none of his grown-ups had yet thought to forbid him to smoke.

His outgrown dresses he saw worn daily by a pretty neighbor named Margaret Finley, who to him might as well have been another boy too little to be of interest, or maybe even a girl, though it hardly mattered—and though, because of a different instinct, she would begin to matter to him a great deal in a dozen years, and after that she would matter to him all his life.

The town of Port William consisted of two rows of casually maintained dwellings and other buildings scattered along a thoroughfare that nobody had ever dignified by calling it a street; in wet times it hardly deserved to be called a road. Between the town's two ends the road was unevenly rocked but otherwise had not much distinguished itself from the buffalo trace it once had been. At one end of the town was the school, at the other the graveyard. In the center there were several stores, two saloons, a church, a bank, a hotel, and a blacksmith shop. The town was the product of its own becoming which, if not accidental exactly, had also been unplanned. It had no formal government or formal history. It was without pretense or ambition, for it was the sort of place that pretentious or ambitious people were inclined to leave. It had never declared an aspiration to become any-thing it was not. It did not thrive so much as it merely lived, doing the things it needed to do to stay alive. This tracked and rubbed little settle-ment had been built in a place of great natural abundance and beauty, which it had never valued highly enough or used well enough, had dam-aged, and yet had not destroyed. The town's several buildings, shaped less by art than by need and use, had suffered tellingly and even becomingly a hundred years of wear.

Though Port William sat on a ridge of the upland, still it was a river town; its economy and its thoughts turned toward the river. Distance impinged on it from the river, whose waters flowed from the eastward mountains ultimately, as the town always was more or less aware, to the sea, to the world. Its horizon, narrow enough though it reached across the valley to the ridgeland fields and farmsteads on the other side, was pierced by the river, which for the next forty years would still be its main thor-oughfare. Commercial people, medicine showmen, evangelists, and other river travelers came up the hill from Dawes Landing to stay at the hotel in Port William, which in its way cherished these transients, learned all it could about them, and talked of what it learned.

Mat would remember the town's then-oldest man, Uncle Bishop Bower, who would confront any stranger, rap on the ground with his long staff, and demand, "Sir! What might your name be?"

And Herman Goslin, no genius, made his scant living by meeting the steamboats and transporting the disembarking passengers, if any, up to the hotel in a gimpy buckboard. One evening as he approached the hotel with a small trunk on his shoulder, followed by a large woman with a parasol, one of the boys playing marbles in the road said, "Here comes Herman Goslin with a fat lady's trunk."

"You boys can kiss that fat lady's ass," said Herman Goslin. "Ain't that tellin' 'em, fat lady?"

The town was not built nearer the river perhaps because there was no room for it at the foot of the hill, or perhaps because, as the town loved to reply to the inevitable question from travelers resting on the hotel porch, nobody knew where the river was going to run when they built Port William.

And Port William did look as though it had been itself forever. To Mat at the age of five, as he later would suppose, remembering himself, it must have seemed eternal, like the sky.

However eternal it might have been, the town was also as temporal, lively, and mortal as it possibly could be. It stirred and hummed from early to late with its own life and with the life it drew into itself from the countryside. It was a center, and especially on Saturdays and election days its stores and saloons and the road itself would be crowded with people standing, sitting, talking, whittling, trading, and milling about. This crowd was entirely familiar to itself; it remembered all its history of allegiances, offenses, and resentments, going back from the previous Saturday to the Civil War and long before that. Like every place, it had its angers, and its angers as always, as everywhere, found justifications. And in Port William, a dozen miles by river from the courthouse and the rule of law, anger had a license that it might not have had in another place. Sometimes violence would break out in one of the saloons or in the road. Then proof of mortality would be given in blood.

And the mortality lived and suffered daily in the town was attested with hopes of immortality by the headstones up in the graveyard, which was even then more populous than the town. Mat knew—at the age of five he had already forgotten when he had found out—that he had a brother and two sisters up there, with carved lambs resting on the tops of their small monuments, their brief lives dated beneath. In all the time he had known her, his mother had worn black.

But to him, when he was five, those deaths were stories told. Nothing in Port William seemed to him to be in passage from any beginning to any end. The living had always been alive, the dead always dead. The world, as he knew it then, simply existed, familiar even in its changes: the town, the farms, the slopes and ridges, the woods, the river, and the sky over it all. He had not yet gone farther from Port William than to Dawes Landing on the river and to his uncle Jack Beechum's place out on the Bird's Branch Road, the place his mother spoke of as "out home." He had seen the steamboats on the river and had looked out from the higher ridgetops, and so he understood that the world went on into the distance, but he did not know how much more of it there might be.

Mat had come late into the lives of Nancy and Ben Feltner, after the deaths of their other children, and he had come unexpectedly, "a blessing." They prized him accordingly. For the first four or so years of his life he was closely watched, by his parents and also by Cass and Smoke, Cass's husband, who had been slaves. But now he was five, and it was a household always busy with the work of the place, and often full of company. There had come to be times, because his grown-ups were occupied and he was curious and active, when he would be out of their sight. He would stray off to where something was happening, to the farm buildings behind the house, to the blacksmith shop, to one of the saloons, to wherever the other boys were. He was beginning his long study of the town and its place in the world, gathering up the stories that in years still far off he would hand on to his grandson Andy Catlett, who in his turn would be trying to master the thought of time: that there were times before his time, and would be times after. At the age of five Mat was beginning to prepare himself to help in educating his grandson, though he did not know it.

His grown-ups, more or less willingly, were letting him go. The town had its dangers. There were always horses in the road, and sometimes droves of cattle or sheep or hogs or mules. There were in fact uncountable ways for a boy to get hurt, or worse. But in spite of her losses, Nancy Beechum Feltner was not a frightened woman, as her son would learn. He would learn also that, though she maintained her sorrows with a certain loyalty, wearing her black, she was a woman of practical good sense and strong cheerfulness. She knew that the world was risky and that she must risk her surviving child to it as she had risked the others, and when the time came she straightforwardly did so.

But she knew also that the town had its ways of looking after its own. Where its worst dangers were, grown-ups were apt to be. When Mat was out of the sight of her or his father or Cass or Smoke, he was most likely in the sight of somebody else who would watch him. He would thus be corrected, consciously ignored, snatched out of danger, cursed, teased, hugged, instructed, spanked, or sent home by any grown-up into whose sight he may have strayed. Within that watchfulness he was free—and almost totally free when, later, he had learned to escape it and thus had earned his freedom. "This was a *free* country when I was a boy," he would sometimes say to Andy, his grandson.

When he was five, and for some while afterward, his mother drew the line unalterably only between him and the crowds that filled the town on Saturday afternoons and election days when there would be too much drinking, with consequences that were too probable. She would not leave him alone then. She would not let him go into the town, and she would not trust him to go anywhere else, for fear that he would escape into the town from wherever else she let him go. She kept him in sight.

That was why they were sitting together on the front porch for the sake of the breeze there on a hot Saturday afternoon in the late summer of 1888. Mat was sitting close to his mother on the wicker settee, watching her work. She had brought out her sewing basket and was darning socks, stretching the worn-through heels or toes over her darning egg and weaving them whole again with her needle and thread. At such work her fingers moved with a quickness and assurance that fascinated Mat, and he loved to watch her. She would have been telling him a story. She was full of stories. Aside from the small movements of her hands and the sound of her voice, they were quiet with a quietness that seemed to have increased as it had grown upon them. Cass had gone home after the dinner dishes were done. The afternoon had half gone by.

From where they sat they could see down into the town where the Saturday crowd was, and they could hear it. Doors slammed, now and then a horse nickered, the talking of the people was a sustained murmur from which now and then a few intelligible words escaped: a greeting, some bit of raillery, a reprimand to a horse, an oath. It was a large crowd in a small place, a situation in which a small disagreement could become dangerous in a hurry. Such things had happened often enough. That was why Mat was under watch.

And so when a part of the crowd intensified into a knot, voices were raised, and there was a scuffle, Mat and his mother were not surprised. They were not surprised even when a bloodied man broke out of the crowd and began running fast up the street toward them, followed by other running men whose boot heels pounded on the road.

The hurt man ran toward them where they were sitting on the porch. He was hatless. His hair, face, and shirt were bloody, and his blood dripped on the road. Mat felt no intimation of threat or danger. He simply watched, transfixed. He did not see his mother stand and put down her work. When she caught him by the back of his dress and fairly poked him through the front door—"Here! Get inside!"—he still was only alert, unsurprised.

He expected her to come into the house with him. What finally surprised him was that she did not do so. Leaving him alone in the wide hall, she remained outside the door, holding it open for the hurt man. Mat ran halfway up the stairs then and turned and sat down on a step. He was surprised now but not afraid.

When the hurt man ran in through the door, instead of following him in, Nancy Feltner shut the door and stood in front of it. Mat could see her through the door glass, standing with her hand on the knob as the clutch of booted and hatted pursuers came up the porch steps. They bunched at the top of the steps, utterly stopped by the slender woman dressed in mourning, holding the door shut.

And then one of them, snatching off his hat, said, "It's all right, Mrs. Feltner. We're his friends."

She hesitated a moment, studying them, and then she opened the door to them also and turned and came in ahead of them.

The hurt man had run the length of the hall and through the door at the end of it and out onto the back porch. Nancy, with the bunch of men behind her, followed where he had gone, the men almost with delicacy, as it seemed to Mat, avoiding the line of blood drops along the hall floor. And Mat hurried back down the stairs and came along in his usual place at the tail end, trying to see, among the booted legs and carried hats, what had become of the hurt man.

Mat's memory of that day would always be partly incomplete. He never knew who the hurt man was. He knew some of the others. The hurt man had sat down or dropped onto a slatted green bench on the porch. He might have remained nameless to Mat because of the entire strangeness of the look of him. He had shed the look of a man and assumed somehow the look of all things badly hurt. Now that he had stopped running, he looked used up. He was pallid beneath the streaked bright blood, breathing in gasps, his eyes too widely open. He looked as though he had just come up from almost too deep a dive.

Nancy went straight to him, the men, the friends, clustered behind her, deferring, no longer to her authority as the woman of the house, as when she had stopped them at the front door, but now to her unhesitating, unthinking acceptance of that authority.

Looking at the hurt man, whose blood was dripping onto the bench and the porch floor, she said quietly, perhaps only to herself, "Oh my!" It was as though she knew him without ever having known him before.

She leaned and picked up one of his hands. "Listen!" she said, and the man brought his gaze it seemed from nowhere and looked up at her. "You're at Ben Feltner's house," she said. "Your friends are here. You're going to be all right."

She looked around at the rest of them who were standing back, watching her. "Jessie, you and Tom go see if you can find the doctor, if he's findable." She glanced at the water bucket on the shelf over the wash table by the kitchen door, remembering that it was nearly empty. "Les, go bring a fresh bucket of water." To the remaining two she said, "Get his shirt off. *Cut* it off. Don't try to drag it over his head. So we can see where he's hurt."

She stepped through the kitchen door, and they could hear her going about inside. Presently she came back with a kettle of water still warm from the noon fire and a bundle of clean rags.

"Look up here," she said to the hurt man, and he looked up.

She began gently to wash his face. Wherever he was bleeding, she washed away the blood: first his face, and then his arms, and then his chest and sides. As she washed, exposing the man's wounds, she said softly only to herself, "Oh!" or "Oh my!" She folded the white rags into pads and instructed the hurt man and his friends to press them onto his cuts to stop the bleeding. She said, "It's the Lord's own mercy we've got so many hands," for the man had many wounds. He had begun to tremble. She kept saying to him, as she would have spoken to a child, "You're going to be all right."

Mat had been surprised when she did not follow him into the house, when she waited on the porch and opened the door to the hurt man and then to his friends. But she had not surprised him after that. He saw her as he had known her: a woman who did what the world put before her to do.

At first he stayed well back, for he did not want to be told to get out of the way. But as his mother made order, he grew bolder and drew gradually closer until he was almost at her side. And then he was again surprised, for then he saw her face.

What he saw in her face would remain with him forever. It was pity, but it was more than that. It was a hurt love that seemed to include entirely the hurt man. It included him and disregarded everything else. It disregarded the aura of whiskey that ordinarily she would have resented; it disregarded the blood puddled on the porch floor and the trail of blood through the hall.

Mat was familiar with her tenderness and had thought nothing of it. But now he recognized it in her face and in her hands as they went out to the hurt man's wounds. To him, then, it was as though she leaned in the black of her mourning over the whole hurt world itself, touching its wounds with her tenderness, in her sorrow.

Loss came into his mind then, and he knew what he was years away from telling, even from thinking: that his mother's grief was real; that her children in their graves once had been alive; that everybody lying under the grass up in the graveyard once had been alive and had walked in daylight in Port William. And this was a part, and belonged to the deliverance, of the town's hard history of love.

The hurt man, Mat thought, was not going to die, but he knew from his mother's face that the man *could* die and someday would. She leaned over him, touching his bleeding wounds that she bathed and stanched and bound, and her touch had in it the promise of healing, some profound encouragement.

It was the knowledge of that encouragement, of what it had cost her, of what it would cost her and would cost him, that then finally came to Mat, and he fled away and wept.

What did he learn from his mother that day? He learned it all his life. There are few words for it, perhaps none. After that, her losses would be his. The losses would come. They would come to him and his mother. They would come to him and Margaret, his wife, who as a child had worn his cast-off dresses. They would come, even as Mat watched, growing old, to his grandson, Andy, who would remember his stories and write them down.

But from that day, whatever happened, there was a knowledge in Mat that was unsurprised and at last comforted, until he was old, until he was gone.

Nell Freudenberger

The Tutor

from *Granta*

S HE WAS an American girl, but one who apparently kept Bombay time, because it was three thirty when she arrived for their one-o'clock appointment. It was a luxury to be able to blame someone else for his wasted afternoon, and Zubin was prepared to take full advantage of it. Then the girl knocked on his bedroom door.

He had been in the preparation business for four years, but Julia was his first foreign student. She was dressed more like a Spanish or an Italian girl than an American, in a sheer white blouse and tight jeans that sat very low on her hips, perhaps to show off the tiny diamond in her belly button. Her hair was shiny, reddish brown—chestnut you would call it—and she'd ruined her hazel eyes with a heavy application of thick, black eyeliner.

"I have to get into Berkeley," she told him.

It was typical for kids to fixate on one school. "Why Berkeley?"

"Because it's in San Francisco."

"Technically Berkeley's a separate city."

"I know that," Julia said. "I was born in San Francisco."

She glanced at the bookshelves that covered three walls of his room. He liked the kids he tutored to see them, although he knew his pride was irrelevant: most didn't know the difference between Spender and Spenser, or care.

"Have you *read* all of these?"

"Actually that's the best way to improve your verbal. It's much better to see the words in context." He hated the idea of learning words from a list; it was like taking vitamin supplements in place of eating. But Julia looked discouraged, and so he added: "Your dad says you're a math whiz, so we don't need to do that."

"He said what?"

"You aren't?"

Julia shrugged. "I just can't believe he said 'whiz.'"

"I'm paraphrasing," Zubin said. "What were your scores?"

"Five hundred and sixty verbal, seven-sixty math."

Zubin whistled. "You scored higher than I did on the math."

Julia smiled, as if she hadn't meant to, and looked down. "My college counselor says I need a really good essay. Then my verbal won't matter so much." She dumped out the contents of an expensive-looking black leather knapsack, and handed him the application, which was loose and folded into squares. Her nails were bitten, and decorated with half-moons of pale pink polish.

"I'm such a bad writer though." She was standing expectantly in front of him. Each time she took a breath, the diamond in her stomach flashed.

"I usually do lessons in the dining room," Zubin said.

The only furniture in his parents' dining room was a polished mahogany table, covered with newspapers and magazines, and a matching sideboard—storage space for jars of pickle, bottles of Wild Turkey from his father's American friends, his mother's bridge trophies, and an enormous, very valuable Chinese porcelain vase, which the servants had filled with artificial flowers: red, yellow and salmon-colored cloth roses beaded with artificial dew. On nights when he didn't go out, he preferred having his dinner served to him in his room; his parents did the same.

He sat down at the table, but Julia didn't join him. He read aloud from the form. "Which book that you've read in the last two years has influenced you most, and why?"

Julia wandered over to the window.

"That sounds okay," he encouraged her.

"I hate reading."

"Talk about the place where you live, and what it means to you." Zubin looked up from the application. "There you go. That one's made for you."

She'd been listening with her back to him, staring down Ridge Road toward the Hanging Garden. Now she turned around—did a little spin on the smooth tiles.

"Can we get coffee?"

"Do you want milk and sugar?"

Julia looked up, as if shyly. "I want to go to Barista."

"It's loud there."

"I'll pay," Julia said.

"Thanks. I can pay for my own coffee."

Julia shrugged. "Whatever—as long as I get my fix."

Zubin couldn't help smiling.

"I need it five times a day. And if I don't get espresso and a cigarette first thing in the morning, I have to go back to bed."

"Your parents know you smoke?"

"God, no. Our driver knows—he uses it as blackmail." She smiled. "No smoking is my dad's big rule."

"What about your mom?"

"She went back to the States to find herself. I decided to stay with my dad," Julia added, although he hadn't asked. "He lets me go out."

Zubin couldn't believe that any American father would let his teenage daughter go out at night in Bombay. "Go out where?"

"My friends have parties. Or sometimes clubs—there's that new place, Fire and Ice."

"You should be careful," Zubin told her.

Julia smiled. "That's so Indian."

"Anyone would tell you to be careful—it's not like the States."

"No," Julia said.

He was surprised by the bitterness in her voice. "You miss it."

"I am missing it."

"You mean now in particular?"

Julia was putting her things back into the knapsack haphazardly—phone, cigarettes, datebook, Chap Stick. She squinted at the window, as if the light were too bright. "I mean, I don't even know what I'm missing."

Homesickness was like any other illness: you couldn't remember it properly. You knew you'd had the flu, and that you'd suffered, but you didn't have access to the symptoms themselves: the chills, the swollen throat, the heavy ache in your arms and legs as if they'd been split open and some-thing—sacks of rock—had been sewn up inside. He had been eighteen, and in America for only the second time. It was cold. The sweaters he'd bought in Bombay looked wrong—he saw that the first week—and they weren't warm enough anyway. He saw the same sweaters, of cheap, shiny wool, in too-bright colors, at the "international" table in the Freshman Union. He would not sit there.

His roommate saw him go out in his T-shirt and windcheater, and offered to loan him one of what seemed like dozens of sweaters: brown or black or wheat-colored, the thickest, softest wool Zubin had ever seen. He went to the Harvard Co-op, where they had a clothing section, and looked at the sweaters. He did the calculation several times: the sweaters were "on sale" for eighty dollars, which worked out to roughly 3,300 rupees. If it had been a question of just one he might have managed, but you needed a minimum of three. When the salesperson came over, Zubin said that he was just looking around.

It snowed early that year.

"It gets, like, how cold in the winter in India?" his roommate, Bennet, asked.

Zubin didn't feel like explaining the varied geography of India, the mountains and the coasts. "About sixty degrees Fahrenheit," he said.

"*Man*," said Bennet. Jason Bennet was a nice guy, an athlete from Nat-ick, Massachusetts. He took Zubin to eat at the lacrosse table, where Zubin looked not just foreign, but as if he were another species—he weighed at least ten kilos less than the smallest guy, and felt hundreds of years older. He felt as if he were surrounded by enormous and powerful children. They were hungry, and then they were restless; they ran around and around in circles, and then they were tired. Five nights a week they'd pledged to keep sober; on the other two they drank systematically until they passed out.

He remembered the day in October that he'd accepted the sweater (it was raining) and how he'd waited until Jason left for practice before put-ting it on. He pulled the sweater over his head and saw, in the second of wooly darkness, his father. Or rather, he saw his father's face, floating in his mind's eye like the Cheshire Cat. The face was making an expression that Zubin remembered from the time he was ten, and had proudly revealed the thousand rupees he'd made by organizing a betting pool on the horse races among the boys in the fifth standard.

He'd resolved immediately to return the sweater, and then he had looked in the mirror. What he saw surprised him: someone small but good-looking, with fine features and dark, intense eyes, the kind of guy a girl, not just a girl from home but any girl—an American girl—might find attractive.

And he wanted one of those: there was no use pretending he didn't. He watched them from his first-floor window, as close as fish in an aquarium tank. They hurried past him, laughing and calling out to one another, in their boys' clothes: boots, T-shirts with cryptic messages, jeans worn low and tight across the hips. You thought of the panties underneath those jeans, and in the laundry room you often saw those panties: impossibly sheer, in incredible colors, occasionally, delightfully torn. The girls folding their laundry next to him were entirely different from the ones at home. They were clearly free to do whatever they wanted—a possibility that often hit him, in class or the library or on the historic brick walkways of the Radcliffe Quad, so intensely that he had to stop and take a deep breath, as if he were on the point of blacking out.

He wore Jason's sweater every day, and was often too warm; the classrooms were overheated and dry as furnaces. He almost never ran into Jason, who had an active and effortless social schedule to complement his rigorous athletic one. And so it was a surprise, one day in late October, to come back to the room and find his roommate hunched miserably over a textbook at his desk.

"Midterms," Jason said, by way of an explanation. Zubin went over and looked at the problem set, from an introductory physics class. He'd taken a similar class at Cathedral; now he laid out the equations and watched as Jason completed them, correcting his roommate's mistakes as they went along. After the third problem Jason looked up.

"Man, thanks." And then, as if it had just occurred to him. "Hey, if you want to keep that—"

He had managed so completely to forget about the sweater that he almost didn't know what Jason meant.

"It's too small for me anyway."

"No," Zubin said.

"Seriously. I may have a couple of others too. Coach has been making us eat like hogs."

"Thanks," Zubin said. "But I want something less preppy."

Jason looked at him.

"No offense," Zubin said. "I've just been too fucking lazy. I'll go tomorrow."

The next day he went back to the Co-op with his almost-new textbooks in a bag. These were for his required classes (what they called the Core, or general knowledge), as well as organic chemistry. If you got to the reserve reading room at nine, the textbooks were almost always there. He told himself that the paperbacks for his nineteenth-century novel class weren't worth selling—he'd bought them used anyway—and when he took the rest of the books out and put them on the counter, he realized he had forgotten the *Norton Anthology of American Literature* in his dorm room. But the books came to $477.80 without it. He took the T downtown to a mall where he bought a down jacket for $300, as warm as a sleeping bag, the same thing the black kids wore. He got a wool watchman's cap with a Nike swoosh.

When he got home, Jason laughed. "Dude, what happened? You're totally ghetto." But there was approval in it. Folding the brown sweater on Jason's bed, Zubin felt strong and relieved, as if he had narrowly avoided a terrible mistake.

Julia had been having a dream about losing it. There was no sex in the dream; she couldn't remember whom she'd slept with, or when. All she experienced was the frustrating impossibility of getting it back, like watching an earring drop and scatter in the bathroom sink, roll and clink down the drain before she could put her hand on it. The relief she felt on waking up every time was like a warning.

She had almost lost it in Paris, before they moved. He was German, not French, gangly but still handsome, with brown eyes and blondish hair. His name was Markus. He was a year ahead of her at the American School and he already knew that he wanted to go back to Berlin for university, and then join the Peace Corps. On the phone at night, he tried to get her to come with him.

At dinner Julia mentioned this idea to her family.

"*You* in the Peace Corps?" said her sister Claudia, who was visiting from New York. "I wonder if Agnès B. makes a safari line?"

When Claudia came home, she stayed with Julia on the fourth floor, in the *chambre de bonne* where she had twin beds and her Radiohead poster, all her CDs organized by record label and a very old stuffed monkey named Frank. The apartment was half a block from the Seine, in an old hotel on the Rue des Saint-Pères; in the living room were two antique chairs, upholstered in red-and-gold-striped brocade, and a porcelain clock with shepherdesses on it. The chairs and the clock were Louis XVI, the rugs were from Tehran, and everything else was beige linen.

Claudia, who now lived with her boyfriend in a railroad apartment on the Lower East Side, liked to pretend she was poor. She talked about erratic hot water and rent control and cockroaches, and when she came to visit them in Paris she acted surprised, as if the houses she'd grown up in—first San Francisco, then Delhi, then Dallas, Moscow and Paris—hadn't been in the same kind of neighborhood, with the same pair of Louis XVI chairs.

"I can't believe you have a Prada backpack," she said to Julia. Claudia had been sitting at the table in the kitchen, drinking espresso and eating an orange indifferently, section by section. "Mom's going crazy in her old age."

"I bought it," Julia said.

"Yeah, but with what?"

"I've been selling my body on the side—after school."

Claudia rolled her eyes and took a sip of her espresso; she looked out the window into the little back garden. "It's so *peaceful* here," she said, proving something Julia already suspected: that her sister had no idea what was going on in their house.

It started when her father's best friend, Bernie, left Paris to take a job with a French wireless company in Bombay. He'd wanted Julia's father to leave with him, but even though her father complained all the time about the oil business, he wouldn't go. Julia heard him telling her mother that he was in the middle of an important deal.

"This is the biggest thing we've done. I love Bernie—but he's afraid of being successful. He's afraid of a couple of fat Russians."

Somehow Bernie had managed to convince her mother that Bombay was a good idea. She would read the share price of the wireless company out loud from the newspaper in the mornings, while her father was making eggs. It was a strange reversal; in the past, all her mother had wanted was for her father to stay at home. The places he traveled had been a family joke, as if he were trying to outdo himself with the strangeness of the cities— Istanbul and Muscat eventually became Tbilisi, Ashkhabad, Tashkent. Now, when Julia had heard the strained way that her mother talked about Bernie and wireless communication, she had known she was hearing part of a larger argument—known enough to determine its size, if not its subject. It was like watching the exposed bit of a dangerous piece of driftwood, floating just above the surface of a river.

Soon after Claudia's visit, in the spring of Julia's freshman year, her parents gave her a choice. Her mother took her to Galeries Lafayette, and then to lunch at her favorite crêperie on the Ile Saint-Louis, where, in between *galettes tomate-fromage* and *crêpe pomme-chantilly*, she told Julia about the divorce. She said she had found a two-bedroom apartment in the West Village: a "feat," she called it.

"New York will be a fresh start—psychologically," her mother said. "There's a bedroom that's just yours, and we'll be a five-minute train ride from Claudie. There are wonderful girls' schools— I know you were really happy at Hockaday—"

"No I wasn't."

"Or we can look at some coed schools. And I'm finally going to get to go back for my master's—" She leaned forward confidentially. "We could both be graduating at the same time."

"I want to go back to San Francisco."

"We haven't lived in San Francisco since you were three."

"So?"

The sympathetic look her mother gave her made Julia want to yank the tablecloth out from underneath their dishes, just to hear the glass breaking on the rustic stone floor.

"For right now that isn't possible," her mother said. "But there's no reason we can't talk again in a year."

Julia had stopped being hungry, but she finished her mother's crêpe anyway. Recently her mother had stopped eating anything sweet; she said it "irritated her stomach" but Julia knew the real reason was Dr. Fabrol, who had an office on the Ile Saint-Louis very near the crêperie. Julia had been seeing Dr. Fabrol once a week during the two years they'd been in

Paris; his office was dark and tiny, with a rough brown rug and tropical plants which he misted from his chair with a plastic spritzer while Julia was talking. When he got excited he swallowed, making a clicking sound in the back of his throat.

In front of his desk Dr. Fabrol kept a sandbox full of little plastic figures: trolls with brightly colored hair, toy soldiers, and dollhouse people dressed in American clothes from the Fifties. He said that adults could learn a lot about themselves by playing "*les jeux des enfants.*" In one session, when Julia couldn't think of anything to say, she'd made a ring of soldiers in the sand, and then without looking at him, put the mother doll in the center. She thought this might be over the top even for Dr. Fabrol, but he started arranging things on his desk, pretending he was less interested than he was so that she would continue. She could hear him clicking.

The mother doll had yellow floss hair and a full figure and a red-and-white polka-dotted dress with a belt, like something Lucille Ball would wear. She looked nothing like Julia's mother—a fact that Dr. Fabrol obviously knew, since Julia's mother came so often to pick her up. Sometimes she would be carrying bags from the nearby shops; once she told them she'd just come from an exhibit at the new Islamic cultural center. She brought Dr. Fabrol a postcard of a Phoenician sarcophagus.

"I think this was the piece you mentioned?" Her mother's voice was louder than necessary. "I think you must have told me about it—the last time I was here to pick Julia up?"

"Could be, could be," Dr. Fabrol said, in his stupid accent. They both watched Julia as if she were a TV and they were waiting to find out about the weather. She couldn't believe how dumb they must have thought she was.

Her father asked her if she wanted to go for an early morning walk with their black labrador, Baxter, in the Tuileries. She would've said no—she wasn't a morning person—if she hadn't known what was going on from the lunch with her mother. They put their coats on in the dark hall with Baxter running around their legs, but by the time they left the apartment, the sun was coming up. The river threw off bright sparks. They crossed the bridge, and went through the archway into the courtyard of the Louvre. There were no tourists that early but a lot of people were walking or jogging on the paths above the fountain.

"Look at all these people," her father said. "A few years ago, they wouldn't have been awake. If they were awake they would've been having coffee and a cigarette. Which reminds me."

Julia held the leash while her father took out his cigarettes. He wasn't fat but he was tall and pleasantly big. His eyes squeezed shut when he smiled, and he had a beard, mostly grey now, which he trimmed every evening before dinner with special scissors. When she was younger, she had looked at other fathers and felt sorry for their children; no one else's father looked like a father to her.

In the shade by the stone wall of the Tuileries, with his back to the flashing fountain, her father tapped the pack, lifted it to his mouth and pulled a cigarette out between his lips. He rummaged in the pocket of his brown corduroys for a box of the tiny wax matches he always brought back from India, a white swan on a red box. He cupped his hand, lit the cigarette and exhaled away from Julia. Then he took back Baxter's leash and said: "Why San Francisco?"

She wasn't prepared. "I don't know." She could picture the broad stillness of the bay, like being inside a postcard. Was she remembering a postcard?

"It's quiet," she said.

"I didn't know quiet was high on your list."

She tried to think of something else.

"You know what I'd like?" her father asked suddenly. "I'd like to watch the sunrise from the Golden Gate—do you remember doing that?"

"Yes," Julia lied.

"I think you were in your stroller." Her father grinned. "That was when you were an early riser."

"I could set my alarm."

"You could set it," her father teased her.

"I'm awake now," she said.

Her father stopped to let Baxter nose around underneath one of the grey stone planters. He looked at the cigarette in his hand as if he didn't know what to do with it, dropped and stamped it out, half-smoked.

"Can I have one?"

"Over my dead body."

"I'm not sure I want to go to New York."

"You want to stay here?" He said it lightly, as if it were a possibility.

"I want to go with you," she said. As she said it, she knew how much she wanted it.

She could see him trying to say no. Their shadows were very sharp on the clean paving stones; above the bridge, the gold Mercury was almost too bright to look at.

"Just for the year and a half."

"*Bombay*," her father said.

"I liked India last time."

Her father looked at her. "You were six."

"Why are you going?"

"Because I hate oil and I hate oilmen. And I hate these goddamn *kommersants*. If I'd done it when Bernie first offered—" Her father stopped. "You do not need to hear about this."

Julia didn't need to hear about it; she already knew. Her father was taking the job in Bombay—doing exactly what her mother had wanted him to do—just as her parents were getting a divorce. The only explanation was that he'd found out about Dr. Fabrol. Even though her mother was going to New York (where she would have to find another psychologist to help her get over Julia's), Julia could see how her father wouldn't want to stay in Paris. He would want to get as far away as possible.

Julia steered the conversation safely toward business: "It's like mobile phones, right?"

"It is mobile phones." Her father smiled at her. "Something you know about."

"I'm not *that* bad."

"No, you're not."

They'd walked a circle in the shade, on the promenade above the park. Her father stopped, as if he wasn't sure whether he wanted to go around again.

"It's not even two years," Julia said. There was relief just in saying it, the same kind she'd felt certain mornings before grade school, when her mother had touched her head and said *fever*.

Her father looked at the Pont Neuf; he seemed to be fighting with himself.

"I'd rather start over in college—with everybody else," she added.

Her father was nodding slowly. "That's something we could explain to your mother."

• • •

As you got older, Zubin noticed, very occasionally a fantasy that you'd been having forever came true. It was disorienting, like waking up in a new and better apartment, remembering that you'd moved, but not quite believing that you would never go back to the old place.

That was the way it was with Tessa. Their first conversation was about William Gaddis; they had both read *Carpenter's Gothic*, and Zubin was halfway through *JR*. In fact he had never finished *JR*, but after the party he'd gone home and lain on his back in bed, semierect but postponing jerking off with the relaxed and pleasant anticipation of a sure thing, and turned fifty pages. He didn't retain much of the content of those pages the next morning, but he remembered having felt that Gaddis was an important part of what he'd called his "literary pedigree," as he and Tessa gulped cold red wine in the historic, unheated offices of the campus literary magazine. He even told her that he'd started writing poems himself.

"Can I read them?" she asked. As if he could show those poems to anyone!

Tessa moved closer to him; their shoulders and their hips and their knees were pressed together.

"Sure," he said. "If you want."

They had finished the wine. Zubin told her that books were a kind of religion for him, that when things seemed unbearable the only comfort he knew was to read. He did not tell her that he was more likely to read science fiction at those times than William Gaddis; he hardly remembered that himself.

"What do you want to do now?" he'd asked, as they stepped out onto the narrow street, where the wind was colder than anything he could have imagined at home. He thought she would say she had class in the morning, or that it was late, or that she was meeting her roommate at eleven, and so it was a surprise to him when she turned and put her tongue in his mouth. The wind disappeared then, and everything was perfectly quiet. When she pulled away, her cheeks and the triangle of exposed skin between her scarf and her jacket were pink. Tessa hung her head, and in a whisper that was more exciting to him than any picture he had ever seen, print or film, said: "Let's go back to your room for a bit."

He was still writing to Asha then. She was a year below him in school, and her parents had been lenient because they socialized with his parents (and because Zubin was going to Harvard). They had allowed him to come over and have a cup of tea, and then to take Asha for a walk along Marine Drive, as long as he brought her back well before dark. Once they had walked up the stairs from Hughes Road to Hanging Garden and sat on one of the benches, where the clerks and shopgirls whispered to each other in the foliage. He had ignored her flicker of hesitation and pointed down at the sun setting over the city: the Spenta building with a pink foam of cloud behind it, like a second horizon above the bay. He said that he wouldn't change the worst of the concrete-block apartments, with their exposed pipes and hanging laundry and water-stained, crumbling facades, because of the way they set off plain Babulnath Temple, made its tinseled orange flag and bulbous dome rise spectacularly from the dense vegetation, like a spaceship landed on Malabar Hill.

He was talking like that because he wanted to kiss her, but he sometimes got carried away. And when he noticed her again he saw that she was almost crying with the strain of how to tell him that she had to get home *right now*. He pointed to the still-blue sky over the bay (although the light was fading and the people coming up the path were already dark shapes) and took her hand and together they climbed up to the streetlight, and turned left toward her parents' apartment. They dropped each other's hand automatically when they got to the driveway, but Asha was so relieved that, in the mirrored elevator on the way up, she closed her eyes and let him kiss her.

That kiss was the sum of Zubin's experience, when he lost it with Tessa on Jason Bennet's green futon. He would remember forever the way she pushed him away, knelt in front of him and, with her jeans unbuttoned, arched her back to unhook her bra and free what were still the breasts that Zubin held in his mind's eye: buoyant and pale with surprising long, dark nipples.

Clothed, Tessa's primary feature was her amazing acceptability; there was absolutely nothing wrong with the way she looked or dressed or the things she said at the meetings of the literary magazine. But when he tried to remember her face now, he came up with a white oval into which eyes, a nose and a pair of lips would surface only separately, like leftover Cheerios in a bowl of milk.

When he returned from the States the second time, Asha was married to a lawyer and living in Cusrow Baug. She had twin five-year-old boys, and a three-year-old girl. She had edited a book of essays by famous writers about Bombay. The first time he'd run into her, at a wine tasting at the Taj President, he'd asked her what she was doing and she did not say, like so many Bombay women he knew, that she was married and had three children. She said: "Prostitution." And when he looked blank, she laughed and said, "I'm doing a book on prostitution now. Interviews and case histories of prostitutes in Mumbai."

When their city and all of its streets had been renamed overnight, in '94, Zubin had had long discussions with Indian friends in New York about the political implications of the change. Now that he was back those debates seemed silly. The street signs were just something to notice once and shake your head at, like the sidewalks below them—constantly torn up and then abandoned for months.

His mother was delighted to have him back. "We won't bother you," she said. "It will be like you have your own artist's loft."

"Maybe I should start a salon," Zubin joked. He was standing in the living room, a few weeks after he'd gotten back, helping himself from a bottle of Rémy Martin.

"Or a saloon," his father remarked, passing through.

He didn't tell his parents that he was writing a book, mostly because only three of the thirty poems he'd begun were actually finished; that regrettable fact was not his fault, but the fault of the crow that lived on the sheet of tin that was patching the roof over his bedroom window. He'd learned to ignore the chain saw from the new apartment block that was going up under spindly bamboo scaffolding, the hammering across the road, the twenty-four-hour traffic and the fishwallah who came through their apartment blocks between ten and ten thirty every morning, carrying a steel case on his head and calling "hell-o, hell-o, hell-o." These were routine sounds, but the crow was clever. It called at uneven intervals, so that just as Zubin was convinced it had gone away, it began again. The sound was mournful and rough, as depressing as a baby wailing; it sounded to Zubin like despair.

When he'd first got back to Bombay, he'd been embarrassed about the way his students' parents introduced him: "BA from Harvard; Henry fellow at Oxford; Ph.D. from Columbia." He would correct them and say that he hadn't finished the Ph.D. (in fact, he'd barely started his dissertation) when he quit. That honesty had made everyone unhappy, and had been bad for business. Now he said his dissertation was in progress. He told his students' parents that he wanted to spend a little time here, since he would probably end up in the States.

The parents assumed that he'd come back to get married. They pushed their children toward him, yelling at them: "Listen to Zubin; he's done three degrees—two on scholarship—not lazy and spoiled like you. Aren't I paying enough for this tutoring?" They said it in Hindi, as if he couldn't understand.

The kids were rapt and attentive. They did the practice tests he assigned them; they wrote the essays and read the books. They didn't care about Harvard, Oxford and Columbia. They were thinking of Boston, London and New York. He could read their minds. The girls asked about particular shops; the boys wanted to know how many girlfriends he had had, and how far they'd been willing to go.

None of his students could believe he'd come back voluntarily. They asked him about it again and again. How could he tell them that he'd missed his bedroom? He had felt that if he could just get back *there*—the dark wood floor, the brick walls of books, the ancient rolltop desk from Chor Bazaar—something would fall back into place, not inside him but in front of him, like the lengths of replacement track you sometimes saw them fitting at night on dark sections of the Western Railway commuter line.

He had come home to write his book, but it wasn't going to be a book about Bombay. There were no mangoes in his poems, and no beggars, no cows or Hindu gods. What he wanted to write about was a moment of quiet. Sometimes sitting alone in his room there would be a few seconds, a silent pocket without the crow or the hammering or wheels on the macadam outside. Those were the moments he felt most himself; at the same time, he felt that he was paying for that peace very dearly—that life, his life, was rolling away outside.

"But why did you wait three years?" his mother asked. "Why didn't you come home right away?"

When he thought about it now, he was surprised that it had taken only three years to extract himself from graduate school. He counted it among the more efficient periods of his life so far.

He saw Julia twice a week, on Tuesdays and Thursdays. One afternoon when his mother was hosting a bridge tournament, he went to her house for the first time. A servant showed him into her room and purposefully shut the door, as if he'd had instructions not to disturb them. It was only four o'clock but the blinds were drawn. The lights were on and the door to her bathroom was closed; he could hear the tap running. Zubin sat at a small, varnished desk. He might have been in any girl's room in America: stacks of magazines on the bookshelf, tacked-up posters of bands he didn't know, shoes scattered across a pink rag rug and pieces of pastel-colored clothing crumpled in with the sheets on the bed. A pair of jeans was on the floor where she'd stepped out of them, and the denim held her shape: open, round and paler on the inside of the fabric.

Both doors opened at once. Zubin didn't know whether to look at the barefoot girl coming out of the bathroom, or the massive, bearded white man who had appeared from the hall.

"Hi, Daddy," Julia said. "This is Zubin, my tutor."

"We spoke on the phone, sir," said Zubin, getting up.

Julia's father shook hands as if it were a quaint custom Zubin had insisted on. He sat down on his daughter's bed, and the springs protested. He looked at Zubin.

"What are you working on today?"

"*Dad.*"

"Yes."

"He just got here."

Julia's father held up one hand in defense. "I'd be perfectly happy if you didn't get into college. Then you could just stay here."

Julia rolled her eyes, a habit that struck Zubin as particularly American.

"We'll start working on her essay today." Zubin turned to Julia: "Did you do a draft?" He'd asked her the same thing twice a week for the past three, and he knew what the answer would be. He wouldn't have put her on the spot if he hadn't been so nervous himself. But Julia surprised him: "I just finished."

"What did you write about?" her father asked eagerly.

"The difficulties of being from a broken home."

"Very interesting," he said, without missing a beat.

"I couldn't have done it without you."

"I try," he said casually, as if this were the kind of conversation they had all the time. "So maybe we don't even need Zubin—if you've already written your essay?"

Julia shook her head: "It isn't good."

Zubin felt he should say something. "The new format of the SAT places much greater emphasis on writing skills." He felt like an idiot.

Julia's father considered Zubin. "You do this full-time?"

"Yes."

"Did you always want to be a teacher?"

"I wanted to be a poet," Zubin said. He could feel himself blushing but mostly he was surprised that he had told these two strangers something he hadn't even told his parents.

"Do you write poems now?"

"Sometimes," Zubin said.

"There are some good Marathi poets, aren't there?"

"That's not what I'm interested in." Zubin thought he'd spoken too forcefully, but it didn't seem to bother Julia's father.

"I'll leave you two to work now. If you want, come to dinner sometime—our cook makes terrible Continental food, because my daughter won't eat Indian."

Zubin smiled. "That sounds good—thank you, sir."

"Mark," Julia's father said, closing the door gently behind him.

"Your dad seems cool."

Julia was gathering up all of her clothes furiously from the bed and the floor. She opened her closet door—a light went on automatically—and threw them inside. Then she slammed it. He didn't know what he'd done wrong.

"Do you want me to take a look at what you have?"

"What?"

"Of the essay."

"I didn't write an essay."

"You said—"

Julia laughed. "Yeah."

"How do you expect to get into Berkeley?"

"You're going to write it."

"I don't do that." He sounded prim.

"I'll pay you."

Zubin got up. "I think we're finished."

She took her hair out of the band and redid it, her arms above her head. He couldn't see any difference when she finished. "A hundred dollars."

"Why do you want me to write your essay?"

Suddenly Julia sank down onto the floor, hugging her knees. "I have to get out of here."

"You said that before." He wasn't falling for the melodrama. "I'll help you do it yourself."

"A thousand. On top of the regular fee."

Zubin stared. "Where are you going to get that much money?"

"Half a *lakh*."

"That calculation even I could have managed," Zubin said, but she wasn't paying attention. She picked up a magazine off her night table, and flopped down on the bed. He had the feeling that she was giving him time to consider her offer and he found himself—in that sealed-off corner of his brain where these things happen—considering it.

With $200 a week, plus the $1,000 bonus, he easily could stop all the tutoring except Julia's. And with all of that time, there would be no excuse not to finish his manuscript. There were some prizes for first collections in England and America; they didn't pay a lot, but they published your book. Artists, he thought, did all kinds of things for their work. They made every kind of sacrifice—financial, personal, moral—so as not to compromise the only thing that was truly important.

"I'll make a deal with you," Zubin said.

Julia looked bored.

"You try it first. If you get really stuck—then maybe. And I'll help you think of the idea."

"They *give* you the idea," she said. "Remember?"

"I'll take you to a couple of places. We'll see which one strikes you." This, he told himself, was hands-on education. Thanks to him, Julia would finally see the city where she had been living for nearly a year.

"Great," said Julia sarcastically. "Can we go to Elephanta?"

"Better than Elephanta."

"To the Gateway of India? Will you buy me one of those big, spotted balloons?"

"Just wait," said Zubin. "There's some stuff you don't know about yet."

· · ·

They walked from his house past the Hanging Garden, to the small vegetable market in the lane above the Walkeshwar Temple. They went down a flight of uneven steps, past small, open electronic shops where men clustered around televisions waiting for the cricket scores. The path wound between low houses, painted pink or green, a primary school and a tiny, white temple with a marble courtyard and a black *nandi* draped in marigolds. Two vegetable vendors moved to the side to let them pass, swiveling their heads to look, each with one hand lightly poised on the flat basket balanced on her head. Inside the baskets, arranged in an elegant multicolored whorl, were eggplants, mint, tomatoes, Chinese lettuces, okra, and the smooth white pumpkins called *dudhi*. Further on a poster man had laid out his wares on a frayed, blue tarpaulin: the usual movie stars and glossy deities, plus kittens, puppies and an enormous white baby, in a diaper and pink headband. Across the bottom of a composite photo— an English cottage superimposed on a Thai beach, in the shadow of Swiss mountains dusted with yellow and purple wildflowers and bisected by a torrential Amazonian waterfall—were the words, *Home is where. When you go there, they have to let you in.* Punctuation aside, it was difficult for Zubin to imagine a more depressing sentiment.

"You know what I hate?"

Zubin had a strange urge to touch her. It wasn't a sexual thing, he didn't think. He just wanted to take her hand. "What?"

"Crows."

Zubin smiled.

"You probably think they're poetic or something."

"No."

"Like Edgar Allan Poe."

"That was a raven."

"Edgar Allan Po*etic*." She giggled.

"This kind of verbal play is encouraging," Zubin said. "If only you would apply it to your practice tests."

"I can't concentrate at home," Julia said. "There are too many distractions."

"Like what?" Julia's room was the quietest place he'd been in Bombay.

"My father."

The steps opened suddenly onto the temple tank: a dark green square of water cut out of the stone. Below them, a schoolgirl in a purple jumper and a white blouse, her hair plaited with two red ribbons, was filling a brass jug. At the other end a laborer cleared muck from the bottom with an iron spade. His grandmother had brought him here when he was a kid. She had described the city as it had been: just the sea and the fishing villages clinging to the rocks, the lush, green hills, and in the hills these hive-shaped temples, surrounded by the tiny colored houses of the priests. The concrete-block apartments were still visible on the Malabar side of the tank, but if you faced the sea you could ignore them.

"My father keeps me locked up in a cage," Julia said mournfully.

"Although he lets you out for Fire and Ice," Zubin observed.

"He doesn't. He ignores it when I go to Fire and Ice. All he'd have to do is look in at night. I don't put pillows in the bed or anything."

"He's probably trying to respect your privacy."

"I'm his *kid*. I'm not supposed to have privacy." She sat down suddenly on the steps, but she didn't seem upset. She shaded her eyes with her hand. He liked the way she looked, looking—more serious than he'd seen her before.

"Do you think it's beautiful here?" he asked.

The sun had gone behind the buildings, and was setting over the sea and the slum on the rocks above the water. There was an orange glaze over half the tank; the other, shadowed half was green and cold. Shocked-looking white ducks with orange feet stood in the shade, each facing a different direction, and on the opposite side two boys played an impossibly old-fashioned game, whooping as they rolled a worn-out bicycle tire along the steps with a stick. All around them bells were ringing.

"I think lots of things are beautiful," Julia said slowly. "If you see them at the right time. But you come back and the light is different, or someone's left some trash, or you're in a bad mood—or whatever. Everything gets ugly."

"This is what your essay is about." He didn't think before he said it; it just came to him.

"The Banganga Tank?"

"Beauty," he said.

She frowned.

"It's your idea."

She was trying not to show she was pleased. Her mouth turned up at the corners, and she scowled to hide it, "I guess that's okay. I guess it doesn't really matter what you choose."

Julia was a virgin, but Anouk wasn't. Anouk was Bernie's daughter; she lived in a fancy house behind a carved wooden gate, on one of the winding lanes at Cumbala Hill. Julia liked the ornamental garden, with brushed-steel plaques that identified the plants in English and Latin, and the blue ceramic pool full of lumpy-headed white-and-orange goldfish. Behind the goldfish pond was a cedar sauna, and it was in the sauna that it had happened. The boy wasn't especially cute, but he was distantly related to the royal house of Jodhpur. They'd only done it once; according to Anouk that was all it took, before you could consider yourself ready for a real boyfriend at university.

"It's something to get over with," Anouk said. "You simply hold your breath." They were listening to the Shakira album in Anouk's room, which was covered with pictures of models from magazines. There were even a few pictures of Anouk, who was tall enough for print ads, but not to go to Europe and be on runways. She was also in a Colgate commercial that you saw on the Hindi stations. Being Anouk's best friend was the thing that saved Julia at the American School, where the kids talked about their fathers' jobs and their vacation houses even more than they had in Paris. At least at the school in Paris they'd gotten to take a lot of trips—to museums, the Bibliothèque Nationale, and Monet's house at Giverny.

There was no question of losing her virginity to any of the boys at school. Everyone would know about it the next day.

"You should have done it with Markus," Anouk said, for the hundredth time, one afternoon when they were lying on the floor of her bedroom, flipping through magazines.

Julia sometimes thought the same thing; it was hard to describe why they hadn't done it. They'd talked about it, like they'd talked about everything, endlessly, late at night on the phone, as if they were the only people awake in the city. Markus was her best friend—still, when she was sad, he was the one she wanted to talk to—but when they kissed he put his tongue too far into her mouth and moved it around in a way that made her want to gag. He was grateful when she took off her top and let him put his hand underneath her bra, and sometimes she thought he was relieved too, when she said no to other things.

"You could write him," Anouk suggested.

"I'd love him to come visit," Julia allowed.

"Visit and come."

"Gross."

Anouk looked at her sternly. She had fair skin and short hair that flipped up underneath her ears. She had cat-shaped green eyes exactly like the ones in the picture of her French grandmother, which stared out of an ivory frame on a table in the hall.

"What about your tutor?"

Julia pretended to be horrified. "Zubin?"

"He's cute, right?"

"He's about a million years older than us."

"How old?"

"Twenty-nine, I think."

Anouk went into her dresser and rummaged around. "Just in case," she said innocently, tossing Julia a little foil-wrapped packet.

This wasn't the way it was supposed to go—you weren't supposed to be the one who got the condom—but you weren't supposed to go to high school in Bombay, to live alone with your father, or to lose your virginity to your SAT tutor. She wondered if she and Zubin would do it on the mattress in his room, or if he would press her up against the wall, like in *9½ Weeks*.

"You better call me, like, the second after," Anouk instructed her.

She almost told Anouk about the virginity dream, and then didn't. She didn't really want to hear her friend's interpretation.

It was unclear where she and Markus would've done it, since at that time boys weren't allowed in her room. There were a lot of rules, particularly after her mother left. When she was out, around eleven, her father would message her mobile, something like: WHAT TIME, MISSY? or simply, ETA? If she didn't send one right back, he would call. She would roll her eyes, at the café or the party or the club, and say to Markus, "My dad."

"Well," Markus would say. "You're his daughter."

When she came home, her father would be waiting on the couch with a book. He read the same books over and over, especially the ones by Russians. She would have to come in and give him a kiss, and if he smelled cigarettes he would ask to see her bag.

"You can't look in my bag," she would say, and her father would hold out his hand. "Everybody else smokes," she told him. "I can't help smelling like it." She was always careful to give Markus her Dunhills before she went home.

"Don't you trust me?" she said sometimes (especially when she was drunk).

Her father smiled. "No. I love you too much for that."

It was pouring and the rain almost shrieked on Zubin's tin roof, which still hadn't been repaired. They were working on reading comprehension; a test two years ago had used Marvell's "To His Coy Mistress." Zubin preferred "The Garden," but he'd had more success teaching "To His Coy Mistress" to his students; they told him it seemed "modern." Many of his students seemed to think that sex was a relatively new invention.

"It's a persuasive poem," Zubin said. "In a way, it has something in common with an essay."

Julia narrowed her eyes. "What do you mean, persuasive?"

"He wants to sleep with her."

"And she doesn't want to."

"Right," Zubin said.

"Is she a virgin?"

"You tell me." Zubin remembered legions of teachers singsonging exactly those words. "Look at line twenty-eight."

"That's disgusting."

"Good," he said. "You understand it. That's what the poet wanted—to shock her a little."

"That's so manipulative!"

It was amazing, he thought, the way Americans all embraced that kind of psychobabble. *Language* is manipulative, he wanted to tell her.

"I think it might have been very convincing," he said instead.

"*Vegetable* love?"

"It's strange, and that's what makes it vivid. The so-called metaphysical poets are known for this kind of conceit."

"That they were conceited?"

"Conceit," Zubin said. "Write this down." He gave her the definition; he sounded conceited.

"The sun is like a flower that blooms for just one hour," Julia said suddenly.

"That's the opposite," Zubin said. "A comparison so common that it doesn't mean anything—you see the difference?"

Julia nodded wearily. It was too hot in the room. Zubin got up and propped the window open with the wooden stop. Water sluiced off the dark, shiny leaves of the magnolia.

"What is that?"

"What?"

"That thing, about the sun."

She kicked her foot petulantly against his desk. The hammering outside was like an echo, miraculously persisting in spite of the rain. "Ray Bradbury," she said finally. "We read it in school."

"I know that story," Zubin said. "With the kids on Venus. It rains for seven years, and then the sun comes out and they lock the girl in the closet. Why do they lock her up?"

"Because she's from Earth. She's the only one who's seen it."

"The sun."

Julia nodded. "They're all jealous."

People thought she could go out all the time because she was American. She let them think it. One night she decided to stop bothering with the outside stairs; she was wearing new jeans that her mother had sent her; purple cowboy boots and a sparkly silver halter top that showed off her stomach. She had a shawl for outside, but she didn't put it on right away. Her father was working in his study with the door cracked open.

The clock in the hall said ten twenty. Her boots made a loud noise on the tiles.

"Hi," her father called.

"Hi."

"Where are you going?"

"A party."

"Where?"

"Juhu." She stepped into his study. "On the beach."

He put the book down and took off his glasses. "Do you find that many people are doing Ecstasy—when you go to these parties?"

"Dad."

"I'm not being critical—I read an article about it in *Time*. My interest is purely anthropological."

"Yes," Julia said. "All the time. We're all on Ecstasy from the moment we wake up in the morning."

"That's what I thought."

"I have to go."

"I don't want to keep you." He smiled. "Well I do, but—" Her father was charming; it was like a reflex.

"See you in the morning," she said.

The worst thing was that her father *knew* she knew. He might have thought Julia knew even before she actually did; that was when he started letting her do things like go out at ten thirty, and smoke on the staircase outside her bedroom. It was as if she'd entered into a kind of pact without knowing it; and by the time she found out why they were in Bombay for real, it was too late to change her mind.

It was Anouk who told her, one humid night when they were having their tennis lesson at Willingdon. The air was so hazy that Julia kept losing the ball in the sodium lights. They didn't notice who'd come in and taken the last court next to the parking lot until the lesson was over. Then Anouk said: "Wow, look—*Papa!*" Bernie lobbed the ball and waved; as they walked toward the other court, Julia's father set up for an overhead and smashed the ball into the net. He raised his fist in mock anger, and grinned at them.

"Good lesson?"

"Julia did well."

"I did not."

"Wait for Bernie to finish me off," Julia's father said. "Then we'll take you home."

"How much longer?"

"When we're finished," said Bernie sharply.

"On sort ce soir."

"On va voir," her father said. Anouk started to say something and stopped. She caught one ankle behind her back calmly, stretched, and shifted her attention to Julia's father. "How long?"

He smiled. "Not more than twenty."

They waited in the enclosure, behind a thin white net that was meant to keep out the balls, but didn't, and ordered fresh lime sodas.

"We need an hour to get ready, at least."

"I'm not going."

"Yes you are."

Anouk put her legs up on the table and Julia did the same and they compared: Anouk's were longer and thinner, but Julia's had a better shape. Julia's phone beeped.

"It's from Zubin."

Anouk took the phone.

"It's just about my lesson."

Anouk read Zubin's message in an English accent: CAN WE SHIFT FROM FIVE TO SIX ON THURSDAY?

"He doesn't talk like that," Julia said, but she knew what Anouk meant. Zubin was the only person she knew who wrote SMS in full sentences, without any abbreviations.

Anouk tipped her head back and shut her eyes. Her throat was smooth and brown and underneath her sleeveless white top, her breasts were outlined, the nipples pointing up. "Tell him I'm hot for him."

"You're a flirt."

Anouk sat up and looked at the court. Now Bernie was serving. Both men had long, dark stains down the fronts of their shirts. A little bit of a breeze was coming from the trees behind the courts; Julia felt the sweat between her shoulders. She thought she'd gone too far, and she was glad when Anouk said, "When are they going to be finished?"

"They'll be done in a second. I think they both just play 'cause the other one wants to."

"What do you mean?"

"I mean, my dad never played in Paris."

"Mine did," Anouk said.

"So maybe he just likes playing with your dad."

Anouk tilted her head to the side for a minute, as if she were thinking. "He would have to though."

The adrenaline from the fight they'd almost had, defused a minute before, came flooding back. She could feel her pulse in her wrists. "What do you mean?"

Her friend opened her eyes wide. "I mean, your dad's probably grateful."

"Grateful for *what*?"

"The job."

"He had a good job before."

Anouk blinked incredulously. "Are you serious?"

"He was the operations manager in Central Asia."

"Was," Anouk said.

"Yeah, well," Julia said. "He didn't want to go back to the States after my mom did."

"My God," Anouk said. "That's what they told you?"

Julia looked at her. *Whatever you're going to say, don't say it.* But she didn't say anything.

"You have it backwards," Anouk said. "Your mother left because of what happened. She went to America, because she knew your father couldn't. There was an article about it in *Nefte Compass*—I couldn't read it, because it was in Russian, but my dad read it." She lifted her beautiful eyes to Julia's. "My dad said it wasn't fair. He said they shouldn't've called your dad a crook."

"Four–five," her father called. "Your service."

"But I guess your mom didn't understand that."

Cars were inching out of the club. Julia could see the red brake lights between the purple blossoms of the hedge that separated the court from the drive.

"It doesn't matter," Anouk said. "You said he wouldn't have gone back anyway, so it doesn't matter whether he *could* have."

A car backed up, beeping. Someone yelled directions in Hindi.

"And it didn't get reported in America or anything. My father says he's lucky he could still work in Europe—probably not in oil, but anything else. He doesn't want to go back to the States anyway—*alors, c'est pas grand chose.*"

The game had finished. Their fathers were collecting the balls from the corners of the court.

"Ready?" her father called, but Julia was already hurrying across the court. By the time she got out to the drive she was jogging, zigzagging through the cars clogging the lot, out into the hot nighttime haze of the road. She was lucky to find an empty taxi. They pulled out into the mass of traffic in front of the Hagi Ali and stopped. The driver looked at her in the mirror for instructions.

"Malabar Hill," she said. "Hanging Garden."

.   .   .

Zubin was actually working on the essay, sitting at his desk by the open window, when he heard his name. Or maybe hallucinated his name: a bad sign. But it wasn't his fault. His mother had given him a bottle of sambuca, which someone had brought her from the duty-free shop in the Frankfurt airport.

"I was thinking of giving it to the Mehtas but he's stopped drinking entirely. I could only think of you."

"You're the person she thought would get the most use out of it," his father contributed.

Now Zubin was having little drinks (really half drinks) as he tried to apply to college. He had decided that there would be nothing wrong with writing a first draft for Julia, as long as she put it in her own words later. The only problem was getting started. He remembered his own essay perfectly, unfortunately on an unrelated subject. He had written, much to his English teacher's dismay, about comic books.

"Why don't you write about growing up in Bombay? That will distinguish you from the other applicants," she had suggested.

He hadn't wanted to distinguish himself from the other applicants, or rather, he'd wanted to distinguish himself in a much more distinctive way. He had an alumni interview with an expatriate American consultant working for Arthur Anderson in Bombay; the interviewer, who was young, Jewish and from New York, said it was the best college essay he'd ever read.

"Zu-bin."

It was at least a relief that he wasn't hallucinating. She was standing below his window, holding a tennis racket. "Hey, Zubin—can I come up?"

"You have to come around the front," he said.

"Will you come down and get me?"

He put a shirt over his T-shirt, and then took it off. He took the glass of sambuca to the bathroom sink to dump it, but he got distracted looking in the mirror (he should've shaved) and drained it instead.

He found Julia leaning against a tree, smoking. She held out the pack.

"I don't smoke."

She sighed. "Hardly anyone does anymore." She was wearing an extremely short white skirt. "Is this a bad time?"

"Well—"

"I can go."

"You can come up," he said, a little too quickly. "I'm not sure I can do antonyms now though."

In his room Julia gravitated to the stereo. A Brahms piano quartet had come on.

"You probably aren't a Brahms person."

She looked annoyed. "How do *you* know?"

"I don't," he said. "Sorry—are you?"

Julia pretended to examine his books. "I'm not very familiar with his work," she said finally. "So I couldn't really say."

He felt like hugging her. He poured himself another sambuca instead. "I'm sorry there's nowhere to sit."

"I'm sorry I'm all gross from tennis." She sat down on his mattress, which was at least covered with a blanket.

"Do you always smoke after tennis?" he couldn't help asking.

"It calms me down."

"Still, you shouldn't—"

"I've been having this dream," she said. She stretched her legs out in front of her and crossed her ankles. "Actually it's kind of a nightmare."

"Oh," said Zubin. Students' nightmares were certainly among the things that should be discussed in the living room.

"Have you ever been to New Hampshire?"

"What?"

"I've been having this dream that I'm in New Hampshire. There's a frozen pond where you can skate outside."

"That must be nice."

"I saw it in a movie," she admitted. "But I think they have them— anyway. In the dream I'm not wearing skates. I'm walking out onto the pond, near the woods, and it's snowing. I'm walking on the ice but I'm not afraid—everything's really beautiful. And then I look down and there's this thing—this dark spot on the ice. There are some mushrooms growing, on the dark spot. I'm worried that someone skating will trip on them, so I bend down to pick them."

Her head was bent now; she was peeling a bit of rubber from the sole of her sneaker.

"That's when I see the guy."

"The guy."

"The guy in the ice. He's alive, and even though he can't move, he sees me. He's looking up and reaching out his arms and just his fingers are coming up—just the tips of them through the ice. Like white mushrooms."

"Jesus," Zubin said.

She misunderstood. "No—just a regular guy."

"That's a bad dream."

"Yeah, well," she said proudly. "I thought maybe you could use it."

"Sorry?"

"In the essay."

Zubin poured himself another sambuca. "I don't know if I can write the essay."

"You have to." Her expression changed instantly. "I have the money—I could give you a check now even."

"It's not the money."

"Because it's dishonest?" she said in a small voice.

"I—" But he couldn't explain why he couldn't manage to write even a college essay, even to himself. "I'm sorry."

She looked as if she'd been about to say something else, and then changed her mind. "Okay," she said dejectedly. "I'll think of something."

She looked around for her racket, which she'd propped up against the bookshelf. He didn't want her to go yet.

"What kind of a guy is he?"

"Who?"

"The guy in the ice—is he your age?"

Julia shook her head. "He's old."

Zubin sat down on the bed, at what he judged was a companionable distance. "Like a senior citizen?"

"No, but older than you."

"Somewhere in that narrow window between me and senior citizenship."

"You're not old," she said seriously.

"Thank you." The sambuca was making him feel great. They could just sit here, and get drunk and do nothing, and it would be fun, and there would be no consequences; he could stop worrying for tonight, and give himself a little break.

He was having that comforting thought when her head dropped lightly to his shoulder.

"Oh."

"Is this okay?"

"It's okay, but—"

"I get so tired."

"Because of the nightmares."

She paused for a second, as if she was surprised he'd been paying attention. "Yes," she said. "Exactly."

"You want to lie down a minute?"

She jerked her head up—nervous all of a sudden. He liked it better than the flirty stuff she'd been doing before.

"Or I could get someone to take you home."

She lay down and shut her eyes. He put his glass down carefully on the floor next to the bed. Then he put his hand out; her hair was very soft. He stroked her head and moved her hair away from her face. He adjusted the glass beads she always wore, and ran his hand lightly down her arm. He felt that he was in a position where there was no choice but to lift her up and kiss her very gently on the mouth.

"Julia."

She opened her eyes.

"I'm going to get someone to drive you home."

She got up very quickly and smoothed her hair with her hand.

"Not that I wouldn't like you to stay, but I think—"

"Okay," she said.

"I'll just get someone." He yelled for the servant.

"I can get a taxi," Julia said.

"I know you *can*," he told her. For some reason, that made her smile.

In September she took the test. He woke up early that morning as if he were taking it, couldn't concentrate, and went to Barista, where he sat trying to read the same *India Today* article about regional literature for two hours. She wasn't the only one of his students taking the SAT today, but she was the one he thought of, at the eight forty subject change, the ten-o'clock break, and at eleven twenty-five, when they would be warning them about the penalties for continuing to write after time was called. That afternoon he thought she would ring him to say how it had gone, but she didn't, and it wasn't until late that night that his phone beeped and her name came up: JULIA: VERBAL IS LIKE S-SPEARE: PLAY. It wasn't a perfect analogy, but he knew what she meant.

He didn't see Julia while the scores were being processed. Without the bonus he hadn't been able to give up his other clients, and the business was in one of its busy cycles; it seemed as if everyone in Bombay was dying to send their sixteen-year-old child halfway around the world to be educated. Each evening he thought he might hear her calling up from the street, but she never did, and he didn't feel he could phone without some pretense.

One rainy Thursday he gave a group lesson in a small room on the first floor of the David Sassoon library. The library always reminded him of Oxford, with its cracked chalkboards and termite-riddled seminar tables, and today in particular the soft, steady rain made him feel as if he were somewhere else. They were doing triangles (isosceles, equilateral, scalene) when all of a sudden one of the students interrupted and said: "It stopped."

Watery sun was gleaming through the lead-glass windows. When he had dismissed the class, Zubin went upstairs to the reading room. He found Bradbury in a tattered ledger book and filled out a form. He waited while the librarian frowned at the call number, selected a key from a crowded ring, and, looking put-upon, sent an assistant into the reading room to find "All Summer in a Day" in the locked glass case.

It had been raining for seven years; thousands upon thousands of days compounded and filled from one end to the other with rain, with the drum and gush of water, with the sweet crystal fall of showers and the concussion of storms so heavy they were tidal waves come over the islands.

He'd forgotten that the girl in the story was a poet. She was different from the other children, and because it was a science fiction story (this was what he loved about science fiction) it wasn't an abstract difference. Her special sensitivity was explained by the fact that she had come to Venus from Earth only recently, on a rocket ship, and remembered the sun—it was like a penny—while her classmates did not.

Zubin sat by the window in the old seminar room, emptied of students, and luxuriated in a feeling of potential he hadn't had in a long time.

He remembered when a moment of heightened contrast in his physical surroundings could produce this kind of elation; he could feel the essay wound up in him like thread. He would combine the Bradbury story with the idea Julia had had, that day at the tank. Beauty was something that was new to you. That was why tourists and children could see it better than other people, and it was the poet's job to keep seeing it the way the children and the tourists did.

He was glad he'd told her he couldn't do it because it would be that much more of a surprise when he handed her the pages. He felt noble. He was going to defraud the University of California for her gratis, as a gift.

He intended to be finished the day the scores came out and, for perhaps the first time in his life, he finished on the day he'd intended. He waited all day, but Julia didn't call. He thought she would've gone out that night to celebrate, but she didn't call the next day, or the next, and he started to worry that she'd been wrong about her verbal. Or she'd lied. He started to get scared that she'd choked—something that could happen to the best students, you could never tell which. After ten days without hearing from her, he rang her mobile.

"Oh yeah," she said. "I was going to call."

"I have something for you," he said. He didn't want to ask about the scores right away.

She sighed. "My dad wants you to come to dinner anyway."

"Okay," Zubin said. "I could bring it then."

There was a long pause, in which he could hear traffic. "Are you in the car?"

"Uh-huh," she said. "Hold on a second?" Her father said something and she groaned into the phone. "My dad wants me to tell you my SAT scores."

"Only if you want to."

"Eight hundred math."

"Wow."

"And six-ninety verbal."

"You're kidding."

"Nope."

"Is this the Julia who was too distracted to do her practice tests?"

"Maybe it was easy this year," Julia said, but he could tell she was smiling.

"I don't believe you."

"Zu*bin*!" (He loved the way she added the extra stress.) "I *swear*."

They ate *coquilles St. Jacques* by candlelight. Julia's father lit the candles himself, with a box of old-fashioned White Swan matches. Then he opened Zubin's wine and poured all three of them a full glass. Zubin took a sip; it seemed too sweet, especially with the seafood. "A toast," said Julia's father. "To my daughter the genius."

Zubin raised his glass. All week he'd felt an urgent need to see her; now that he was here he had a contented, peaceful feeling, only partly related to the two salty dogs he'd mixed for himself just before going out.

"Scallops are weird," Julia said. "Do they even have heads?"

"Did any of your students do better?" her father asked.

"Only one, I think."

"Boy or girl?"

"What does *that* matter?" Julia asked. She stood up suddenly: she was wearing a sundress made of blue-and-white printed Indian cotton, and she was barefoot. "I'll be in my room if anyone needs me."

Zubin started to get up.

"Sit," Julia's father said. "Finish your meal. Then you can do whatever you have to do."

"I brought your essay—the revision of your essay," Zubin corrected himself, but she didn't turn around. He watched her disappear down the hall to her bedroom: a pair of tan shoulders under thin, cotton straps.

"I first came to India in 1976," her father was saying. "I flew from Moscow to Paris to meet Julia's mom, and then we went to Italy and Greece. We were deciding between India and North Africa—finally we just tossed a coin."

"Wow," said Zubin. He was afraid Julia would go out before he could give her the essay.

"It was February and I'd been in Moscow for a year," Julia's father said. "So you can imagine what India was like for me. We were staying in this pension in Benares—Varanasi—and every night there were these incredible parties on the roof.

"One night we could see the burning ghats from where we were— hardly any electricity in the city, and then this big fire on the ghat, with the drums and the wailing. I'd never seen anything like that—the pieces of the body that they sent down the river, still burning." He stopped and refilled their glasses. He didn't seem to mind the wine. "Maybe they don't still do that?"

"I've never been to Benares."

Julia's father laughed. "Right," he said. "That's an old man's India now. And you're not writing about India, are you?"

Writing the essay, alone at night in his room, knowing she was out somewhere with her school friends, he'd had the feeling, the delusion really, that he could hear her. That while she was standing on the beach or dancing in a club, she was also telling him her life story: not the places she'd lived, which didn't matter, but the time in third grade when she was humiliated in front of the class; the boy who wrote his number on the inside of her wrist; the weather on the day her mother left for New York. He felt that her voice was coming in the open window with the noise of the motorbikes and the televisions and the crows, and all he was doing was hitting the keys.

Julia's father had asked a question about India.

"Sorry?" Zubin said.

He waved a hand dismissively in front of his face. "You don't have to tell me—writers are private about these things. It's just that business guys like me—we're curious how you do it."

"When I'm here, I want to write about America and when I'm in America, I always want to write about being here." He wasn't slurring words, but he could hear himself emphasizing them: "It would have made *sense* to stay there."

"But you didn't."

"I was homesick, I guess."

"And now?"

Zubin didn't know what to say.

"Far be it from me, but I think it doesn't matter so much, whether you're here or there. You can bring your home with you." Julia's father smiled. "To some extent. And India's wonderful—even if it's not your first choice."

It was easy if you were Julia's father. He had chosen India because he remembered seeing some dead bodies in a river. He had found it "wonderful." And that was what it was to be an American. Americans could go all over the world and still be Americans; they could live just the way they did at home and nobody wondered who they were, or why they were doing things the way they did.

"I'm sure you're right," Zubin said politely.

Finally Julia's father pressed a buzzer and a servant appeared to clear the dishes. Julia's father pushed back his chair and stood up. Before disappearing into his study, he nodded formally and said something—whether "Good night," or "Good luck," Zubin couldn't tell.

Zubin was left with a servant, about his age, with big, southern features and stooped shoulders. The servant was wearing the brown uniform from another job: short pants and a shirt that was tight across his chest. He moved as if he'd been compensating for his height his whole life, as if he'd never had clothes that fit him.

"Do you work here every day?" Zubin asked in his schoolbook Marathi.

The young man looked up as if talking to Zubin was the last in a series of obstacles that lay between him and the end of his day.

"Nahin," he said. *"Mangalwar ani guruwar."*

Zubin smiled—they both worked on Tuesdays and Thursdays. "Me too," he said.

The servant didn't understand. He stood holding the plates, waiting to see if Zubin was finished and scratching his left ankle with his right foot. His toes were round and splayed, with cracked nails and a glaucous coating of dry, white skin.

"Okay," Zubin said. *"Bas."*

Julia's room was, as he'd expected, empty. The lights were burning and the stereo was on (the disc had finished), but she'd left the window open; the bamboo shade sucked in and out. The mirror in the bathroom was steamed around the edges—she must've taken a shower before going out; there was the smell of some kind of fragrant soap and cigarettes.

He put the essay on the desk where she would see it. There were two Radiohead CDs, still in their plastic wrappers, and a detritus of pens and pencils, hairbands, fashion magazines—French *Vogue, Femina* and *YM*—gum wrappers, an OB tampon and a miniature brass abacus, with tiny ivory beads. There was also a diary with a pale blue paper cover.

The door to the hall was slightly open, but the house was absolutely quiet. It was not good to look at someone's journal, especially a teenage girl's. But there were things that would be worse—jerking off in her room, for example. It was a beautiful notebook with a heavy cardboard cover that made a satisfying sound when he opened it on the desk.

"It's empty."

He flipped the diary closed but it was too late. She was climbing in through the window, lifting the shade with her hand.

"That's where I smoke," she said. "You should've checked."

"I was just looking at the notebook," Zubin said. "I wouldn't have read what you'd written."

"My hopes, dreams, fantasies. It would've been good for the essay."

"I finished the essay."

She stopped and stared at him. "You wrote it?"

He pointed to the neatly stacked pages, a paper island in the clutter of the desk. Julia examined them, as if she didn't believe it.

"I thought you weren't going to?"

"If you already wrote one—"

"No," she said. "I tried but—" She gave him a beautiful smile. "Do you want to stay while I read it?"

Zubin glanced at the door.

"My dad's in his study."

He pretended to look through her CDs, which were organized in a zippered binder, and snuck glances at her while she read. She sat down on her bed with her back against the wall, one foot underneath her. As she read she lifted her necklace and put it in her mouth, he thought unconsciously. She frowned at the page.

It was better if she didn't like it, Zubin thought. He knew it was good, but having written it was wrong. There were all these other kids who'd done the applications themselves.

Julia laughed.

"What?" he said, but she just shook her head and kept going.

"I'm just going to use your loo," Zubin said.

He used it almost blindly, without looking in the mirror. Her towel was hanging over the edge of the counter, but he dried his hands on his shirt. He was drunker than he'd thought. When he came out she had folded the three pages into a small square, as if she were getting ready to throw them away.

Julia shook her head. "You did it."

"It's okay?"

Julia shook her head. "It's perfect—it's spooky. How do you even know about this stuff?"

"I was a teenager—not a girl teenager, but you know."

She shook her head. "About being an American I mean? How do you know about that?"

She asked the same way she might ask who wrote *The Fairie Queene* or the meaning of the word "synecdoche."

Because I am not any different, he wanted to tell her. He wanted to grab her shoulders: *If we are what we want, I am the same as you.*

But she wasn't looking at him. Her eyes were like marbles he'd had as a child, striated brown and gold. They moved over the pages he'd written as if they were hers, as if she were about to tear one up and put it in her mouth.

"This part," Julia said. "About forgetting where you are? D'you know, that *happens* to me? Sometimes coming home I almost say the wrong street—the one in Paris, or in Moscow when we used to have to say '*Pushkinskaya.*'"

Her skirt was all twisted around her legs.

"Keep it," he said.

"I'll write you a check."

"It's a present," Zubin told her.

"Really?"

He nodded. When she smiled she looked like a kid. "I wish I could do something for *you.*"

Zubin decided that it was time to leave.

Julia put on a CD—a female vocalist with a heavy bass line. "This is too sappy for daytime," she said. Then she started to dance. She was not a good dancer. He watched her fluttering her hands in front of her face, stamping her feet, and knew, the same way he always knew these things, that he wasn't going anywhere at all.

"You know what I hate?"

"What?"

"Boys who can't kiss."

"All right," Zubin said. "You come here."

Her bed smelled like the soap—lilac. It was amazing, the way girls smelled, and it was amazing to put his arm under her and take off each thin strap and push the dress down around her waist. She made him turn off the lamp but there was a street lamp outside; he touched her in the artificial light. She looked as if she were trying to remember something.

"Is everything okay?"

She nodded.

"Because we can stop."

"Do you have something?"

It took him a second to figure out what she meant. "Oh," he said. "No—that's good I guess."

"I have one."

"You do?"

She nodded.

"Still. That doesn't mean we have to."

"I want to."

"Are you sure?"

"If you do."

"If I do—yes." He took a breath. "I want to."

She was looking at him very seriously.

"This isn't—" he said.

"Of course not."

"Because you seem a little nervous."

"I'm just thinking," she said. Her underwear was light blue, and it didn't quite cover her tan line.

"About what?"

"America."

"What about it?"

She had amazing gorgeous perfect new breasts. There was nothing else to say about them.

"I can't wait," she said, and he decided to pretend she was talking about this.

Julia was relieved when he left and she could lie in bed alone and think about it. Especially the beginning part of it: she didn't know kissing could be like that—sexy and calm at the same time, the way it was in movies that were not *9½ Weeks*. She was surprised she didn't feel worse; she didn't feel regretful at all, except that she wished she'd thought of something to say afterward. *I wish I didn't have to go,* was what he had said, but he put on his shoes very quickly. She hadn't been sure whether she should get up or not, and in the end she waited until she heard the front door shut behind him. Then she got up and put on a T-shirt and pajama bottoms, and went into the bathroom to wash her face. If she'd told him it was her first time, he would've stayed longer, probably, but she'd read enough magazines to know that you couldn't tell them that. Still, she wished he'd touched her hair the way he had the other night, when she'd gone over to his house and invented a nightmare.

Zubin had left the Ray Bradbury book on her desk. She'd thanked him, but she wasn't planning to read it again. Sometimes when you went back you were disappointed, and she liked the rocket ship the way she remembered it, with silver tail fins and a red lacquer shell. She could picture herself taking off in that ship—at first like an airplane, above the hill and the tank and the bay with its necklace of lights—and then straight up, beyond the sound barrier. People would stand on the beach to watch the launch: her father, Anouk and Bernie, everyone from school, and even Claudie and her mother and Dr. Fabrol. They would yell up to her, but the yells would be like the tails of comets, crusty blocks of ice and dust that rose and split in silent, white explosions.

She liked Zubin's essay too, although she wasn't sure about the way he'd combined the two topics; she hoped they weren't going to take points off. Or the part where he talked about all the different perspectives she'd gotten from living in different cities, and how she just needed one place where she could think about those things and articulate what they meant to her. She wasn't interested in "articulating." She just wanted to get moving.

Zubin walked all the way up Nepean Sea Road, but when he got to the top of the hill he wasn't tired. He turned right and passed his building, not quite ready to go in, and continued in the Walkeshwar direction. The market was empty. The electronics shops were shuttered and the "Just Orange" advertisements twisted like kites in the dark. There was the rich, rotted smell of vegetable waste, but almost no other trash. Foreigners marveled at the way Indians didn't waste anything, but of course that wasn't by choice. Only a few useless things flapped and flattened themselves against the broad, stone steps: squares of folded newsprint from the vendors' baskets, and smashed matchbooks—extinct brands whose labels still appeared underfoot: "export-quality premium safety matches" in fancy script.

At first he thought the tank was deserted, but a man in shorts was standing on the other side, next to a small white dog with stand-up, triangular ears. Zubin picked a vantage point on the steps out of the moonlight, sat down and looked out at the water. There was something different about the tank at night. It was partly the quiet; in between the traffic sounds a breeze crackled the leaves of a few desiccated trees growing between the paving stones. The night intensified the contrast, so that the stones took on a kind of sepia, sharpened the shadows and gave the carved and whitewashed temple pillars an appropriate patina of magic. You could cheat for a moment in this light and see the old city, like taking a photograph with black-and-white film.

The dog barked, ran up two steps and turned expectantly toward the tank. Zubin didn't see the man until his slick, seal head surfaced in the black water. Each stroke broke the black glass; his hands made eddies of light in the disturbed surface. For just a moment, even the apartment blocks were beautiful.

Ben Fountain

Fantasy for Eleven Fingers

from *Southwest Review*

S O LITTLE is known about the pianist Anton Visser that he belongs more to myth than anything so random as historical fact. He was born in 1800 or 1801, thus preceding by half a generation the Romantic virtuosos who would transform forever our notions of music and performer. Liszt, more charitable than most, called him "our spiritual elder brother," though he rather less kindly described his elder brother's playing as "affectation of the first rank." Visser himself seems to have been the source of much confusion about his origins, saying sometimes that he was from Brno, at other times from Graz, still others from Telc or Iglau. "The French call me a German," he is reported to have told the Countess Koeniggratz, "and the Germans call me a Jew, but in truth, dear lady, I belong solely to the realm of music."

He was fluent in German, Slovak, Magyar, French, English, and Italian, and he could just as fluently forget them all when the situation obliged. He was successful enough at cards to be rumored a cheat; he liked women, and had a number of vivid affairs with the wives and mistresses of his patrons; he played the piano like a human thunderbolt, crisscrossing Europe with his demonic extra finger and leaving a trail of lavender gloves as souvenirs. Toward the end, when Visser-mania was at its height, the mere display of his naked right hand could rouse an audience to hysterics;

his concerts degenerated into shrieking bacchanals, with women alternately fainting and rushing the stage, flinging flowers and jewels at the great man. But in the early 1820s Visser was merely one of the legion of virtuosos who wandered Europe peddling their grab bags of pianistic stunts. He was, first and foremost, a *saloniste*, a master of the *morceaux* and flashy potpourri that so easily enthralled his wealthy audiences. He seems to have been something of a super-cocktail pianist to the aristocracy—much of what we know of him derives from diaries and memoirs of the nobility—although he wasn't above indulging the lower sort of taste. His specialty, apparently, was speed-playing, and he once accepted a bet to play six million notes in twelve hours. A riding school was rented out, flyers printed and subscriptions sold, and for eight hours and twenty minutes Visser incinerated the keyboard of a sturdy Erard while the audience made themselves at home, talking, laughing and eating, playing cards and roaming about, so thoroughly enjoying the performance that they called for an encore after the six millionth note. Visser shrugged and airily waved a hand as if to say, Why not?, and continued playing for another hour.

No likeness of the virtuoso has survived, but contemporaries describe a tall man of good figure with black, penetrating eyes, a severe, handsome face, and a prominent though elegantly shaped nose. That he was a Jew was widely accepted, and loudly published by his rivals; there is no evidence that Visser bothered to deny the consensus. His hands, of course, were his most distinguishing feature. The first edition of *Grove's Dictionary* states that Visser had the hands of a natural pianist: broad, elastic palms, spatulate fingers, and exceptionally long little fingers. He could stretch a twelfth and play left-hand chords such as A-flat, E-flat, and A-flat and C, but it was the hypnotically abnormal right hand that ultimately set him apart. "The two ring fingers of his right hand," the critic Blundren wrote, "are perfect twins, each so exact a mirror image of the other as to give the effect of an optical illusion, and in action possessed of a disturbing crablike agility. Difficult it is, indeed, to repress a shudder when presented with Visser's singular hand."

Difficult, indeed, and as is so often the case with deformity, a sight that both compelled and repelled. Visser seems not to have emphasized his singular hand during the early stages of his career, but the speed with which he played, to such cataclysmic effect, in time gave rise to unsettling stories. It was his peculiar gift to establish the melody of a piece with his thumbs in the middle register of the piano, then surround the melody with arpeggios, tremolos, double notes, and other devices, moving up and down the keyboard with such insane rapidity that it seemed as if four hands rather than two were at work. His sound was so uncanny that a certain kind of story—tentative, half-jesting at first—began to shadow the pianist: Satan himself was playing with Visser, some said, while others ventured that he'd sold the devil his soul in exchange for the extra finger, which enabled him to play with such hectoring speed.

That Visser had emerged from the mysterium of backward Eastern Europe gave the stories an aura of plausibility. "There is something dark, elusive, and unhealthy in Visser," remarked Field, while Moscheles said that his rival's playing "does not encourage respectable thoughts." His few surviving compositions show a troublingly oblique harmonic stance, a cracked Pandora's box of dissonance and atonal sparks, along with the mournful echoes of gypsy songs and the derailed melodies of Galician folk tunes. He became known as the Bohemian Faust, and was much in demand; neither the sinister flavor of his stage persona nor his string of love affairs seemed to diminish his welcome in fashionable salons.

In 1829, however, there was a break. Some say it was due to an incident at the Comte de Gobet's, where Visser was accused of cheating at cards; his legendary success and extra finger had long made him an object of suspicion, though others said that he was discovered making free with the fifteen-year-old daughter of a baron. Visser was, whatever the cause, refused by society, forced out into *le grand public* to make his living, this at a time when there were few adequate venues for touring virtuosos and concert managers tended to have the scruples of slave traders. Visser billed himself as the Man with Eleven Fingers, the freak-show aspect of virtuosity made explicit for once, and over the next two years of playing in rowdy beer gardens and firetrap opera houses he perfected his florid stagecraft: the regal entrance, the lavender gloves portentously removed, then the excruciating pause before his hands fell on the keyboard like an avalanche. It was early noted that his audiences were disproportionately female; more remarkable was the delirium that his performances induced, a feature that grew even more pronounced with the addition of the *Fantaisie pour Onze Doigts* to his repertoire. Hummel, who heard it played in a ballroom in Stuttgart, called it "a most strange and affecting piece, with glints of dissonance issuing from the right hand like the whip of a lash, or very keen razor cuts." Kalkenbrenner, who happened on it at a brewery in Mainz, compared the chill of the strained harmonies of the loaded right hand to "a trickle of ice-cold water running down one's back," and added: "I believe that Visser has captured the very sound of Limbo."

The effect on audiences was astonishing. From the first reported performance, in October 1831, there were accounts of seizures, faintings, and fits of epilepsy among the spectators; though some accused Visser of paying actors to mimic and encourage such convulsions, the phenomenon appears to have been accepted as genuine. Mass motor hysteria would most likely be the diagnosis today, though a physician from Gossl who witnessed one performance proposed theories having to do with electrical contagion; others linked the *Fantasy* to the Sistine Chapel Syndrome, the hysterics to which certain foreign women—English spinsters, chiefly—sometimes fell prey while viewing the artistic treasures of Italy. In any event, the *Fantasy* was a short-lived sensation. From its debut in the fall of 1831 until his death the following January, Visser performed the piece perhaps thirty times. He was said to be traveling to Paris to play for the Princess Tversky's salon—the fame of the *Fantasy* had, conveniently, paroled his reputation—when he was killed stupidly, needlessly, in a tavern in Cologne, knifed in a dispute over cards, so the story goes.

People naturally believed that the *Fantasy* died with him; even the stupendously gifted Liszt refused to attempt it, rather defensively dismissing the piece as "a waste of time, an oddity based on an alien formation of the hand." One might study the score as scholars study the texts of a dead language, but the living sound was thought to be lost forever, until that day in 1891 when Leo and Hermine Kuhl brought their six-year-old daughter to the Vienna studio of Herr Moritz Puchel. Herr Puchel listened to the girl play Chopin's "Aeolian Harp" étude; he gave her a portion of Beethoven's A-flat Sonata to sight-read, which she did without stress; he confirmed, as her current teacher, Frau Holzer, had told him, that the child did indeed have perfect pitch. Finally he asked Anna Kuhl to stand before him and place her hands on his upturned palms.

"Yes," he said gravely, much in the manner of a doctor giving an unhappy diagnosis, "someday she will play Visser's *Fantasy*."

Herr Puchel himself had been a prodigy, a student of Czerny's, who in turn had been a student of Beethoven's; though he was an undeniably brilliant musician, Puchel's own career as a virtuoso had been thwarted by the misfortune of thin, bony hands. He had, instead, made his reputation as a teacher, and by the age of sixty had achieved such a degree of eminence that he accepted only those students who could answer in the affirmative the following three questions:

Are you a prodigy?

Are you of Slavic descent?

Are you Jewish?

This, the Catholic Puchel believed, was the formula for greatness, and Anna Kuhl qualified on all counts. The Kuhls came from Olomouc, in Moravia—a town, as would often be noted, that has some claim as Visser's birthplace—where Anna's grandfather founded the textile factory on which the family fortune was based; by the time of Anna's birth, Leo and his brothers had built a textile empire substantial enough to be headquartered in the Austrian capital. The Kuhls were typical of Vienna's upper-class Jewry: politically liberal, culturally and linguistically German, their Judaism little more than a pious family memory, they devoted themselves to artistic and intellectual attainment as a substitute for the social rank which would always be denied them. And yet the desire to assimilate, to be viewed as complete citizens, was strong; theirs was a world in which any departure from convention provoked intense, if grimly decorous, fear, and the Kuhls were so horrified by Anna's deformity that they considered amputation in the hours after her birth. When the doctor could not assure them that the infant would survive the shock, the parents relented, though one may reasonably wonder if they were ever completely rid of their instinctive revulsion, or of the more rarefied, if no less desperate, fear that Anna's condition threatened their tenuous standing in society.

Great pianists manifest the musical impulse early, usually around age four; for Anna Kuhl the decisive moment came at two, when Frau Holzer, giving a lesson to Anna's older brother, discovered that the little girl had perfect pitch. On further examination the child revealed astonishing powers of memory and muscular control, as well as profound sensitivity to aural stimulus—she wept on hearing Chopin for the first time, burst into fierce, agonal sobs as if mourning some inchoate yet powerfully sensed memory. Frau Holzer undertook to form the child's talent; by age four Anna had composed her first song, "Good Morning," and by age six had mastered the *Versuch, The Well-Tempered Clavier* and most of Chopin's *Études*. That year she performed at an exhibition of the city's young pianists, playing with such artistry that Grunfeld, the notoriously saccharine court pianist, was seen shaking his head and mumbling to himself as he left the hall.

"A prodigy," Frau Holzer wrote in her recommendation to Herr Puchel. "Memorizes instantly; staggering technique and maturity of expression; receptive to hard work, instruction, challenge." Regarding what Frau Holzer chose to call the child's "unique anatomy," Puchel was matter-of-fact to the point of brusqueness, devising technical drills suited to Anna's conformation but otherwise focusing, for the present, on the traditional repertoire. Herr Puchel—stout, bushy-bearded, with a huge strawberry of a nose and endearingly tiny feet—had concluded after forty years of teaching that his students would never be truly happy unless coaxed and cudgeled to that peak of performance in which nervous breakdown is a constant risk. Students, by definition, could not reach Parnassus alone; they were too weak of will, too dreamy and easily distracted; they had to be cultivated into that taut, tension-filled state without which pure and lasting art is impossible. Thus it was that visitors to Herr Puchel's studio could hear "*Falsch!*" regularly screamed from the teaching room. "*Falsch!*" *der Meister* would shriek at the first missed note, "Start over!," his screams punctuated in summer by the *swack* of the flyswatter with which he defended his territory against Vienna's plague of flies. In moments of extreme aesthetic crisis he would push aside his student and sit at the piano, hike up his legs and pound the keyboard with his dainty feet, legs churning like a beetle stuck on its back. "You sound like this!" he would howl at the offender, though his gruff tenderness could be equally effective. "Don't be afraid to stick your neck out," he is said to have told one student after a risky, rubato-laced polonaise. "You might find that it gets stroked instead of chopped off."

A dangerous man, yet prodigious in his results, and apparently Anna responded to this sort of treatment. By all accounts she was a preternaturally serious little girl, self-assured, disposed to silence but precise in speech, with an aura of unapproachability that discouraged all but the very determined or very frivolous. A photographic portrait made at the time shows a girl as slender and graceful as a tulip stem, with long, ringletted masses of black hair, deep-set dark eyes, high Slavic cheekbones and skin as pale as January snow. At this age she seems unconscious of her unique right hand, or perhaps trusting is a better word; she has allowed herself to be posed with her fingers draped to full effect across the back of a Roentgen chair.

"A perfect breeze of a girl," is how the *Salonblatt*, Vienna's snob-society newspaper, described the young Anna. "A perfect breeze who turns into an exquisite storm when seated before the eighty-eight black and white keys." Puchel believed that the loftiest musical heights could be reached only through the ordeal of performance; he wanted Anna to start playing in public immediately, and arranged through court connections her society debut at a soirée of the Princess Montenuovo. *Salonblatt* rhapsodized over the playing of this "mystical" child whose arpeggios "flashed and shimmered like champagne," while the Baroness Flotow left an account in her diary of a charmingly poised little girl who devastated the company with Chopin's *Nocturnes*, ate cakes and drank Turkish coffee with the ladies, and complained about the quality of the piano.

She continued awing the impressionable aristocracy for several years, until Puchel judged that she was seasoned enough for her concert debut. In October 1895, the Berlin Philharmonic was scheduled to perform in Vienna; when Julius Epstein, the featured pianist, fell ill, Puchel arranged for Anna to take his place, and after the monumental program of Beethoven's C major Concerto, a set of Rameau variations, the Weber-Liszt *Pollacca*, and a Chopin group consisting of the "Berceuse," the E-flat "Nocturne," and the E-minor Waltz, the girl prodigy left Vienna gasping for air. Brahms toasted her *in absentia* that night, at a banquet intended to honor the suddenly forgotten Epstein; Mahler enthused over her sonorities and golden tone, while both traditional and Secessionist critics marveled at her luminously refined technique, her uncalculated emotion and spontaneity. Agents and concert managers came seething; after interviewing numerous candidates, Leo and Hermine settled on the well-known agent Sigi Kornblau, who appears to have been the kind of dry, hustling administrator that every genius needs, although Anna reportedly told her cousins that visits with Herr Kornblau were "not much fun," and "rather like going to the dentist." Within weeks the young virtuoso and her entourage—her mother, her French governess, a servant girl named Bertha, and Herr Puchel, who carried along a dummy keyboard for practice on the train— had embarked on her first European tour, and for the next three years she alternated between prolonged seasons of close-packed concert dates, and equally demanding, if more solitary, periods of study and practice.

Many have speculated as to the brutalizing effect of such a life on someone who was, after all, a mere child. Regulating Anna's program would seem to have been within the power of her parents, but it appears that Leo and Hermine were no less susceptible than their fellow bourgeois to validation by the aristocracy. Through Anna they might cross, for brief moments at least, the glacis separating them from the remote nobility. Their daughter's labors brought them acceptance, and whatever the cost to Anna in personal terms, the strain seemed not to diminish—perhaps even enhanced?—the remarkable message of her playing. Like all virtuosos, she had exemplary technique: critics wrote of her fluent, almost chaste clarity, the pinpoint accuracy of her wide skips and galloping chords, the instinctive integrity of her rubato and her broad dynamic range, from shadowlike *pianissimo* to artillery-grade *forte*. But more than that there was the singularity of her sound, the "golden sound" that the critics never tired of describing, along with a tenderness of expression that ravished her listeners. This was not yet another robotic prodigy pumping out notes like a power sewing machine; there was, rather, a quality of innocence in her playing, an effusion of trust and vulnerability all the more remarkable for being conveyed through supreme artistry.

"The child," wrote Othmar Wieck, a critic not known for charity, "is a veritable angel come down to earth." And in Vienna, a city that more than cherished art, that craved it as an escape from the gloom and pessimism that had settled over the empire in the century's final years, it was perhaps only natural that people would project their fears and longings onto the young virtuoso. *Haut bourgeois* concertgoers openly wept at her performances, while for others she became an object of obsession, her name turning up with arcane frequency in suicide notes or the vertiginous ramblings of the mentally disturbed. But even those of sturdier, less enervated natures would lapse into deep melancholy after one of her concerts, as if they'd sensed within their grasp some piece of information crucial to existence, only to feel it slip away as the last note was played.

Her first "phase," as the family neatly termed such episodes, seems to have occurred in the autumn of her thirteenth year. Engagements in Brussels, Paris, and Berlin were abruptly canceled, due to "temporary illness," according to the notice released by Herr Kornblau's office, though even then there were rumors of a nervous attack. Some said that Anna was under the care of the famous Professor Meynert; others, that she was in residence at the luxurious psychiatric retreat of Professor Leidesdorf, where doctors in white gloves and silk top hats administered the latest in electric and water-immersion therapies. In any event, the young virtuoso's reemergence several weeks later marks the first known instance in which she kept her right hand purposely concealed. Anna, along with her parents and a number of family friends, attended the opening of the Kunstlerhaus exhibition in late October; she was observed wearing a tailored suit of steel-grey bengaline, the long sleeves that grazed her palms even further extended by a ruffled trim of Irish lace. She carried in addition an embroidered silk kerchief wrapped as if casually about her right hand, and from that time forward the young pianist never showed her hand in public until the instant she sat before the keyboard.

Commentators have noted in this eccentricity all the characteristics of a neurotic symptom. Without doubt, the compulsively veiled hand, as well as the "phases" during which she retreated from the outside world, indicate significant stress in the girl's life. Some have portrayed these symptoms as a response to her treatment by the pan-German press, which, in the course of advocating the union of Austria's German-speaking regions with the Reich, had begun to review her performances in the manner of anti-Semitic diatribes. Others surmise that these were a sensitive girl's reactions to the more general malaise hanging over the city, although the pursuit of art, with its constant, debilitating risk of failure, not to mention the solitude and unwholesome narcissism that sustained concentration necessarily entails, is, even in the best of circumstances, enough to induce the entire range of pyschopathy. That Anna was merciless with herself, and suffered accordingly, is evident from her cousin Hugo's diaries. For instance, in the entry dated 11 November 1898, we find Anna telling Hugo:

It's only when I'm with you that I'm allowed not to work.

And on 5 December, in response to Hugo's entreaties not to strain herself:

She looked down at her shoes and smiled to herself, as if I were a rather dense little boy who'd asked her to make the river stand still.

"To play well—I suppose I've always assumed that it's a matter of life and death."

It was Hugo to whom the family turned when Anna lapsed into one of her phases. Hugo Kuhl was destined to become a minor celebrity of the age, an ironic, deliciously blasé *feuilletoniste* for the liberal press and the author of a number of drawing-room plays, of which *The Escape Artist* and *Dinner with Strangers* are still known to scholars. But at the time in question Hugo was merely a literary-minded student at the university, known to his circle as a stylish, handsome wit of no defined vocational goal, also an accomplished amateur pianist with a sec touch. It seems that he alone, out of all Anna's siblings and numerous cousins, could give some organizing principle to the drift of her phases, during which Anna managed to dress and feed herself but little else.

21 March
To Uncle Leo's flat in the P.M.
Anna listless, almost catatonic, Hermine tearing around like a fishwife, railing at her to practice—
Shame on you, Anna, for shame! Herr Puchel will be so furious!
Anna silent, tears in her eyes; I could have cheerfully throttled dear aunt at that moment. Chose instead to move A into the afternoon sun, onto the cut-velvet sofa by the window. Sat for a peaceful hour while I read *Tantchen Rosmarin* aloud, A's head on my shoulder. For me, a perfect hour. For her, I imagine that existence was almost tolerable.

In fact Hugo was basically helpless when confronted with a phase, and admitted as much in his diaries. His therapy seemed to consist of taking her out for long walks on the Ringstrasse, or among the earthier amusements and shops of the Prater. The two cousins were often seen strolling arm in arm, a strikingly handsome, fashionably dressed young couple, and yet mismatched for all their good looks and evident wealth: Hugo obviously too old to be Anna's suitor, Anna clearly too young to be Hugo's wife. Even so, some have suggested that their devotion to one another surpassed the usual bond of sympathetic cousins, and, indeed, there are aspects of the diaries that imply infatuation. Hugo notes even their most casual physical contact, as when Anna places her arm on his, or their legs happen to brush while riding in a carriage. He remarks frequently on her beauty, variously describing it as "radiant," "precocious," and "disabling," and once comparing her, without his usual irony, to Rembrandt's sublime portraits of Jewish women. And then there are the insights which come of close observation, as when he tries to make sense of Anna's stern artistic will:

> When one is sickened by ugliness, tedium, stupidity, false feeling—by daily life, in other words—one must construct rigorous barriers of tact and taste in order to survive.

They walked in all weathers, at all times of day, sometimes covering the entire four kilometers of the Ringstrasse. After one such outing Hugo made this terse entry:

> Walking with A today on the Ring.
> Insolent thugs holding a meeting in the park opposite the Reichsrat, chanting, singing vile Reform Union songs.
> Cries of *ostjuden*—they actually threatened us!
> I have never been so furious in my life. Still trembling six hours later, as I write this.
> A in a state of collapse.

Witnesses gave a decidedly sharper account of the incident, which arose not in connection with a Reform Union "meeting," but rather a demonstration by some Christian Social toughs over the language rights bill currently paralyzing Parliament. These witnesses—including a *Dienstmann* on break and the note-bearer to the Emperor's First Lord Chamberlain—said that perhaps thirty demonstrators strutted out of the park and approached the young couple chanting "Jew, where is your patch? Jew, where is your patch?," an obvious reference to the triangular yellow patch that Jews were required to wear before emancipation. It was unknown whether the mob specifically recognized the Kuhls, or simply assumed they were Jewish on the basis of looks; in any event, they continued chanting as they surrounded the couple, crowding in so closely that there was, as a nearby coachman put it, "a good deal of mushing about, not blows exactly." With one arm around Anna, the other fending off the mob, Hugo maintained a slow but determined progress past the park. Eventually the mob broke into laughter and fell away, manifesting a mood that was, on that day at least, more sportive than resolutely bloody.

Months later Hugo was still brooding in his diary, his humiliation evident; as for the young virtuoso, if the incident put her in a state of collapse, she recovered quickly. Within the week she traveled to Budapest and performed a program of Beethoven's C minor Concerto and Brahms's *Paganini Variations*. Her novel handling of Brahms's octave glissandos was especially stunning, the way she took them *prestissimo*, *staccato*, and *pianissimo* all in one, producing a feverish, nearly unbearable nervous effect which electrified the critics no less than the crowd.

"The child," Heuberger wrote in the *Neue freie Presse*, "does not play like a child, but with the mastery of genius powered by long and serious study." The pan-German press reviewed the performance in typically viperish tones. "Like glass shattering," the *Deutsche Zeitung* said of the sounds she produced. "Her hair is almost as beautiful as Paderewski's," the *Deutsches Volksblatt* sarcastically remarked, adding, "the position of her fingers on the keys reminded one of spiders." Her fingers: though Puchel's technical exercises ensured that all fingers developed equally, the teacher had not, to this point, chosen to emphasize her sixth finger in performance, though it could be heard, or perhaps more accurately, *felt*, in the cascades of her arpeggios and brass-tinged double notes, the dizzying helium lift of her *accelerando*. But at some point during the spring or summer of 1899 Herr Puchel sat Anna before the *Fantasy*. Even from the beginning, practice sessions devoted to that work took place in the privacy of the Kuhls' comfortable Salesianergasse apartment, rather than in Puchel's more accessible Rathaus studio. In the interest of maximizing box-office receipts, Kornblau had decreed to Anna's inner circle that the dormant and presumed-lost *Fantasy* would be presented to the public with all the drama and mystery of a Strauss debut.

"Such an odd piece," Hugo recorded after hearing it for the first time. "And needlessly difficult; Visser's rolled chords seem impossible even for Anna's hands." Several days later he makes this entry:

> Lunch at Sacher Garden w/ Anna, Hermine, Mother.
> When I brought up the *Fantasy*, the weirdness of it, A simply smiled. "Visser was enjoying himself when he wrote that," she said. "He was *being* himself, perhaps for the first time in his life. I suppose it felt like taking a deep breath after holding it in for all those years."

"But do you like it?" I asked her. "The sound of the thing, I mean."

Answer: "I like *him*. I like him in that particular piece, though he scares me."

Scares you?

She laughed. "Yes, because he's flaunting it. The thing that made him different. Which seems dangerous, in a way."

Engagements throughout Europe were scheduled for the fall, among them a series in London in which she would play twenty-two of Beethoven's sonatas. In the midst of her preparations Anna was approached by officials from the Ministry of Culture, requesting her, as the child prodigy and pride of Vienna, to take part in a special Wagner program. In an attempt to defuse rising political tensions, the government was promoting those aspects of culture that all of the empire's competing factions shared. Thus it was no coincidence that Anna, a Jew, was being asked to perform Wagner, the champion of pagan vigor and Teutonic mysticism so beloved by the pan-German zealots.

And beloved, incidentally, by Anna as well; she agreed. The evening approached with much fanfare; even the Emperor Franz Josef would attend, emerging from high mourning for the late empress, stabbed to death in Geneva the previous year by the anarchist Luccheni. The program began well enough. Winkelmann roused the audience with "Der Augen leuchtendes Paar"; Schmedes and Lehman lifted them further with the "Heil dir, Sonne!" from *Siegfried*. Anna took the stage and was fairly into the Prelude from *Tristan* when jeers of "Hep! Hep!" rang out from the audience. Within moments everyone understood: a contingent of pan-Germans had taken a block of seats near the stage, and on prearranged signal they began braying the classic anti-Semitic insult. Others in the audience tried to shout them down while a phalanx of policemen came scurrying down the aisle; in the meantime Anna set her jaw and played on, furnishing heady background music for the impending riot. At the last moment, just as the police were poised to wade into the seats, the pan-Germans rose and marched out in ranks, singing "Deutschland über Alles" at the top of their lungs.

Until now the pan-German press had, however thinly, veiled its attacks in the rhetoric of musical criticism, but now they savaged Anna with unrestrained glee. "No Jew," declared one reviewer, "can ever hope to understand Wagner," and to the list of Jew bankers, Northern Railway Jews, Jew peddlers, Jew thieves and subversive press Jews, they now added "this Jew-girl, this performing metronome with her witch's hand and freakish impro-vising." And when word leaked of her intention to perform the *Fantasy* the following January, her enemies were livid. "A perversion," the *Kyffhauser* shrieked of the *Fantasy*, seizing at once on Visser's putative Jewish origins, "an immoral composition born of the ghetto's fetid mewlings and melan-cholies," while the *Deutsches Volksblatt* called it "degenerate, antisocial music, full of contempt for all great ideals and aspirations." The liberal press counterattacked with accusations of revanchism and demagoguery, the pan-Germans fired back in shrill paranoid-racist style, and the battle was joined.

Herr Kornblau, of course, could not have been more pleased. The con-tract had already been signed for Anna's performance at the Royal Opera House on the twentieth of January; she would present the *Fantasy* in a program that, calculated for balancing effect, would include such stan-dards as Liszt's *Love Dreams* and Beethoven's "Moonlight" sonata, along with works by Mozart, Schumann, and Chopin. Meanwhile Anna contin-ued her rigorous schedule of practice and performance. She played in Berlin's Kroll Hall, battling the poor acoustics, then Leipzig, Paris, and London, which brought her back to fractious Vienna in mid-November with a scathing cough and bruiselike discs beneath her eyes. Hugo was clearly worried for his cousin; "*elle travaille comme une negresse*," he con-fided to his diary, and then there is this entry for November 29: "I feel as if Anna is being slowly ground up." Her name figured in the parliamentary debates over the new, allegedly decadent, art; *Deutsches Volksblatt*, the paper of the ascendant Christian Socials, warned that "fists will have to go into action on January 20," while the writers of the Young Vienna move-ment published a pro-Kuhl manifesto, vowing to meet the "barbarization" of public life with an equal strength of purpose.

She gave her final concert of the century in December, at the Royal German Theater in Prague. It was, at her insistence and over her man-agers' objections, a program consisting entirely of Chopin. Those present said that she looked pale and strained; critics noted a fragile, almost glass-ine quality in her playing, which seemed to heighten rather than diminish the emotional effect. "She was dreaming," the Countess Lara von Pergler recorded in her memoirs, "and she allowed us to dream with her. It is a dream which, after all these years, haunts me still." And indeed, it appears that Anna captured the rare essence of Chopin that night. Romantic and expressive, yet aristocratic and restrained, it is difficult even for masters to convey the spirit of Chopin, which is, ultimately, sadness. Not the sadness of great tragedy, but the irredeemable sadness of time itself: days pass, the world changes, and that which we most treasure must inevitably be lost.

Wednesday 20 December
To Uncle's; pretended to read while Anna practiced, then got her bundled in her cloak and out the door before Hermine et al. could come along, thank God.

Grey skies, bitter cold; plane trees along the Ring limned in snow. Walked in contented silence for a kilometer, her arm on mine. Blessed moments! We understand silence, cousin and I.

"How do you do it?" I finally asked. "What you create on the piano, how do you do it?"

A: "I concentrate, and I hear it. But I must concentrate very hard—that's the value of practice, really, learning to concentrate properly, but in a way it's not me, it's something coming through me. If I concentrate very hard it comes through me."

"Then there's this." She pulled her right hand out of her muff, shot back her sleeve and held up her hand, examining it as one might judge a piece of fruit.

"You see this." She was smiling! Smiling as she waggled her extra finger, and blushing, her breath rapid. I was excited too. "This isn't mine either."

"Nonsense," I said. "It's yours and it's wonderful, just as everything about you is wonderful." But she only shrugged and slipped her hand back inside the muff.

At the time she was trying to master the nearly impossible fingering of the *Fantasy*, a task made harder by the fact that her hands were much smaller than Visser's—she could stretch somewhat past an octave with her left, and marginally better than that with her right. In the midst of her efforts Christmas came and went, followed by the turning of the century. Hugo duly noted the fireworks and balls in his diary, along with the latest crises in Parliament, new ideas for plays, and his obsessive running count of the city's suicides, a not unusual preoccupation in Vienna—to the mystification and endless fascination of its citizens, the Austrian capital led Europe in the self-murder statistic. He rather dryly records as well his engagement to Flora Lanner, the blond, beautiful, magnificently wealthy daughter of Oskar Lanner, manufacturer of fruit conserves. By all appearances it would be a brilliant match, not least for the families' smooth pragmatism regarding matters of faith; though Jewish, the Lanners were so fully assimilated that two of Flora's brothers had been baptized in order to join the Imperial Officer Corps. Whether Hugo's engagement had any bearing on his cousin's fate—whether, bluntly put, he and Anna were in love, and the engagement a source of despair to her—is impossible, at this late date, to say; the chaos of two world wars, not to mention a highly efficient program of genocide, have erased much evidence which we otherwise might have had, and Hugo demonstrates in his surviving diaries a sure talent for glossing over his own emotional turbulence.

In any case, his famous cousin soon found herself the object of a nerve-shredding public hysteria. The pan-Germans continued their threats to disrupt the concert, citing as justification the "occult" fits and seizures which the *Fantasy* had induced seventy years before. The Secessionist and Young Vienna movements appropriated the young pianist as their champion, while a congeries of beards from the conservatory accused Anna and her managers of sensationalism, fomenting needless conflict for publicity purposes. An obsessed fan worked out a dizzying mathematical correlation between the date of Visser's death and Anna's birthday, which the *Abendpost* featured in a front-page story. Professors of neurology and musicology were invited to propose theories explaining the *Fantasy*'s violent effect on listeners, while Sigmund Freud—obscure, struggling, no longer young, shunned by the medical establishment and passed over for professorship—followed the controversy from his office on the Berggasse, where he read the newspapers and wrote *The Interpretation of Dreams* in the long stretches between patient appointments.

"You don't have to do this, you know," Hugo told Anna on January 11. "Nobody would blame you for backing out." "Nor you," is the curt answer which he recorded—apropos of Flora? Mayor Lueger of the Christian Social party said that he could not guarantee security outside the Royal Opera on the evening of the twentieth, citing "forces beyond all but the Almighty's control." But the young virtuoso was nevertheless resolved. Those with access to the Kuhl household at this time reported that Anna was the very essence of composure; though it seems that a phase was widely feared, and perhaps secretly desired, among her inner circle, she practiced unstintingly each day, the Beethoven, the Liszt, her beloved Chopin, and the *Fantasy* over which her fingers were gradually gaining control. Pianists will tell you that they practice in order to reduce the risk of catastrophe, but they know that to play with complete safety is an insult to their art. Music demands risk, a condition that Anna seems to have embraced with near-manic devotion, as if by engaging the demons inherent in her art she could destroy all claims they might have on her.

Overwrought fans, and on several occasions journalists, were caught infiltrating the Kuhls' apartment house in hopes of overhearing Anna practice. An old man, one Zolmar Magg of Lvov, a tanner, was discovered to have heard Visser perform the *Fantasy* in 1831, and the local music society appealed for funds to send him to Vienna for the revival. And on January 16 Hugo makes this entry:

> To Uncle's in the P.M. I can hardly bear to listen to the thing now, this *Fantasy*, this nightmare—it's like a dream in which you're trying to flee some hideous creature, yet for all your terror your legs refuse to move.

The following day the Ministry of Culture announced that it was unilaterally canceling Anna's engagement at the Royal Opera House, citing security concerns and the previous autumn's Wagner debacle, for which, the Ministry's communiqué suggested, Fräulein Kuhl was in part responsible. Even as shock resolved into shrill outcry a second announcement was made, this time issuing from the Theater an der Wien, one of Vienna's oldest theaters and its leading operetta house. The impresario Alexandrine von Schonerer, owner and director of the theater and, incidentally, estranged sister of the notorious anti-Semite George von Schonerer, had offered to suspend her current production of *Die Fledermaus* so that Anna might perform the *Fantasy* as scheduled. Kornblau publicly conveyed the Kuhls' acceptance of the offer, noting that the Theater an der Wien had generously chosen to honor all tickets for the Royal Opera venue; the following day, the eighteenth, the pan-German press went into convulsions, calling for vengeance on "the Semitic vampires and their insipid hangers-on" and once again vowing to enjoin the concert. That afternoon the adjutant general announced that the emperor's own First Hussars would be deployed in the streets around the theater, with orders to ensure the strictest security.

Thursday 18 January

Anna detached, quite removed from the outer chaos. What Kornblau, Leo, everyone fears most is a phase—Puchel looks to be on the verge of a stroke, so great is his anxiety—but it doesn't occur to any of them that a phase might be the most normal response to all of this.

And yet she carries on—meals, lessons, study, practice, all in the coolest way imaginable. A method of storing up energy, I suppose. Tonight I played "Soirées de Vienne" for her after dinner, then read Goethe aloud, *Italian Journey*.

"I will be at your side, every step," I told her, which she acknowledged with a grave nod. "God bless you, Hugo."

"God bless you"—the truly blessed would get her out of here, had he the slightest scrap of courage.

For the performance she chose a black, full-skirted gown with dark brocade roses, a shirred waist and a high collar of mousseline de soie. A light snow was falling that evening as she and her entourage departed the Salesianergasse, the flakes fine and dry as ash, forming brilliant silver aureoles around the street lamps. Approaching the theater they began to pass mounted hussars at the street corners, the soldiers magnificent in their blue capes with sable trim, their crested helmets and gold-edged riding boots. Soon the streets were filled with carriages all moving in a thick yet peaceable flow toward the theater. As the pan-Germans had vowed, the virtuoso experienced difficulty in reaching her destination, but it was this mass of coaches, rather than virile nationalism, which proved to be her sole hindrance—Anna was delayed by her own traffic jam, in effect.

Frau von Schonerer received her at an obscure side entrance to the theater, along with a captain of the hussars, six uniformed police, the theater superintendent and three muscular assistants, as well as two plainclothes agents from the emperor's secret police. Anna was escorted first to her dressing room to remove her cloak, then to a basement rehearsal space where a Bösendorfer grand stood waiting for her final warm-up. Puchel entered with Anna and shut the door, leaving the others to endure the chilly hall while Anna ran through fragments of her repertoire, the glorious bursts of notes and supple noodlings followed by Puchel's muffled voice as he delivered last-minute instructions.

"So small," the hussar captain later remarked, describing Anna as she left the rehearsal room. "So frail and small, it seemed impossible that this delicate girl could be the cause of so much furor." With the theater superintendent and police in the lead, Puchel and Frau von Schonerer on either side, Anna walked amid a vast entourage back to her dressing room, thirty or more people snaking with her through the backstage labyrinth. The captain was close at her heels, then her parents, her uncles, Hugo and several other cousins, Kornblau and his mistress, then a trailing flotsam of stagehands and well-connected journalists. For twenty minutes Anna sat in a corner of the dressing room while this crowd was allowed to mingle about, sampling the sumptuous buffet of meats and cheeses and admiring the flowers and telegrams sent by well-wishers. Hermine and Kornblau, still in mortal dread of a phase, sought to distract the young pianist with trivial chatter. Hugo positioned himself nearby, saying nothing, while Frau von Schonerer furnished periodic updates on the size and eminence of the audience.

"She seemed to withdraw into herself," Hugo wrote later, "to seek some deep, unfathomable place within her soul, a refuge from this ridiculous melee." Finally, at ten minutes to eight, Anna announced that she wished to be alone. Her parents and managers protested, fearing a collapse, but the girl was firm.

"I must have these last few minutes to myself."

"But at least Herr Puchel—" Hermine began.

"No one."

"Then Hugo, dear Hugo—"

"No one," Anna insisted. "I won't set foot on that stage unless I have this time alone." With difficulty, amid pleas and anxious protestations, the room was cleared and the door shut. For several minutes the entourage was forced to stare at itself out in the hall; presently the stage manager arrived to inform Frau von Schonerer that the audience was seated, the scheduled hour had come. Kornblau relayed this information through the closed door. Some said that what followed came within moments, others, that at least a minute had passed—in any event everyone heard it, a crack, a sharp report within the dressing room.

"Like a small-caliber pistol," one of the policemen said later; the captain compared it to the bark of a smartly snapped whip, while Hugo described it as the sound of a block of ice spontaneously splitting in two. For a moment no one moved, then several of the men leaped for the door, piling into an absurd heap when it refused to yield. The superintendent was pushing forward with his ball of keys when Anna spoke from within.

"I'm fine," she called in a flat, faintly disgusted voice. "I just fell, that's all. I'm fine."

The superintendent hesitated. He was still standing there, frozen, when Anna unlocked the door and stepped into the hall, her eyes firm, her carriage irreproachably straight, her face pale and fixed as a carnival mask. She proceeded down the hall with the measured walk of a bride; Hugo, who happened to be standing near the superintendent, fell into step beside her, taking her arm and guiding her through the crowd, which closed ranks behind them in a flurry of whispers. He later recounted how he spoke to her several times as they made their way to the backstage area, asking if she was well, if she'd injured herself; so great was her concentration that she seemed not to hear. He stood with her in the wings as Frau von Schonerer, with all the force of her dramatic training, gave a prolonged and eloquent introduction in which the significance of the performance was justly noted. When she concluded, as previously agreed, Anna did not appear at once; rather, she waited until Frau von Schonerer had left the stage, then stepped onto a platform empty of all save the piano and bench.

To those standing in the wings, the ovation which greeted Anna swept over the stage like a shock wave. The audience rose to its feet as if physically impelled, the thunder of hands rippling with cries of "Brave girl! Beautiful girl!" Anna walked toward the piano, then unaccountably veered toward the front of the stage, proceeding to the apron's far edge as if to acknowledge, even encourage the volcanic applause. Slowly, almost shyly, she removed the kerchief with which her right hand was concealed, then extended her hand toward the audience. Witnesses said later that the effect was one of indescribable horror, how the applause of those who failed to understand mixed with the gasps and shrieks of those who did, until, at the very last, a kind of groan, a mass, despairing sigh seemed to rise from the audience.

For, in the end, they all saw and understood. A glistening rose of blood had taken root on Anna's hand, shining from the stump of her severed extra finger. This was, in effect, her final performance, the last instance on record in which she appeared in public; indeed, from that point forward Anna Kuhl disappears so thoroughly from history that she might have been plucked from the face of the earth. No explanation for her self-mutilation was ever forthcoming, neither from Anna, nor her family, nor the concert-making industry which had so stringently run the better part of her life. Some have surmised that heartbreak was the primary cause; others, the strain of performing in such a charged and poisonous atmosphere, of finding herself the prey of a new, peculiarly intoxicating politics of hate. Or perhaps she sensed, through the harrowing susceptivity of her art, where these forces would lead us in the new century? But we remain as pitifully ignorant as her audience, which for many moments could do no more than stare at her ruined hand. They were in shock; many sank as if numbed to their chairs, while others staggered in a daze toward the exits, and only later, much later, would it occur to them that the *Fantasy* was now lost forever, its score as useless as a mute artifact, or the vaporous relic of a forgotten dream.

Charles D'Ambrosio

The High Divide

from *The New Yorker*

AT THE Home I'd get up early, when the Sisters were still asleep, and head to the ancient Chinese man's store. The ancient Chinese man was a brown, knotted, shriveled man who looked like a chunk of gingerroot and ran one of those tiny stores that sell grapefruits, wine, and toilet paper, and no one can ever figure out how they survive. But he survived, he figured it out. His ancient Chinese wife was a little twig of a woman who sat in a chair and never said a word. He spoke only enough English to conduct business, to say hello and good-bye, to make change, although every morning, when I came for my grapefruit, I tried to teach him some useful vocabulary.

I came out of the gray drizzle through the glass door with the old Fishback Appliance Repair sign still stenciled on it, a copper cowbell clanging above me, and the store was cold, the lights weren't even on. I went to the bin and picked through the grapefruits and found one that wasn't bad, a yellow ball, soft and square from sitting too long in the box, and then I went to the counter. The Chinese man wasn't there. His tiny branchlike wife was sitting in her chair, all bent up. I searched my pockets for show, knowing all along that I'd be a little short. I came up with twenty-seven cents, half a paper clip, a pen cap, and a ball of blue lint. I put the money in her hand and she stared at it. By the lonesome sound my nickels and pennies made when she sorted them into their slots I also knew that the till was empty.

I looked behind her through the beaded curtain to the small apartment behind the shop. Next to the kitchen sink was an apple with a bite out of it, the bite turned brown like an old laugh.

I held my grapefruit, tossed it up in the air, caught it.

Where is he? I asked.

She was chewing on a slice of ginger and offered me a piece, which I accepted. In the morning, they chewed ginger instead of drinking coffee.

Husband? I said.

She blinked and spat on the floor.

Meiyou xiwang, she said. *Meiyou xiwang*.

She folded her hands, tangling the tiny brown roots together. *Meiyou xiwang*, she said, touching her heart, and sending her hands flying apart. Her singsong voice beat an echo against the bare walls. Her hands flapped like a bat. I shook my head. *Meiyou xiwang*, she insisted. Huh? I said, but I knew we could go on forever not making any sense. She hugged herself, like she was cold. I didn't know what to say. She'd traveled all this way, she'd left China and crossed the ocean and come to Bremerton and opened a little store and put grapefruit in the bins and Mogen David on the shelves, but she'd gone too far, because now she couldn't tell anybody what was happening to her anymore.

I had two projects at the Home. I was reading the encyclopedia, working through the whole circle of learning available to man, as the introduction said. I'd started with Ignatius Loyola, because I'm named after him, and the Inquisition, and this led me right into the topic of torture.

My other project involved learning Latin so I could be an altar boy. I got the idea one morning at Sacred Heart while I was staring at the cold altar and the Cross and winking at the nailed-up Christ to see if he'd wink back. Our priest said that he didn't go for the vernacular because it was vulgar. If you were God Eternal, he said, would you want to listen to such yowling? He said that everything in the Church was a sign for something else, and a priest was a man who knew all the signs, but an altar boy knew a few of them, too. I looked around the sanctuary. With the snowy marble slab of altar, the gilt dome of the tabernacle and its tiny doors, the chalices and cruets, the fresh-cut flowers, the sparkling candlelight, the sanctuary was like a foreign country, and if I knew the language I could go there.

Several times I read the Missal as far as the Minor Elevation, the part of the Mass just after you pray for the dead. *Per omnia saecula saeculorum. Amen.* World without end. Amen. But I was trying to learn Latin with phonetics—the Missal was Latin on one side, English on the other—and, needless to say, my comprehension was zero, and I was always finding myself back at the beginning, starting over. *Per omnia saecula saeculorum, amen!*

Most of our schoolwork focused on how to get into Heaven. Sister Eulalia, the catechism nun, taught us about sin and the opportunities for salvation. She was a short, wide old woman with thick glasses and blue eyes that drifted behind them like tropical fish. She kept calling Jesus the Holy Victim and the Word Made Flesh and the Unspotted Sacrifice. She said that sacrifice didn't mean to kill but to make holy. We are made in the image of God's great mystery but through our ignorance and despair our vision is clouded. Salvation, she told us, is our presence in a bright light where we at last become the perfect image and reflection of our Creator.

We saw a slide show on the scapular. A boy was riding by a gas station on his bicycle. A man was pumping gas and a family was waiting in a car. Then the gas station was blowing up and the boy was flying through the air. Everybody died but the boy, who was wearing his scapular. Sister Eulalia passed around blank order forms and said to fill them out and bring $2.50 if you thought it was prudent to have a scapular for yourself. I'd spent all my money on grapefruits, though.

At night, in bed, I practiced my prayers. We had to memorize so many at the Home: Our Father, Hail Mary, Glory Be, Act of Faith, of Hope, of Love, of Contrition. Praying either put me to sleep or made me think of girls. Once, I passed a girl a note during class and Sister Josephine, the discipline nun, intercepted it and said someone my age doesn't know the least thing about love and shouldn't use that word the way I did. That kind of love is special, she said. It's a rare gift from God, it's the consummation of a union, and it's certainly nothing for children. Sister Josephine called it The Marriage Act. It's embarrassing for me to admit, but she made me cry, she was yelling so much. I never sent another note. Still, I attached a vague feeling of hope to different girls, a feeling of, I don't know, of whatever, that came out, some nights, when I said prayers.

We had to learn the prayers because we prayed for everything: we prayed for food, we prayed for sleep, we prayed for new basketballs. Three times a day, Sister Catherine, the food nun, took us to the church cafeteria for our meals. Volunteer ladies served us—they were all old and kind and had science-fiction hair, clouds of blue gas, burning white-hot rocket fuel, explosions of atomic frizz. I loved the endless stacks of white bread and the cold slabs of butter. When the nuns said I was underfoot, I went downstairs and studied the encyclopedias or read Latin or went outside and shot buses with my pump gun. Buses passed the Home every twenty-six minutes. I built up my arm pitching rocks at a tree until a circle of pulpy white wood was exposed in the bark. One afternoon I planted a sunflower in a milk carton.

I longed to go somewhere but there wasn't anywhere good that I knew of. Then one day I found the public-school yard.

What're you doing here, you stupid shit? asked one kid, a pudgy boy with skin like a baby.

He and some other boys pushed around me in a circle.

The pudge said, Who are you?

When I didn't answer, he said, You're one of those orphan bastards, right?

The boys crowded in closer and I was afraid to speak. People could tell you were from the Home by your haircut. We were all shaved up like the Dalai Lama.

Finally, I smiled and mumbled, If you say so.

What? the pudge said. I didn't hear you.

The circle of boys cinched like a knot. Their looming heads were way up in the sky.

Yeah, I said.

After that I sat below the monkey bars and chewed a butter sandwich and watched pudge-boy and his gang over by the water fountain with some girls and I knew I was going to have to kick his ass sooner or later. Everything else was new and strange but this seemed predictable and something I could rely on.

That spring the pudge had the nerve to try out for baseball. He wore brand-new cleats and threw like a fem and his mitt, also brand-new, very orange and stiff, wouldn't close. He might as well have been standing in right field with a piece of toast. He dropped everything. The second day of practice, we had an intrasquad game and I nailed him three times. I just chose places on his fat body and threw the ball at them. Eventually, pudge-boy was afraid to stand in the batter's box. The coach thought I had a control problem but I didn't. My control was perfect.

I whiffed nine guys and made the team and the pudge was cut. He walked away, crying. I ran down the hill and jumped on his back. I hit him in the face and the neck and beat on his ear over and over. You hear that? I shouted. You hear that, you fat fucker? Now that I had him alone I was insane. The pudge rolled away on the grass, holding his ear. Blood was coming out. He was bawling, and I hawked a gob of spit right into his black, wailing mouth and said, You bastard.

That night, I was asleep with the encyclopedia pitched like a tent over my nose when Sister Celestine, the head nun, came in.

Why weren't you at dinner?

I could hear the polished rocks of Sister Celestine's rosary rattling as she worried them between her fingers.

She pulled the encyclopedia off my head.

Won't you talk? Sister said.

She tucked a dry, stray shaft of hair back beneath her habit. Maybe you'd feel more comfortable making a confession?

I picked at the fuzzballs on my blanket.

I just got off the phone with that boy's mother, she said.

She touched a cut on my lip and took a deep breath. She said you called him a name. Do you know what that name means?

I shook my head.

She took off her scapular and put it around my neck. Two small pieces of brown wool hung on a cord, one in back, the other in front.

I rubbed the wool between my finger and thumb.

It's not magic, she said.

No?

More like a sign, she said, that helps guide people—she paused—like us. When you pray to it you never say Amen, because the prayer is continuous. It doesn't have an end. Before I received my calling, she said, I used to be a lot like you. I felt trapped. It was like I lived in a dark little corner of my own mind. She sighed. Ignatius, do you know what the opposite of love is?

Hate, I said.

Despair, Sister said. Despair is the opposite of love.

. . .

When the pudge came to the yard, he was obviously beat up and everybody wanted to know what happened. Before I could say anything, he came charging across the lot and said, Truce, truce. We shook hands and sat under the monkey bars, which had become my private territory.

I thought Catholics were pansies, he said.

Ignatius Loyola was a warrior, I said.

That's a weird name, the pudge said. My name's Donny.

Ignatius, I told him.

I'm sorry I called you a bastard, Donny said. He peeled a strip of red rubber off his tennis shoe and stretched and snapped it in the air. Then he put it in his mouth and chewed on it.

You should meet my dad, he said.

My dad used to race pigeons, I said. He had about a hundred of them.

Donny looked impressed. How do you race pigeons? he asked.

You just drive out to the country and let them go—they always find their way back to the coop. You can use pigeons to send messages.

My dad ate a pigeon once, Donny said. In France.

Donny told me about the Eurckan Territory, which was something he'd made up on summer vacation. The Eurekan Territory came from Eureka, California, where he had relatives he didn't like. All they did was drink greyhounds, he said, and talk about people you didn't know. They were always slapping their knees and saying Gosh, isn't that funny? when nothing was funny.

Donny wasn't a Catholic but I let him wear my scapular, which he kept on calling a spatula.

You should come over to our house, Donny said. It's big. My dad rakes it in.

I said, You want to go see my dad?

Donny looked at me. Where? he said.

What do you mean, where?

Isn't he dead?

Follow me, I said.

St. Jude's Hospital was a huge old brick building. A hurricane fence caged in a patio that was scattered with benches and garbage cans. We walked around the fence, plucking the cold wires with our fingers.

My dad was sitting on a bench with a loaf of bread and an orange. He wore a paper nightgown with snaps in the back. His eyes were like blown fuses, and dry white yuck made a crust around his mouth. Wind ruffled his hair. It was too cold to be outside in a paper outfit.

Don't you want a sweater? I said.

I climbed up the chain-link fence.

This is my friend Donny, I said. Donny, this is my dad, Tony Banner.

Dad was barefoot on one foot and wore a foam-rubber slipper on the other. He grabbed the fence and the links shivered. He looked out west, toward the Olympic Mountains, and we looked, too. It was getting dark.

Hey, Dad?

What?

He dropped a piece of bread through the fence, and a couple of cooing pigeons bobbed along the gutter and fought each other for it. They were ugly pigeons, dirty like a sidewalk. They were right under me and Donny's feet. I kicked one in the head. It fell over, and beat the dirt with its wings.

I'm learning quite a lot of prayers at school, I said.

That got him to laugh. The cuts on his hands were healing. That last week at our house he emptied all the soup cans in the garage and kept the rusty nails in his pockets. One morning for breakfast he served me a bowl of nails with milk and then squeezed a fistful of them in his hand until blood came out. He kept saying with his voice very loud and fast, I got the nails, I got the nails right here, boy—where's my cross, eh? Now he was gentle. He pushed bread through the fence until the loaf was gone and the pigeons flew away, except the one I'd kicked.

I gotta go home and eat, Donny said to me.

Donny's gotta go home and eat, I told my dad, translating for him. I've got to go eat, too.

I turned around once, real quick, and he was gripping the fence, looking off nowhere, then Donny and I crawled through a hole in the hedge.

Donny's dad asked us, Who wants to get the hell out of here? Who wants to go hiking in the Olympics? I'd spent most of my summer at Donny's house, so I knew his parents. Mrs. Cheetam was a beautiful woman with silver-and-gold hair. Mr. Cheetam was a traveling salesman and wasn't home much, but it was true, he raked it in. They bought Donny everything. Donny told me he had a sister who died of leukemia. He played me a cassette of her last farewell. Near the end of the tape she said, Donny? I love you, remember that. I want you to know that wherever I am, and wherever you are, I'll be watching. I'll be with you always. I love you. Do you hear me? Donny?

When she said that—I love you. Do you hear me? Donny?—I got a lonely sort of chill.

We're now leaving the Eurekan Territory! Donny said as we drove away, and I said, That's right. Good-bye, Eurekan Territory!

Mr. Cheetam listened to different tapes from a big collection he kept in a suitcase. They were old radio shows, and one I liked was called *The Shadow*: Who knows what evil lurks in the hearts of men? Mr. Cheetam and Donny knew all the words and talked right along with the tapes. The Shadow knows, they said, ha ha ha!

Later Donny woke up and asked, Where are we? Mr. Cheetam said, You see that river there, Donny? That's the Quinault River, and we're going to hike up along what's called the High Divide, and when we get to the top we'll be at the source of that river. You'll be able to skip right over it, he said, so remember how big it is now. Donny asked, What if we see the Sasquatch? I said we'd be famous, if we captured it. Or took a picture, Donny said. But I don't want to see it, he added. We parked at the ranger station and signed in. It was silent and we could hear our feet crunching the gravel. We cinched up our pack straps and looked at each other. This is it, Mr. Cheetam said. He looked up the trail. This is where we separate the men from the boys.

After about an hour, we cut off the main path and headed toward the river. This is where I buried my dad, Mr. Cheetam explained. I always visit once a year. Right beside the river was a tree, hanging over the water and shadowing everything. Initials were carved in the tree on the side facing the river. B.C. is Billy Cheetam, Donny said. That's my grandpa. Is he under the tree? I asked. No, no, Mr. Cheetam laughed. He was cremated and I scattered his ashes in the river. But this is the spot, he said. The river was deep and wide at that point. Mr. Cheetam asked if he and Donny could be alone to think and remember and I hiked back out to the main trail. I sat against a fallen log until Donny came back. He talks to him, Donny said. What's he say? I asked, but Donny didn't know.

Our first camp was disappointing because we could hear Boy Scouts hooting and farting around, a troop of about sixty in green uniforms with red or yellow hankies around their necks. It was like the army, with pup tents everywhere. Mr. Cheetam said not to worry, higher up there wouldn't be any Scouts.

We found wood and lit a campfire and made dinner—beef Stroganoff— and I sopped up all the gravy with my fingers. We washed the pots and pans with pebbles and sand in the river. Mr. Cheetam drank whiskey from a silver flask, wiping his lips and saying, Aaahhh, this is living!

The Boy Scouts sounded off with taps. Donny and I shared a smoke-wood stogie—a kind of gray stick you could smoke—and when it was quiet Mr. Cheetam cupped his hands around his mouth and moaned, Who stole my Golden Arm? Whooooo stoooole myyyy Goool-den Aaaarm? You could hear his voice echoing in the forest. Whoo stoooole my Gooolden Aaarm? You did! Mr. Cheetam shouted, grabbing Donny. We crawled into our tents and I started laughing and Donny got hysterical, too. Mr. Cheetam had a different tent and told us to shut up.

Donny whispered how he hated the Japs and never wanted to be captured by them—they knew how to make you talk. I told him about the Inquisition and all the tortures they'd invented for getting confessions.

They had this one thing called the press, I said. If you were accused of a crime and didn't make a plea, the King ordered you to lie down. Then he piled rocks on you until you confessed the truth or got crushed.

How big were the rocks? Donny asked.

I don't know.

What if you had thirty—what if you had a hundred—no, wait, what if you had a thousand rocks on you and then you decided to tell the truth?

You could, I said. But if you said you *didn't* do anything, the King didn't want to hear that, and he'd just go ahead with another rock, until you admitted you *did* do it.

Donny hesitated, and I thought I understood.

I know, I said. *I know.*

At the next camp, only two people were around, a man and a woman, who were sitting naked on a rock in the river when we first arrived, but kept to themselves afterward. Donny and Mr. Cheetam fished for a while but quit after Donny's hook got caught in the trees too many times. Mr. Cheetam said, Don't worry about it, Donny. It's no good down here. Higher up the water's colder and we'll catch tons of rainbows, maybe some Dolly Varden.

We ate a great meal of dehydrated chicken tetrazzini and pilot biscuits and chocolate for dessert. Donny and I shared more smokewood. Now and then we added sticks to the fire and the light breathed out and made a circle around us. I love getting away from it all, Mr. Cheetam said.

He tipped back his flask and in the bright curved silver I could see the fire flaming up.

Once upon a time, Mr. Cheetam said, there was a boy and girl who were very much in love.

Where was this? Donny asked.

Oh, Mr. Cheetam said, it doesn't matter, does it? Love's the same everywhere you go, so let's just make up a place.

How about the Eurekan Territory? I said.

O.K., Mr. Cheetam said. The Eurekan Territory, that's where they were in love. It was a small place, and everybody knew everybody else, so eventually people figured out this boy and girl had a thing going. You know what a thing is, right?

Donny said he did.

Good for you, Mr. Cheetam said. Well, this thing was frowned on by everyone. People took different sides, against the boy, or against the girl, everybody blaming everybody else. But the boy and girl were madly in love and you can't stop love, not when it's the real thing.

He went to his pack and pulled out a big bottle and refilled his flask. When he came back he said, You know what that's like, to have a real thing?

Donny said, Yeah, I know.

I mean really real, Mr. Cheetam said.

How real? I said.

Mr. Cheetam ignored me. To hell with what anybody thinks, these kids, these lovers, said. So one night the boy meets the girl on the edge of town and they drive up a dark winding road to a lover's leap. They can see everything from up there, but they're not looking. No sirree, Bob. The boy and the girl sit in the car, spooning, as we used to call it back in the day— making out, and listening to love songs on the radio, until one of the songs is interrupted by a special bulletin. A prisoner has escaped!

Does the prisoner have hooks instead of hands? I asked.

Yeah, Mr. Cheetam said, that's the guy.

How'd you know? Donny asked.

I knew because the story wasn't true. The girl hears something outside, and the boy says, Oh, baby, baby, don't worry, we're way up here above everything, we're safe. The boy tries to get at the girl, and the girl keeps hearing something outside. Eventually it's no fun, and they go home. When the boy opens the door for the girl to drop her out he finds a hook clawing and banging at the door handle, just clinging there, ripped right off the prisoner's arm.

Mr. Cheetam didn't scare me, but Donny was scared.

We were quiet for a minute, and then I told them about when my dad was driving in his car. The other car came out of nowhere, I said. And my dad was hanging half out the door. His foot was stuck under the clutch and his head was banging on the road. He was dragged about two hundred feet. He was in the hospital for a month. My mom died.

No one said anything, so I added, That's a true life story.

You don't think mine was? Mr. Cheetam asked. He looked at me strangely and winked.

Well, I said, yeah, I do. I know it is. I heard about those lovers before.

Mr. Cheetam stood up, stretched, and fell down. Donny and I looked at each other, then we got in our sleeping bags.

Your dad sure enjoys whiskey, I said.

In the middle of the night, Donny said, Hey, you hear that?

Come off it, I said.

I swear I heard something.

There's nothing out there, I said, but Donny went over to sleep in his dad's tent anyway.

We reached a sign that pointed different ways: the High Divide and the Low Divide. We took the high, up and up. There were fewer trees, and we climbed on loose rock called scree, and the air was thinner. Donny had an ugly blister on his heel and complained, and Mr. Cheetam got impatient with him. Just pull yourself up and get going, he said. Don't fall behind.

Finally we crossed a field full of pink and yellow wildflowers, and at the far end, where the path ended, was a lake. The surface was perfectly clear and placid and we could see ourselves.

Here we are, Mr. Cheetam said.

Skinny-dipping, Donny said.

First things first, girls, Mr. Cheetam said, so we hopped to, setting up camp and scrounging enough wood for the night.

Donny and I stripped naked and jumped off the cliffs. No one else was around but when we swam and shouted and splashed our voices bounced back and forth off the rocks. Ricochet, we yelled. We dove and dove. Then we lay on a hot flat rock. I noticed that Donny had hair on his balls and he probably noticed so did I. You want to smoke a stogerooni? Donny asked. Nah, later, I said. We were stretched out and quiet: blue sky, yellow sun, white mountain—everything was perfect but Donny got antsy doing nothing for so long and took another dip. He came up fast and said, A fish! I saw a fish! And he got his fishing pole and caught a rainbow, like pulling a prayer from the water.

Good work, Donny, Mr. Cheetam said.

The fish wasn't all the way dead yet and Mr. Cheetam had to slap its head against a rock. Blood came out the eyes. The knife blade sank into the skin with a ripping sound. What do we do with the guts? I asked. Toss 'em in the lake, Mr. Cheetam said. We don't want any animals coming into camp. Bears? Donny said. It's not impossible, Mr. Cheetam said, but not likely, either. Maybe the Sasquatch, Donny said. Mr. Cheetam said to shut up about that damned Sasquatch. It's time you grow up, he said, shaking Donny's arm. Jesus, Donny said, rubbing himself.

Mr. Cheetam wrapped the fillets in foil and set them on the fire. It was soft out now, not dark but not light, either. Our shadows were weak around the fire, and Mt. Olympus was tinged pink and purple, and the wind died down.

Hey, I said, what about the Quinault?

Yeah, the Quinault! Donny said. You said I'd get to walk across it.

Oh crap, what was I thinking? Mr. Cheetam asked himself. You already did and I forgot, God damn it!

We ran back through the darkening wildflowers. We found a little stream about a foot wide and three inches deep that you would never think was a river but it was. There's your mighty Quinault, Donny, Mr. Cheetam said. Donny asked if we built a dam would the river dry up below and Mr. Cheetam laughed, saying, No, I'm afraid it doesn't work that way. We bent down and drank and splashed our faces in the water. We listened to the little river, trickling in a whisper. It was almost like nothing.

The fish was all burned to hell when we got back to camp. Donny was upset and kept whining. I'm sorry, Mr. Cheetam said, but things happen. What can I say? Then he offered, Tomorrow? You want to stay another day? Donny looked at me, then said, Stay! Stay! O.K., Mr. Cheetam said, I think we've got everything we need—plenty of provisions—and we'll catch some more fish.

After dinner, Mr. Cheetam drew out his flask again. His face was like my dad's had been in the last days, rough and black. One night toward the end I'd found him, my dad, in our broom closet. He had all his Bob Dylan records out and was writing new lyrics on them with a nail. Other things happened that I prefer to keep to myself. All week his loud voice was like the echo of thoughts he'd had a long time ago. Then one morning at the very end I heard him calling me in the rain. He was on top of our house in boxer shorts, yelling. Our neighbor tried to drive him off the roof by throwing a pot of geraniums at him. My dad started ripping apart the chimney and pitching bricks down on me and everybody else on the front lawn. We had to call the authorities. For a while he thought he was Jesus in a hospital called St. Judas, but it was really St. Jude's and my dad, of course, wasn't Jesus. The same people who took him to the hospital brought me to the Home. I hadn't eaten in three days.

Nearby we saw field mice hopping around, and Mr. Cheetam said that we'd better keep our packs inside the tents tonight. He hooked his arm around Donny's neck and said, How'd you like to go to California?

Not Eureka, Donny said.

No, Mr. Cheetam said, L.A.

Donny said he didn't know anything about L.A. Mr. Cheetam fussed with the fire, arranging the coals. When that goes out that's it until morning, he said. He tipped back the flask. Then he capped it and said, That's it for that, too. He stretched and groaned and walked out where the firelight failed. I heard him whistling in the dark.

Son? Mr. Cheetam said.

What? Donny asked.

Come on over here a minute, Mr. Cheetam said.

They were in the shadows. I heard Donny say, What does Mom think?

That's the thing, Mr. Cheetam said. Your mother would stay.

I don't know, Donny said. How long would we be gone?

Donald, Mr. Cheetam said, don't be stupid. We're divorcing, your mom and I. You see, we won't come back—we'll live in a brand-new house there.

Donny begged, But why?

Donald, come on. You see how things are.

The two of them were quiet and staring ahead, like their next thoughts might fall out of the sky.

What can I say? Mr. Cheetam said.

Nothing, Donny said.

I love you, Donald. You know that.

I crawled inside our tent. A little while later, Donny got in his bag, buried down inside. He was crying and choking. I whispered, Donny, hey, hey, Donny? Donny? I think I hear something out there. Do you hear it? Let's go look! I hugged my arm around him and he started jerking in his bag and sat up and cried to me, Here's your stupid spatula! Then he crossed over into Mr. Cheetam's tent but kept crying and begging even louder for no divorce.

Look, I heard Mr. Cheetam say, after your sister died—His voice fell apart. That's too easy, he said. I've met someone else. He was quiet a minute. That's the truth.

I thought the crying would go on forever, but eventually Donny must have fallen asleep.

I turned over and over in my sleeping bag, and then I put on Sister Celestine's scapular and grabbed the flashlight and crawled out of the tent. The fire made a hiss and I kicked the last few embers around in the bed of ash. Mr. Cheetam snorted in his sleep and I heard Donny say, Dad? And Mr. Cheetam say, What? but there was nothing after that, even though I stood outside their tent a long time, listening.

I aimed my flashlight ahead to the flat rock rim of the lake and followed the narrow beam up there. I sat, dangling my feet, and snapped off the light. I think I was feeling sorry for myself. Suddenly it felt like we'd been gone for ages. Was it Sunday? I gathered up ten rocks for a rosary, to count my prayers. I rattled them in my hands and started the Our Father but my voice was weird. I shook the rocks in my fist like dice. I threw one in the lake, and a little while later I heard the splash. Circles opened out where the stone had vanished. I thought of saying something in Latin but couldn't recall a single word, except amen. I yelled out, A-men! and heard back, Hey-men, hey-men, hey-men, smaller and smaller.

I stretched out on the rock. Sister Celestine's scapular was old, the wool worn soft from handling. Once, at the Home, I had climbed the stairs, six flights up from my room in the basement, to see where she lived. We weren't supposed to go up there. I saw why. Hosiery hung from the water pipes. Candy wrappers were crumpled on the floor. A black habit lay like an empty sack beside the bed. The bed was unmade, and I could see the hollow where Sister Celestine slept. A pale-green blanket and a thin yellow top sheet had been twisted into a tight braid and kicked off the end of the mattress. The only decoration was a black wooden crucifix, nailed on the wall above the bed like a permanent shadow.

I was still lying there when Donny and Mr. Cheetam came running up the rock in their undies. Hey, what's going on? they asked. They said they'd heard me shouting and were afraid I'd got lost or seen something.

Maybe the Sasquatch, Donny said.

God damn it, Donald, there is no such thing, Mr. Cheetam said. That's just a myth.

Oh yeah, Donny said. How do you know?

Don't worry, I said. It was nothing.

You sure? Donny said.

It was nothing, I said. I'm sure.

A wind was blowing and it was a little cold on that rock. Nobody knew what to say.

See out there? Above Mt. Olympus? That green star? Mr. Cheetam said, pointing. We all looked—a vague white shadow, a green light. It's not really a star. That's a planet—that's Venus, Mr. Cheetam said. The goddess of love.

That's just a *myth*, Donny said, looking at his father. Bastard.

I didn't hear you, Mr. Cheetam said. What did you say?

Nothing, Donny said.

Nothing? It didn't sound like nothing to me.

I pitched another rock in the lake, way out there, as far as possible. We all listened. Across the water a circle spread out, wider and wider. Then, shaking with cold, Donny folded his arms around himself and yelled out, Hey, and we heard back, Hey, hey, hey, and then I yelled out, Hey, and even Mr. Cheetam joined in, and we kept hearing back, Hey, hey, hey, like there were millions of us everywhere.

Gail Jones

Desolation

from *The Kenyon Review*

1

A MELANCHOLY seriousness settles on the faces of people attending concerts; it is a look both distracted and concentrated, disturbed and imperturbable. Something says: we shall endure this, it will eventually pass; we shall orient our serried faces to the irresistible stage, and hope for suspension in the glorious no-time of music. Everyone is the same; everyone feels this. Concerts impose a rude aura of collectivity and the tense AC/DC of the serious/glorious.

She had noticed it last night at a piano recital, in which a slim Chinese woman, beautifully intense, played Rachmaninoff with superhuman celerity; and she notices it here, listening to Death in Vegas. Faces shining in the dark, riveted, young, are replicating the expression. The music they are listening to is electronically synthesized, and has a quality of pounding and insistent stammer: the squeal of a keyboard and the whine of electric guitars are encased in an overamplified throb.

Repetition, repetition, repetition, she thinks.

On the stage, absurdly familiar, is a skull-and-crossbones flag, and behind it hangs a screen of fluctuating and synchronized projections. Images loop, and loop again, then accelerate to crescendo. There are soldiers marching in formation, dancers whirling out of focus, machinery, lightbulbs, a weather balloon ascending.

She wonders what meaning operates here, that employs the visual as mere flash. The bald head of the keyboard player is her stable sign; throughout the concert it is variously and fantastically lit—red, blue, purple, and then gold—but it remains somehow definite, a human globe, a wonderfully absolute, pure, and untechnical thing.

Ragged applause: then the system of repetitions restarts.

There is too much sound and too much light: she is feeling denuded and swathed in excess. Ordinary and strobe lights rake the dark crowd, and at some point this young woman, who has come to the concert alone, covers her eyes with one hand to counter the bluish-light blindness. Even with her eyes closed she can still see the fulgurous strobe, and she is even more willfully and emphatically alone; she is locked into some solitary concert and closed to community. She is a foreigner, people will know it, she does not belong here.

Someone reaches over and holds gently her other hand.

The young woman can feel the touch, which she takes as a gesture of solicitude. Perhaps, seeing her shade her eyes, someone has imagined her distressed. Perhaps it is simple kindness, a vague gesture of concert solidarity. When she reopens her eyes, blinking against the renewed brightness, a man is standing beside her: an Algerian, possibly, or an Indian, or a Moroccan. They are listening to music in Paris, foreign together. The venue for the concert is the Elysée Montmartre, an old cabaret—*belle-époque*-looking, even in dereliction—a hall gutted and transformed for dance parties and concerts. The plaster ceiling is decorated with eight women's faces. They are gigantic and smiling and have flowing *fin de siècle* hairstyles; scarlet lights sit at their chins, so that they appear mean and infernal.

Here they are then, an instant couple, beneath eight scarlet-faced women. The man is staring at the stage; he has not attempted conversation. The music is now so loud that it has materialized as a physical force; the wooden floor vibrates with seismic shivers that move upwards through every body.

Quaker, the woman is thinking. *This is like being possessed.*

The Elysée Montmartre is becoming hot and stuffy. Patrons are removing layers of clothes and buying more beer. The room is filled with cigarette smoke and everyone wears black. Afraid that she will faint or swoon, overcome by whatever bodily, existential, or foolish conundrum, the woman pulls the foreign man with her, drags him through the dense crowd, and leaves the building, still quaking.

2

How to tell this compassionately? How to preserve his vulnerability? It was a small encounter, saturated with contingent sadness.

In the street the strangers faced each other, mutually embarrassed. They were exactly the same height, and she has discovered that he is handsome and possibly ten years her junior. Light from pink neon burnished his features.

Eleanor, she said, and extended her hand formally.

Rashid. I am Rashid.

He took her hand again and performed an Indian affirmation, a brief sideways tilt and motion of the head.

Australia.

India.

We rhyme, she joked.

You have excellent cricketers, Rashid said politely.

Cricketers, yes.

International value; how arcane it is, how transparent.

She was relieved to speak English, but disconcerted by her own uncharacteristic assertiveness. She was already wondering if she would sleep with him, this Rashid, this young man, this youth she had dragged from a loud concert as her hysterical accessory. They left for a nearby bar, walking side by side, careful not to touch each other or forge obligation, and then soon after, more trusting, to his rented room. It was a pitifully small studio, on the fifth floor of an old building in the nineteenth *arrondissement*. Paint blistered on the walls; unintelligible graffiti inscribed all the surfaces. In Rashid's room the lighting was yellow-brown and spilled from a glass tulip depending at an angle from the wall. The air was hung with persistent scents of Indian cooking. There was a small basin, a single chair, a pile of stacked dirty dishes.

Eleanor fought to repress a powerful intuition: *What am I doing here?*

Then she noticed a shudder, like an aftershock from the Death in Vegas concert. She assumed it was the Metro, somewhere deep beneath them. She heard its thunderous sound trailing into the night, and imagined the tunnel, and the tired driver, and the headlights flashing on walls lined with innards of cable and pipe, then the sequence of lit chambers and dark tunnels, lit chambers and dark tunnels, repeating on an efficient exhausted circuit; and she saw then the passengers of many nations embarking and disembarking, and heard the *shoosh* of electric doors, opening and closing; and she thought *repetition, repetition, repetition, repetition. . . .*

You get used to it, said Rashid. You get used to the Metro.

He prepared cups of tea in the Indian style, milky and with sugar, and they sat together on the single bed, sipping and making self-conscious small talk.

When they made love, it was in darkness; Rashid was shy and inexpert. Eleanor held his body closely, but he felt absent, anonymous.

The kindness of strangers. (She almost adopts a southern accent.)

Pardon? said Rashid.

In the companionable quiet, she could hear a dripping tap and his soft, murmurous breathing.

And then, clothed in darkness, Rashid began to confess:

I should tell you, Miss Eleanor, that I have great shame, he announced in a low and slightly hoarse whisper. I was sent to France by my father—at huge expense—to do a computer course, technology: that was the deal. Why not United States or England? He knew a family here. They said they would look out for me. Take me in. For the first two months or so I tried very hard but my French was poor and I could not understand the technical terms. I studied, and I tried, but fell further and further behind. The other students in the course were all confident and cool. They called me *le singe*, the monkey, and they laughed behind my back. Finally, I could stand it no more, so I left the course. I did not tell the Guptas, the family I was staying with—kind people, good people, from Bombay like my family—but left every day with my hair combed and my books under my arm. I would wait in the parks, or wander the streets, looking into shop windows. I became an expert at wandering and wasting time.

But then one day I received a letter from home, from my father, asking me how I was doing—was I well? was I successful?—and I felt suddenly such shame and such deception. I left the Guptas that day and simply disappeared. I knew another Indian, a Bengali—he rents this place—who agreed to let me use his room while I looked for work. He works on night shift, so I use the bed at night, and he has it in the day. I have found work here and there—I am a cleaner, part-time, at the Elysée Montmartre, so I get to see all the concerts—but because I am illegal, I am poorly paid. I have no hope at all of repaying my father. No hope at all of saving a fare back home. And I live in dread of seeing the Guptas appear on the street. I avoid the Indian areas, and get my friend to do the shopping.

I am stranded here; I am lost. I don't know what to do.

Sometimes I feel I have become invisible.

Eleanor held Rashid in the now abysmal darkness. He curled away from her, his body distant and demonstrating shame. She became aware once again of the Metro, shuddering the whole building. It rolled beneath them both, in its corridor of hot air, in its unceasing, predictable circumnavigation of the city, carrying figures whose faces were blurred and carried away as they zipped into the underground night, like people dragged, fast motion, beyond any reliable identification.

3
six disquisitions she tells herself

FOREIGNNESS

This man, this Rashid, carries the metaphysic of the stranded. He lies awake at night, in someone else's bed, thinking of a home that becomes more precious with each new remembering. He knows too that his lost home is their found exotic. Everywhere in this city are chichi boutiques stocked with small objects from his country, familiar things relocated.

He is another kind of object: he has entered a state of abstraction. He imagines himself becoming phantom, almost invisible. Making love, even making love, has not embodied him wholly.

CITY

One's own city is always stable; it rests, we reside. But the traveler and the refugee and the phantomized stranded know the secret instability of every city. They have felt the ground move and shift beneath their foreign feet, and know that collapse of many kinds is always possible. Sometimes this is an experience of excitation; sometimes it is the tremor of lives on the annihilating brink. She inhabits the touristic decadence of the casual encounter; he is her object and she has unintentionally compounded his desolation.

MUSIC

It was the democracy—or was it the fascism?—of music that united them. They listened together. They bobbed their bodies in sync. Each moved with a kind of instinctive and elated obedience. This transcultural age is the age of music. Words are disparaged, too difficult and too absurdly imperative. Young people everywhere hallow the names of musicians and seek their lost sacred in a riff or in a resonating chord. She dragged him away. She broke his tense AC/DC.

PARENTS

He is enchained to them. We all are, even when they die. Of all the authorities in the world parents are the most sovereign, and they follow like a double and separate shadow, everywhere we go. Here is a young woman traveling, wondering: *What would my parents think?* The trouble we cause them. The loving shame that they wield. If life were a blindman's bluff, we would always touch them in the darkness; they would always be there, somewhere.

SEX

When he came inside her, his body responded with a chorealike shiver; she found it somehow anguishing. The sigh he gave up was such a distant and sad-sounding relinquishment. This certainty, then: that in the effacements and anonymities of the night, other things find metaphorical definition. The physical body in crisis and its transphysical continuation are like the indivisible image and afterimage of the blinding strobe.

NIGHT

As a child she was obsessed with the idea that the planet is always half night. It symbolized, even to her child-mind, the impermanence of all states and the principle of alterity and radical conversion. Now she knows it more boldly: that night is a mode of magnification. Depression. Insomnia. Concerts. Sex. The enhancement of both misery and its forms of consolation. This is banal knowledge but now, in this lightly shaking room, it somehow reassures her.

4

They were lying together asleep, on the narrow borrowed bed, when Rashid woke with a start and switched on a nearby lamp. His face was damp and shining with tears.

Eleanor turned drowsily toward her lover, her shanghaied youth, and saw his red swollen eyes and his look of taut dishevelment.

I dreamed. . . .

There is more, he said slowly, there is more I didn't tell you.

Rashid leaned away. His face was not visible.

When I left Bombay, my mother was dying of cancer. She was very, very thin, and had dark rings beneath her eyes. I knew then that she was dying—and she knew that I knew—but my father nevertheless insisted that I leave. She wept so much; I shall never forget it. I said: I will return soon and make a journey, and bring you some Ganga water; I will return and get the holy water and you will be cured. I think I believed it then. I was confident when I left. I thought all the time about going to Europe, about money, about success. In the letter, my father's letter, he told me that my mother had died. I left the Guptas' house because my mother had died. Just that. Because my mother had died. I could not bear to be with people. I could not bear the knowledge of her death.

I dreamed just now a dream that I have had three times. I dreamed that my mother came to me wearing the white sari of a widow. She was looking like a skeleton, and her voice was strange and very quiet. She said: I wrote you a letter and you didn't answer. Where is my answer, Rashid? Where is my answer? She began to pound her chest in mourning, as if I were the one who had died. I remember that there was spittle on her chin, like an old person, like a cancer patient. I wanted to wipe her face with a cloth but I could not stretch far enough to touch her.

Here Rashid paused. He was silent for a long minute.

She wept so much, he repeated, I can never forget it.

And then Rashid too began to weep. Eleanor had never seen a man cry with such disinhibition. His whole body sobbed; he was like a small child. He clenched his fists against his eyes, as if trying to contain his dreamy sorrow.

Je suis desolé, he said. *Desolé. Desolé.*

Please leave, he said. *Desolé. Desolé.*

5

Eleanor is on the street, at four in the morning. The look of things is black glass—it has recently rained or the streets have been washed and cleaned—and everything appears remarkably still and settled. Her lonesome footsteps echo down the tunnel of the rue de Meaux. She has returned to her habit of itemization; she begins to replay her nighttime memories.

This is what she is remembering:

She is remembering that the only lyrics in the Death of Vegas concert were "All gods suck, all gods suck," combined with a spinning Shiva image and the round surface of some dark, possibly planetary, object. Did it hurt him, this crude and flashy combination? Did it recall some childhood moment of a more holy and private life?

She is remembering the scarlet women peering down from the ceiling; how gigantic and superintending they seemed, how ambiguous in their presences. They rested somewhere between benevolence and malevolence, between charm and grotesquerie.

This night has made every detail retrospectively symbolic. Their hair. Their oversize, European smiles.

She is remembering his face under pink neon, how young he appeared. He had large lustrous eyes and a patina of electrical shine. He had a shy expression and a quality of good-looking tenderness. Yet she desired him, quite simply, because he held her hand. When he first touched her, she could not have guessed that he was so insubstantial.

She is remembering the woman playing Rachmaninoff, the Chinese woman, and the bald head of the keyboard player, repetitiously recoloring. She is remembering too the precise look of melancholy seriousness that begins in a concert, extends into gestures and confessions, and then moves outwards, traveling like vibrations, traveling so mysteriously—not like the Metro at all, not regular and entrammeled—but fanning open, invisibly, like vibrations in the body, into all the glories and desolations of a black city night.

Edward P. Jones

A Rich Man

from *The New Yorker*

H ORACE AND LONEESE Perkins—one child, one grandchild—lived most unhappily together for more than twelve years in Apartment 230 at Sunset House, a building for senior citizens at 1202 Thirteenth Street NW. They moved there in 1977, the year they celebrated forty years of marriage, the year they made love for the last time—Loneese kept a diary of sorts, and that fact was noted on one day of a week when she noted nothing else. "He touched me," she wrote, which had always been her diary euphemism for sex. That was also the year they retired, she as a pool secretary at the Commerce Department, where she had known one lover, and he as a civilian employee at the Pentagon, as the head of veteran records. He had been an Army sergeant for ten years before becoming head of records; the Secretary of Defense gave him a plaque as big as his chest on the day he retired, and he and the Secretary of Defense and Loneese had their picture taken, a picture that hung for all those twelve years in the living room of Apartment 230, on the wall just to the right of the heating-and-air-conditioning unit.

A month before they moved in, they drove in their burgundy-and-gold Cadillac from their small house on Chesapeake Street in Southeast to a Union Station restaurant and promised each other that Sunset House would be a new beginning for them. Over blackened catfish and a peach cobbler that they both agreed could have been better, they vowed to devote themselves to each other and become even better grandparents. Horace had long known about the Commerce Department lover. Loneese had told him about the man two months after she had ended the relationship, in 1969. "He worked in the mailroom," she told her husband over a spaghetti supper she had cooked in the Chesapeake Street home. "He touched me in the motel room," she wrote in her diary, "and after it was over he begged me to go away to Florida with him. All I could think about was that Florida was for old people."

At that spaghetti supper, Horace did not mention the dozens of lovers he had had in his time as her husband. She knew there had been many, knew it because they were written on his face in the early years of their marriage, and because he had never bothered to hide what he was doing in the later years. "I be back in a while. I got some business to do," he would say. He did not even mention the lover he had slept with just the day before the spaghetti supper, the one he bid good-bye to with a "Be good and be sweet" after telling her he planned to become a new man and respect his marriage vows. The woman, a thin school-bus driver with clanking bracelets up to her elbows on both arms, snorted a laugh, which made Horace want to slap her, because he was used to people taking him seriously. "Forget you, then," Horace said on the way out the door. "I was just tryin to let you down easy."

Over another spaghetti supper two weeks before moving, they reiterated what had been said at the blackened-catfish supper and did the dishes together and went to bed as man and wife, and over the next days sold almost all the Chesapeake Street furniture. What they kept belonged primarily to Horace, starting with a collection of six hundred and thirty-nine record albums, many of them his "sweet babies," the 78s. If a band worth anything had recorded between 1915 and 1950, he bragged, he had the record; after 1950, he said, the bands got sloppy and he had to back away. Horace also kept the Cadillac he had painted to honor a football team, paid to park the car in the underground garage. Sunset had once been intended as a luxury place, but the builders, two friends of the city commissioners, ran out of money in the middle and the commissioners had the city-government people buy it off them. The city-government people completed Sunset, with its tiny rooms, and then, after one commissioner gave a speech in Southwest about looking out for old people, some city-government people in Northeast came up with the idea that old people might like to live in Sunset, in Northwest.

Three weeks after Horace and Loneese moved in, Horace went down to the lobby one Saturday afternoon to get their mail and happened to see Clara Knightley getting her mail. She lived in Apartment 512. "You got this fixed up real nice," Horace said of Apartment 512 a little less than an hour after meeting her. "But I could see just in the way that you carry yourself that you got good taste. I could tell that about you right off." "You swellin my head with all that talk, Mr. Perkins," Clara said, offering him coffee, which he rejected, because such moments always called for something stronger. "Whas a woman's head for if a man can't swell it up from time to time. Huh? Answer me that, Clara. You just answer me that." Clara was fifty-five, a bit younger than most of the residents of Sunset House, though she was much older than all Horace's other lovers. She did not fit the city people's definition of a senior citizen, but she had a host of ailments, from high blood pressure to diabetes, and so the city people had let her in.

Despite the promises, the marriage, what little there had been of it, came to an end. "I will make myself happy," Loneese told the diary a month after he last touched her. Loneese and Horace had fixed up their apartment nicely, and neither of them wanted to give the place up to the other. She wanted to make a final stand with the man who had given her so much heartache, the man who had told her, six months after her confession, what a whore she had been to sleep with the Commerce Department mailroom man. Horace, at sixty, had never thought much of women over fifty, but Clara—and, after her, Willa, of Apartment 1001, and Miriam, of Apartment 109—had awakened something in him, and he began to think that women over fifty weren't such a bad deal after all. Sunset House had dozens of such women, many of them attractive widows, many of them eager for a kind word from a retired Army sergeant who had so many medals and ribbons that his uniform could not carry them. As far as he could see, he was cock of the walk: many of the men in Sunset suffered from diseases that Horace had so far escaped, or they were not as good-looking or as thin, or they were encumbered by wives they loved. In Sunset House he was a rich man. So why move and give that whore the satisfaction?

They lived separate lives in a space that was only a fourth as large as the Chesapeake Street house. The building came to know them as the man and wife in 230 who couldn't stand each other. People talked about the Perkinses more than they did about anyone else, which was particularly upsetting to Loneese, who had been raised to believe family business should stay in the family. "Oh, Lord, what them two been up to now?" "Fight like cats and dogs, they do." "Who he seein now?" They each bought their own food from the Richfood on Eleventh Street or from the little store on Thirteenth Street, and they could be vile to each other if what one bought was disturbed or eaten by the other. Loneese stopped speaking to Horace for nine months in 1984 and 1985, when she saw that her pumpkin pie was a bit smaller than when she last cut a slice from it. "I ain't touch your damn pie, you crazy woman," he said when she accused him. "How long you been married to me? You know I've never been partial to pumpkin pie." "That's fine for you to say, Horace, but why is some missing? You might not be partial to it, but I know you. I know you'll eat anything in a pinch. That's just your dirty nature." "My nature ain't no more dirty than yours."

After that, she bought a small icebox for the bedroom where she slept, though she continued to keep the larger items in the kitchen refrigerator. He bought a separate telephone, because he complained that she wasn't giving him his messages from his "associates." "I have never been a secretary for whores," she said, watching him set up an answering machine next to the hide-a-bed couch where he slept. "Oh, don't get me started 'bout whores. I'd say you wrote the damn book." "It was dictated by you."

Their one child, Alonzo, lived with his wife and son in Baltimore. He had not been close to his parents for a long time, and he could not put the why of it into words for his wife. Their boy, Alonzo, Jr., who was twelve when his grandparents moved into Sunset, loved to visit them. Horace would unplug and put away his telephone when the boy visited. And Loneese and Horace would sleep together in the bedroom. She'd put a pillow between them in the double bed to remind herself not to roll toward him.

Their grandson visited less and less as he moved into his teenage years, and then, after he went away to college, in Ohio, he just called them every few weeks, on the phone they had had installed in the name of Horace and Loneese Perkins.

. . .

In 1987, Loneese's heart began the countdown to its last beat and she started spending more time at George Washington University Hospital than she did in the apartment. Horace never visited her. She died two years later. She woke up that last night in the hospital and went out into the hall and then to the nurses' station but could not find a nurse anywhere to tell her where she was or why she was there. "Why do the patients have to run this place alone?" she said to the walls. She returned to her room and it came to her why she was there. It was nearing three in the morning, but she called her own telephone first, then she dialed Horace's. He answered, but she never said a word. "Who's this playin on my phone?" Horace kept asking. "Who's this? I don't allow no playin on my phone." She hung up and lay down and said her prayers. After moving into Sunset, she had taken one more lover, a man at Vermont Avenue Baptist Church, where she went from time to time. He was retired, too. She wrote in her diary that he was not a big eater and that "down there, his vitals were missing."

Loneese Perkins was buried in a plot at Harmony Cemetery that she and Horace had bought when they were younger. There was a spot for Horace and there was one for their son, but Alonzo had long since made plans to be buried in a cemetery just outside Baltimore.

Horace kept the apartment more or less the way it was on the last day she was there. His son and daughter-in-law and grandson took some of her clothes to the Goodwill and the rest they gave to other women in the building. There were souvenirs from countries that Loneese and Horace had visited as man and wife—a Ghanaian carving of men surrounding a leopard they had killed, a brass menorah from Israel, a snow globe of Mt. Fuji with some of the snow stuck forever to the top of the globe. They were things that did not mean very much to Alonzo, but he knew his child, and he knew that one day Alonzo, Jr., would cherish them.

Horace tried sleeping in the bed, but he had been not unhappy in his twelve years on the hide-a-bed. He got rid of the bed and moved the couch into the bedroom and kept it open all the time.

He realized two things after Loneese's death: His own "vitals" had rejuvenated. He had never had the problems other men had, though he had failed a few times along the way, but that was to be expected. Now, as he moved closer to his seventy-third birthday, he felt himself becoming ever stronger, ever more potent. God is a strange one, he thought, sipping Chivas Regal one night before he went out: he takes a man's wife and gives him a new penis in her place.

The other thing he realized was that he was more and more attracted to younger women. When Loneese died, he had been keeping company with a woman of sixty-one, Sandy Carlin, in Apartment 907. One day in February, nine months after Loneese's death, one of Sandy's daughters, Jill, came to visit, along with one of Jill's friends, Elaine Cunningham. They were both twenty-five years old. From the moment they walked through Sandy's door, Horace began to compliment them—on their hair, the color of their fingernail polish, the sharp crease in Jill's pants ("You iron that yourself?"), even "that sophisticated way" Elaine crossed her legs. The young women giggled, which made him happy, pleased with himself, and Sandy sat in her place on the couch. As the ice in the Pepsi-Cola in her left hand melted, she realized all over again that God had never promised her a man until her dying day.

When the girls left, about three in the afternoon, Horace offered to accompany them downstairs, "to keep all them bad men away." In the lobby, as the security guard at her desk strained to hear, he made it known that he wouldn't mind if they came by to see him sometime. The women looked at each other and giggled some more. They had been planning to go to a club in Southwest that evening, but they were amused by the old man, by the way he had his rap together and put them on some sort of big pedestal and shit, as Jill would tell another friend weeks later. And when he saw how receptive they were he said why not come on up tonight, shucks, ain't no time like the present. Jill said he musta got that from a song, but he said no, he'd been sayin that since before they were born, and Elaine said thas the truth, and the women giggled again. He said I ain't gonna lie bout bein a seasoned man, and then he joined in the giggling. Jill looked at Elaine and said want to? And Elaine said what about your mom? And Jill shrugged her shoulders and Elaine said O.K. She had just broken up with a man she had met at another club and needed something to make the pain go away until there was another man, maybe from a better club.

At about eleven thirty, Jill wandered off into the night, her head liquored up, and Elaine stayed and got weepy—about the man from the not-so-good club, about the two abortions, about running away from home at seventeen after a fight with her father. "I just left him nappin on the couch," she said, stretched out on Horace's new living-room couch, her shoes off and one of Loneese's throws over her feet. Horace was in the chair across from her. "For all I know, he's still on that couch." Even before she got to her father, even before the abortions, he knew that he would sleep with her that night. He did not even need to fill her glass a third time. "He was a fat man," she said of her father. "And there ain't a whole lot more I remember."

"Listen," he said as she talked about her father, "everything's gonna work out right for you." He knew that, at such times in a seduction, the more positive a man was the better things went. It would not have done to tell her to forget her daddy, that she had done the right thing by running out on that fat so-and-so; it was best to focus on tomorrow and tell her that the world would be brighter in the morning. He came over to the couch, and before he sat down on the edge of the coffee table he hiked up his pants just a bit with his fingertips, and seeing him do that reminded her vaguely of something wonderful. The boys in the club sure didn't do it that way. He took her hand and kissed her palm. "Everything's gonna work out to the good," he said.

Elaine Cunningham woke in the morning with Horace sleeping quietly beside her. She did not rebuke herself and did not look over at him with horror at what she had done. She sighed and laid her head back on the pillow and thought how much she still loved the man from the club, but there was nothing more she could do: not even the five-hundred-dollar leather jacket she had purchased for the man had brought him around. Two years after running away, she had gone back to where she had lived with her parents, but they had moved and no one in the building knew where they had gone. But everyone remembered her. "You sure done growed up, Elaine," one old woman said. "I wouldna knowed if you hadn't told me who you was." "Fuck em," Elaine said to the friends who had given her a ride there. "Fuck em all to hell." Then, in the car, heading out to Capitol Heights, where she was staying, "Well, maybe not fuck my mother. She was good." "Just fuck your daddy then?" the girl in the back-seat said. Elaine thought about it as they went down Rhode Island Avenue, and just before they turned onto New Jersey Avenue she said, "Yes, just fuck my daddy. The fat fuck."

She got out of Horace's bed and tried to wet the desert in her mouth as she looked in his closet for a bathrobe. She rejected the blue and the paisley ones for a dark-green one that reminded her of something wonderful, just as Horace's hiking up his pants had. She smelled the sleeves once she had it on, but there was only the strong scent of detergent.

In the half room that passed for a kitchen, she stood and drank most of the orange juice in the gallon carton. "Now, that was stupid, girl," she said. "You know you shoulda drunk water. Better for the thirst." She returned the carton to the refrigerator and marveled at all the food. "Damn!" she said. With the refrigerator door still open, she stepped out into the living room and took note of all that Horace had, thinking, A girl could live large here if she did things right. She had been crashing at a friend's place in Northeast, and the friend's mother had begun to hint that it was time for her to move on. Even when she had a job, she rarely had a place of her own. "Hmm," she said, looking through the refrigerator for what she wanted to eat. "Boody for home and food. Food, home. Boody. You shoulda stayed in school, girl. They give courses on this. Food and Home the first semester. Boody Givin the second semester."

But, as she ate her eggs and bacon and Hungry Man biscuits, she knew that she did not want to sleep with Horace too many more times, even if he did have his little castle. He was too tall, and she had never been attracted to tall men, old or otherwise. "Damn! Why couldn't he be what I wanted and have a nice place, too?" Then, as she sopped up the last of the yolk with the last half of the last biscuit, she thought of her best friend, Catrina, the woman she was crashing with. Catrina Stockton was twenty-eight, and though she had once been a heroin addict, she was one year clean and had a face and a body that testified not to a woman who had lived a bad life on the streets but to a nice-looking Virginia woman who had married at seventeen, had had three children by a truck-driving husband, and had met a man in a Fredericksburg McDonald's who had said that women like her could be queens in D.C.

Yes, Elaine thought as she leaned over the couch and stared at the photograph of Horace and Loneese and the Secretary of Defense, Catrina was always saying how much she wanted love, how it didn't matter what a man looked like, as long as he was good to her and loved her morning, noon, and night. The Secretary of Defense was in the middle of the couple. She did not know who he was, just that she had seen him somewhere, maybe on the television. Horace was holding the plaque just to the left, away from the Secretary. Elaine reached over and removed a spot of dust from the picture with her fingertip, and before she could flick it away a woman said her name and she looked around, chilled.

She went into the bedroom to make sure that the voice had not been death telling her to check on Horace. She found him sitting up in bed, yawning and stretching. "You sleep good, honey bunch?" he said. "I sure did, sweetie pie," she said and bounded across the room to hug him. A breakfast like the one she'd had would cost at least four dollars anywhere in D.C. or Maryland. "Oh, but Papa likes that," Horace said. And even the cheapest motels out on New York Avenue, the ones catering to the junkies and prostitutes, charged at least twenty-five dollars a night. What's a hug compared with that? And, besides, she liked him more than she had thought, and the issue of Catrina and her moving in had to be done delicately. "Well, just let me give you a little bit mo, then."

Young stuff is young stuff, Horace thought the first time Elaine brought Catrina by and Catrina gave him a peck on the cheek and said, "I feel like I know you from all that Elaine told me." That was in early March.

In early April, Elaine met another man at a new club on F Street Northwest and fell in love, and so did Horace with Catrina, though Catrina, after several years on the street, knew what she was feeling might be in the neighborhood of love but it was nowhere near the right house. She and Elaine told Horace the saddest of stories about the man Elaine had met in the club, and before the end of April he was sleeping on Horace's living-room floor. It helped that the man, Darnell Mudd, knew the way to anyone's heart, man or woman, and that he claimed to have a father who had been a hero in the Korean War. He even knew the name of the Secretary of Defense in the photograph and how long he had served in the Cabinet.

By the middle of May, there were as many as five other people, friends of the three young people, hanging out at any one time in Horace's place. He was giddy with Catrina, with the blunts, with the other women who snuck out with him to a room at the motel across Thirteenth Street. By early June, more than a hundred of his old records had been stolen and pawned. "Leave his stuff alone," Elaine said to Darnell and his friends as they were going out the door with ten records apiece. "Don't take his stuff.

He loves that stuff." It was eleven in the morning and everyone else in the apartment, including Horace, was asleep. "Sh-h-h," Darnell said. "He got so many he won't notice." And that was true. Horace hadn't played records in many months. He had two swords that were originally on the wall opposite the heating-and-air-conditioning unit. Both had belonged to German officers killed in the Second World War. Horace, high on the blunts, liked to see the young men sword fight with them. But the next day, sober, he would hide them in the bottom of the closet, only to pull them out again when the partying started, at about four in the afternoon.

His neighbors, especially the neighbors who considered that Loneese had been the long-suffering one in the marriage, complained to the management about the noise, but the city-government people read in his rental record that he had lost his wife not long ago and told the neighbors that he was probably doing some kind of grieving. The city-government people never went above the first floor in Sunset. "He's a veteran who just lost his wife," they would say to those who came to the glass office on the first floor. "Why don't you cut him some slack?" But Horace tried to get a grip on things after a maintenance man told him to be careful. That was about the time one of the swords was broken and he could not for the life of him remember how it had happened. He just found it one afternoon in two pieces in the refrigerator's vegetable bin.

Things toned down a little, but the young women continued to come by and Horace went on being happy with them and with Catrina, who called him Papa and pretended to be upset when she saw him kissing another girl. "Papa, what am I gonna do with you and all your hussies?" "Papa, promise you'll only love me." "Papa, I need a new outfit. Help me out, willya please?"

Elaine had become pregnant not long after meeting Darnell, who told her to have the baby, that he had always wanted a son to carry on his name. "We can call him Junior," he said. "Or Little Darnell," she said. As she began showing, Horace and Catrina became increasingly concerned about her. Horace remembered how solicitous he had been when Loneese had been pregnant. He had not taken the first lover yet, had not even thought about anyone else as she grew and grew. He told Elaine no drugs or alcohol until the baby was born, and he tried to get her to go to bed at a decent hour, but that was often difficult with a small crowd in the living room.

Horace's grandson called in December, wanting to come by to see him, but Horace told him it would be best to meet someplace downtown, because his place was a mess. He didn't do much cleaning since Loneese died. "I don't care about that," Alonzo, Jr., said. "Well, I do," Horace said. "You know how I can be bout these things."

In late December, Elaine gave birth to a boy, several weeks early. They gave him the middle name Horace. "See," Darnell said one day, holding the baby on the couch. "Thas your grandpa. You don't mind me callin you his granddad, Mr. Perkins? You don't mind, do you?" The city-government people in the rental office, led by someone new, someone who took the rules seriously, took note that the old man in Apartment 230 had a baby and his mama and daddy in the place and not a single one of them was even related to him, though if one had been it still would have been against the rules as laid down in the rule book of apartment living.

By late February, an undercover policeman had bought two packets of crack from someone in the apartment. It was a woman, he told his superiors at first, and that's what he wrote in his report, but in a subsequent report he wrote that he had bought the rocks from a man. "Start over," said one of his superiors, who supped monthly with the new mayor, who lived for numbers, and in March the undercover man went back to buy more.

It was late on a warm Saturday night in April when Elaine woke to the crackle of walkie-talkies outside the door. She had not seen Darnell in more than a month, and something told her that she should get out of there because there might not be any more good times. She thought of Horace and Catrina asleep in the bedroom. Two men and two women she did not know very well were asleep in various places around the living room, but she had dated the brother of one of the women some three years ago. One of the men claimed to be Darnell's cousin, and, to prove it to her, when he knocked at the door that night he showed her a Polaroid of him and Darnell at a club, their arms around each other and their eyes red, because the camera had been cheap and the picture cost only two dollars.

She got up from the couch and looked into the crib. In the darkness she could make out that her son was awake, his little legs kicking and no sound from him but a happy gurgle. The sound of the walkie-talkie outside the door came and went. She could see it all on the television news— "Drug Dealing Mama in Jail. Baby Put in Foster Care." She stepped over the man who said he was Darnell's cousin and pushed the door to the bedroom all the way open. Catrina was getting out of bed. Horace was snoring. He had never snored before in his life, but the drugs and alcohol together had done bad things to his airway.

"You hear anything?" Elaine whispered as Catrina tiptoed to her.

"I sure did," Catrina said. Sleeping on the streets required keeping one eye and both ears open. "I don't wanna go back to jail."

"Shit. Me, neither," Elaine said. "What about the window?"

"Go out and down two floors? With a baby? Damn!"

"We can do it," Elaine said, looking over Catrina's shoulder to the dark lump that was Horace mumbling in his sleep. "What about him?"

Catrina turned her head. "He old. They ain't gonna do anything to him. I'm just worried bout makin it with that baby."

"Well, I sure as hell ain't gonna go without my child."

"I ain't said we was," Catrina hissed. "Down two floors just ain't gonna be easy, is all."

"We can do it," Elaine said.

"We can do it," Catrina said. She tiptoed to the chair at the foot of the bed and went through Horace's pants pockets. "Maybe fifty dollars here," she whispered after returning. "I already got about three hundred."

"You been stealin from him?" Elaine said. The lump in the bed turned over and moaned, then settled back to snoring.

"God helps them that helps themselves, Elaine. Les go." Catrina had her clothes in her hands and went on by Elaine, who watched as the lump in the bed turned again, snoring all the while. Bye, Horace. Bye. I be seein you.

The policeman in the unmarked car parked across Thirteenth Street watched as Elaine stood on the edge of the balcony and jumped. She passed for a second in front of the feeble light over the entrance and landed on the sloping entrance of the underground parking garage. The policeman was five years from retirement and he did not move, because he could see quite well from where he sat. His partner, only three years on the job, was asleep in the passenger seat. The veteran thought the woman jumping might have hurt herself, because he did not see her rise from the ground for several minutes. I wouldn't do it, the man thought, not for all a rich man's money. The woman did rise, but before she did he saw another woman lean over the balcony dangling a bundle. Drugs? he thought. Nah.

Clothes? Yeah, clothes more like it. The bundle was on a long rope or string—it was too far for the man to make out. The woman on the balcony leaned over very far and the woman on the ground reached up as far as she could, but still the bundle was a good two feet from her hands.

Just let them clothes drop, the policeman thought. Then Catrina released the bundle and Elaine caught it. Good catch. I wonder what she looks like in the light. Catrina jumped, and the policeman watched her pass momentarily in front of the light, and then he looked over at his partner. He himself didn't mind filling out the forms so much, but his partner did, so he let him sleep on. I'll be on a lake fishin my behind off and you'll still be doin this. When he looked back, the first woman was coming up the slope of the entrance with the bundle in her arms and the second one was limping after her. I wonder what that one looks like in a good light. Once on the sidewalk, both women looked left, then right, and headed down Thirteenth Street. The policeman yawned and watched through his sideview mirror as the women crossed M Street. He yawned again. Even at three o'clock in the morning people still jaywalked.

The man who was a cousin of Darnell's was on his way back from the bathroom when the police broke through the door. He frightened easily, and though he had just emptied his bladder, he peed again as the door came open and the light of the hallway and the loud men came spilling in on him and his sleeping companions.

Horace began asking about Catrina and Elaine and the baby as soon as they put him in a cell. It took him that long to clear his head and understand what was happening to him. He pressed his face against the bars, trying to get his bearings and ignoring everything behind him in the cell. He stuck his mouth as far out of the bars as he could and shouted for someone to tell him whether they knew if the young women and the baby were all right. "They just women, y'all," he kept saying for some five minutes. "They wouldn't hurt a flea. Officers, please. Please, Officers. What's done happened to them? And that baby . . . That baby is so innocent." It was a little after six in the morning, and men up and down the line started hollering for him to shut up or they would stick the biggest dick he ever saw in his mouth. Stunned, he did quiet down, because, while he was used to street language coming from the young men who came and went in his apartment, no bad words had ever been directed at him. They talked trash with the filthiest language he had ever heard but they always invited him to join in and "talk about how it really is," talk about his knowing the Secretary of Defense and the Mayor. Usually, after the second blunt, he was floating along with them. Now someone had threatened to do to him what he and the young men said they would do to any woman that crossed them.

Then he turned from the bars and considered the three men he was sharing the two-man cell with. The city-jail people liked to make as little work for themselves as possible, and filling cells beyond their capacity meant having to deal with fewer locks. One man was cocooned in blankets on the floor beside the tiered metal beds. The man sleeping on the top bunk had a leg over the side, and because he was a tall man the leg came down to within six inches of the face of the man lying on the bottom bunk. That man was awake and on his back and picking his nose and staring at Horace. His other hand was under his blanket, in the crotch of his pants. What the man got out of his nose he would flick up at the bottom of the bunk above him. Watching him, Horace remembered that a very long time ago, even before the Chesapeake Street house, Loneese would iron his handkerchiefs and fold them into four perfect squares.

"Daddy," the man said, "you got my smokes?"

"What?" Horace said. He recalled doing it to Catrina about two or three in the morning and then rolling over and going to sleep. He also remembered slapping flies away in his dreams, flies that were as big as the hands of policemen.

The man seemed to have an infinite supply of boogers, and the more he picked the more Horace's stomach churned. He used to think it was such a shame to unfold the handkerchiefs, so wondrous were the squares. The man sighed at Horace's question and put something from his nose on the big toe of the sleeping man above him. "I said do you got my smokes?"

"I don't have my cigarettes with me," Horace said. He tried the best white man's English he knew, having been told by a friend who was serving with him in the army in Germany that it impressed not only white people but black people who weren't going anywhere in life. "I left my cigarettes at home." His legs were aching and he wanted to sit on the floor, but the only available space was in the general area of where he was standing and something adhered to his shoes every time he lifted his feet. "I wish I did have my cigarettes to give you."

"I didn't ask you bout *your* cigarettes. I don't wanna smoke them. I ask you bout *my* cigarettes. I wanna know if you brought *my* cigarettes."

Someone four cells down screamed and called out in his sleep: "Irene, why did you do this to me? Irene, ain't love worth a damn anymore?" Someone else told him to shut up or he would get a king-sized dick in his mouth.

"I told you I do not have any cigarettes," Horace said.

"You know, you ain't worth shit," the man said. "You take the cake and mess it all up. You really do. Now, you know you was comin to jail, so why didn't you bring my goddam smokes? What kinda fuckin consideration is that?"

Horace decided to say nothing. He raised first one leg and then the other and shook them, hoping that would relieve the aches. Slowly, he turned around to face the bars. No one had told him what was going to happen to him. He knew a lawyer, but he did not know if he was still practicing. He had friends, but he did not want any of them to see him in jail. He hoped the man would go to sleep.

"Don't turn your fuckin back on me after all we meant to each other," the man said. "We have this long relationship and you do this to me. Whas wrong with you, Daddy?"

"Look," Horace said, turning back to the man. "I done told you I ain't got no smokes. I ain't got your smokes. I ain't got my smokes. I ain't got nobody's smokes. Why can't you understand that?" He was aware that he was veering away from the white man's English, but he knew that his friend from Germany was probably home asleep safely in his bed. "I can't give you what I don't have." Men were murdered in the D.C. jail, or so the *Washington Post* told him. "Can't you understand what I'm sayin?" His back stayed as close to the bars as he could manage. Who was this Irene, he thought, and what had she done to steal into a man's dreams that way?

"So, Daddy, it's gonna be like that, huh?" the man said, raising his head and pushing the foot of the upper-bunk man out of the way so he could see Horace better. He took his hand out of his crotch and pointed at Horace. "You gon pull a Peter-and-Jesus thing on me and deny you ever knew me, huh? Thas your plan, Daddy?" He lowered his head back to the black-and-white-striped pillow. "I've seen some low-down dirty shit in my day, but you the lowest. After our long relationship and everything."

"I never met you in my life," Horace said, grabbing the bars behind him with both hands, hoping, again, for relief.

"I won't forget this, and you know how long my memory is. First, you don't bring me my smokes, like you know you should. Then you deny all that we had. Don't go to sleep in here, Daddy, thas all I gotta say."

He thought of Reilly Johnson, a man he had worked with in the Pentagon. Reilly considered himself something of a photographer. He had taken the picture of Horace with the Secretary of Defense. What would the bail be? Would Reilly be at home to receive his call on a Sunday morning? Would they give him bail? The policemen who pulled him from his bed had tsk-tsked in his face. "Sellin drugs and corruptin young people like that?" "I didn't know nothin about that, Officer. Please." "Tsk. Tsk. An old man like you."

"The world ain't big enough for you to hide from my righteous wrath, Daddy. And you know how righteous I can be when I get started. The world ain't big enough, so you know this jail ain't big enough."

Horace turned back to the bars. Was something in the back as painful as something in the stomach? He touched his face. Rarely, even in the lost months with Catrina, had he failed to shave each morning. A man's capable demeanor started with a shave each morning, his sergeant in boot camp had told him a thousand years ago.

The man down the way began calling for Irene again. Irene, Horace called in his mind. Irene, are you out there? No one told the man to be quiet. It was about seven and the whole building was waking up and the man calling Irene was not the loudest sound in the world anymore.

"Daddy, you got my smokes? Could use my smokes right about now."

Horace, unable to stand anymore, slowly sank to the floor. There he found some relief. The more he sat, the more he began to play over the arrest. He had had money in his pocket when he took off his pants the night before, but there was no money when they booked him. And where had Catrina and Elaine been when the police marched him out of the apartment and down to the paddy wagon, with the Sunset's female security guard standing behind her desk with an "Oh, yes, I told you so" look? Where had they been? He had not seen them. He stretched out his legs and they touched the feet of the sleeping man on the floor. The man roused. "Love don't mean shit anymore," the man on the lower bunk said.

It was loud enough to wake the man on the floor all the way, and that man sat up and covered his chest with his blanket and looked at Horace, blinking and blinking and getting a clearer picture of Horace the more he blinked.

Reilly did not come for him until the middle of Monday afternoon. Somebody opened the cell door and at first Horace thought the policeman was coming to get one of his cellmates.

"Homer Parkins," the man with the keys said. The doors were supposed to open electronically, but that system had not worked in a long time.

"Thas me," Horace said and got to his feet. As he and the man with the keys walked past the other cells, someone said to Horace, "Hey, Pops, you ain't too old to learn to suck dick." "Keep moving," the man with the keys said. "Pops, I'll give you a lesson when you come back."

As they poured his things out of a large manila envelope, the two guards behind the desk whispered and laughed. "Everything there?" one of them asked Horace. "Yes." "Well, good," the guard said. "I guess we'll be seein you on your next trip here." "Oh, leave that old man alone. He's somebody's grandfather." "When they start that old," the first man said, "it gets in their system and they can't stop. Ain't that right, Pops?"

He and Reilly did not say very much after Reilly said he had been surprised to hear from Horace and that he had wondered what had happened to him since Loneese died. Horace said he was eternally grateful to Reilly for bailing him out and that it was all a mistake as well as a long story that he would soon share with him. At Sunset, Reilly offered to take him out for a meal, but Horace said he would have to take a rain check. "Rain check?" Reilly said, smiling. "I didn't think they said that anymore."

The key to the apartment worked the way it always had, but something was blocking the door, and he had to force it open. Inside, he found destruction everywhere. On top of the clothes and the mementos of his life, strewn across the table and the couch and the floor were hundreds and hundreds of broken records. He took three steps into the room and began to cry. He turned around and around, hoping for something that would tell him it was not as bad as his eyes first reported. But there was little hope—the salt and pepper shakers had not been touched, the curtains covering the glass door were intact. There was not much beyond that for him to cling to.

He thought immediately of Catrina and Elaine. What had he done to deserve this? Had he not always shown them a good and kind heart? He covered his eyes, but that seemed only to produce more tears, and when he lowered his hands the room danced before him through the tears. To steady himself, he put both hands on the table, which was covered in instant coffee and sugar. He brushed broken glass off the chair nearest him and sat down. He had not gotten it all off, and he felt what was left through his pants and underwear.

He tried to look around but got no farther than the picture with the Secretary of Defense. It had two cracks in it, one running north to south and the other going northwest to southeast. The photograph was tilting, too, and something told him that if he could straighten the picture it all might not be so bad. He reached out a hand, still crying, but he could not move from the chair.

He stayed as he was through the afternoon and late into the evening, not once moving from the chair, though the tears did stop around five o'clock. Night came and he still did not move. My name is Horace Perkins, he thought just as the sun set. My name is Horace Perkins and I worked many a year at the Pentagon. The apartment became dark, but he did not have it in him to turn on the lights.

The knocking had been going on for more than ten minutes when he finally heard it. He got up, stumbling over debris, and opened the door. Elaine stood there with Darnell, Jr., in her arms.

"Horace, you O.K.? I been comin by. I been worried about you, Horace."

He said nothing but opened the door enough for her and the baby to enter.

"It's dark, Horace. What about some light?"

He righted the lamp on the table and turned it on.

"Jesus in Heaven, Horace! What happened! My Lord Jesus! I can't believe this." The baby, startled by his mother's words, began to cry. "It's O.K.," she said to him. "It's O.K.," and gradually the baby calmed down. "Oh, Horace, I'm so sorry. I really am. This is the worst thing I've ever seen in my life." She touched his shoulder with her free hand, but he shrugged it off. "Oh, my dear God! Who could do this?"

She went to the couch and moved enough trash aside for the baby. She pulled a pacifier from her sweater pocket, put it momentarily in her mouth to remove the lint, then put it in the baby's mouth. He appeared satisfied and leaned back on the couch.

She went to Horace, and right away he grabbed her throat. "I'm gonna kill you tonight!" he shouted. "I just wish that bitch Catrina was here so I could kill her, too." Elaine struggled and sputtered out one "please" before he gripped her tighter. She beat his arms but that seemed to give him more strength. She began to cry. "I'm gonna kill you tonight, girl, if it's the last thing I do."

The baby began to cry, and she turned her head as much as she could to look at him. This made him slap her twice, and she started to fall, and he pulled her up and, as he did, went for a better grip, which was time enough for her to say, "Don't kill me in front of my son, Horace." He loosened his hands. "Don't kill me in front of my boy, Horace." Her tears ran down her face and over and into his hands. "He don't deserve to see me die. You know that, Horace."

"Where, then!"

"Anywhere but in front of him. He's innocent of everything."

He let her go and backed away.

"I did nothin, Horace," she whispered. "I give you my word, I did nothin." The baby screamed, and she went to him and took him in her arms.

Horace sat down in the same chair he had been in.

"I would not do this to you, Horace."

He looked at her and at the baby, who could not take his eyes off Horace, even through his tears.

One of the baby's cries seemed to get stuck in his throat, and to release it the baby raised a fist and punched the air, and finally the cry came free. How does a man start over with nothing? Horace thought. Elaine came near him, and the baby still watched him as his crying lessened. How does a man start from scratch?

He leaned down and picked up a few of the broken albums from the floor and read the labels. "I would not hurt you for anything in the world, Horace," Elaine said. Okeh Phonograph Corporation. Domino Record

Co. RCA Victor. Darnell, Jr.,'s crying stopped, but he continued to look down at the top of Horace's head. Cameo Record Corporation, N.Y. "You been too good to me for me to hurt you like this, Horace." He dropped the records one at a time: "It Takes an Irishman to Make Love." "I'm Gonna Pin a Medal on the Girl I Left Behind." "Ragtime Soldier Man." "Whose Little Heart Are You Breaking Now." "The Syncopated Walk."

Dale Peck

Dues

from *The Threepenny Review*

F IRST OF all, Adam. He creaked up beside me on a bicycle that seemed welded of leftover plumbing parts. "Pull over," he said with all the authority of a Keystone Cop.

He was cute enough. In particular, the hair: black, thick, sticking out of his head in a dozen directions. His long thin legs straddled the flared central strut of his bicycle like denim-covered tent poles and he stared down at my own bike with eyes the color of asphalt—the old gray kind, with glass embedded in it to reflect light.

But this wasn't a pickup.

"That is my bicycle," he announced. A trace of an accent?

"I'm sure there's some misunderstanding," I said. "I paid for this bike."

"Then you bought stolen merchandise," he said, his consonants soft. Eastern European. *Shtolen mershendise.* "I think you should show me where."

I'd gone on a tip. Benny's East Village. "You won't believe his prices," a friend had told me. "Isn't that the burrito place?" I'd said. In fact my friend had said, "They're probably all stolen, but what you don't know won't hurt you." "He steals burritos?" I'd said. "*Bicycles*," my friend said. "Come *on*."

By the time Adam and I arrived the shop had closed for the day. Adam's thin legs had labored to turn his creaking pedals, and it occurred to me I could have outrun him, but I didn't. The sun was setting at our backs and our shadows stretched out in front of us like twinned towers. I thought we were a pair. I thought we were in it together.

Benny sat on a swivel chair on the sidewalk, a television propped in front of him on a pair of milk crates; a tin of rice and beans wobbled on his lap. We'd been there only a few minutes when a man half carried, half pushed a bike up the street. He held it by the seat, lifting the back wheel off the ground because it couldn't turn: it was still locked to the frame. After inspecting the bicycle, Benny paid the man from a roll of bills he pulled from the breast pocket of his T-shirt, stowed the bicycle under the grate of his store, and returned to his chair.

I turned to Adam.

"I guess I should have investigated further."

"You should have."

He was pulling the kryptonite U-lock from its frame-mounted holder, and I inferred from this action that he wanted to trade bikes. I dismounted, and was unwinding my chain from the seat post when his lock caught me in the side of the head, just behind and below my left eye. Fireflies streaked through my field of vision when the lock struck me, but I didn't actually lose consciousness until the sidewalk hit me in the forehead.

Charlie sponged the grit from my face. What was stuck to solid skin washed away easily, but the bits of gravel embedded in the gashes on my cheek and forehead resisted, had to be convinced to relinquish their berth. I closed my eyes against the water trickling from his rag.

One summer when I was seven or eight I carried cupfuls of water from a stream and poured them down chipmunk holes. The chipmunks would remain underground for as long as possible until, wobbling like drunken sailors, they staggered into the sunshine. Gently I lifted them into a tinfoil turkey tray I'd habitated with rocks, plants, a ribbed tin can laid on its side (a sleeping den, I'd thought), and then I watched as the chipmunks revived, explored their playground tentatively, and then, inevitably, hurdled the shiny wall and scrambled back down their holes.

"I'm afraid I'm going to have to use a tweezers for the last of it."

I opened my eyes. Charlie was making a face, as if performing this surgery hurt him instead of me.

He asked me if it hurt me.

I was still remembering the way that last chipmunk had lain on its side after I'd fished it from its home, eyes closed, chest fluttering as rapidly as a bee's wings. I'd dared to stroke its heaving ribs. The chipmunk curled itself into a ball around my finger, its mouth and the claws of all four paws digging at me until I flung it away and it scurried to safety.

"It hurts," I said, then caught Charlie's arm as he flinched. "My head hurts," I said. "What you're doing doesn't hurt."

Benny's East Village sold bikes every day except Sunday from eleven until seven, but seemed always to be bustling with activity. In the mornings a young woman worked on the bicycles. This was Deneisha, who seemed to live on the third floor. Every ten minutes a younger version of her leaned out the window to relay a request: "Deneisha, Mami says why you didn't get no more coffee if you used the last of it?" "Deneisha, Benny says to call him back on his cell phone." "Deneisha, Eduardo wants to know when are you gonna take the training wheels off my bike so I can go riding with him?" Deneisha, her thick body covered in greasy overalls, inky black spirals of hair rubberbanded off her smooth round face, ignored these interruptions, working with Allen wrenches and oil cans and tubes of glue on gears, brakes, tires. For bicycles that still had a chain fastened to them she had an enormous pair of snips, their handles as long as her meaty arms, and for U-locks she had a special saw that threw sparks like a torch as it chewed through tempered steel.

After the shop closed there was a lull until the sun went down, and then the bicycles began to arrive. Every thief was different. Some skulked, others paraded their booty openly, offering it to anyone they passed on the sidewalk, but few spent any time bargaining with Benny. The more nervous the thief, the less interest Benny showed, the less money he pulled from the roll of bills. He seemed completely untroubled by his illicit enterprise, absorbing stolen bikes with the same equanimity with which he absorbed tins and cartons of delivered food. Only the white kids, the college-age junkies selling off the first or the last of their ties to a suburban past, tried his patience. "I said ten bucks," I heard him say once. "Take it or leave it."

· · ·

Charlie couldn't understand my obsession. We'd only been together for three months, and what I'd learned about him was that he absorbed information with a stenographer's Zen. "Existence is the sum of experience," he'd shrugged that first night, as though the events of our lives were drops of water and we the puddles at the end of their runneled paths, little pools of history. When I still wouldn't let it go he prodded harder.

"Is it the coincidence that bothers you, or the fact that he hit you? Or is it that you pretended innocence of what you were getting when you bought the bike in the first place, and now it's come back and bitten you in the ass?"

At the time I couldn't answer him, and of course hindsight makes it that much less clear. I offered him words like "cleave" and "hew," words that could mean both cutting and binding, but Charlie waved my rhetoric away. "Context makes meaning clear," he said. And then, more bluntly: "*Choose.*"

But I couldn't choose. My life felt splayed on either side of the incident with Adam like his long thin legs straddling the ancient bicycle which he did, in fact, leave for me. Like conjoined twins, my two selves were linked at the hip, sharing a common future but divided as to which past to claim. And so every day I rode Adam's creaking iron bike to a stoop across from Benny's and waited for something like Denelsha's saw or snips to sever my old unmolested self, leaving my new scarred body to get on with things.

At a party Charlie took me to I told the story behind the bandages on my cheek and forehead a half dozen times. By then the two bruises had joined into one, across my forehead, down my left cheek, vanishing into the hairline. The single bruise was mottled black, purple, blue, green, yellow, but, like the story I told over and over again, essentially painless, and as the night wore on Charlie added his own coda to my words. "Victim," he would say, turning my mottled left profile to the audience. "Thief," he said, showing them my right.

"Uh-oh," he said at one point, "here comes trouble." Trouble was a man around our age, one hand holding shaggy bangs off his unlined forehead as though he were taking in a sight, the Grand Canyon, a caged animal. From across the room I heard his cry. "Now *where* did I leave that man?" His gaze fell on Charlie. "*There* he is."

Charlie introduced him as Fletcher. From the name I knew this to be his ex-boyfriend, who had dumped Charlie last summer after a five-year relationship that Charlie referred to by the names of various failed political unions: Czechoslovakia, Upper and Lower Egypt, the Austro-Hungarian Empire. His arms around Charlie's waist, Fletcher pulled him a few feet away, as if together they were examining my bruised face. "Is this *really* the new model," Fletcher said, "or just something you picked up at Rent-a-Wreck?" Charlie offered me a wan smile but, like the Orangeman that he was, seemed content in Fletcher's possessive embrace. Under his questions, I recited once again the story of the two bicycles, the single blow, adding this time the week of camping out across from Benny's shop. Fletcher's assessment: "I don't know why you're focusing on *him*, he's just a businessman. It was the Slav who sucker-punched you."

On the bicycle ride to Benny's, Adam had told me he came from Slovenia. He came here on a student visa, stayed on after his country seceded from the Yugoslavian republic; that was a decade ago. "Back home," he told me, "the terrain is hills and mountains but everyone rides bicycles like this." He smacked the flecked chrome of his handlebars. "Often you see people, not just grandmothers but healthy young men, pushing their bicycles up inclines too steep to pedal. I wanted a mountain bike."

He told me he was illegal, worked without a green card, had almost to live like a thief himself; he had a degree in computer science and an MBA, had emigrated to get in on the dot-com boom but ended up tending bar at Windows on the World. After Fletcher's harangue I bought two books on Balkan history at a used bookstore, a novel and a book of journalism, and I read them on the stoop across from Benny's in an effort to understand what Adam meant by telling me about his stunted furtive existence, the two kinds of bicycles, the broadside with the lock. Why *did* he need a mountain bike, if he was only going to ride the swamp-flat streets of the East Village?

But then: Grace.

I was sitting on the stoop across from Benny's absorbed in the cyclical tale of centuries of avenged violence that is Balkan history. Two plaster lions flanked me, their fangs dulled beneath years of brown paint. A woman stopped in front of me and hooked a finger around one of the lion's incisors. "That is a *great* book," she said with the kind of enthusiasm only a middle-aged counterculturalist can summon. She pointed not to the book I was reading but to the novel on the concrete beside me. Against the heat of early September she wore green plastic sandals, black spandex shorts, a halter top that seemed sewn from a threadbare bandanna. The spandex was worn and semitransparent on her thin thighs and her stomach was so flat it was concave; a ruby glowed from her navel ring, an echo of the bindi dot on her forehead. She could have been thirty or fifty. She let go of the lion's tooth and picked up the novel even as I told her I looked forward to reading it. "Like, wow," she exclaimed, and when she blinked it seemed to me her eyes were slightly out of sync. She held the book up to me, the cover propped open to the first set of endpapers. An ex libris card was stuck on the left-hand side with a name penned on it in black ink: *Grace* was the first name, followed by a polysyllabic scrawl ending in *-itz*. The same card adorned the book I was reading and, nervously, my index finger traced the hard shell of scab above my left eye. What she said next would have seemed no more unlikely had the lion behind her spoken it himself: "That's *my* name."

She didn't ask for her books back—they weren't stolen, she'd bought them for a class at the New School and sold them after it was over so she could afford a course in elementary Sanskrit—but I insisted she take them anyway, sensing that a drama was unfolding somewhat closer than the Balkans. In the end she accepted the novel but told me to finish the history. Over coffee I told her about Adam and the bicycle, and Grace was like, wow.

"Once I got the same cabdriver twice," she said. She blinked: her left eye and then, a moment later, her right. "I mean, I got a cabdriver I'd had before. I tried to ask him if he'd ever, you know, randomly picked up the same person twice, besides me of course, but he didn't speak English so I don't know." Her face clouded for a moment, then lit up again. Blink blink. "Oh and then once I got in the same car on the F train. I went to this winter solstice party out in Park Slope, and the kicker is we went to a bar afterward so I didn't even leave from the same stop I came out on. I think I got off at Fourth Avenue or whatever it is, and then we walked all the way to like Seventh or something, it was fucking freezing is all I remember, but whatever. When the train pulled into the station it was the same train I'd ridden out on, the same car. Totally spooky, huh?"

"How'd you know it was the same one?"

"Graffiti, duh. 'Hector loves Isabel.' Scratched into the glass with a razor blade in, like, really big letters."

"And the cabdriver?"

"His name was Jesus."

"Just Jesus?"

"Just Jesus."

The incident with Adam had been painful but finite. A city tale, one of those chance meetings leading to romance or, in this case, violence; already the bruise was fading. But the incident with Grace was more troubling, awoke in me a creeping dread. What if life was just a series of borrowed items, redundant actions, at best repetitious, at worse theft? "Those who cannot remember the past are condemned to repeat it." But what if repetition happened regardless of memory? What if we were all condemned? I felt then that I understood the history I was reading, began to sympathize with the urge to destroy something that continually reminded you of your derivative status. Like most people, I first bought used items out of poverty, but after my fortunes improved I continued to buy secondhand from a sense of a different debt. Clothes, books, bicycles: I wanted to pay my dues to history, wanted to wear it on my back, carry it in my hands, ride it through the streets. But now it seemed history had rejected my tithing, rejected it scornfully. The past can be sold, it mocked me, but it can never be bought.

Charlie was less blasé about Grace than he'd been about Adam, but ultimately dismissed it.

"It takes three events to form a narrative. Two is just coincidence."

"But a coincidence which is made up of two coincidences. What's that?"

"Proof that New York, as someone once said, is just a series of small towns."

The first night, after cleaning and bandaging my wounds, Charlie had put me to bed and spooned himself behind me, his arms around me, the outline of his erect penis palpable through two pairs of underwear. At the time it was so familiar I didn't really notice it, but later it came to preoccupy my thoughts. It was like Adam's mountain bike, misplaced, a tool for which the pertinent scenario existed only at a remembered remove. Or Grace's ex libris cards, a claim of ownership on something she had no intention of keeping, like a gravestone on an abandoned grave. The night I met Grace, Charlie and I had sex for the first time since Adam had whacked me in the head, and the whole time I was unable to shake an image of Fletcher's face next to Charlie's crotch. "See this? This is *mine*." Later that night, when I was dozing off and Charlie was leafing through the book that had fallen from my hands, I suddenly sat up.

"*Fletcher.*"

"What about Fletcher?"

"You used to belong to him." Silently but victoriously, I ticked off forefinger, middle finger, ring finger. Then: "That's three."

The next day, after Charlie went to work, I stayed in the apartment. At first I wasn't aware that I was doing it. Staying in. I worked in the morning, ordered lunch from an Italian place around the corner. I read while I ate tepid fettuccine and kept reading after I'd finished my meal; all this was normal, or had been normal, if you disregarded the weeks I'd spent in front of Benny's. On a pad made up of reused sheets from early drafts of stories was written "shaving cream, milk," but after I'd finished the history I neglected my shopping and instead took a nap. I didn't wake until Charlie called that evening after he got off work.

"Dinner? There's that new French place on Twelfth."

"Oh," I said. "I'm sorry, I was hungry, I ordered in. Mexican."

"That's fine," Charlie said. "I've got some chicken in the fridge, and some work I really should get done. My place tonight?"

"Oh," I said again. "I'm sorry. I, um. My head's pounding. Do you mind?"

Charlie didn't say *that's fine* the second time. He said, "Sure," and it seemed to me his voice wasn't annoyed but instead relieved. "I'll give you a call tomorrow."

The next day I stayed in again, working. I'd been trying to write about Adam since I'd met him, but after I met Grace the story suddenly fell into place.

In the story I am afraid to leave my apartment. I am afraid that a stranger will stop me on the sidewalk and put their hand on my Salvation

Army chest. "That's my shirt." Someone else claims my pants. Nearly naked, I skulk indoors. But not even my home is safe. A visitor runs his hand over my sofa (Housing Works, $250). "I used to *love* this couch." Another pulls open the drawers of my desk (Regeneration, $400): "What *are* the odds?" Finally someone waves their arms, taking in the time-smudged dimensions of my tiny apartment. "This used to be *my* home." My throat is dry, and I go to the faucet for a drink. But as the water runs I wonder: how many bodies has this passed through to get to me?

But it was worse than all that. When Charlie came over that evening he glanced through the story I'd written and said, "Haven't I read this before?"

On the third day I didn't leave my apartment Charlie called me and told me a story:

"Once I wanted to hack all my hair off with a pair of scissors. But I had a crew cut at the time. So I went out and bought next year's calendar and marked the date a year hence with a big red X. For the next twelve months I didn't touch my hair, and when the day with the X came up I looked in the mirror and realized I liked my hair long. I realized that my crew cuts had been a way of hacking off my hair all along."

I said the only thing I could think of.

"Huh?"

"Your whole shut-in thing," Charlie said. "It's not real. Or it's not new. It's just a symbol of something you already do. You've already done. Think about it. Where is it you're *really* afraid to go?"

I thought about it.

"But you have a crew cut now," I said.

"Give me a break, will you? I'm going bald, it's the dignified thing to do."

When we met Charlie gave me a road map. This was on our third date. Oh, okay, our second. We'd gone back to his apartment and he spread the map out on his kitchen table (IKEA, $99). The table, like everything else in Charlie's apartment, was new and neat, but the map was old and wrin-kled, a flag-sized copy of the continental U.S., post-Alaska, pre-Hawaii. Some of the creases were so worn they'd torn, or were about to.

"Now," Charlie said. "Fold it."

There were four long creases, twelve short, and folding the map proved as hard as solving Rubik's cube. I got it wrong a half dozen times before I finally got the front and back covers in the right place and, a little chagrined, handed it to Charlie.

"Did I fail?"

"You passed," Charlie said. "With flying colors. Anyone who can fold a map on the first try is far too rational for me."

"And what about people who can't fold one at all?"

In answer, Charlie pulled open the white laminate-fronted drawer of one of those nameless pieces of furniture, a "storage unit." Inside were several maps practically wadded up, as well as dozens of takeout menus and hundreds of crooked twist ties. He had to scrunch the pile down before the drawer would close again.

"Wow," I said. "The map test *and* your messy drawer. You must really like me."

Charlie grinned, sheepish but pleased. "It's about time I entered into a new alliance."

By the time I understood what that meant, I thought I was ready to sign. And then Adam came along.

On the fourth day, Grace called. When I asked her how she'd gotten my number she said, "Out of the book," and when I started to ask how she knew my last name she interrupted me and said, "Honey, I think you'd better turn on the television."

Months later, when the indemnity claims began to be discussed in the press, New Yorkers would learn that the opposing sides, the insurance companies and the property owners, differed on a crucial issue: whether the collapse of the towers constituted one event, or two. The World Trade Center, it turned out, was insured for three billion dollars, but if it was deemed that the crash of the second plane into the south tower, not quite twenty minutes after the north tower was hit, constituted a distinct historical event, the insurers would have to pay the full amount twice, in effect saying that the buildings had been destroyed not once but two times. A lot of the argument, as it turned out, was rhetorical: to the insurers, the World Trade Center was a single site—maps marked it with a single X, guidebooks gave it only one entry—that had been destroyed by a united terrorist attack. But to the property owners, the Twin Towers were, architecturally, structurally, visibly, two buildings destroyed by two separate planes, either one of which could have missed its target. Which argument began to make more and more sense to me as time went on and details about what had happened came out. Nearly three-quarters of the people who died were in the north tower, and, of those, more than ninety percent were on floors above those hit by the plane, including dozens of people attending a breakfast conference at Windows on the World. The reason why far fewer people died in the second tower, which stood for less than an hour, as opposed to the hundred minutes the north tower remained intact, is that people in the south tower saw what had happened to the north tower and evacuated their offices. Regardless of whether you considered the two plane crashes coincidence or concerted assault, the planes had struck separately—and people in the second incident had learned from the first.

The antonym to history is prophecy. Historical patterns only emerge when we look back in time; they exist in the future as nothing more than guesses. That we make such projections speaks of a kind of faith, though whether that faith is in the past or the future, the predictability of human nature, or physics, or God, is anybody's guess. But in the end, it always takes you by surprise. By which I mean that when I fought my way through the clouds of dust and crowds of dusty people to Charlie's apartment, I found Fletcher had beaten me there. Who could have foreseen that?

In the days to come, I rode my bike around the city, watched as walls and windows and trees and lampposts filled up with pictures of the missing. Dust clogged my lungs and coated the chain of Adam's creaking bicycle, making it harder and harder to turn the pedals, but it was three days before I stopped wandering aimlessly and actually started looking for him.

I found him, finally, a day and a half later, at the armory on Lexington and Twenty-sixth. Indian restaurants lined that stretch of Lex, and the air was usually tinged with curry, but all the restaurants had been closed for days. There were thousands of pictures taped to the wall of the armory, hundreds of people queuing to look at them. Many of the pictures were printed by inkjets and had smeared into unrecognizable blurs after two days of thunderstorms. Where there was a television crew, dozens of people holding up Polaroids and snapshots and flyers jockeyed to get on camera.

By common will the line moved from left to right. Heads nodded up and down as feet shuffled side to side. I tried not to look in anyone's eyes, living or photographed. I did look at the living, just in case, but mostly I looked at the pictures on the wall.

Sometimes A leads to Z. But sometimes Z leads to A. What I mean is, I was looking for Adam, but I found Zach. Zach: "You won't believe his prices." Zach: "They're probably all stolen, but what you don't know won't hurt you." "*Bicycles,*" Zach had said. "Come *on.*"

I looked at his face for a long time. He hadn't been a close friend, but someone I'd known off and on for almost fifteen years, and as I looked at him I was suddenly reminded of everyone I'd known who had died of AIDS in the eighties and nineties, the tragic consequences of being in the wrong place at the wrong time. The memory was as unexpected as Adam's blow to my head but produced in me an odd, almost eerie sense of calm. Z had led to A, and A to Z, and Z back to A, but now it was a different A. History wasn't even a circle but a diminishing spiral, twisting into a tinier and tinier point.

And then:

"Keith? Keith, is that you?"

I didn't recognize him at first. He was shorter than I remembered, his features less fine. His eyes weren't gray but blue. But the hair was the same, thick and black and sticking out of his head in a dozen directions. It was streaked with soot now too, as if he hadn't washed in days. His T-shirt was also filthy, and pinned to his chest were three pictures which I hardly had time to take in—there were two women and one man, all smiling the hopelessly naive smiles of the doomed—before Adam grabbed me up in a huge embrace. His arms collapsed around me, one and then the other, and his tears salved the faded remnants of my wounded face.

"Oh my God, Keith!" Adam cried. "You're alive!"

Ron Rash

Speckle Trout

from *The Kenyon Review*

LANNY CAME upon the pot plants while fishing Caney Creek. It was a Saturday, and after helping his father sucker tobacco all morning, he'd had the truck and the rest of the afternoon and evening for himself. He'd changed into his fishing clothes and driven the three miles of dirt road to the French Broad. He drove fast, the rod and reel clattering side to side in the truck bed and clouds of red dust rising in his wake like dirt devils. He had the windows down and if the radio worked he would have had it blasting. The driver's license in his billfold was six months old but only in the last month had his daddy let him drive the truck by himself.

He parked by the bridge and walked upriver toward where Caney Creek entered. Afternoon sunlight slanted over Brushy Mountain and tinged the water the color of cured tobacco. A big fish leaped in the shallows but Lanny's spinning rod was broken down and even if it hadn't been he would not have bothered to make a cast. There was nothing in the river he could sell, only stocked rainbows and browns, knottyheads, and catfish. The men who fished the river were mostly old men, men who would stay in one place for hours, motionless as the stumps and rocks they sat on. Lanny liked to keep moving, and he fished where even the younger fishermen wouldn't go.

In forty minutes he was half a mile up Caney Creek, the spinning rod still broken down. There were trout in the lower section where browns and rainbows had worked their way up from the river, and Old Man Jenkins would not buy them. The gorge narrowed to a thirty-foot wall of water and rock, below it the deepest pool on the creek. This was the place where everyone else turned back. He waded through waist-high water to reach the left side of the waterfall, then began climbing, using juts and fissures in the rock for leverage and resting places. When he got to the top he put the rod together and tied a gold Panther Martin on the line.

The only fish this far up were what fishing magazines called brook trout, though Lanny had never heard Old Man Jenkins or anyone else call them anything other than speckle trout. Jenkins swore they tasted better than any brown or rainbow and paid Lanny fifty cents apiece no matter how small they were. Old Man Jenkins ate them head and all, like sardines.

Mountain laurel slapped against Lanny's face and arms, and he scraped his hands and elbows climbing straight up rocks there was no other way around. The only path was water now. He thought of his daddy back at the farmhouse and smiled to himself. The old man had told him never to fish a place like this alone, because a broken leg or a rattlesnake bite could get you stone-dead before anyone found you. That was near about the only kind of talk he got anymore from the old man, Lanny thought to himself as he tested his knot, always being lectured about something—how fast he drove, who he hung out with—like he was eight years old instead of sixteen, like the old man himself hadn't raised all sorts of hell when he was young.

The only places with enough water to hold fish were the pools, some no bigger than a washbucket. Lanny flicked the spinner into the pools and in every third or fourth one a small, orange-finned trout came flopping out onto the bank, the spinner's treble hook snagged in its mouth. Lanny would slap the speckle's head against a rock and feel the fish shudder in his hand and die. If he missed a strike, he cast again into the same pool. Unlike browns and rainbows, the speckles would hit twice, occasionally even three times. Old Man Jenkins had told Lanny when he was a boy most every stream in the county was thick with speckles, but they'd been too easy caught and soon enough fished out, which was why now you had to go to the back of beyond to find them.

He already had eight fish in his creel when he passed the No Trespassing sign nailed in an oak tree. The sign was scabbed with rust like the ten-year-old car tag on his granddaddy's barn, and he paid no more attention to the sign than he had when he'd first seen it a month ago. He knew he was on Toomey land, and he knew the stories. How Linwood Toomey had once used his thumb to gouge a man's eye out in a bar fight and another time opened a man's face from ear to mouth with a broken beer bottle. Stories about events Lanny's daddy had witnessed before, as his daddy put it, he'd got straight with the Lord. But Lanny had heard other things. About how Linwood Toomey and his son were too lazy and hard drinking to hold steady jobs. Too lazy and drunk to walk the quarter-mile from their farmhouse to the creek to look for trespassers too, Lanny told himself.

He waded on upstream, going farther than he'd ever been. He caught more speckles, and soon ten dollars' worth bulged in his creel. Enough money for gas, maybe even a couple of bootleg beers, he told himself, and though it wasn't near the money he'd been making at the Pay-Lo bagging groceries, at least he could do this alone and not have to deal with some old bitch of a store manager with nothing better to do than watch his every move, then fire him just because he was late a few times.

He came to where the creek forked and that was where he saw a sudden high greening a few yards above him on the left. He left the water and climbed the bank to make sure it was what he thought it was.

The plants were staked like tomatoes and set in rows the same way as tobacco or corn. He knew they were worth money, a lot of money, because Lanny knew how much his friend Travis paid for an ounce of pot and this wasn't just ounces but maybe pounds.

He heard something behind him and turned, ready to drop the rod and reel and make a run for it. On the other side of the creek a gray squirrel scrambled up a blackjack oak. He told himself there was no reason to get all jumpy, that nobody would have seen him coming up the creek.

He let his eyes scan what lay beyond the plants. He didn't see anything moving, not even a cow or chicken. Nothing but some open ground and then a stand of trees. He rubbed a pot leaf between his finger and thumb, and it felt like money to him, more money than he'd make even at the Pay-Lo. He looked around one more time before he took the knife from its sheath and cut down five plants.

That was the easy part. Dragging the stalks a mile down the creek was a lot harder, especially while trying to keep the leaves from being stripped off. When he got to the river he hid the plants in the underbrush and walked the trail to make sure no one was fishing. Then he carried the plants to the road edge, stashed them in the ditch, and got the truck. He emptied the creel into the ditch, the trout stiff and glaze-eyed. He wouldn't be delivering Old Man Jenkins any speckles this evening.

Lanny drove back home with the stalks hidden under willow branches and potato sacks. He planned to stay only long enough to get a shower and put on some clean clothes, but as he walked through the front room his father looked up from the TV.

"We ain't ate yet."

"I'll get something in town," Lanny said.

"No, your momma's fixin supper right now, and she's set the table for three."

"I ain't got time. Travis is expecting me."

"You can make time, boy. Or I might take a notion to go somewhere in that truck myself this evening."

It was seven thirty before Lanny drove into the Hardee's parking lot and parked beside Travis's battered Camaro. He got out of the truck and walked over to Travis's window.

"You ain't going to believe what I got in back of the truck."

Travis grinned.

"It ain't that old prune-faced bitch that fired you, is it?"

"No, this is worth something."

Travis got out of the Camaro and walked around to the truck bed with Lanny. Lanny looked around to see if anyone was watching, then pulled back enough of a sack so Travis could see one of the stalks.

"I got five of em."

"Holy shit. Where'd that come from?"

"Found it when I was fishing."

Travis pulled the sack back farther.

"I need to start doing my fishing with you. It's clear I been going to the wrong places."

A car pulled up to the drive-through and Travis pulled the sack over the plant.

"What you planning to do with it?"

"Sell it, if I can figure out who'll buy it."

"Leonard would buy it, I bet."

"He don't know me though. I ain't one of his potheads."

"Well, I am," Travis said. "Let me lock my car and we'll go pay him a visit."

"How about we go over to Dink's first and get some beer."

"Leonard's got beer. His is cheaper and it ain't piss-warm like what we got at Dink's last time."

They drove out of Marshall, following 221 toward Mars Hill.

"You in for a treat, meeting Leonard," Travis said. "They ain't another like him, leastways in this county."

"I heard tell he was a lawyer once."

"Naw, he just went to law school a few months. They kicked his ass out because he was stoned all the time."

After a mile they turned off the blacktop and onto a dirt road. On both sides of the road what had once been pasture was now thick with blackjack oak and broomsedge. They passed a deserted farmhouse and turned onto another road no better than a logging trail, trees on both sides now.

The woods opened into a small meadow, at the center a battered green-and-white trailer, its windows painted black. On one side of the trailer a satellite dish sprouted like an enormous mushroom, on the other side a Jeep Cherokee, its back fender crumpled. Two Dobermans scrambled out from under the trailer, barking as they ran toward the truck. They leaped at Lanny's window, their claws raking the passenger door as he quickly rolled up the window.

The trailer door opened and a man with a gray ponytail and wearing only a pair of khaki shorts stepped onto the cinder-block steps. He yelled at the dogs and when that did no good he came out to the truck and kicked at them until they slunk back from where they had emerged.

Lanny looked at a man who wasn't any taller than himself and looked to outweigh him only because of a stomach that sagged over the front of his shorts like a half-deflated balloon.

"That's Leonard?"

"Yeh. The one and only."

Leonard walked over to Travis's window.

"I got nothing but beer and a few nickel bags. Supplies are going to be low until people start to harvest."

"Well, we likely come at a good time then." Travis turned to Lanny. "Let's show Leonard what you done brought him."

Lanny got out and pulled back the branches and potato sacks.

"Where'd you get that from?" Leonard said.

"Found it," Lanny said.

"Found it, did you? And you figured finders keepers."

"Yeh," said Lanny.

Leonard let his fingers brush some of the leaves.

"Looks like you dragged it through every briar patch and laurel slick between here and the county line."

"There's plenty of leaves left on it," Travis said.

"What you give me for it?" Lanny said.

Leonard lifted each stalk, looking at it the same way Lanny had seen buyers look at tobacco.

"Fifty dollars."

"You trying to cheat me," Lanny said. "I'll find somebody else to buy it."

As soon as he spoke Lanny wished he hadn't, because he'd heard from more than one person that Leonard Hamby was a man you didn't want to get on the wrong side of. He was about to say that he reckoned fifty dollars would be fine but Leonard spoke first.

"You may have an exalted view of your entrepreneurial abilities," Leonard said.

Lanny didn't understand all the words but he understood the tone. It was smart-ass but it wasn't angry.

"I'll give you sixty dollars, and I'll double that if you bring me some that doesn't look like it's been run through a hay baler. Plus I got some cold beers inside. My treat."

"OK," Lanny said, surprised at Leonard but more surprised at himself, how tough he'd sounded. He tried not to smile as he thought how when he got back to Marshall he'd be able to tell his friends he'd called Leonard Hamby a cheater to his face and Leonard hadn't done a damn thing about it but offer more money and free beer.

Leonard took a money clip from his front pocket and peeled off three twenties and handed them to Lanny. Leonard nodded toward the meadow's far corner.

"Put them over there next to my tomatoes. Then come inside if you got a notion to."

Lanny and Travis carried the plants through the knee-high grass and laid them next to the tomatoes. As they approached the trailer Lanny watched where the Dobermans had vanished under the trailer. He didn't lift his eyes until he reached the steps.

Inside, it took Lanny's vision a few moments to adjust, because the only light came from a TV screen. Strings of unlit Christmas lights ran across the walls and over door eaves like bad wiring. A dusty-looking couch slouched against the back wall. In the corner Leonard sat in a fake-leather recliner patched with black electrician's tape. Except for a stereo system, the rest of the room was shelves filled with books and CDs. Music was playing, music that didn't have any guitars or words.

"Have a seat," Leonard said, and nodded at the couch.

A woman stood in the foyer between the living room and kitchen. She was a tall, bony woman and the cutoff jeans and halter top she wore had little flesh to hold them up. She'd gotten a bad sunburn and there were pink patches on her skin where she'd peeled. To Lanny she mostly looked wormy and mangy, like some stray dog around a garbage dump. Except for her eyes. They were a deep blue, like a jaybird's feathers. If you could just keep looking into her eyes, she'd be a pretty woman, Lanny told himself.

"How about getting these boys a couple of beers, Wendy," Leonard said.

"Get them your ownself," the woman said, and disappeared into the back of the trailer.

Leonard shook his head but said nothing as he got up. He brought back two longneck Budweisers and a sandwich bag filled with pot and some wrapping papers.

He handed the beers to Travis and Lanny and sat down. Lanny was thirsty and he drank quickly as he watched Leonard carefully shake some pot out of the bag and onto the paper. Leonard licked the cigarette paper and twisted it at both ends, then lit it.

The orange tip brightened as Leonard drew the smoke in. He handed the joint to Travis, who drew on it as well and handed it back.

"What about your buddy?"

"He don't smoke pot. Scared his daddy would find out and beat the tar out of him."

"That ain't so," Lanny said. "I just like a beer buzz better."

Lanny lifted the bottle to his lips and drank until the bottle was empty. "I'd like me another one."

"Quite the drinker, aren't you," Leonard said. "Just make sure you don't overdo it. I don't want you passed out and pissing on my couch."

"I ain't gonna piss on your couch."

Leonard took another drag of the joint and passed it back to Travis.

"They're in the refrigerator," Leonard said. "You can get one easy as I can."

Lanny stood up and for a moment he felt off plumb, maybe because he'd drunk the beer so fast. When the world steadied he got the beer and sat back down on the couch. He looked at the TV, some kind of western but without the sound on he couldn't tell what was happening. He drank the second beer quick as the first as Travis and Leonard finished smoking the pot.

Travis had his eyes closed.

"Man, I'm feeling good," Travis said.

Lanny studied the man who sat in the recliner, trying to figure out what it was that made Leonard Hamby a man you didn't want to mess with. Leonard looked soft, Lanny thought, white and soft like bread dough. Just because a man had a couple of mean dogs didn't make him such a badass, he told himself. He thought about his own daddy and Linwood Toomey, big men you could look at and tell right away were badasses, or, like his daddy, once had been. Lanny wondered if anyone would ever call him a badass and wished again that he didn't take after his mother, who was short and thin-boned.

"What's this shit you're listening to, Leonard," Lanny said.

"It's called 'Appalachian Spring.' It's by Copland."

"Ain't never heard of them."

Leonard looked amused.

"Are you sure? They used to be the warm-up act for Lynyrd Skynyrd."

"I don't believe that."

"No matter. Copland is an acquired taste, and I don't anticipate your listening to a classical music station anytime in the future."

Lanny knew Leonard was putting him down, talking over him like he was stupid, and it made him think of his teachers at the high school, teachers that used smart-ass words against him when he gave them trouble because they were too old and scared to try anything else. He got up and made his way to the refrigerator, damned if he was going to ask permission. He got the beer out and opened the top but didn't go back to the couch. He went down the hallway to find the bathroom.

The bedroom door was open, and he could see the woman sitting up in the bed reading a magazine. He pissed and then walked into the bedroom and sat down on the bed.

The woman laid down the magazine.

"What do you want?"

Lanny grinned.

"What you offering?"

Even buzzed up with beer he knew it was a stupid thing to say. It seemed to him that ever since he'd got to Leonard's his mouth had been a faucet he couldn't shut off.

The woman's blue eyes stared at him like he was nothing more than a sack of shit somebody had dumped on her bed.

"I ain't offering you anything," she said. "Even if I was, a little pecker-head like you wouldn't know what to do with it."

The woman looked toward the door.

"Leonard," she shouted.

Leonard appeared at the doorway.

"It's past time to get your Cub Scout meeting over."

Leonard nodded at Lanny.

"I believe you boys have overstayed your welcome."

"I was getting ready to leave anyhow," Lanny said. As he got up, the beer slipped from his hand and spilled on the bed.

"Nothing but a little peckerhead," the woman said.

In a few moments he and Travis were outside. The evening sun glowed in the treetop like a snagged orange balloon. The first lightning bugs rode over the grass as though carried on an invisible current.

"You get more plants, come again," Leonard said and closed the trailer door.

Lanny went back the next Saturday, two burlap sacks stuffed into his belt. After he'd been fired from the Pay-Lo, he'd about given up hope on earning enough money for his own truck, but now things had changed. Now he had what was pretty damn near a money tree and all he had to do was get its leaves to Leonard Hamby. He climbed up the waterfall, the trip up easier without a creel and rod. Once he passed the No Trespassing sign, he moved slower, quieter. I bet Linwood Toomey didn't even plant it, Lanny told himself. I bet it was somebody who figured the Toomeys were too sorry to notice pot was growing on their land.

When he came close to where the plants were, he crawled up the bank, slowly raising his head like a soldier in a trench. He scanned the tree line across the field and saw no one. He told himself even if someone hid in the trees, they could never get across the field to catch him before he was long gone down the creek.

Lanny cut the stalks just below the last leaves. Six plants filled the sacks. He thought about cutting more, taking what he had to the truck and coming back to get the rest, but he figured that was too risky. He made his way back down the creek. He didn't see anyone on the river trail, but if he had he'd have said it was poke shoots in the sacks if they'd asked.

When he drove up to the trailer, Leonard was watering the tomatoes with a hose. Leonard cut off the water and herded the Dobermans away from the truck. Lanny got out of the truck and walked around to the truck bed.

"How come you grow your own tomatoes but not your own pot?"

"Because I'm a low-risk kind of guy. Since they've started using the planes and helicopters, it's gotten too chancy unless you have a place way back in some hollow."

One of the Dobermans growled from beneath the trailer but did not show its face.

"Where's your partner?"

"I don't need no partner," Lanny said. He lifted the sacks from the truck bed and emptied them onto the ground between him and Leonard.

"That's one hundred and twenty dollars' worth," Lanny said.

Leonard stepped closer and studied the plants.

"Fair is fair," Leonard said, and pulled a money clip from his pocket. He handed Lanny five twenty-dollar bills and four fives.

Lanny crumpled the bills in his fist and stuffed them into his pocket, but he did not get back in the truck.

"What?" Leonard finally said.

"I figured you to ask me in for a beer."

"I don't think so. I don't much want to play host this afternoon."

"You don't think I'm good enough to set foot in that roachy old trailer of yours."

Leonard looked at Lanny and smiled.

"Boy, you remind me of a banty rooster, strutting around not afraid of anything, puffing your feathers out anytime anyone looks at you wrong. You think you're a genuine, hardcore badass, don't you?"

"I ain't afraid of you, if that's what you're getting at. If your own woman ain't scared of you, why should I be."

Leonard looked at the money clip in his hand. He tilted it in his hand until the sun caught the metal and a bright flash hit Lanny in the face. Lanny jerked his head away from the glare.

Leonard laughed and put the money clip back in his pocket.

"After the world has its way with you a few years, it'll knock some of the strut out of you. If you live that long."

"I ain't wanting your advice," Lanny said. "I just want some beer."

Leonard went into the trailer and brought out a six-pack of cans.

"Here," he said. "A farewell present. Don't bother to come around here anymore."

"What if I get you some more plants?"

"I don't think you better try to do that. Whoever's pot that is will be harvesting in the next few days. You best not be anywhere near when they're doing it either."

"What if I do get more?"

"Same price, but if you want any beer you best be willing to pay bootleg price like your buddies."

The next day soon as Sunday lunch was finished, he put on jeans and a T-shirt and tennis shoes and headed toward the French Broad. The day was hot and humid, and the only people on the river were a man and two boys swimming near the far bank. By the time he reached the creek his T-shirt was sweat-soaked and sweat stung his eyes.

Upstream the trees blocked out most of the sun and the cold water he splashed on his face and waded through cooled him. At the waterfall, an otter slid into the pool. Lanny watched its body surge through the water, straight and sleek as a torpedo, before disappearing under the far bank. He wondered how much an otter pelt was worth and figured come winter it might be worth finding out. He knelt and cupped his hand, the pool's water so cold it hurt his teeth.

He climbed the left side of the falls, then made his way upstream until he got to the No Trespassing sign. If someone waited for him, Lanny believed that by now the person would have figured out he'd come up the creek, so he stepped up on the right bank and climbed the ridge into the woods. He followed the sound of water until he figured he'd gone far enough and came down the slope slow and quiet, stopping every few yards to listen. When he got to the creek, he looked upstream and down before crossing.

The plants were still there. He pulled the sacks from his belt and walked toward the first plant, his eyes on the trees across the field.

The ground gave slightly beneath his right foot. He did not hear the spring click. What he heard was the sound of bone shattering. Pain raced like a flame up his leg to consume his whole body.

When he came to, he was on the ground, his face inches from a pot plant. This ain't nothing but a bad dream, he told himself, thinking that if he believed it hard enough it might become true. He used his forearm to lift his head enough to look at the leg and the leg twisted slightly and the pain hit him like a fist. The world turned deep blue and he thought he was going to pass out again, but in a few moments the pain eased a little.

He looked at his foot and immediately wished he hadn't. The trap's jaws clenched around his leg just above the ankle. Blood soaked the tennis shoe red, and the leg angled back on itself in a way that made bile surge up from his stomach. Don't look at it anymore until you have to, he told himself and laid his head back on the ground.

His face looked toward the sun now, and he guessed it was still early afternoon. Maybe it ain't that bad, he told himself. Maybe if I just lay here a while it'll ease up some, and I can get the trap off. He lay still as possible, breathing long shallow breaths, trying to think about something else. He remembered what Old Man Jenkins had said about how one man could pretty much fish out a stream of speckle trout by himself if he took a notion to. Lanny wondered how many speckle trout he'd be able to catch out of Caney Creek before they were all gone. He wondered if after he did he'd be able to find another way-back trickle of water that held them.

He must have passed out again, because when he opened his eyes the sun hovered just above the tree line. When he tested the leg, pain flamed up every bit as fierce as before. He wondered how late it would be tonight before his parents would get worried and how long it would take after that before someone found his truck and got people searching. Tomorrow at the earliest, he told himself, and even then they'd search the river before looking anywhere else.

He lifted his head a few inches and shouted toward the woods. No one called back, and he imagined Linwood Toomey and his son passed-out drunk in their farmhouse. Being so close to the ground muffled his voice, so he used a forearm to raise himself a little higher and called again.

I'm going to have to sit up, he told himself, and just the thought of doing so made the bile rise again in his throat. He took deep breaths and used both arms to lift himself into a sitting position. The pain smashed against his body again but just as quickly eased. The world began draining itself of color until everything around him seemed shaded with gray. He leaned back on the ground, sweat popping out on his face and arms like blisters.

Everything seemed farther away, the sky and trees and plants, as though he were being lowered into a well. He shivered and wondered why he hadn't brought a sweatshirt with him.

Two men came out of the woods. They walked toward him with no more hurry or concern than men come to check their tobacco for cutworms. Lanny knew the big man in front was Linwood Toomey and the man trailing him his son. He could not remember the son's name but had seen him in town a few times. What he remembered was the son had been away from the county for nearly a decade and that some said he'd been in the marines and others said prison. The younger man wore a dirty white T-shirt and jeans, the older, blue coveralls with no shirt underneath. Grease coated their hands and arms.

They stood above him but did not speak. Linwood Toomey took a rag from his back pocket and rubbed his hands and wrists. Lanny wondered if they weren't there at all, were nothing but some imagining the hurting caused.

"My leg's broke," Lanny said, figuring if they spoke back they must be real.

"I reckon it is," Linwood Toomey said. "I reckon it's near about cut clear off."

The younger man spoke.

"What we going to do?"

Linwood Toomey did not answer the question, but eased himself onto the ground beside the boy. They were almost eye level now.

"Who's your people?"

"My daddy's James Burgess. My momma was Ruthie Candler before she got married."

Linwood Toomey smiled.

"I know who your daddy is. Me and him used to drink some together, but that was back when he was sowing his wild oats. I'm still sowing mine, but I switched from oats. Found something that pays more."

Linwood Toomey stuffed the rag in his back pocket.

"You found it too."

"I reckon I need me a doctor," Lanny said. He was feeling better now, knowing Linwood Toomey was there beside him. His leg didn't hurt nearly as much now as it had before, and he told himself he could probably walk on it if he had to, once Linwood Toomey got the trap off.

"What we going to do?" the son said again.

The older man looked up.

"We're going to do what needs to be done."

Linwood Toomey looked back at Lanny. He spoke slowly and his voice was soft.

"Coming back up here a second time took some guts, son. Even if I'd figured out you was the one done it I'd have let it go, just for the feistiness of your doing such a thing. But coming back up here a third time was downright foolish, and greedy. You're old enough to know better."

"I'm sorry," Lanny said.

Linwood Toomey reached out his hand and gently brushed some of the dirt off Lanny's face.

"I know you are, son."

Lanny liked the way Linwood Toomey spoke. The words were soothing, like rain on a tin roof. He was forgetting something, something important he needed to tell Linwood Toomey. Then he remembered.

"I reckon we best get on to the doctor, Mr. Toomey."

"There's no rush, son," Linwood Toomey said. "The doctor won't do nothing but finish cutting that lower leg off. We got to harvest these plants first. What if we was to take you down to the hospital and the law started wondering why we'd set a bear trap. They might figure there's something up here we wanted to keep folks from poking around and finding."

Linwood Toomey's words had started to blur and swirl in Lanny's mind. They were hard to hold in place long enough to make sense. But what he did understand was Linwood Toomey's words weren't said in a smart-ass way like Leonard Hamby's or Lanny's teachers or spoken like he was still a child the way his parents did. Lanny wanted to explain to Linwood Toomey how much he appreciated that, but to do so would mean having several sentences of words to pull apart from one another, and right now that was just too many. He tried to think of a small string of words he might untangle.

Linwood Toomey took a flat glass bottle from his back pocket and uncapped it.

"Here, son," he said, holding the bottle to Lanny's lips.

Lanny gagged slightly but kept most of the whiskey down. He tried to remember what had brought him this far up the creek. Linwood Toomey pressed the bottle to his lips again.

"Take another big swallow," he said. "It'll cut the pain while you're waiting."

Lanny did as he was told and felt the whiskey spread down into his belly. It felt warm and soothing, like an extra quilt on a cold night. Lanny thought of something he could say in just a few words.

"You reckon you could get that trap off my foot?"

"Sure," Linwood Toomey said. He slid over a few feet to reach the trap, then looked up at his son.

"Step on that lever, Hubert, and I'll get his leg out."

The pain rose up Lanny's leg again but it seemed less a part of him now. It seemed to him Linwood Toomey's words had soothed the bad hurting away.

"That's got it," Linwood Toomey said.

"Now what?" the son said.

"Go call Edgar and tell him we'll be bringing the plants sooner than we thought," Linwood Toomey said. "Bring back them machetes and we'll get this done."

The younger man walked toward the house.

"The whiskey help that leg some?" Linwood Toomey asked.

"Yes, sir," Lanny mumbled, his eyes now closed. Even though Linwood Toomey was beside him the man seemed to be drifting away along with the pain.

Linwood Toomey said something else but each word was like a balloon slipped free from his grasp. Then there was silence except for the gurgle of the creek, and he remembered it was the speckle trout that had brought him here. He thought of how you could not see the orange fins and red flank spots but only the dark backs in the rippling water, and how it was only when they lay gasping on the green bank moss that you realized how bright and pretty they were.

Timothy Crouse

Sphinxes

from *Zoetrope*

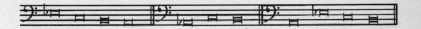

I CAN still hear the satisfaction in Roberto's voice: he'd talked Miguel into shepherding Rosario on her trip to the seashore. And the roguishness: "Everybody knows about Miguel."

Not long after he began taking lessons from me, Roberto one day looked up from the keyboard and asked: "Do you like Rosario?"

"Rosario? What Rosario?"

He said her full name.

"She's a student of mine."

"I'm going to marry her."

At the period I remember best, Roberto and Rosario had a little girl, Lilí, and lived in an apartment looking out on the mountains. French windows opened onto a dramatic wrought-iron balcony, which Roberto had designed himself. The apartment smelled of geraniums. I always associated this with Rosario's sense of order. Everything in its place, immaculate.

Though I generally required my students to come to me, I made an exception as often as possible for Rosario, since being away from Lilí impaired her concentration. She was preoccupied with every aspect of her daughter's well-being. This concern extended to Roberto, even to myself. She always had waiting for me a draft of her "magic immunizer"—an orchard squeezed into one tall glass—and entreated me to drink every drop. Something majestically selfless lent a becoming gravity to her solicitude.

Late one sultry afternoon I arrived to find Roberto—lank, tan, with the nose of a Caesar—lounging in an armchair. At the piano, Rosario was helping Lilí, in her lap, pick out a tune. They all looked fresh and trim—congenitally undisheveled. Rosario put the child down: "If you're quiet-quiet, you can stay." With a smile to Roberto: "You, too." Lilí pondered for a moment, chin in fist, then parked herself in a miniature chair. She sat through the entire hour without a peep. Rosario leapt up afterward and cuddled her. "You were so good! Let's play our game." She pinched her ears, nuzzled her neck, pulled faces at her. To each sally Lilí responded in kind, with squeals.

Roberto leaned back and pronounced: "I feel envious of myself."

Many of my students wanted to confide in me. I used this as an incentive to conscientious preparation: do your lesson well and afterward you can unburden yourself. One-way confessional; no penance, no absolution. The more they revealed, the better I could tailor their assignments. If they pressed me for a reply, I would point to the sounding board of the piano.

One of the stories that Roberto told me dealt with a younger friend of his named Miguel, also a pupil of mine. How they knew each other, I'm not sure; it may have been a professional connection, since Roberto was an engineer and Miguel, at the time I met him, had recently wound up his training as an architect.

"We went sailing together, and the wind quit on us. We'd brought a picnic hamper—it was so chock-full the top wouldn't close. With nothing else to do, we cleaned it out. Then I dove into the water and began showing off my butterfly stroke. Miguel hollered at me to come back, or I'd get a cramp. I called him a sissy and kept on going, to tease him. A spasm jack-knifed me, crunched the air right out of me. I couldn't stay afloat. Just as I was giving up—I remember thinking rather calmly of Rosario for the last time—an arm grappled my chest. Somehow Miguel tugged my dead-weight to the boat. Hauling me over the gunwale was too much for him: he injured his spine. He still has to wear a brace."

Other stories that he passed on to me, always in an affectionate tone, centered on Miguel's penchant for strapping youths, which Roberto took to be a commonly known fact since with him Miguel was impishly open about it. He was fascinated by his friend's descriptions of a spangled, promiscuous netherworld, and amused by his ardors. "In the street, Miguel will spot some foxy *muchacho*, and *ayayay!*—he trembles, he staggers, he has to cling to my arm, or Rosario's."

Both men had slender silhouettes. It would have been difficult to tell them apart at a distance, if not for Miguel's gait. Lumbar twinges caused him to stiffen his naturally balletic glide, like a dancer working on a treacherous floor. He had curly hair (Roberto's was bristly), and his face was longer than Roberto's, with sharper features, nostrils that flared. Each man had a peculiar way of actuating his attention. When I put a problem to Roberto, he would flick the tip of his nose, as though rapping his intellect awake. Miguel would bite down on one side of his underlip, and slowly release it. Roberto used to scold Miguel for this habit, warning him that he'd get canker sores.

Of the three, Rosario had the most pianistic talent. With her octave-spanning fingers, autonomous left hand, knack for sight-reading, and affluent musicality, she could have surmounted the drawback of a delayed start and made a career for herself. (She had a lovely voice, too, and might have become a singer.) Scales, arpeggios, the "Gradus ad Parnassum" never wearied her. Exercises that Miguel and Roberto would have done with clenched teeth, such as practicing pieces a half tone higher or lower than written, she regarded as a lark. While the two men were still plunking away at "The Little Orphan," she bounded through *Anna Magdalena Bach* and Tchaikovsky's *Children's Album*. Her great ambition was to graduate to Schubert's *Impromptus* and Chopin's *Nocturnes*. She achieved it with exhilarating dispatch. I had to dissuade her from tackling the Études: fragile wrists.

She had one odd weakness—rushing the final measure of a piece.

"Look, Rosario: there's a fermata at the end. The composer wants that note prolonged."

She would blush.

"A work isn't finished until the last resonance has faded."

She assented. But as soon as she approached a double bar, she seemed to go blank.

"What happens to you?"

"The piano gets snatched away from me."

I'd been teaching Miguel for almost a year when he told me: "A lot of people think I'm homosexual. It's an act I put on, to lull husbands."

He was no doubt capable of bringing it off, what with his fine-drawn lineaments, his wounded dancer's grace, his streak of flamboyance (which I had to curb repeatedly in his music-making).

"I only sleep with married women," he went on. "Fewer complications that way. Except sometimes . . . There was an underage pantheress who used to prowl the nightclubs. Her husband—a bulldog, with a pencil mustache—came up to here on her" (he sketched her bust) "and liked to exhibit her, doing tangos. She always managed to brush me on the dance floor.

"I redecorated their apartment for them, as a favor. Nouveaux riches, unsure of their taste. We did a heap of shopping for furniture and fabrics. I flirted, ostentatiously, with the brawnier clerks.

"They had a country place. He said I must spend a weekend, go deer hunting. I recoiled—the poor helpless Bambis and so forth. He chuckled: 'You can keep my wife company while I'm off in the woods. I don't suppose you'll object to a nice haunch of venison.'

"So I rode the train to a whistle-stop in the hills. He met me. 'My bride is under the weather, unfortunately, and couldn't make it out. Maybe tomorrow. There's someone here I think you'll like, though.' He drove me to their chalet, and did the honors. The walls were studded with antlers; each rack involved a saga. At last, he excused himself. After a few minutes, he reappeared—in a geisha wig and a kimono, mustache powdered over, rouge everywhere. . . ."

The memory of it turned Miguel ashen.

Gazing into Rosario's naked eyes was like dropping your vision down a well. The first time I met her, all I saw was a pair of sapphires with a woman appended; they reduced the rest of her face to a mere perfect setting, a blur of high cheekbones framed by lustrous red hair. It helped that, during lessons, she put on glasses for her myopia.

In all but the coldest months, she went about in sleeveless blouses and short skirts. Her arms and legs were slim, sinuous. Matter-of-factly, she would say: "I enjoy looking at them." It did not occur to her to begrudge others the same pleasure.

Her bearing—back perpendicular, hands folded, thighs together—turned any seat she occupied into a throne. She told me that once, due to some domestic emergency, she had arrived less than prepared for an oral exam at the university, where she was taking courses in pedagogy. "As luck would have it, the professor started ogling my legs. The first tough question he asked me, I put on a meek, respectful expression and opened my knees. He gaped. He stammered. Without realizing that I hadn't answered, he moved on. The longer I sat like that, the more flustered he became. He had no idea what I was or wasn't saying. Finally he spluttered, 'Get out,' and dismissed me—with the top grade!"

Periodically I invited my students to a class in harmony or analysis. It wasn't unusual for a dozen or more of them to cram into my studio, pitching on every available chair and scrap of carpet. Prodigies gearing up for international careers, a radiologist mad for Debussy, an octogenarian widow who practiced four hours a day . . . I wished for them all to cohere, cross-pollinate—and to some extent they did. Their attitudes toward Rosario, however, exposed their frailties like a dye: the women acknowledged her with a sullenness that betrayed their envy, while the men fought shy of her, although they hobnobbed easily enough with Roberto and Miguel.

After concerts, there would be ad hoc suppers at cafés. Roberto, Rosario, and Miguel, who never missed a musical event of any importance, usually took part. It was on these occasions that I observed the mixture of humility and histrionics which Miguel displayed in public toward Rosario. He held her coat, repaired her mussed hair with a deft pat. Once, he sashayed into a ladies' room with her to help mend a broken spaghetti strap. He used to lift her hands like chalices and venerate them with caresses. Installing himself across from her, he would stare moonily into her eyes: "Think of me as your adoring mirror. I swear I'll die if you don't let me have my fill." One evening our party included another student of mine, an official at the foreign ministry, who witnessed Miguel's behavior with mounting indignation.

"You permit this?" he hissed at Roberto.

"I encourage it! It redounds to my glory."

• • •

Roberto began to mention affairs he was having. He sought out different companions, he claimed, so as to slake his urges without overtaxing his wife. Under the guise of divulgence, he would fish for advice. Describing some demand his mistress was making of him, he might slip in, expectantly: "Have you ever had to cope with that sort of thing?"

I'd laugh: "You need more Schumann!"

Rosario was wise to what was going on and saw no reason to protest. For her, the essence of the marriage was maternity. "I'm a scatterbrain," she would say, "but *this* I take seriously"—indicating the zone of her womb.

Roberto and Rosario were accustomed to spending a week or two at the beach every summer. This year, one of Roberto's partners had fallen ill, saddling him with an extra load at the office. Also, Roberto had just embarked on a liaison with a young ballerina. If he could persuade Rosario to go on vacation without him, he would provide himself an open field while affording her a rest. Sending her off unprotected would, for him, have been out of the question. He had thought of the ideal escort: Miguel, who combined the most expedient features of a bodyguard and a *dame de compagnie*. At first, Miguel balked. It required a lot of wheedling on Roberto's part to bring him around. He didn't have an easy job with Rosario, either.

I listened to her deliberate: "Naturally, Lilí would come with me. But can I trust Roberto to eat properly? And Miguel has been overworked. Wouldn't he be happier unwinding with his handsome friends than chaperoning me?"

They went. While they were away, I attended a recital by Claudio Arrau. During the intermission I noticed Roberto, at the rail of one of the boxes, deep in conversation with a wiry, chignoned gamine. After the last encore, filing out of the auditorium, we ran into each other. He hesitated for a moment, then introduced his chum, the dancer.

"What a terrific evening!" he said a bit too loudly.

I concurred.

"That *Carnaval* was a real treat," he rattled on. "Such a charming piece, isn't it?"

At his next lesson he asked: "Why did you look at me that way when I said I liked his *Carnaval*?"

"You called it charming."

"Well, sure. *Papillons* and all that. You can't deny it's pretty stuff."

"A cadaver comes up to you and wants to dance—you consider that charming?"

"What are you talking about?"

"Listen to *Carnaval.*"

When Miguel returned from the vacation, his playing grew soberer, solider, focused. Some chronic misgiving seemed to have been resolved, some inner reorganization effected: the same chord, voiced more cogently. Yet he was also feverish, brooding; one day a confession, long pent up, gushed out of him:

"We took the train down to the coast. The motion of the carriage kept jogging our arms against each other—hers cool, mine hot. I was in a sweat. The craving in me! What I'd felt for the others was—froth. All that time longing for Rosario, courting her from behind my mask—and now to have this chance. It gave me qualms. And there was Lilí, curled up across our thighs, sucking her thumb.

"The train arrived late. The hotel clerk informed us that we'd forfeited our reservations: the only thing he had available was a room with a double bed and a cot for the little girl. Rosario winked at me: 'I don't think it would kill either of us to sleep together.' Was it that I couldn't bring myself to abuse her naïveté? Or pure cowardice? I slipped the clerk a thin wad. Adjacent rooms materialized. Rosario and Lilí, at least, got a good night's sleep.

"The next morning, early, I heard them stirring. I washed up and joined them for breakfast on Rosario's terrace. As soon as we'd finished, we grabbed our bathing gear and made for the beach. I hired a cabaña. While Rosario and Lilí changed, I scanned the panorama. The sand, the air, the sea—all sparkling. I felt sparkling myself. The cabaña's door opened, and Lilí flittered out. Then Rosario stepped onto the deck. She tossed her mane, loosening it to the breeze. I couldn't swallow. I could hardly breathe. It hadn't occurred to me to prepare for this sight—not that I could have. The swimsuit was a sleek one-piece, modest compared to the bikinis that many other women were sporting—but what it concealed, it revealed more than nudity itself, including the precise, sand-dollar forms of the nipples. It was her utter lack of self-consciousness, as much as anything, that undid me. I scuttled into the dressing room.

"When I emerged, Rosario was sitting on the sand, watching Lilí romp with some children in a tidal pool. I sank down beside her. She stretched her limbs and let out a groan of relaxation, as if only at that moment had she shed her burdens. 'Would you rub some lotion on my back?' she asked, not taking her attention off her daughter. The swimsuit was cut low in the rear, almost to the sacrum. The flesh was smooth as meerschaum, except for a tiny heart-shaped mole near the fifteenth vertebra (I counted them in an effort to calm myself). My hand was on fire. A crushing ache had me in torment. I tried to relieve this through speech, telling Rosario how voluptuous I found her. The liberties I allowed myself only inflamed me more. Of course, I was also testing the waters. 'Oh, Miguel,' she said, 'you and your flattery!'

"*Don't do anything rash*, I cautioned myself. *Bide your time.* Didn't the sheer freedom to luxuriate in Rosario's presence amount to progress?

"We had lunch on the patio. Lilí was transfixed by the fan-pleated napkins, the staff's uniforms, the Noah's ark of new faces. A waiter brought her a cushion to perch on and helped her choose from the menu. He was lame. After he left, she said to us, quite stricken: 'That poor man, he's like Esmeralda'—her doll, who had lost a foot. She laid out the seashells she'd collected, and aligned them by order of preciousness. When the waiter presented the check, she shyly pushed her three prize specimens in his direction.

"While Lilí had her nap, Rosario and I sat on the terrace. The canvas awning cast a shadow that stopped on her thighs just at the line where her skirts usually fall. The sun floodlit those legs of hers. I kept glancing at them, insatiable. She appeared to be drowsing. It sounds absurd, but I would swear her knees caught me spying. More than once I've been unnerved by the way that her gaze—which I live for—suddenly retracts. Well, now she locked her legs—rigid, canted off to one side—and her entire body seemed to retract. I actually shivered. Then they did something negligible, and momentous—to this day, I have the impression it was the legs alone, independent, that did it. They opened far enough for a fist to slide in between them, and the farther one slowly rose about an inch, as if to gauge my reaction. The movement was so—brazen.

"Somebody began to whisper with furious intensity, telling Rosario all my secrets. Only as the torrent subsided did I realize who was talking. Rosario jumped to her feet. Had I outraged her? Was she storming off to phone Roberto? A hoarse cry—'Mommy!'—came from the room. Rosario must have picked up an earlier cry that I, in my agitation, had missed. For a second, she stared at me."

The doorbell rang. Miguel, stranded on the sunstruck terrace, blinked.

"My next student."

"Ah."

"Roberto."

I went and let him in. Seeing Miguel, he smiled.

"Did you mention my idea?" Roberto asked him.

"No . . . I wanted you to."

"Miguel and I both need to work on mechanics, right? Why not coach each other, to accelerate the process? One week, say, Miguel practices leaps: I zero in on the problems. The next week he does the same for me. That way, we'll get to the four-hand repertoire before we grow long beards! Maybe once a month, we could have a joint session with you, to make sure we're not leading each other astray."

"Bravo! How soon do you start?"

They set up an appointment on the spot.

The following time, Miguel did an impressive job with some exercises by Clementi. He was anxious to finish telling me his story:

"That afternoon, after my outburst, the world seemed to be holding its breath. Rosario behaved as though nothing had happened. On the beach, I sought refuge in Lilí—her uncomplicated light. Together we built a sand castle—a château, in fact, with all the fairy-tale trappings—and I spun tales in which she starred as its resident princess. We had supper around five, for her sake. Both Rosario and I spontaneously dressed up for the hotel's rather pretentious restaurant, and Lilí got to wear her 'royal gown' (a velvet frock). Rosario had somehow managed to manicure her nails. I refused to let myself believe she had done this for me. I half convinced myself that if I indulged such a presumptuous fantasy, those crimson rake-teeth would lash out and flay me. A tasty terror.

"Afterward I lay on my bed, clothed, letting myself be mesmerized by the revolutions of the ceiling fan. The dimness around me thickened. I was conscious only of a thudding right beneath my Adam's apple. Someone knocked. Rosario—in a silk nightgown that tied behind the neck.

Without a word, she floated past me and tiptoed to the door that communicated with her room, opened it a crack, listened. I began to say something. Her palm muzzled me, warmly. I kissed it. She stepped back. My hopes froze. She reached behind her neck and undid the bow.

"I've usually found in even the most alluring woman some falsity, some tinge of coarseness that diminishes my respect for her. It was just the opposite with Rosario. One detail made our intimacy especially poignant: she was both with me and with her sleeping child. An instinctive vigilance radiated from her—a wave of tenderness combined with a coiled readiness to spring, if necessary, to her daughter's defense. I sensed this as palpably as one feels the sun on one's skin.

"Then the idyll was over. Dismal! In the last eighty-one days, I've seen Rosario alone exactly four times. I mustn't push for more. She's devoted to Lilí and Roberto.

"Every day I'm not with her weighs like jail. All I want to do is hibernate—but I can't fall asleep, thinking about her. It's turning me into a zombie. I play a lot, to distract myself." He paused. "Can I study that new piece you gave her?"

"Which one?"

"By Mompou." He hummed the theme. "It won't leave me alone."

I produced a score for him. "Start by working out the fingerings."

"What's the title?"

"*Secreto.*"

His teeth clamped down on his lip.

It was around then that I performed Prokofiev's *Paysage* for Miguel, to demonstrate what delights lay in store if he stuck at his drills. I finished, and he exclaimed, "You don't mean to tell me that's how all women are!"

"Of course not."

It puzzled him that Roberto disallowed this sort of comprehension: "We'll hear a piece at a concert. His only comment is 'I liked it' or 'I didn't like it'—as if it were a flan. When I try to discuss what it's about, he gets sarcastic: 'I don't need to make up stories to go with the soundtrack.'"

Even with me, Roberto practically brandished this incapacity. (Or was it puerile resistance, a stance adopted in order to distinguish himself from his more aesthetic friend?) "I honestly can't see anything more in music than a formally pleasing arrangement of melodies, harmonies, and rhythms."

"Only that, Roberto?"

He would shrug.

One day, having played a piece by Schumann, he said: "This moves me."

"Why?"

He flicked his nose. "I just feel an affinity. . . ."

I launched into my own rendition, emphasizing certain of the ideas.

"Wait! Is it his family?"

"He and his wife and his children, all joined in some activity—that's his heaven. They're a hearth that cheers him and drives off the world's chill. . . ."

He became keen to learn the language of music, notwithstanding his limited aptitude. Every week he would turn up with some new revelation. Frequently he was guessing rather than hearing; nevertheless, he gained increasing trust in his own ear. "This passage demands a crescendo here," I would tell him, demonstrating. He would acquiesce but venture: "Maybe a tad softer, eh?"

Rosario, for her part, had a vivid sympathy with the Romantic repertoire, so much so that she was often disturbed by the anguished passions it depicted. Like a child who cannot bear stories in which dumb beasts are threatened, she shied away from extreme emotions. If she was unsettled by one of Chopin's evocations of jealousy, say, she felt free to leaven it with some congenial sentiment of her own, or simply to use the music as a vehicle for her mood of the moment. Although this disqualified her as an interpreter, it need not have prevented her from developing into a competent instrumentalist. She could have cloaked her failing beneath the ensemble of a chamber group, or excelled as a soloist in those grandiloquent calliopes which are the warhorse piano concertos. Empty compositions would have come out sounding expressive with her.

As the summer receded, I had less time for my students beyond the ambit of their lessons. Miguel gradually resigned himself to scant, sporadic trysts. He and Roberto carried on their reciprocal coaching. Soon they were plodding through Schubert's *Ländler*, D. 814. I advised Roberto to prepare a similar piece with Rosario. He contended it was too difficult to coordinate their schedules. The flimsiness of the alibi made me suspect that what really thwarted him was the fear that playing side by side with her would show him to poor advantage.

He declared his intention to acquire a grand piano.

"What's the matter with your upright?" I asked him.

"I don't do things by halves," he retorted. "Besides, Rosario should have an instrument worthy of her talent."

At his insistence, I referred him to el señor Alvear, proprietor of the Casa de Pianos. Soon afterward, I was hurrying along a street downtown when a tubby, florid figure up the block began bouncing toward me, waving: el señor Alvear. He had on a beret and a muffler (no overcoat), and as usual he toted a wicker basket filled with bonbons. "Catch, catch!" he cried in his flügelhorn voice, and lobbed foil-wrapped candies at me.

Flushed, beaming, he bussed me on the cheek. "You've sent me a tycoon! The man has to have a full-size grand, no less."

"You didn't sell him one. . . ."

"Anything larger than three-quarters was excessive, I told him. That only made him want to buy a full-size more."

"A baby grand will do him fine."

He cocked his head. "A smaller piano means a smaller commission for you."

"Así es."

When I next stopped at Roberto's and Rosario's, a Blüthner Aliquod baby grand loomed in the twilight of the living room. Rosario went to get me a glass of juice from the kitchen, where Lilí was being given dinner by the maid. Roberto was talking on the telephone in the study. An odd dissonance charged the atmosphere. I sat down at the piano to try it out. Feathery action, pedals that yielded without the slightest creak, ringing tones in every range.

Roberto sauntered in. "How do you like it?"

"How do *you* like it, is the question."

"Not bad for its size, I suppose."

"But it's magnificent!"

"He knows it's magnificent," Rosario said, stepping into the room. "He's just grumpy because he won't be playing it himself."

"What do you mean?"

"Well, not for a while," he conceded, chagrined. "My company bid for a job down south. It's so much bigger than anything we've done before, we didn't think we'd win it. The word came yesterday. I've been put in command."

"Everybody agrees that Roberto is the one best qualified," said Rosario. "And it's such an opportunity. Still, what a wrench . . ."

"I'll be marooned, away from my family." Roberto made a gesture encompassing his wife, the Blüthner, me.

"You won't quit practicing," I growlingly admonished him.

"That I promise! Even if I have to use one of those mute keyboards."

It was pouring outside. With his wet slicker and dripping curls, Miguel seemed to sweep the whole hectic vigor of the cloudburst into my apartment. From his sodden briefcase we extracted his music, damp at the edges. I brought him a towel, and he rubbed his crown into a spume of fluffy ringlets. "I have a message for you from Rosario," he announced. "She's canceling her lesson tomorrow."

Rosario had always notified me of such changes herself, and in good time. After weeks of specially assigned exercises, she had been eager to attack Scriabin's *Prelude for the Left Hand*.

"She's well?"

"Wonderful." A manic treble suggested that he had shared a delicious secret with me. "She's gone to see Roberto," he added, in the manner of one obliged to furnish a gross hint.

"Ah."

"He's been away for over *two months*." Then, as if discarding all restraint: "She needed to see him."

"That's a long separation."

Miguel couldn't shake his itchiness. When he played, he hit many wrong notes. Suddenly he seized my arm: "She's pregnant!"

As soon as Rosario returned, I went to give her a lesson. She greeted me with news of her husband. An efficient housekeeper was fixing him wholesome meals. His project, though formidable, was advancing smoothly; if the weather continued mild, he would finish it on schedule. "And you'd be proud of him. He's rented a spinet: no matter how busy the day, he does scales for at least twenty minutes."

I signed for her to sit down at the keyboard. She did, but remained motionless, looking straight ahead. Mainly to herself she said: "I missed Roberto. It was a mistake to sleep with him. Now he'll inevitably presume . . . It will be that much harder to tell him. I'll have to wait for the proper moment. Isn't there some music about this?"

At the end of the session, I answered: *Transfigured Night.*"

"That's it!" She brightened. "Schoenberg will be my patron saint."

Rosario was one of those women who live on easy terms with pregnancy. Her condition remained almost imperceptible. A gossamer smile betokened the dreaminess that enveloped her and that seemed only to enrich her faculties. She devoured pieces as fast as I fed them to her, wanting to spend all her time at the piano when she was not with Lilí.

Once he had made his disclosure, Miguel kept his own counsel—except for issuing the occasional contented sigh, and offhandedly mentioning his conviction that Rosario was carrying a boy.

I was early. The maid let me in. Believing that Rosario was not yet home, and tempted by the Blüthner, I began to toil over the Liszt sonata. I don't recall how far I got before I became conscious of her standing in a doorway. She wore a look of horrified rapture.

"Please, don't stop."

"It may not be healthy for you to hear this when you're . . ."

"I've never been stronger. It's now that I can face such things."

I glanced at my watch. "We'd better start your lesson."

The next week she told me that she had been listening to recordings of the sonata.

"Horowitz's version is all about Horowitz. Arrau conveys perhaps half of what's there."

"Even that much is a miracle."

"Then how to describe what you convey?"

"He has a vast repertoire. I don't."

She began a campaign to get me to perform the entire piece for her. Soon Miguel took up the same refrain. She must have spoken to Roberto about it as well: he wrote me a postcard appealing for a future "Liszt recital."

That sonata is an intelligent, seductive cobra.

. . .

Rosario's labor commenced on a frosty afternoon about seven months after her initial visit to Roberto. In order to spare him anxiety, she put off alerting him until the last possible moment. Within a couple of hours, she was able to report to him that it was a boy, astonishingly robust. Ecstatic, he flew back on the next plane. His first impression: "The spit and image of Rosario!" The engineering project was so close to completion that he was able to turn it over to a partner and stay home to be with his son.

Miguel had accompanied Rosario throughout her accouchement. Inspired by his friend's devotion, Roberto insisted that the baby's name incorporate both of theirs: Guelberto. Following some discussion, this became Gilberto, which quickly, via Gilbertito, contracted to Tito.

A few weeks after the birth, Roberto and Rosario held an intimate soirée where Miguel and I were the only guests—if one could apply that term to Miguel, a virtual member of the family in his capacity of tireless volunteer sitter, burper, bather, and diaper-changer. No sooner was my coat off than the two men bustled me into the nursery to behold the gurgling scion. Roberto urged me to offer him a pinkie: "He has the grip of a rock climber." Miguel fussed with Tito's bedding and got him to smile. I noticed that he was neglecting his pose. Over dinner, he slipped back into it to act out the befuddled reactions of various hospital personnel who, on the night of the delivery, had taken him for Rosario's spouse and were at a loss to fathom how "this hysterical peacock," as he described himself, could have managed to sire an heir. His mimicry had Roberto in stitches.

Rosario gave a recital in Roberto's honor, surprising him with Scriabin's *Prelude* and *Nocturne for the Left Hand*, along with several études by Kessler. Roberto, a stranger to all of these pieces, sat beside Miguel on the sofa, with Lilí, in her nightgown, on his lap. His face assumed its satisfied cast. Miguel's was set in an identical expression.

Toward the tail of the evening, Rosario pulled me aside: "I don't know how to laugh."

"I've never seen you laugh. It's true."

"Can't you teach me?"

"Are you happy?"

"How could I not be!"

"Then you don't need to laugh."

. . .

At the time I accepted Rosario as a student, we settled on the fee for my services. Week after week elapsed without my receiving any payment. I had to tell her: "This cannot go on."

"You mustn't think I don't value your . . ."

"It violates your orderliness, Rosario."

"The one thing I haven't ever been able to keep straight is my accounts," she owned. "I stick my bills in an old hatbox. I always mean to get to them, but the pile just grows, and I can't deal with it."

"Before our next session, you'll send me what you owe me. The rule will be: you pay me first thing."

Rosario respected this disposition faithfully for as long as she remained my pupil. Otherwise, she did not mend her ways. Eventually Roberto took over the administration of her finances. "If she wasn't so good-looking, she'd be in debtor's prison," he joked.

Soon after the evening of my audience with Tito, Rosario asked to come to me for her lesson. She moved listlessly, seemed to peer out through an indigo haze. Having played a few notes, she thumped a sour chord and let her hands plummet to her lap. "Fool!" she muttered.

"What is it?"

"While Roberto was gone, I vowed that I would surprise him by keeping up with the bills. I did stay on top of the really dire ones, but most of them were still unopened when he got home. He didn't rebuke me—just shook his head. The other night, he sat down to pay them. I was in bed. He stalked in, snapped on the light, flung one at me with 'Third Notice' stamped on it: 'What's this?' I supposed he was angry because we might be dunned. I apologized. 'No, read it.' It was for the pregnancy test I'd had a couple of weeks before my first trip to visit him. 'What's the meaning of this!' he shouted. For months I'd been considering how best to present the facts to him. I was positive I could make him understand. But I didn't take enough time—I blurted out: '*He's not yours.*' Roberto looked like he'd been stabbed."

The next morning Miguel appeared at my door, though it wasn't the day for his lesson. He begged me to spend a few minutes with him. Since I was just leaving, I suggested that he walk with me to an appointment I had. I set a brisk pace and he jounced along at my side, fitfully grasping me by the arm as he spoke.

"Rosario talked to you—I know. Listen, the last thing I wanted to do was to hurt Roberto. I never thought there'd be consequences. I never thought he'd find out. If it had been me Roberto confronted with that bill, I'd have invented a story. But Rosario did what she did—which upset everything. I couldn't let Roberto simply hang like that, not knowing who the father was. I was sure I could break it to him in a way so he'd feel—not excluded. I had this idea I could tell him the truth as if I were lying. . . ."

He stepped off the curb and I yanked him back as a bicycle whizzed by. He didn't seem to notice.

"I reached him at the office: 'Can you come over, it's urgent.' Ten minutes later, we were both standing in my alcove. It just popped out of me. 'I'm the father.' He glared: 'Ah, so Rosario told you. Who are you trying to cover for?' He started getting all worked up: 'Don't hide this from me!' 'I am the father.' 'You're mocking me!'—and he stomped out. I called Rosario to tell her what had happened. She was angry: 'Why didn't you speak to me first? There was no reason for him to know.'"

We were at my destination. I reached out and thrummed on his shoulder a theme from the rondo he was studying. "Tomorrow at five."

It was seventeen after the hour when an elated Miguel sailed in. "I've just left Roberto. Do you know what he did? He hugged me—hugged me!—and asked me to forgive him. He said: 'With Rosario so attractive . . . even for you, Miguel. You needed to have a son, man! Besides—aren't two fathers better than one?' What a friend! I would give my life for him!"

"Your life, Miguel?"

"Yes!"

I had to handle Miguel sternly for several weeks to get him back in harness. Rosario settled down of her own accord. Roberto did not alter his demeanor, except to introduce a shade of punctilio into our relations, a heightened sense of his own dignity. A different tone crept into his remarks about Rosario and Miguel: not so much paternal as paternalistic, a benevolent grandfather speaking of slightly errant grandchildren. He had lost ground pianistically while away, and drove himself to catch up with Miguel. They kept on meeting regularly to critique each other, and we had a joint lesson monthly.

One of these took place at Roberto's. I was struck by his warmth as a host. In a hundred gracious ways he had insinuated Miguel as an ornament of the household. A favorite armchair was reserved for him. He was encouraged to regard the kitchen as his own, and sometimes on the maid's day off he cooked dinner. When I got there that evening, Lilí was bawling over some grievance. Roberto, who was building a fire in the grate, let Miguel assuage her. Rosario, placidly ensconced on the sofa, suckled Tito.

At random intervals, I would ask my students to play something they had not practiced for many months, to ascertain whether it had stayed in their fingers. During one of his private lessons, I said to Roberto: "Let's hear that Schumann piece you were affected by."

"I've forgotten it," he snapped.

"Go ahead, give it a try. You may be surprised how much of it comes back."

Reluctantly, he complied. He acquitted himself so well, one would almost have sworn he had been reviewing the score.

"Excellent."

He scowled. "Never again!"

"Roberto—"

"Schumann. Bah! If he had such a happy hearth, why was he obsessed with death? Those dancing skeletons in *Carnaval*? I see them every day around my house. Grimacing." He mashed some keys cacophonously. "Don't mind me. I still haven't recovered from the strain of that job."

To disperse the gloom, I served tea with cakes and played him Mac-Dowell's *Dance of the Gnomes*.

"Ah," said Roberto, "a piece with nothing but charm."

It was as though I had unwittingly opened a drawer deep inside Roberto and glimpsed some venomous insect feeding on the darkness. Whatever that noxious energy may have been, he seemed to harbor it as a mortifying reminder of hazards to be shunned. He showed Miguel and Rosario the most exquisite consideration. They, in turn, deferred to him as the generous ruler of their garden.

Miguel was ambushed by the ferocity of his attachment to the baby. Tito's smiles and yawns, imperious appetites, budding quirks became his only topic. He buttonholed everyone he met to flaunt photos of his "godson." To me, he chafed at the façade he had adopted: "Will I always have to talk to my boy through this mask?" When an earache set the child wailing in agony, Miguel couldn't eat or sleep; he later confessed to me that the ordeal had brought him a guilty relief, since it supplied him a pretext to haunt the nursery at all hours, wring his hands, moan, and for once vent his feelings for Tito with fully licensed abandon.

I remember the coziness of the household throughout that wintry season: dense crystal vases spilled over with flowers that sunned in the blaze of the fireplace, and the vista of snowcapped peaks made the living room all the more snug. Rosario seemed burnished with well-being. Roberto, prospering in his business, bought for her any number of expensive outfits, which soon had their fronts stained with mother's milk. Rosario said that she was "addicted" to feeding the baby. One evening, as Tito gorged, Roberto poked Miguel in the ribs: "Don't you wish you were him? When Rosario nursed Lilí, she was ravishing enough, but the boy stimulates a whole other set of glands in her. What a pity it would have been to miss this, eh? It sometimes seems to me that I was destined to have only a daughter, but that Fate had the good sense to change its mind."

Rosario told me: "Before I married Roberto, I asked him: 'What if I fall in love with someone else?' He answered: 'Just so you don't stop loving me. . . .' 'It's impossible for me to stop loving you,' I said. And that's how it's turned out.

"There's something incestuous in me. Roberto excites me more as a brother. With Miguel, it's different. He's more of a son. What would it be like with a real son! That's what I've secretly dreamed of, ever since I began to desire men. Maybe that's why I had a boy." She gave a quick smile: "It's not going to happen, though." Suddenly earnest: "I'll die soon."

"Rosario!"

"Today I'm crazy."

Weeks before Tito's first birthday, Roberto set about planning a party. He liked to ruminate the guest list out loud. A legion of relatives, colleagues, and neighbors had to be included, especially those with tots of their own. He petitioned Miguel for the names of his *muchachos*. "I'm in a bind," Miguel told me. He managed to extricate himself by claiming that they were such a jealous bunch, to invite any of them would cause hostilities.

Roberto was determined that I too should attend. I had a conflicting engagement. "In that case," he said, "you might help celebrate the occasion in another way. Would you, one evening, give us the Liszt sonata?"

Roberto and Miguel wore dinner jackets; Rosario, a hyacinth sheath. Candles shone; a tall vase on the Blüthner bristled with gladiolas. A few streamers, some stray specks of confetti, and a balloon lolling in an upper corner testified to the recent festivity.

As I entered, a small pink whirlwind darted at me and enfolded my legs.

"Lilí just wanted to welcome you," Rosario explained.

"My mommy said I can't stay."

"Then we have to obey her."

"But why can't I hear the music?"

"Another time, I'm going to play something specially for you."

"You are? What?"

"Wait and see."

Lilí contemplated this briefly, then went to kiss Roberto and Miguel good night. Tripping back to me, she motioned me down and mouthed: "Don't forget." Rosario led her off.

"We missed you at the party," said Roberto. "A resounding success, wouldn't you say, Miguel?"

"Tito howled through most of it, that's for sure," Miguel laughed. "What a pair of lungs that kid has!"

I offered my score to Roberto: "You might like to follow—though it may be awkward for the three of you together. . . ."

"Not to worry." With a flourish, he drew a tight new edition from a stack on the coffee table. I passed my wilted old folio to Miguel, who nestled into "his" armchair and leafed through the pages. Moving to the piano, I adjusted the bench and took some deep breaths. Rosario came back and sat down on the sofa beside Roberto. At that moment, I pounced.

The whole piece is daunting, but the first two notes are nearly insuperable: terminal heartbeats. How to play *those?* The keys have to be touched as if they were red-hot irons. I pinged off that opening salvo—vitality's parting shots—and plunged ahead, in a kind of conscious trance . . . until at last, in the closing measures, the dawn appeared and outfaced the destroyer. The final note whispered: *Death, even you will die.*

Miguel stood up and began to pace: "This never sank in before—yet I can't say I didn't know."

Roberto, who had been lost in scrutiny of the ceiling, bent forward and addressed me: "Rosario was right. You really put it across. I almost wish you hadn't. . . ."

"The beauty transforms it into something tolerable," said Miguel.

Borne on her own current, Rosario reflected: "People live such different lives. Why shouldn't they experience death differently? For one it might be an eternal catastrophe. . . . For another, nothing at all." She stood up; I thought she was going to leave. Instead, with a soft gesture she signaled for me to surrender the bench. She occupied my place with such a magisterial posture that an electric hush seemed to descend upon a crowded hall. "Number Five, from Schoenberg's *Six Little Piano Pieces*," she announced. "In celebration of our heartbeats."

An hour before her next lesson, Rosario telephoned me, asking to have it at my house. She turned up well-groomed as always but had circles under her eyes. She was quiet, rather stiff. We worked on a *Prelude and Fugue*. At the end, I fetched her coat from the closet.

She wrapped it about her as if suddenly chilled, and sniffed sharply. "Roberto delivered an ultimatum: 'If Miguel ever tries to see Tito again, I'll kill him.'"

"Kill Miguel?"

"No, Tito." She clawed her hair back. "All this time. Engineering it."

The bell jangled. I opened the door: Miguel, unshaven, bedraggled. Rosario manifested no surprise at his apparition. He seemed on the verge of pleading for something. She laid her hand over his mouth.

The following day, I got in at four o'clock from doing errands. Two students of mine, teenage twin sisters, were waiting outside my apartment in their matched jumpers, stealing glances at Miguel, who leaned against a wall, weeping.

"Miguel, what is it?"

"How can he cut me off from my head? *Never?* I don't want to live!"

"Come in, why don't you? I have to give these girls their lesson. Yours isn't till five."

"I'll stay here."

The twins were unabashedly gawking. I shooed them in.

When I ushered them out, Miguel was standing in the same spot, more composed. I led him in to the piano. He said nothing—for fear, I guessed, of dissolving again. His hands shook so, he could scarcely play. Midway through the hour, he sprang up, embraced me, and bolted.

Roberto requested that I come to him for his lesson. It was dusk; he left the lamps unlit. No one else seemed to be around. The gladiolas, still in their tall vase, exhaled a sickly smell.

He worked attentively. At one moment he mumbled to no one in particular: "Even flirted with me."

At the end, he pressed down middle C with his fifth finger and intoned, "Good-bye." Was he saying this to me or to the piano?

As I walked home, I remembered that once, at a gathering, I had seen Miguel clasp Roberto around the waist, dance a few steps with him, and yell, "How hot this man is!" Roberto joined in the act, stroking Miguel's chin: "Look who's talking!" Everybody had laughed, except Rosario, who asked me, "Why are they laughing?"

I recalled one of Miguel's first lessons. A stifling summer day. He had on a fitted silk shirt, shorts, espadrilles. I got up to pour him some water. When I turned around, he had unbuttoned his shirt. He flashed me a broad grin.

"Is something funny?'

"Sorry." He buttoned up.

Another time—I'd praised him for having performed a piece well—he took my index finger and put it to his lips.

"What are you doing?"

He held my finger there for a few more seconds and, with a subtle smile, answered: "Shushing my pride."

I was expecting Rosario at three o'clock. Three thirty came, and no sign of her. I phoned. The maid answered: "Something terrible, *Dios mío* . . . Lilí fell off the balcony."

"What?"

"Dead."

. . .

The day after the funeral, Rosario arrived punctually for her lesson. She was dressed in a gray suit and had on dark glasses, which she did not remove.

"Just Bach," she said.

Every so often, a shudder convulsed her and she had to stop. At one point she retired to the other room for a few minutes. She strode back in: "I need to play."

Week by week, she made progress.

From her spring, she passed directly to her autumn. Her red foliage turned gray. She took to wearing a hat, and gray weeds. More stunning than ever. She reminded me of the elm in the field behind the house where I grew up. A squall of hailstones fractured its branches, yet the tree stood firm.

Roberto decided to relocate to another city. Rosario moved with him. At our last meeting, she clutched my hands. "You've taught me to take care with endings," she said. "We'll probably never see each other again. I am not an unfinished symphony. The double bar has come."

The metronome tapped away, prestissimo. Six years? Seven?

One summer afternoon, the sun closed down like an iris, the sky let loose a barrage, and I, who had been trying to outrun the storm, found myself huddling beneath a leaky cornice. Each time the blast seemed to have reached its utmost vehemence it would swell anew. I was thinking of a three-legged mongrel I'd seen, hoping the poor cur hadn't drowned, when suddenly a shape bodied forth out of the swirl. A bald shape, with an umbrella. It slowed, squinted through the murk, advanced, halted, pushed its nose almost up to mine.

"Roberto!"

He glowered, brought the drumming black canopy over my head. "Music!" His jaw quivered. "The best music is silence." His incisors dug into his lower lip till it bled. He planted his umbrella in my hand with a solicitous squeeze, and tromped off into the deluge.

I tried to conjure up Rosario's two sapphires. In her presence I had always forbidden myself to blink, not wanting to lose sight of their dazzle even for an instant. Now, in order to recapture her eyes, I needed to press my own tight shut.

Paula Fox

Grace

from *Harper's Magazine*

O NCE THEY were out on the street, Grace, his dog, paid no attention to John Hillman, unless she wanted to range farther than her leash permitted. She would pause and look back at him, holding up one paw instead of lunging ahead and straining against her collar as John had observed other dogs do.

On her suddenly furrowed brow, in the faint tremor of her extended paw, he thought he read an entreaty. It both touched and irritated him. He would like to have owned a dog with more spirit. Even after he had put her dish of food on the kitchen floor, she would hesitate, stare fixedly at his face until he said, heartily, "Go ahead, Grace," or, "There you are! Dinner!"

He entered Central Park in the early evening to take their usual path, and the farther he walked from the apartment house where he lived the more benign he felt. A few of the people he encountered, those without dogs of their own, paused to speculate about Grace's age or her breed.

"The classical antique dog," pronounced an elderly man in a long raincoat, the hem of which Grace sniffed at delicately.

John had decided she was about three years old, as had been estimated by the people at the animal shelter where he had found her. But most of the people who spoke to him in the park thought she looked older.

"Look at her tits. She's certainly had one litter. And some of her whiskers are white," observed a youngish woman wearing a black sweatshirt and baggy gray cotton trousers. As she looked at John her expression was solemn, her tone of voice impersonal. But he thought he detected in her words the character of a proclamation: "Tits" was a matter-of-fact word a woman could say to a man unless he was constrained by outmoded views.

What if, he speculated, inflamed by her use of the word, he had leaped upon her and grabbed her breasts, which, as she spoke, rose and fell behind her sweatshirt like actors moving behind a curtain?

"You're probably right," he said as he glanced up at a park lamp that lit as he spoke, casting its glow on discarded newspapers, fruit-juice cartons, crushed cigarette packs, and empty plastic bottles that had contained water. He had seen people, as they walked or ran for exercise, pausing to nurse at such bottles, holding them up at an angle so that the water would flow more quickly into their mouths. Perhaps they were merely overheated.

"I don't know much about dogs," he added.

She was pleasant-looking in a fresh, camp-counselor style, around his age, he surmised, and her stolid-footed stance was comradely. He would have liked to accompany her for a few minutes, a woman who spoke with such authority despite the ugliness of her running shoes. He knew people wore such cartoon footwear even to weddings and funerals these days. Meanwhile, he hoped she wouldn't suddenly start running in place or stretch her arms or do neck exercises to ease whatever stress she might be experiencing, emitting intimate groans as she did so.

When he was speaking with people, he found himself in a state of apprehension, of nervous excitement, lest he be profoundly offended by what they said or did. For nearly a year, he had dated a girl who did such neck cycles at moments he deemed inappropriate. After completing one she had done in a bar they frequented, she had asked him, "Didn't I look like a kitty-cat?" "No!" he replied, his voice acid with distaste. At once he regretted it. They spent the night lying in her bed like wooden planks. The next morning she dressed in silence, her face grim. He had tried to assuage her with boyish gaiety. She had broken her silence with one sentence: "I don't want to see you anymore."

"Have a good day," said the woman in the baggy trousers, crimping her fingers at him as she sloped down the path. He bent quickly to Grace and stroked her head. "But it's night," he muttered.

. . .

Was the interest expressed by people in the park only for his dog? Was he included in their kindly looks? When the walk was over, John felt that he was leaving a country of goodwill, that the broad avenue he would cross when he emerged from the park to reach his apartment house was the border of another country, New York City, a place he had ceased to love this last year.

Grace made for frequent difficulty at the curb. If the traffic light was green and northbound cars raced by, she sat peacefully on her haunches. But when the light changed to red and the traffic signal spelled WALK, Grace balked, suddenly scratching furiously at the hardened earth at the base of a spindly tree or else turning her back to the avenue. John would jerk on the leash. Grace would yelp. It was such a high, thin, frightened yelp. John would clench his jaw and yank her across the avenue, half wishing a car would clip her.

In the elevator, a few seconds later, he would regret his loss of control. If only Grace would look up at him. But she stared straight ahead at the elevator door.

The trouble with owning a dog is that it leaves you alone with a private judgment about yourself, John thought. If a person had accused him of meanness, he could have defended himself. But with a dog—you did something cheap to it when you were sure no one was looking, and it was as though you had done it in front of a mirror.

John hoped that Grace would forget those moments at the curbside. But her long silky ears often flattened when he walked by her, and he took that as a sign. The idea that she was afraid of him was mortifying. When she cringed, or crept beneath a table, he murmured endearments to her, keeping his hands motionless. He would remind himself that he knew nothing about her past; undoubtedly, she'd been abused. But he always returned, in his thoughts, to his own culpability.

To show his good intentions, John brought her treats, stopping on his way home from work at a butcher shop to buy knucklebones. When Grace leaped up and whimpered and danced as John was opening the door, he would drop his briefcase and reach into a plastic bag to retrieve and show Grace what he had brought her. She would begin at once to gnaw the bone with the only ferocity she ever showed. John would sit down in a chair in the unlit living room, feeling at peace with himself.

After he gave her supper he would take her to the park. If all went well, the peaceful feeling lasted throughout the evening. But if Grace was pigheaded when the traffic light ordered them to walk—or worse, if the light changed when they were in the middle of the avenue and they were caught in the rush of traffic and Grace refused to move, her tail down, her rump turned under—then John, despite his resolution, would jerk on the leash, and Grace would yelp. When this happened, he had to admit to himself that he hated her.

This murderous rage led him to suspect himself the way he suspected the men who walked alone in the park, shabbily dressed and dirty, men he often glimpsed on a path or standing beneath the branch of a tree halfway up a rise. In his neighborhood there were as many muggings during the day as there were at night. Only a week earlier a man had been strangled less than one hundred yards from the park entrance. Now that it was early summer, the foliage was out, and it was harder to see the direction from which danger might come.

A day after the murder, he wondered if his cry would be loud enough to bring help. He had never had to cry out. He stood before his bathroom mirror, opened his mouth, and shut it at once, imagining he had seen a shriek about to burst forth, its imminence signaled by a faint quivering of his uvula.

Grace didn't bark—at least he'd never heard her bark—and this fact increased his worry. Would she silently observe his murder, then slink away, dragging her leash behind her?

Sometimes he wished she would run away. But how could she? He didn't let her off the leash as some owners did their dogs. Were he to do so, she was likely to feel abandoned once again.

He had got Grace because he had begun to feel lonely in the evenings and on weekends since the end of his affair with the kitty-cat girl, as he named her in memory. In his loneliness, he had begun to brood over his past. He had been slothful all his life, too impatient to think through the consequences of his actions. He had permitted his thoughts to collapse into an indeterminate tangle when he should have grappled with them.

When regret threatened to sink him, he made efforts to count his blessings. He had a passable job with an accounting firm, an affectionate older sister living in Boston with whom he spoke once a month, and a rent-controlled apartment. He still took pleasure in books. He had been a comparative-literature major in college before taking a business degree, judging that comp lit would get him nowhere. His health was good. He was only thirty-six.

Only! Would he tell himself on his next birthday that he was *only* thirty-seven, and try to comfort himself with a word that mediated between hope and dread?

He had little time to brood over the past during work, yet in the office he felt himself slipping into a numbness of spirit and body broken only by fits of the looniness he had also observed in colleagues and acquaintances. He called the phenomenon "little breakdowns in big cities."

His own little breakdowns took the form of an irritability that seemed to increase by the hour. He became aware of a thick, smothering, oily smell of hair in the packed subway trains he rode to and from work. There was so much hair, lank or curly, frizzed or straight, bushy or carved in wedges, adorned with wide-toothed combs, metal objects, bits of leather, rubber bands. There were moments when John covered his mouth and nose with one hand.

Then there was the bearded man he shared an office with. Throughout the day, with his thumb and index finger, he would coil a hair in his beard as though it were a spring he was trying to force back into his skin. When John happened to look up and catch his office mate at it, he couldn't look away or take in a single word the man was saying.

He was in a fire of rage. Why couldn't the man keep his picking and coiling for private times?

That was the heart of it, of course: privacy. No one knew what it meant anymore. People scratched and groomed themselves, coiled their hair, shouted, played their radios at full volume, ate, even made love in public. Not that anyone called it lovemaking.

On a scrap of paper that he found on his desk, John wrote:

Name's Joe Sex
You can call me Tex
You kin have me, have me
At 34th and Lex.

He rolled it up into a ball and aimed at but missed the wastebasket. Later that day, a secretary retrieved it and read it aloud to the staff. People grew merry and flirtatious. He was thanked by everyone for cheering them up, for lightening the day.

On the weekend before he found Grace at the animal shelter, he wrote three letters to the *New York Times*. The first was to a noted psychiatrist who had reviewed a study of child development, calling it an "instant classic." John wrote: "An instant classic is an oxymoron. A classic is established over time, not in an instant."

The second was sent to a book reviewer who had described a detective story as *lovingly* written. "Lovingly," John wrote, "is not an adverb that applies to literature, especially thrillers when they concern criminal activity."

His third letter was about a term, "street smart," used by a writer to describe a novel's heroine. "This is a superficially snappy but meaningless cliché that trivializes reality," he wrote. "On the street, the truth is that people stumble about in confusion and dismay even when they are making fortunes selling illegal drugs. People are smart for only a few minutes at a time."

While he was writing the letters he felt exalted. He was battling the degradation of language and ideas. But the intoxication soon wore off. He stared down at the letters on his desk. They looked less than trivial. He crumpled them and threw them into a wastebasket.

He came to a decision then. What he needed was a living creature to take care of; an animal would be a responsibility that would anchor him in daily life.

On weekends, Grace was a boon. John played with her, wearing an old pair of leather gloves so her teeth wouldn't mark his hands. He bought rubber toys in a variety store, and she learned to chase and fetch them back to him. Once, while he lay half-asleep in his bathtub, she brought him a rubber duck. "Why Grace," he said, patting her with a wet hand, "how appropriate!"

Perhaps dogs had thoughts. How else to explain the way Grace would suddenly rise from where she was lying and go to another room? Something must have occurred to her.

She followed him about as he shaved, made breakfast, washed his socks, dusted the furniture with an old shirt. When he sat down with his newspaper, she would curl up nearby on the floor. In the three months he had owned her, she had grown glossy and sleek. He liked looking at her. Where had she come from?

As if feeling his gaze, she stared up at him. At such moments of mutual scrutiny, John felt that time had ceased. He sank into the natural world reflected in her eyes, moving toward an awareness to which he was unable to give a name.

But if he bent to pet her, she would flatten her ears. Or if he touched her when she was up, her legs would tremble with the effort to remain upright yet humble. Or so he imagined.

One day he came home from work at noon. He had felt faint while drinking coffee at his desk in the office. Grace was not at the door to welcome him. He called her. There was no response.

After a thorough search, surprised by the violent thumping of his heart, he discovered her beneath the box springs of his bed. "Oh, Grace!" he exclaimed reproachfully. As soon as he had extricated her, he held her closely, her small hard skull pressed against his throat. After a moment he put her down. "You gave me a scare," he said. Grace licked her flank. Had his emotion embarrassed her?

John's throat was feeling raw and sore, but he took Grace for a walk right away. She might have been confused by the change in her routine. At the park entrance, she sat down abruptly. He tugged at the leash. She sat on—glumly, he thought. He picked her up and walked to a patch of coarse grass and placed her on it. Dutifully, she squatted and urinated. A dozen yards or so away, John saw a black dog racing around a tree while its owner watched it, swinging a leash and smiling.

Grace seemed especially spiritless today. Later, propped up by pillows in bed and drinking tea from a mug printed with his initials—a gift from the kitty-cat girl—he wondered if Grace, too, was sick.

She was lying beneath the bedroom window, her paws twitching, her eyes rolled back leaving white crescents below her half-closed lids. He tried to forget how he had dragged her back home after their brief outing.

Of course, animals didn't hold grudges. They forgave, or forgot, your displays of bad temper. Yet they must have some form of recollection, a residue of alarm that shaped their sense of the world around them. Grace would have been as exuberant as the black dog circling the tree if her puppyhood had been different. She pranced and cried when John came home from work, but wasn't that simply relief? My God! What did she do in the apartment all day long, her bladder tightening as the hours accumulated, hearing, without understanding, the din of the city beyond the windows?

John felt better toward dusk, after waking from a nap. He determined to take Grace to a veterinarian. He ought to have done so long ago. In the telephone directory, he found a vet listed in the West Eighties, a few blocks from his apartment house.

The next morning he called his office to say that he wouldn't be in until after lunch; he had to go to the doctor. Did the secretary sense an ambiguity in his voice when he mentioned a doctor? She didn't know that he had a dog. No one in the office knew.

Yet was it possible that his evasions, his lies, were transparent to others? And they chose not to see through them because the truth might be so much more burdensome?

He recognized that people thought him an oddball at best. His friends warned him that, at worst, he would dry up, he was so wanting in emotion. But he considered most of them to be sentimentalists, worshiping sensations that they called feelings.

"You have a transient sensation. At once you convert it into a conviction," he said to a woman sitting beside him at a dinner party. The hostess heard him, sprang to her feet, grabbed the salad bowl, with its remaining contents, and emptied it onto his head. He was dismayed, but he managed to laugh along with the other guests, who helped to pick leaves of lettuce and strips of carrot and radish from his collar and neck.

For the rest of the evening, desolation wrapped itself around him like a mantle. Everyone, including himself, was wrong. Somehow he knew he was alive. Life was an impenetrable mystery cloaked in babble. He couldn't get the olive-oil stains out of his shirt and had to throw it out.

In the vet's waiting room, Grace sat close to John's feet, her ears rising and falling at the cries of a cat in a carrier. The cat's owner tapped the carrier with an index finger and smiled at John. "Sorry about the noise," she said. "We all get scared in the doctor's office."

She may have been right, but he shied away from her all-encompassing "we." He smiled minimally and picked up a copy of *Time* magazine from a table.

When the receptionist told him to go to Room One, Grace balked. He picked her up and carried her, turning away from the cat owner's sympathetic gaze. He placed Grace on a metal examination table in the middle of a bare cubicle. A cat howled in another room.

As the doctor entered, his lab coat emanating the grim, arid smell of disinfectant, he nodded to John and looked at Grace. She had flattened herself against the table; her head was between her paws. The doctor's pink hands moved Grace's envelope of fur and skin back and forth over her bones as he murmured, "Good girl, good dog."

He took her temperature, examined her teeth, and poked at her belly. With each procedure, Grace grew more inert. "Distemper shots?" the doctor asked. John shook his head mutely. The doctor asked him more questions, but John couldn't answer most of them. Finally John explained that he'd found her in an animal shelter. The doctor frowned. "Those places weren't great even before the city cut funding for them," he said. John nodded as though in agreement, but it was all news to him. What he'd known about dogs was that they could get rabies and had to be walked at least twice a day.

The doctor said that Grace had a bit of fever. It would be best to leave her overnight for observation. John could pick her up in the morning on Saturday.

John went to his office. People remarked on his paleness and asked him what the doctor had said. "I had a fever yesterday. Probably a touch of flu," he replied. After his words they kept their distance. A secretary placed a bottle of vitamin C tablets on his desk, averting her face as she told him they were ammunition in the war against colds.

"I have leprosy," John said.

She giggled and backed away from his desk. She doesn't know what leprosy is, he guessed, or senses that it's vaguely un-American.

He kept to his section of the office the rest of the day. He was gratified that his colleagues had him pegged as a bit crazy. He had no desire to dislodge the peg. It made it easier. Thinking about that now, as he drank his third carton of tea, he didn't know what the it was that was made easier.

After work, with no special reason to go home, he stopped at a bar on Columbus Avenue. He ordered a double whiskey. As he drank it, his brain seemed to rise in his skull, leaving a space that filled up with serene emptiness. He ordered a repeat, wanting to sustain the feeling, which recalled to him the moments that followed lovemaking, almost a pause of being. But as he lifted his glass, he became cautious at the thought of four whiskeys on an empty stomach, and asked a passing waiter for a steak, medium. He took his drink to a booth.

The steak, when it came, was leathery, and it reminded him of the gloves he wore when he played with Grace. At this very moment she was in a cage in the dark, bewildered but stoical. Long-suffering was more like it, poor thing, carried along on the current of existence. No wonder she suddenly got up and went to another room to lie down. It wasn't thought that roused her, only a need for a small movement of freedom inside of fate. Why, after all, had he stopped in this awful, shadowy bar?

He had a few friends, most of them cocooned in partial domesticity, living with someone or seeing someone steadily. His oldest friend was married, the father of a child. Occasionally someone would introduce him to a woman in an attempt at matchmaking, feebly disguised as a dinner party.

One showed no interest in him, but another had taken him aside and asked him why he had lent himself to what was, basically, a slave auction. His impulse was to remark that no one had bid for her. Instead he asked why she had agreed to meet him. She replied that she had a sociological interest in the lifestyles of male loners in New York. He observed that life, like death, was not a style. She called him a dinosaur.

The only woman over the years for whom he had felt even a shred of interest was the mother of his friend's child. When he recognized the interest, stirred once more to life after he stopped seeing the kitty-cat girl, a sequence of scenes ran through his mind like a movie: betrayal, discovery, family disruption, himself a stepfather, late child-support checks. She was steadfast and not especially drawn to him.

There had been a time when he took the kitty-cat girl out for social evenings with his friends. Their enthusiasm for her was tinged by hysteria, he noted, as though he'd been transformed from a lone wolf to a compliant sheep. Walking away from a friend's apartment where they had spent an evening, he felt like a figure in a heroic illustration: a woman-saved prodigal son.

Now he was down to a sick dog. An apartment filled with unattractive furniture awaited him. But Grace would not be there.

He was dizzy after downing such a quantity of whiskey. His fork slid from his hand to fall beneath the table. He didn't bother to search for it but continued to sit motionless in the booth, most of the steak uneaten on the plate.

It might be only the strange weakness that had come over him like a swoon, but he imagined he could feel his bodily canals drying up, his eyes dimming, the roots of his hair drying with tiny explosions like milkweed pods pressed between two fingers.

His resounding No to the kitty-cat girl, from months ago, echoed in his ears. What had prevented him from saying yes? She might have laughed and embraced him. By that magic of affection that can convert embarrassment into merriment, they might have averted all that followed. Instead she had turned away and, he thought, gone to sleep, leaving him in an agitated wakefulness in which his resentment at her fatuity kept at bay, he knew now, a harsh judgment on his own nature.

She was, after all, a very nice woman: kind, generous, full hearted. What did it matter that in bending to someone's pet or a friend's small child she assumed a high, squeaky voice, that she held her hand over her heart when she was moved, that she struck actressy poses when she showed him a new outfit or hairstyle? What had it mattered? Body to body—what did it all really matter?

He sighed and bent to retrieve the fork. In the darkness beneath the table he found a whole cigarette lying among the damp pickle ends and crumpled napkins. *Smoke it*, he told himself as he felt the strength returning to his arms and hands. Smoking was the one thing that aroused the kitty-cat girl to anger. He'd been startled by it, so much so that he'd given up the pleasure of an infrequent cigarette after dinner in the evening. "Don't make it a religion," he'd chided her. "It's only one of a thousand things that kill people."

He summoned a waiter and asked him for a match. While he was speaking, he heard a voice boom out, ". . . and this will impact the economy." Someone at the bar had turned up the volume on a suspended television set. John glimpsed the speaker on the screen, an elderly man wearing steel-rimmed eyeglasses. "Impact is a noun, you stupid son of a bitch," he muttered, puffing on the cigarette.

"Always correcting my English," she had protested to him more than once. It suddenly came to him that he'd been lying to himself about how the affair had ended. He'd convinced himself that she had left his apart-ment, angrily, the morning after their quarrel about "kitty-cat." In fact it had taken a week, during which they met at the end of the day in his or her apartment, ate together, went to a movie, slept in bed side by side. They had not made love. When they spoke, it was of mundane matters, and when they parted in the morning, he to his office and she to the pri-vate school where she taught first grade, she had briefly pressed her cheek against his. Life has its rhythms, he told himself.

But at the end of the week, after staring down at the light supper he'd prepared, she burst out at him in words that suggested a continuation of an angry interior monologue, "—and it's not only the way I talk. You're trying to change the way I am!" She paused, then shouted, "Why don't you say anything you really mean? My God! You wouldn't acknowledge the Eiffel Tower if it fell right on you!"

He had laughed, startled at such an extravagant image. "I'd be speech-less then, all right," he'd said. But he admitted he'd been clumsy.

She asked then, as she wept, how he could have said No to her so savagely. Afterward, when she was dying inside, he'd walked around the apartment with a foolish smile—as though nothing had happened between them.

She picked up her purse from the chair where she'd been sitting, not eating while he ate and kept on talking cheerfully.

"You're one big NO!" she burst out. "And you're smiling this instant. . . ."

He recalled touching his face. What she'd said was true. "I don't mean to smile," he'd said. She got up and dropped her key on a kitchen counter and left the apartment.

He'd eaten her untouched supper, his mind like an empty pail. Then he'd waited for her to telephone him. He'd waited for himself to telephone her. But something had gone out of him. He had slumped into a mulelike opposition to her: she skirted life's real troubles, chirping platitudes.

He dropped the cigarette the waiter had lit for him, got to his feet, and hurried from the bar. Behind him came the waiter. John paid his bill on the sidewalk, all too aware of the stares of the public.

I will not think about her, he ordered himself as he walked home. I have cleared the decks. I'm better off.

As he unlocked the door, he called, "Grace!" Then he remembered. "Oh, Christ . . ." he said aloud.

He took a long hot shower, emerging slack-limbed and unpleasantly warm. Naked, he walked through the rooms, letting the air dry him, waving his arms, a heavy object trying to fly.

He paused before the bedroom window that looked out on Central Park. Perhaps the comradely woman out for a run, who had remarked on Grace's tits, would look up and observe to a friend, "See the cock hanging up there in the window?" But he was on the seventh floor, invisible to everything but passing birds.

He put on a ragged T-shirt and turned on the television set. As a rule he watched opera, a Friday-evening news program, and now and then an old movie. Tonight he would settle for diversion. He was finding it hard to keep his mind off the way he'd left the bar without paying his check.

A news anchor was saying, "The crisis centers around . . ." He switched channels and turned up a psychologist with devilish red hair and a sharp jaw who was discussing role models and sharing. "We must share," she asserted in a tone John found menacing. "Share what?" he asked the screen. "Give me a noun or give me death. And isn't 'role model' a tautology?"

On another channel a middle-aged actress declared that after years of substance abuse—"yeah, cocaine, the whole megillah"—and loveless promiscuity, she had become a sexually mature woman, in charge of her body and her life. The male interviewer smiled and nodded without pause.

On a call-in interview, a very large Arab emir was addressed as Abdul by a caller who then asked him, "How ya doin'?" The emir's expression of stolid indifference didn't change, but he appeared to send out a glow like a hot coal.

John switched channels more quickly. In every mouth that spoke from the screen, that word, "hopefully," ownerless, modifying nothing, inserted itself amid sentences like the white synthetic packing material that protected china or glasses.

The telephone rang. Startled—no one called at this time of evening—he picked it up, and a buoyant male voice asked, "John?"

The voice was not familiar. Perhaps he'd forgotten its owner; he wasn't good with voices. "Yes," he answered. He discovered at once that it was a selling call. "Do you know me?" John asked. The voice chuckled. "Well, no, John. I don't," it replied. John hung up.

It was nearly midnight when he turned off the set and went to bed. On a nearby table lay a volume of short stories by a British writer. In one of them, the writer had stated: "You can't help having the diseases of your time."

He thought of the letters to the newspaper he'd thrown away. Why had he bothered? The apocalypse would not be brought about by debased language, would it? "I've been cracked in the head, Grace," he said to the absent dog.

His body, his brain, began a slow descent into the formless stuff of sleep. His hands fluttered at the light switch until, with what felt like his last particle of energy, he pressed it off.

At once his heart began to pound. His eyelids flew open, and he was fully awake, recalling the kitty-cat's account of her only brother's death. It had happened several months before he met her. Her brother was visiting her from the Midwest. While shaving one morning in her bathroom, he toppled over, dead from a heart attack. He had been twenty-eight.

She'd telephoned the news to their mother in Norman, Oklahoma. Their father had died of the same ailment several years earlier.

"Oh, Lord—where will we get the money to fly him home and bury him?" were her mother's first words, she'd told John.

He had expressed indignation at such petty concerns in a woman whose son had died.

"You don't understand," she had cried. "She was putting something in front of her grief—like you bar a door against a burglar. And money isn't petty when there's so little of it!"

She had been right and wrong, as he had been. But he could hardly have pursued the subject while her cheeks were covered with tears.

He turned the light back on and picked up the book of short stories, opening it at random. He read several sentences. Unable to make sense of them, he dropped the book on the table. The phone rang. He grabbed it, aware that he was breathless with hope it would be the girl. "Hello, hello?" he pleaded. A muffled voice at the other end asked, "Manuel?"

The next morning he returned to the vet's office. The waiting room was crowded with animals and their owners. Dogs panted or moved restlessly or whimpered. A brilliant-eyed cat sat on a man's lap, one of its ears nearly severed from its bloodied head.

To John's relief, the receptionist sent him at once to an examining room. The doctor was waiting for him with a grave expression on his face.

"I'm sorry to inform you that"—he turned to glance at a card lying on the table—"Grace has passed away."

John was astonished to hear himself groan aloud. The doctor gripped his arm. "Steady! Relationships with pets are deeply meaningful," he said softly. "You shouldn't blame yourself. Grace was a casebook of diseases. But it was the heartworm that finished her off."

"Heartworm!" cried John.

"It's carried by mosquitoes," the doctor replied. He relinquished John's arm.

"She didn't seem that sick," John said dully, leaning against the examining table.

"She was," the doctor stated brusquely. "And please don't lean against the table or it'll give way. Let me advise a grieving period, after which, hopefully, you'll move on. Get a new pet. Plenty of them need homes." He nodded at the door.

John held up a hand. "Wait! Had she littered?"

The doctor frowned momentarily. "Yes, I believe she had."

"What do you do with the bodies?" John asked at the door.

"We have a disposal method in place. You'll be notified," the doctor answered, taking a bottle of pink liquid from a shelf and shaking it.

On the sidewalk, John stood still, trying to compose himself. He felt a jab of pain over his navel. He loosened his belt, and the pain ceased. He had been eating stupidly of late and had certainly gained weight. He set off for his apartment.

The ceiling paint in the living room was flaking. Really he ought to do something about it. He took a dust mop from a closet and passed it over the floor. The dust collected in feathery little piles, which he gathered up on a piece of cardboard.

Had any of Grace's puppies survived? For a few minutes, he rearranged furniture. He discovered a knucklebone beneath an upholstered chair, where Grace must have stored it. A question formed in his mind as he stooped to pick it up. Was it only her past that had made her afraid? Her puppies lost, cars bearing down on her, endless searching for food, the worm in her heart doing its deadly work. He stared at the bone, scored with her teeth marks.

As if suddenly impelled by a violent push, he went to the telephone. In a notebook written down amid book titles, opera notices, and train schedules to Boston was a list of phone numbers. He had crossed out kitty-cat's name but not her phone number. Still clutching Grace's bone, he dialed it.

On the fifth ring, she answered.

"Hello, Jean," he said.

He heard her gasp. "So. It's you," she said.

"It's me," he agreed.

"And what do you want?" She was breathing rapidly.

"I'd like to see you."

"What for?"

"Jean. I know how bad it was, the way I spoke to you."

"You were so—contemptuous!"

"I know. I had no right—"

She broke in. "No one has."

They fell silent at the same moment. Her breathing had slowed down.

"I haven't just been hanging around, you know," she said defiantly.

"I only want to speak to you."

"You want! You have to think about what other people want once a year!"

"Jean, please . . ." He dropped the bone on the table.

In a suddenly impetuous rush, she said, "It was so silly what I asked you! I'll never forget it. I can't even bear describing it to myself—what happened. All I feel is my own humiliation."

"We are born into the world and anything can happen," he said.

"What?"

"Listen. I had a dog. Grace. She got sick. Last night she died at the animal hospital. I guess I wanted to tell someone."

"I don't know what I'm supposed to do with that news," she said. "But I'm really sorry." She paused, then went on. "Poor thing," she said gently, as if speaking to someone standing beside her.

Something painful and thrilling tore at his throat. He held his breath, but still a sob burst from him. Despite its volume, he heard her say, "John? Are you all right?"

"Yes, yes . . . I don't know."

"Oh, John, I can come over this minute. I've been running, but I can change clothes in a jiffy. I don't feel you're all right."

The few tears had already dried on his cheeks. They stood in their apartments, hanging on to their telephones, trying to make up their minds if they really wanted to see each other again.

Liza Ward

Snowbound

from *The Georgia Review*

THE EVENING my mother left, the newscasters were talking about two high-wire circus performers who had plummeted to their deaths, and the storm. Snow was falling heavily all over the Midwest. Travel advisories were in effect.

My father took his feet off the ottoman and set his drink on the end table beside my grandmother's collection of ceramic frogs. He leaned forward, his arms on his knees as we studied the laced pattern of snowflakes on the television screen decorating our section of the map. He got up, went to the window, and put his hands in his pockets. "What time did she leave?" He checked his watch.

"I don't know," I said.

My father was convinced my mother had gone on vacation, to visit "somebody-or-other" Reynolds in Kansas City, one of those panty-raid girls. But just that afternoon I'd found a telephone number with a strange area code tucked in the box beside her engagement ring. I knew my mother had secrets, and one of them was that she didn't plan on coming back.

My father stared out at Van Dorn as if the hooded glaze of streetlights might tell him something. "Well, they didn't mention a storm in Missouri," he sighed.

"But the snowflakes were covering it." I could tell he was worried, and I wanted to show him I was worried too. I took a ruler off the letter desk, opened the French doors, and stepped into the blue glow of the garden. The patio was covered in snow, the table and chairs draped in sheets like a room closed up to keep out the dust. I turned my face upward, feeling the flakes burn my cheeks. It looked as if the sky ended right there above me, over our house. Perhaps it was only my father and I stuck in this white frozen world while everything else stirred with life.

I pressed the ruler into the snow to test how many inches had fallen. When I was a little girl in Chicago, there had been a blizzard the day after my parents' annual New Year's party. Some of the guests who had passed out in the spare rooms or on couches were trapped, and my mother was making them mimosas. My father and I had closed ourselves in the library to watch the snow. He had pretended to pull a quarter out of my ear, and I had screamed, thinking everything inside me had turned to silver. "Things could be worse," he'd said. "Some people only produce pennies," which had made me even more upset. I remember his face looking worried as he sat me down and showed me how he'd done the trick. Then we put on our boots and ventured outside, and my father had plunged a yardstick into the snow. We walked through the hushed city streets hand in hand, making guesses about how much new snow was falling.

"Three inches, Daddy," I said, stepping back into the living room and closing the door behind me. "Do you think she's all right?"

"Of course. She's probably already in Kansas City." My father turned off the television and sat back down. "I've been thinking." He drummed his finger on the side of his head. "About getting a new couch. She'd like that, don't you think?"

I shrugged my shoulders.

"Oh, yes," he said, slapping his hand across his thigh. "She definitely would." Then my father lay down, put one of the old couch cushions over his face, and sighed into the crease of it.

"What are you doing?" I said.

My father didn't answer.

I went up to my parents' bedroom and wandered through the dark, running my fingers over the bedspread, the nightstand, the cool glass surface of my mother's vanity table. In the mirror, my faced glowed blue with snow light. I imagined my blond hair turning into icicles, my lips sickly blue, and my mother floating beneath the surface of a frozen pond in a far-off place. I went over to the jewelry box and took out the number.

I moved the telephone off the nightstand and threaded the cord into my mother's dressing room. I turned on the light, closed the door, and crouched in the plastic curtain of my mother's bagged dresses.

I let it ring for a long time.

"Hello?" he said, finally.

"Hello." My hands were shaking. "Listen, you don't know me but— I'm calling to see if my mother's there."

"Well, that all depends on who your mother is," he said slowly, and laughed as if it were some sort of joke.

"Ann Peyton Hurst."

There was a pause on the other end of the line as if the phone had gone dead. I brushed a bit of plastic off my face and cinched forward on my knees. "Hello?" I said.

"How did you get this number?"

"I found it."

"Who *is* this?"

"This is her daughter; who's this?"

"Nils Ivers," he said. "Maybe you haven't heard of me. Your mother was an Ivers once. For about two weeks."

"I really need to get in touch with her," I said. "There's a blizzard."

"Well, there isn't any snow *here*." He paused. "Is she leaving someone else now?"

I didn't say anything.

"Where are *you*?" he said.

I didn't answer for a second. Then I told him.

"Well, you're on the line with LA, sugar. This is a long-distance call."

"That doesn't matter," I said suddenly. "We're rolling in money."

"Sounds nice. How old are you?"

I paused. Fourteen was too young. "Seventeen."

"I bet you're beautiful."

"Everyone says so." I felt like my mouth was moving without my mind telling it what to say.

"I bet you look just like her."

"I do," I lied. "People can't believe it." It was the strangest feeling I had, like being a puppet, with someone else pulling the strings.

"You sound like quite a sparkler. A real Roman candle. Have you ever thought about the movies? I always thought your mother should be in the movies."

"Sometimes," I said. "But I'm more interested in other things."

"Like what?"

"Horses and stuff. I can't talk anymore. I have to go," I said.

"What's the rush? Is it a betrayal?"

"I'm tying up the line."

"Ahhh," he said. "I get it. There's a guy, right? He give you his jacket?"

"He told me he'd call," I said. "I have to go."

"Wait," he said quickly. "People thought I didn't love her. They were wrong about me. I did love her."

I hung up the phone.

I leaned my head back against the wall and the beaded hems of dresses stirred inside bags as hangers knocked on the rack. My heart was thumping so hard I thought it might break my chest, and beat its way across the floor. My skin electrified my mind in strange directions, confusing *wanting* with *not wanting*. I saw my mother's Studebaker half-buried in a snowdrift on the side of the highway, the paint catching police lights like the gold wings of an angel. I pressed my face into the folds of a long black evening gown, and breathed deeply. I smelled plastic and, beneath it, my mother's spiced perfume.

More than a foot of snow fell during the night, and the following day it kept on coming. Shapes in the garden dulled, then changed, leaving alien imprints on living room walls like the last sigh of a sinking ship.

The morning *Star* didn't arrive until evening. The people of Lincoln wondered what was happening, though there wasn't anything to wonder about. Time had stopped. My father worked in his study with the door shut, and I couldn't imagine what he was doing. It didn't seem like anyone could possibly be working anywhere else in the world. I put on my boots and forced my way down the drive. The snow was almost up to my knees. It was hard to find my feet. You couldn't make out the stumps of the elms anymore. The tops of the rhododendrons swelled like bubbles trapped on a frozen surface. When I opened the mailbox, the metal door creaked with cold. Snow tumbled off the top, a tiny avalanche—*nothing inside*. I watched the lights of a plow round the corner with the steadiness of a tank coming to rescue Lincoln from an invading army. *Bring provisions*, the neighbors wanted to scream, but no one had a voice. The world wouldn't listen. Everyone had lost someone, and they were going to keep on losing for the rest of time.

I imagined my mother to be the stuff of legends, torn from the arms of her true love, keeping Nils's telephone number for years like a secret treasure inside the box of the ring he had once given her. I imagined that my mother's first marriage had never been annulled, that she had never actually been married to my father at all, that I had been born out of wedlock, and it was therefore no wonder I found myself so alone in the world. *The planets are not aligned*, the fortune-tellers had declared on the day of my birth.

Stories were easier to imagine in a snowstorm. History was that much closer with the present so muffled, and it didn't really matter what was true and what wasn't when it was just one mind thinking alone. I wrote this down on a pad of paper and read it over and over to myself. It made me feel brilliant. I became so excited by what I'd written I wanted to scream it from the rooftops. Instead, I lurked outside my father's study door until he finally opened it.

"You startled me!" he said. I shoved the paper at him without explanation. He held it out at a distance and squinted down at my writing because he wasn't wearing his reading glasses. "It doesn't really matter . . . what's true and what isn't true," my father read slowly, "when it's just one mind thinking about something alone." He seemed to consider this for a moment. Then he nodded his head and raised his eyebrows. "Where did you get that idea?"

"From my head," I said.

"I'm impressed, Susan. That's intelligent." He handed it back to me. "You've got a point. I don't agree with it though."

"Why?"

"Because I believe in fact. A fact is a fact. I'm a rational thinker," he said. "Drives your mother crazy."

I hoped he wasn't going to start talking about her.

"So, I've got a question for you," he said instead. "If a tree falls in the woods and there's no one there to hear, does it make a sound?"

I considered this a moment. "No," I said, finally.

"Whereas, I say yes. Most definitely, yes. A sound makes a sound regardless. This is a very important point of dissension between us," he said, holding me away from him. "I hope in spite of all this we can agree on something for lunch."

I put my arms around his waist and gave him a sideways hug. "There isn't any choice," I said. "We're like people in the war."

My father ruffled my hair the way he had when I was a little girl. I hoped the snow would go on falling forever.

We ate what we could find in the cupboards, canned foods collecting dust on the shelves left over from the days when my grandfather had been alive. I imagined stories trapped inside cans for years, denting the metal with angry little shouts, and the need to be heard. When the lids were opened, swollen metal sighed with relief.

My father and I ate peaches with forks right out of the can. "It's funny," he said in between bites. "I was just remembering that time my sister Portia tried to bury herself in the yard, and then yelled for someone to come and dig her out. I'd entirely forgotten until now."

"Why did she try to bury herself?" I asked.

"It had to do with a story our mother told us about our grandparents," my father said. "There was a terrible blizzard in McCook. Your great-grandparents Elsa and Hans were recently married and had just come from Sweden. They barely knew anyone in Nebraska, and they barely knew each other."

"Why did they get married if they barely knew each other?"

"Oh, I don't know, it was different then." My father frowned. "Marriage wasn't always about love."

"Was it about love with Elsa and Hans?"

"Not at first. Feet and feet of snow fell, trapping them inside with no food for days, and nothing to keep them warm. My mother always said that by being snowbound, they were forced to endure an entire lifetime in one week. And only then did they fall in love. She always said it was love that kept them alive. Neither could bear to watch the other die. So they lived—for a long time, anyway."

"How did they keep each other alive with love?" I wanted to know.

My father shrugged. "Oh, I don't know, it's just a story."

My grandmother liked to tell that story, my father said, in an effort to point out the positive. Though families without heat were freezing, good men who had lost jobs lined up downtown in the hopes of laying their hands on a government shovel. My grandfather had always paid my father to dig out the driveway, but now he hired men, the first three strangers who came to the back door wearing ragged coats and desperate faces.

When Aunt Portia first heard about Elsa and Hans, she went directly to her room and cut the hair off all her dolls. Then she took off the clothes and examined the plastic bodies, turning them over and over in her hands, looking between legs at nothing, tapping hollow chests, pulling arms and legs so the elastic ligaments snapped.

My father found her standing beside a pile of mutilated dolls examining her auburn braids suspiciously in the mirror, as if she meant to cut them next. "What did you do that for?" my father said, picking up a bald glassy-eyed doll, and dropping it back on the pile.

"I cut off the hair," she said bitterly. "They are what they are now, and they're not real. I'm done with dolls. I'm done with games. Somebody loves me, and I'm running away with him."

"Nobody loves ten-year-olds," my father said.

Aunt Portia marched downstairs and put on her coat and hat and slid the mittens my grandmother had knitted over her freckled little hands. She opened the French doors and stepped out into the snowy garden. My father tracked her around the side of the house, and watched her secretly from the cover of darkness. Portia dug a hole in the snow with her hands, lay down in the shallow grave, and covered herself as best she could. She had positioned herself outside the study, and through the window she could see my grandmother knitting sweaters for the Johannsons who had lost their farm in the dust storms. My grandfather put down his book and lit a cigarette, then went to the window. He couldn't see Portia because of the reflection, but Portia didn't understand this, and when she called for help, he couldn't hear her either. "Save me," Portia screamed. My grandfather peered out at the darkness for a moment, and then went back to his chair. "Help," Portia said, and then she started crying. My father paused before making his presence known. He was thirteen. He didn't want to seem like he cared too much.

"Save me," she sniffed.

"Stand up," he said.

"I'm stuck, Thatcher."

"You're not stuck, Portia," my father said, but he crouched down and cleared the snow off her anyway. He offered Portia his hand and pulled her up, and tried to shake the snow out of her coat.

"I killed my dolls," she said. "I want them back."

"They're not real. Remember?"

"I killed a promise."

"You're crazy," my father said, taking her hand in his and dragging her back around the side of the house.

"I promised myself I'd give them to Katharine Johannson," she said. "Now *she* won't even want them." My aunt's teeth were chattering.

"Come on," my father said. "Come inside. I'll make hot chocolate."

But Aunt Portia sat down in the snow against the French doors and refused to move. I pictured my aunt sitting there crying in the same garden, the same snow into which, years later, I'd press the ruler on the night my mother disappeared.

After that they watched Portia carefully, my father told me. She was too serious for a girl her age, easily excitable. She wrote anonymous love letters addressed to no one and left them in places for people to find: *Meet me behind the elm in the garden. I'll be swinging from the branches. I love you _____, I love you_____, I love you.* Was there a suggestion of suicide in those words? Could a ten-year-old even be capable of suicide? My grandparents studied the notes carefully for a clue, but none revealed itself. And then one day, Aunt Portia stopped writing. She got her hair cut short in a bob and waited for love to find her.

"Uncle Freddy was love?" I said.

"There were men before him, but I'm not getting into it," my father said. "She was older than you though. Keep that in mind. You know, your mother found *me*. We were at a party. She turned to me and said, 'Don't you wish you were black?'" My father laughed. "I should have known what I was getting into."

"Was she drunk?" I said.

"Of course not, Susan. Why would you say that?"

"Well, it's kind of a stupid question."

My father shook his head and got up and put the cans in the sink. "It was charming. I thought it was charming." Peach juice had dripped over the table in sticky little trails. The snow had begun to let up.

"So Daddy, why do *you* think Aunt Portia buried herself?" I said.

"I don't know," he said. "Maybe she just wanted to be saved."

"From what?"

"Well, don't we all want that in some way?" my father said.

I wanted to know what it was he wanted to be saved from.

"From humanity, Susan. There's too much brutality and unfairness in the world. People do horrible things to hurt each other."

"Like Starkweather," I said.

"And Hitler. And all the Communists." But we both knew what we were really talking about. Loving my mother scratched you raw, and that rawness only made you want to be more tender.

There was no school for two days, but on the second day, my father went to work, and I was left all alone to wander the house. I took an old album off the bookcase and opened it to a photograph of my father and Aunt Portia standing on either side of the elm tree in the garden. My father looked about my age. His face was smooth without the creases of worrying, and one of his arms snaked around the back of the trunk, the hand reaching out to pull my aunt's long auburn braid. My aunt's eyes were piercing. She stared directly at the camera without smiling, unaware of what her brother was about to do. I could see the future in that shot, the tug of hair, the pulling away the very second after the picture was taken, but I could not see any farther, even though I knew all that had come to pass. The elm looked tall and stately, as if it could never die, and there was no hint of my father's coming back to the very same house to fill his father's shoes, or that my mother would leave him just before a crippling blizzard in November of 1962. There was no hint of plumpness in Aunt Portia's features, or Uncle Freddy, or the three unremarkable children she would bear him. Portia and Thatcher were names that held the promise of Victorian love affairs. What had they dreamed of in their beds at night?

The snow had stopped falling, but the world was still hushed under its spell, and it seemed to me like everything would be frozen forever. The sun flitted in and out behind the clouds. The icy voices of wind rustled in the hedges and icicles dripped from the roof with the rhythm of metronomes. *You're beautiful*, the wind told me. *I love you*, the drops spelled out. It felt like something was about to happen.

I put on an Everly Brothers record and fluttered around the living room wringing my hands. I confused that sensation of waiting with the prickle of love, the anticipation of a first kiss though none was coming. My mind went to a dark unimaginable place where my mother's first husband took my face in his hands and kissed my lips. I couldn't see him, but I knew he was there. He spoke sweet words to me. *You're a real Roman candle.*

I don't know why I wanted to hear that voice again. It was like, if I heard that voice enough, I could actually become the way I wanted to be, which was beautiful, which was seductive, which was a woman loved and desired.

I went into the foyer and sat down at the telephone table, and dialed the number I had committed to memory.

He answered right away.

"Hello," I said. "It's me again, Susan."

"Well, hello, honey," Nils said. "Find your mother yet?"

"No," I said. "That's why I'm calling."

"That hurts. I thought you'd call because you missed me. Do you?"

I wasn't sure *what* I felt. "I don't know. Do you miss *her*?"

I could hear him fumbling around with something, a pot or a dish. "No," Nils sighed.

"Is that because she's with you?"

"No," he said. "You're sharp. You sound like a jealous lover. I kind of like it."

"Why are you home in the middle of the day?" I wanted to know. "Don't you work?"

"What are you, a detective? Why are you home from school?"

"It's a snow day."

"Hmmm," he said. "Can your boyfriend make it to come and visit or are you all alone?"

"He isn't allowed over," I said. "It's against my father's rules."

"I bet you break the rules sometimes, though, don't you? Your mother sure did." Nils laughed.

"You mean when she ran away with you?"

"And other times. Never mind. What's he like, your boyfriend?"

"Well, he's wonderful and strong. He's faced a lot of tragedy, and that's what I've been trying to help him through."

"How do you do that?"

I paused. "He's tough in front of everyone, but when he's with me he whispers all the things he's secretly scared of. I just let him cry it all out," I said. "Sometimes he cries so much my hair gets wet with his tears."

"What color is your hair?"

"Black."

"Like your mother's?"

"Yes."

"What else do you do with your boyfriend to help him through?"

His voice sounded different. Angry somehow, as if he were getting revenge for something, but I was getting revenge for something too. The idea of that revenge made me tingle. "We take walks," I said.

"That can't be it," Nils said. "Boys want more than walks. It's why they waste time taking walks to begin with."

I didn't know what to say anymore, so I just sat there with the receiver to my ear, my heart thudding against my ribs. The line was still as a held breath. I imagined Nils reading my silence in ways I was too shy to actually speak of. A line had been crossed. Was it possible to fall in love this way?

"Anybody there?" he said softly, as if he was afraid of waking me up.

I gave him a sign that was more of a sound than a word.

He spoke in that same hushed voice, like he was trying to imagine or remember a particular moment. "Tell me, did he take your virginity, Susan?"

I hung up the phone.

The walls seemed to close in around me and squeeze my lungs like a fist. The curtains rustled, and to me, they were souls of my grandparents who had died in our house whispering, *You shook the tree.* And for the first time I wasn't happy to think of people coming back after they were dead, because they probably wouldn't be happy with what they saw in me.

All at once, Nils was right there inside me, seeing the things I saw, feeling what I felt, twisting it all around. He could move through wires and tangle up my heart. There wasn't any space between Los Angeles and Lincoln, Nebraska. Distance came together at a broken stoplight, and time, my mother and I, and Nils were all crashing into each other head-on. I had caused the accident, the crossing of paths, and *Bang!* The Forty-fifth Parallel disappeared.

The ring of the telephone broke the stillness. My heart flipped over. It jangled my nerves. I bit my fist. It rang, and rang. Three, four times. I got up and went into the living room and covered my ears with the couch cushions and mashed my lips up against the arm. It kept on ringing. Nils could do anything. He had lost my mother's money. He had made her crazy. He had done something horrible to her, I knew that now, something unforgivable, and yet she couldn't let herself forget. What had Nils done to her? The telephone went silent. I needed to know.

I went up to my parents' bedroom and took it apart. I emptied out drawers and ran my fingers along the cracks looking for false bottoms containing secret stashes of love letters. I poked my fingers into cold dark holes and pried apart hinges. I took out the insoles in heels and dumped the contents of purses on the dressing room floor. I found nothing. I sat on my knees staring in amazement at the mess I had made. The room looked burglarized. I left it that way, and went downstairs and opened the drawers in the letter desk where my mother kept addresses. I sifted through stacks of postcards from people I had never heard of, but none was from Nils. I took the books off the shelves and shook each one by the binding, but there wasn't any note tucked between the pages, not even in *Wuthering Heights*.

A shaft of sunlight spilled into the living room, and then disappeared behind a cloud, leaving a shimmer of dust in its wake. And when the telephone rang for the second time, it was a sign. I watch my hand pass over the rotary, my fingers wrap around the receiver. The cold line tickled my arm. It was the only thing I could feel. "Hello?" I said.

"Susan?"

"Yeah?"

"It's Cora. Something happened."

The cat was frozen solid, stuck on its hind legs, its claws tangled in the mesh of the Lessings' screen door. A layer of snow had fallen over his black fur, and beneath a white dome piled high like a Klan hood, the green eyes were glassy, opaque with frost.

Cora and I stood on the back steps, staring at the cat in disbelief. "I thought you'd want to see it," she said, wiping tear streaks off her round cheeks. "Toby boomeranged pop-tops at Cinders, so he didn't think it was safe to come home until it was too late. You're the first person I called."

"Thanks," I said, which sounded more insincere than I had wanted it to. I watched my breath float up in the sunlight like a cloud of dust, and then returned my eyes to the cat.

"What do I do with him?" Cora said.

"What about your parents?"

"Poppy's away on business. Mummy's working up in the studio. That means she's in an artistic fugue."

"Is she an artist?"

"Well, Mummy's working in new mediums. She collects feathers and makes sculptures." Cora looked down at the cat again and sniffled into her glove. "It's not like I can bury him. I can't even touch him. Toby won't come out of his room. He's put something against the door so I can't get in."

I stole a glance over my shoulder at the Harringtons' house, where everyone said there had once been a murder. A light was on in an upstairs window, but I couldn't see anyone inside. I imagined a woman removing her jewels, sitting down on her knees in the very spot where the bodies had been found, putting her face in her hands. The snow reminded her of things she had never experienced. The walls held in memories no one had lived to remember, and it all stayed there, sleeping under snow. For some people, quiet was not a good thing. Quiet meant being alone in the worst kind of way.

"I'll touch him," I said. I crouched down on my knees and knocked the dome of snow off the cat's head. I had never touching anything dead before. But I wasn't really touching death, I assured myself. There were my fingers inside a glove, reaching out for ice and snow. "It almost doesn't look real," I said. "It's like wax."

"He's real to me," Cora said. "He's Cinders. He sleeps on my pillow. He was waiting all night in a blizzard for me to let him inside, wondering what he'd done to deserve this. I should have left the door open."

"In a blizzard?" I put my hand on her shoulder because that's what I figured a friend should do. "There wasn't anything you could do. It's your brother's fault for chasing him off."

Her pale eyes narrowed bitterly beneath the edge of a striped knit hat. "I guess," she said.

We decided to build a sepulchre in the snow where the cat could be kept until the earth softened, or until Mr. Lessing came back for his business trip with a better idea. It's what people did in the "hinterland," Cora said, when the ground was too frozen for burial. We fashioned a hut out of snow in the back of the garden beside the stand of trees, with a mouth just wide enough for the cat's body.

I told her my great-grandparents were snowed in without food, that they had survived on the plains of Nebraska against impossible odds by keeping each other warm with their love.

"That sounds made up," Cora said, sitting back in the snow to catch her breath. She'd stopped crying. "Nobody can keep each other warm with love. Unless you mean by doing it."

"That's not what I mean," I said. "I think people in love can keep each other alive just by the power of feeling." I remembered sneaking downstairs when I was twelve, watching my parents dance around the living room in the middle of the night, and how in love they had seemed to me then, like they were holding each other up with love, like they'd crumble without it.

"How do you know?" Cora said.

"Trust me. I know." I pretended to concentrate on fortifying a wall. I thought of Nils in Los Angeles waiting by the telephone. Or maybe he'd get sick of waiting and come after me, drive all the way to Lincoln and do something horrible when he found out I wasn't like my mother.

"Who is he?" Cora said.

"No one you know." A wind sent a fresh storm swirling down from tree limbs. Snowflakes shimmered like crystal in the bright sun, beautiful little pinpricks that made you squint your eyes. I imagined someone, the Harringtons' son maybe, watching me from an upstairs window in the neighboring house. I wondered if it was possible to love someone you had never met.

We got up, and walked back to the house in our own footprints without speaking a word. Together, Cora and I freed the frozen cat from the mesh screen and carried him back through the tunnel of snow to the sepulchre. The legs stuck out like branches. The whiskers were stiff and clear, brittle as burnt sugar. One snapped against my coat when I lifted Cinders. I was afraid of where our hands and breath made prints of warmth. In places we had touched, the layer of ice melted away to reveal wet black fur beneath. We reached the edge of the trees and set the cat down in the snow. "Toby should be doing this," Cora said. Her voice was breaking again.

"Don't worry," I assured her. "We'll make him pay." I liked the sound of those words in my mouth. They were powerful, like Dr. No, or John Wayne in *The Alamo*.

"You'll help me?"

"Sure," I said. "I'm your friend." I picked up the cat again to prove my point, guided it into the chamber, and started packing in the hole without a second thought.

The sun was sinking low behind the trees, casting emaciated shadow trunks in the snow.

"Since we're friends now, I have to tell you something," Cora said. "I don't have any other friends."

"That's okay, I don't either," I said. "My mother's gone. She thinks my father fired the housekeeper without telling her, but that was only an excuse. She's always wanted to leave. Mother didn't even know she was pregnant with me until Daddy saw the bulge when they were jumping through a sprinkler. I think she has a secret lover."

Cora bit the inside of her cheek. "Your parents jump through sprinklers?"

"Not anymore," I said.

Cora gathered a bit of snow off the sepulchre and pressed it to her cheek. When she took her hand away, an angry red splotch stayed behind as if the cold had burned her.

"I'm making a wish," she said. "I wish things were different. I wish I had Cinders—What do you wish?"

"I don't have any wishes." I stared up into the frost-covered branches.

"Everyone has wishes." Cora took off her mitten. She leaned forward and carved *Cinders* in the side of the sepulchre.

"I want someone to love me," I said.

"I thought someone did."

"No. Not really."

"Me too," Cora said. "I want that too."

When I got home, my mother's belongings were still scattered in the foyer. Her brown coat with the fur collar lay draped over the chair, the belt trailing on the rug. Shoes and shirts and wrinkled skirts spilled over the top of the stairs, as if she'd been frantically looking for something when the bomb had struck. One high heel teetered on the edge of a step. Strange shapes fluttered along the walls in spotty sunlight. Everything looked caught, frozen underwater. I was lost, stuck between worlds, diving for treasure in a sunken ship.

"Hello," I called, "hello?" to see if anyone was there. The house was silent.

I went into the living room. Sharp light cut through the French doors like a thousand diamonds, and feeling the urge to let in some air, I swung them open. An icy wind tore through the garden and into the living room. I stepped back as the cold ripped through me. My mother's note cards blew off the letter desk and circled on a sudden gust, before coming to rest on the Oriental rug in the stillness that followed.

I shut the doors and lay down in the scatter of white cards. I thought I could see them cramped with words: *Meet me by the elms—I'll be swinging from the branches.* I closed my eyes. Outside, icicles broke free of gutters, piercing hedges like sparkling arrows. Snow shuddered past living room windows in sudden bursts of flour. Somewhere deep below, the boiler pumped. Knitting needles tapped radiators, and my grandfather's ghost stared out into the night as Hans and Elsa dug through decades of snow.

A terrible blizzard hit McCook, Nebraska, early that first spring. Snow kept on falling for days. Even before kissing like newlyweds were supposed to, Elsa and Hans scurried down the ladder and looked out the window in the hopes that the storm had passed while they'd been asleep. But one day they woke up to find there wasn't any morning. Snow had covered the windows and buried the house almost entirely. In the barn, a calf had died of cold trying to nurse from its mother's frozen udder. An icicle had formed around her tail. But Hans couldn't get to the animals. They had nothing left. Their stomachs groaned with hunger. They drank melted snow for water. Hans and Elsa lay in bed under blankets holding each other, but they never slept. They lost track of time, living by the light of candles and lanterns, waiting for the sod roof Hans had just finished to buckle beneath the weight of snow, freezing them on the bed where they lay, clutching each other like twins foot to forehead in a womb.

Each assumed the other asleep, and thought, "I don't want to die. I don't want to die beside this stranger. I am completely alone." When Elsa peeked at her husband through half-closed lids, she saw a face that was blank with sleep, and knew Hans was dreaming about her hair. After all, it was the only reason he had married her. And when Hans wrapped his arms around his wife and touched a golden strand with the tip of his finger, he felt as if he were touching an impossible emptiness. He had heard somewhere about woman's intuition and wondered how it was that this girl could spend the last moments of her life asleep, never telling him what would happen. It was selfish.

Somewhere in the middle of a day after what seemed like years, a fierce wind shook the hut and a piece of the roof fell in. Hans grabbed Elsa's hair in his fist. "What's going to happen?" he screamed.

"Let go!" she cried, and pushed him away. "How should I know. You're the man. You're supposed to do something."

Hans stared down at the piece of sod. "But what is a man supposed to do?" he said, reaching out for the beacon of her hair again.

Elsa slapped his hand away and climbed down the ladder. Sweeping her fingers over surfaces, she opened and closed drawers in the dark until she felt the cold metal shears. Anger burned her heart with a fire, and she wasn't chilled or hungry anymore. Anger filled her up entirely.

"Don't try to go outside or anything," Hans said, coming down the ladder. "You'll only drown in snow."

"That isn't possible," she said, lifting her arms above and behind her. "You can't drown in snow. You suffocate." Her nightgown spread out like wings, her golden hair caught for a moment in candlelight. Hans saw how long and beautiful it was, surprised by waves every now and then, like sudden rapids in a river. And then he saw the scissors. "Don't be stupid," he said.

"I'm not. I'm being smart." Elsa held out the curtain of her hair.

Hans tried to imagine what his father would have done. His father had been a sergeant. "I am your husband, Elsa," he said. "I command you not to cut your hair."

Elsa brought the shears to her scalp. Golden hair fell in piles. Hans pushed his chest against her nose. Elbows met jaws, met knees, met teeth. Hans grabbed. Elsa bit. Loose hair caught like corn silk in the corners of mouths. Scissors sliced skin. Hans stepped back and pressed the cut with his thumb. Elsa covered her mouth with her hand, and stared at the hair on the floor between them, and a drop of her husband's blood that had fallen. Then Elsa tasted blood in Hans's mouth. The horse bucked, and Hans bit his tongue. She knew what he'd been wondering. How fast had his father ridden, before falling on that field outside Stockholm? Hans's mother claimed he'd gone down fighting, but Hans couldn't make himself believe. He'd found the box beneath the bed with the uniform, the mustard stain, the holes in the back of the coat where the bullets had gone in. Hans was thinking how no one else's father had fallen in battle. It wasn't fair. And then Hans, too, fell. Elsa could smell it: the leather, the sweat, the dung, as rocks in the road rose up to meet him. She felt the pebble bury in his scalp, and found the jagged white scar with his fingers, only they weren't just his fingers, they were his father's fingers, and they were her fingers. "Hans," she said, "I'm sorry I cut you."

"You didn't," Hans said.

"I did."

"Really," he said. "I didn't notice." There was a bump in Elsa's nose he had never noticed, and a dimple where the right cheek met the smooth rise of lips, and in the premature crease in her forehead from too much frowning, he found the first boy Elsa had kissed. He'd lured her behind the crates in her parents' storeroom with stories of spiders having babies. But Elsa knew that spiders did not "have" babies. "They're not babies," she'd said, bending down. "They're not even spiders," and then he'd grabbed her. His lips had been like cardboard: Hans could feel them. His spit like the glue Elsa had used to fix the button eyes on her "Mookey" doll after the dog had bitten them off. Hans could feel that glue, and Elsa's disappointment, the frown when the buttons wouldn't stick. "You should have sewn them on," Hans said.

"I suppose." Elsa pressed a rag to his finger to stop the bleeding. Hans liked the smell of her ear. He liked it so much he couldn't let his breath go. He kept breathing in and in until his face turned blue. "Stop," Elsa said quietly. "I'm afraid you'll die."

"What are you most afraid of?"

"You, Hans."

"Don't be."

"What makes you feel most alone?"

"You, Elsa."

"Not anymore though."

"No. Not anymore."

Elsa touched Hans's jawbone, and Hans ran his fingers through the scruff on Elsa's scalp. The hair was patchy and ragged, but it felt to Hans like a field of wheat. Hans's jaw was smooth in Elsa's hand, like the graceful bones in a wing. Hans traced the outline of ribs beneath Elsa's nightgown. "This one points out in a funny direction," he said.

Elsa found the scar on his scalp. She laughed. "You're losing your hair."

"Come on, Elsa, let me touch it more."

"Hands," Elsa said in English. "I'm going to call you Hands."

Hans and Elsa lay intertwined on the floor like two figures petrified in lava. Their breathing slowed. Crystals formed in the creases of smiles. A pick scraped wood as snow fell away, and each felt the other's heart stir.

Hans and Elsa blinked in confusion and covered their eyes to keep out the sudden light. The men stood in the doorway, holding shovels and lantern, their mouths hanging open like woodpecker holes. Ice had collected in their beards. To Hans and Elsa, it could have been any moment in history. Their rescuers could have been Vikings on a frozen shore, or explorers discovering a secret cave. It could have been the ice age.

The men put their hands over their hearts and cried for joy. "It's been so hard. So many are dead. But you're alive. You're alive!"

"Oh," Hans said, stretching and yawning and peering at the men through half-closed lids. "I forgot."

"Yes," Elsa said, rubbing sleep out of her eyes. "Remember? We were going to die."

Nancy Reisman

Tea

from *Michigan Quarterly Review*

I T WASN'T always the handsome men Lillian wanted: she liked a certain
assurance, a scent, the way ordinary men were transformed by desire.
How beautiful they became, their bodies shimmering, muscular legs stretching, broad backs, and thick arms bending around her, cocks hard in the
dimness of hotel rooms, balls delicate against her thighs. She chose men
who only in private revealed their sweeter natures: all had unforgiving
lives, all wanted forgiveness. Even, it seemed, begged for such a thing, not
simply sex but the transcendence sex might confer, a wild impossible
blessing. Was it delusion, seeing them this way? Imagining her fingers
slipping past a man's ribs, palm cupping his heart. She wanted that and in
certain moments, the men—their faces bathed in yearning—seemed to
want it too. But for all their spur-of-the-moment appearances and near-
desperate fucking and orgasmic proclamations—*I love you Lillian I love
you Lillian Oh Lillian Lillian Oh*—the men quickly vanished, never left
their wives. It was a story she'd heard elsewhere. How it became hers she
did not know.

But one way or another, your life unspools. Lillian saw the ways it
could go. Take her parents, her father oafish and generous and dead; her
mother fish-pale and morose, an ineffectual, complaining woman. Carp
under river ice, nibbling ancient disappointments. The smallest pleasures—
hot bath, tea, orange dusk through the bare elms—dissipated in Lillian's

mother's house. Lillian could, at least, choose her own loneliness: at seventeen she took a tiny flat, a job as a shop clerk.

Years tick. You pass certain men in the street. Some you pull into your body, briefly, always too briefly, singular tastes and scents with you even when you're sure you have forgotten. And then, at a holiday party, a wedding reception, there's the quick peck on the cheek, close enough for you to catch the scent again. A sexual thrill rushes through you: you have to brace against it as the next in line, maybe his wife, maybe his daughter, also kisses your cheek, and other men you have known and their wives look on.

In 1927, the year she turned thirty-five, Lillian was plush. Zaftig. Dark lipstick, flowery perfumes, plunge neckline blue satin and beautiful shoes. In a tiny shop on Main Street, Maxwell's, she sold stationery, fountain pens, account ledgers, dark leather diaries. When Abe Cohen appeared, she made no assumptions: for years he had lived on the outskirts of her thinking. Dull. Handsome. Relentlessly upstanding. A friend of her older brother's, respectable in ways her brother Moshe was not. A family man, which is to say he slaved to bring his wife over from Russia, then kept her pregnant for a decade, his life increasingly obscured by that strange brood of daughters, one pleasure-loving son. There had once been rumors—a romance with a Polish girl before his wife arrived—dusty now, insignificant. He himself insignificant, but for his jewelry store, display cases stocked with opals, rubies, diamond studs, pearls she could pull across her tongue.

"Hello." Abe Cohen smiled, removed his hat, and made a show of examining leather-bound account books and watermarked paper. He sorted through the ivory letter stock and asked, "Would you like tea?" as if in midconversation.

"Pardon?"

He gestured at the street. "Miss Schumacher, would you like a cup of tea?"

His thumb moved across the ivory paper in small deliberate circles. Cultured pearls, she thought, *tea*? He dampened his lips with his tongue, and his gaze was direct, chestnut. She'd forgotten his eyes were chestnut, if she had ever known. Bits of white in his hair now, charcoal overcoat like an unbuttoned pelt and beneath it the three-piece suit. Trim for his age, trim for any age except boy and the thumb circling and circling, and when had he unbuttoned the coat? Fedora in his left hand, deeper charcoal. "May I take you to tea?" A soft grit in his voice—this was what sold jewelry to women, of course, that landscaped baritone, and the three-piece suit with all the buttons suggesting their opposite, a continued unbuttoning, and those thumbed circles on the notepaper saying what he meant by tea.

His wife was ill, she'd heard, *failing*. "That's kind of you," she said. This was the moment to decline, or at least steer their meeting to a public venue, sanctioned commiseration: *How is your wife today? Is she feverish? Walking? Eating? Can she take soup?* Tea and pastry. He had beautiful hands. She wanted to touch his mouth, the point on his lip he reached for with his tongue. "I would like that."

She closed the shop early, aware of him watching her hands as she locked the windowed oak door, pulled on her leather gloves, wrapped her blue scarf around her neck. He stood out on the sidewalk a respectful distance, easily a chaperon sent by her brother. When did she decide? In a shopping bag, she carried a box of notepaper and a box of envelopes. The air smelled of snow, the daylight weak behind pillowing gray clouds. Wind pushed east from the lake. She hesitated. Paper in paper in snow, she thought. Wet scraps. He was pressing his tongue against his upper lip. "Would you mind if I stopped home?" She gestured at the shopping bag.

She didn't pause in the foyer of her building, even when he fell behind her, slowed, presumably readying to wait. He followed her up the stairs to the second floor and her apartment. And she was thinking then of the cold outside and the heat of her apartment, the charcoal coat and the buttons, forgetting already his larger life, almost forgetting the tearoom down the street. *Please come in*, she said, and he removed his overshoes and followed her into the small parlor. A reserved breathiness to him. Lillian touched her palm to his right cheek, and he kissed her hand, and then her mouth. There was no hesitation, only a brief awkwardness in the undressing: her fingers pulling open his shirt buttons. *Oh*, his checked step back, as if he'd always undressed himself. His face bore the near drunk, desperate expression of men who have been fighting desire and given over to it—men who might later soberly admit *I have broken a commandment*—tiresome as that was. Best to see him with this expression, beyond caring. In her bed he entered her and moved slowly and then rapidly, climaxing quickly. He touched her for an hour, then rose and washed and kissed her forehead and left.

Two weeks later he reappeared, plied her with cakes from a Polish bakery, good gin smuggled from Canada, moved his fingers over her face and kissed her on the mouth, all gratitude and lust, before running his hands over her breasts and belly and down between her legs, stroking then entering her: it was staggering and deeply pleasurable, bitter to relinquish.

In the first months, Abe's courtship seemed to her a kind of truth, his attentions and her pleasures contradicting all other absence. *Shana* he called her, beautiful one, and during their hours together she believed him. How easily she could forget all previous courtships, the fickle nature of men and romance, the impermanence of passion, the moment at which unalloyed sweetness begins to change. Abe liked ritual, and in the first months held to the rituals of cake and gin and tenderness, intense sex during which his desire seemed to meet her own. But in the spring Abe came to her restless and unhappy and without gifts. She offered him holiday wine, which he refused. What he wanted was hard and unsparing: he took her from behind, not kissing her, not looking her in the eye. It was something men did. *Oh*, she thought, *this*. She gave over to him and her body seemed a separate thing and she dissolved beneath him. He wanted her to say *yes, I like it*. "Yes, I like it," she said, both lying and in some way meaning it. A strange release when he pinned her down, as if she had reached the end of fear. Her lungs refilled only after he'd left her apartment. He returned the next week with fruit and chocolate, kissed her, caressed her, and did not mention his previous visit.

No one seemed to notice the affair, Abe's biweekly visits to Lillian's apartment, although he was known in her neighborhood. Or perhaps no one would believe it of Abe, who after all was her brother's dear friend, a man suffering the burden and sorrow of his wife's illness. Lillian did not meet him in public or ask for more time. She did not want Rebecca Cohen's life: she wanted Abe as she had found him in her flat that first day, a man shaken loose from the world, immersed in the pleasures and wilder demands of his body and her own. For the first year, the trysts at her apartment were enough. For the first year she did not stop seeing other men.

And then another January. Rebecca Cohen collapsed on a streetcar and was confined to bed. This was the word from Lillian's sister-in-law Bertha, the word in the markets and beauty parlors. A brief note from Abe: my wife is ill. And nothing. Slow ticking days, desire accumulating, a honeyed thickness becoming ever more dense, the surfaces of each day coated with the repeating question *where's Abe where's Abe where's Abe*, which did not stop when she drank or slept. And sleep was instead a drifting, the bed an ice floe, lake winds pushing her further and further into arctic realms. She tried the remedies she knew: bootleg gin, reefer, mechanical sex with other men, *not-Abe*, through which the thrumming persisted, without return or release. There seemed no end to her awareness of him in the world. Downtown, almost daily, she saw walking reminders: his daughters, a small army, everywhere. The sourest one, Jo, now worked in Moshe's law office; the strangest, Celia, wandered the city, regularly stopping at Maxwell's to touch and sometimes steal sheets of paper. The eldest was forever at the druggist buying syrups and pills for her mother; the married, stylish one appeared at dress shops Lillian preferred. Two daughters had his eyes, the others his mouth and brow but favored Rebecca, whom Lillian now thought of only as *her*. This required effort. At the butcher shop, the fruit market, in department stores and tearooms, in beauty parlors, in the post office, on the streetcars, in the lobby of the Hippodrome, women clucked and murmured *poor Rebecca*, and *Rebecca's girls look pinched* (hadn't they always?) and *Rebecca's Abe is so pale, poor Abe*.

By mid-February Lillian was half-eaten with desire and mute grief. What reprieve she found came late at night when the arctic drifting deepened and the night seemed a translucent haze, bits of other winters resurfacing as if new: a burgundy reading chair, air colored by men's voices—her father's, his friends'—boisterous and gravelly sweet, tobacco smoke, hot tea. Peppermints. Her father's tone of hilarity, his off-key singing, his calloused hand resting on the crown of her head. The chair and voices and smoke blurred into a single feeling pulled from that other decade, a feeling as immediate as the streetlight through her bedroom window or her white duvet or the freckles on her forearm. And yet it was intangible, a feeling yoked to empty space.

The hazy merging of *then* and *now* quietly leaked from a night into a morning, and then into a day, and another day, as Abe's absence solidified. On Main Street, Lillian would hear and immediately lose not Abe's baritone but a graveled laugh—perhaps the exact laugh she remembered, or a stranger's, or just a misinterpreted squeal of streetcar brakes. The burgundy chair would swim up at her while she restocked sheets of onionskin, as if it had been there all along, waiting for her, as if it might even restore the tea and tobacco smoke and peppermints, the gravelly voice, the hand on her head, all of what she could and could not name. Say the burgundy chair was waiting for her, say it was *that* chair—would the room and by extension the house it had occupied also wait for Lillian? There was a single Brunswick Boulevard address, a house her father had chosen and paid for, a house her mother inherited and from which Lillian had fled. Yet in her mind there seemed two separate houses, one she wanted to visit and one she did not. Was one hidden inside the other? Throughout the city, snow fell in thick flakes, day after day, and the wind came in off the lake, the air itself blurring, and on these, the blurriest of days, it seemed possible the Brunswick house was still her father's. On a Friday evening Lillian set out through the snow to the two-story wood-frame off Humboldt Parkway, the painted steps and snowdrifted porch and thick brass mezuzah in the doorway convincingly belonging to the house of memory.

Lillian's mother, Isabel, appeared in the doorway in a dark blue dress and glass beads, lipstick brightening her face, but the red mouth shifted between a flat pucker and a frown. She kissed Lillian on the cheek, an unfishy kiss. Lillian tried to decide what parts of her mother to believe: the kiss or the furrowed brow and intermittent frown. And what parts of the house to believe. The kitchen smelled of bread and roast chicken; in the dining room, the linen tablecloth was spread, the table set with her mother's wedding silver and white china and brass candlesticks. But the living room seemed eerie and hard to navigate: three card tables covered with picture puzzles—half an Eiffel Tower, and two scrambled landscapes—occupied the space between the sofas. Porcelain figurines of forest animals crowded the old bookshelf and mantel. And where was the chair? Had there ever been a burgundy chair?

Isabel lit the candles and murmured the Sabbath blessings, and the frown and furrowing vanished. She must have been beautiful, Lillian thought, and it seemed a new thought, though her mother had been called beautiful and still sometimes was. During Isabel's prayer, you could almost see her as someone else, someone gracious. The house as that peppermint house. Then the blessings ended and Isabel's mouth reverted to a carp's and she took the carving knife to the chicken. "Nice you decided to visit, Lillian," she said. "And for Shabbat. Who would have guessed?"

"I wanted to see you," Lillian said, but the sentence came out as a question. The word "you" seemed to wobble.

"So you say. Shabbat shalom," Isabel said. "You need money you go see your brother Moshe."

Lillian felt a sharp prickle in her temples. Already, the beginnings of headache, her beautiful forgetting unraveling. How fast the turn—had it always been this fast? Had the Brunswick house ever been anyone's but Isabel's? In the dining room's flat cool, fishmouthed Isabel slapped potatoes onto wedding plates, and below the aromas of dinner lurked the house's trace scents of ammonia and talc and chicken fat. As always. The absence of deeper voices as always, a bitter, heart-stopping *always*. How could Lillian have thought otherwise? In her belly she felt a sharp pull, an impulse to hit. "I don't need money," she said, and reached for the sweet wine.

"You going to bring me more of that?" Isabel said. "I got that from Rabbi Greenberg."

"Moshe will. I brought you paper from the shop."

"Paper I can buy," Isabel said. "But thank you."

"If you don't want it, Ma, I'll take it with me."

"Did I say thank you? I like the paper. It's good what you bring."

And maybe *good* suggested another opening, slim, evanescent, but still a crack in a door through which Lillian might see through her mother to her father. She waited, ate in silence. The chicken tasted of rosemary and onion and salt, there were roast carrots, and Isabel set out honey for the challah. Poppy cake. Strong tea which Lillian cut with lemon.

"You met someone?" Isabel said.

"No."

"You going to tell me or not?"

"There's nothing to tell."

Isabel sipped at her tea with exaggerated care. "He must be no good."

"Ma, what did I just say?"

"Your brother Moshe, he's a good man. A schemer but a good man. Bertha too, you should take a lesson from her. Stop with the nogoodnik."

Had her father's friends actually visited? Lillian couldn't have made them all up. Couldn't have made him up.

"Lillian? You hear what I'm telling you?"

"What else do you want, Ma?"

"You already got pearls."

"What?"

"You think I don't know you. I know you. You want more pearls, you ask your brother Moshe."

She had not invented Abe Cohen, his hands moving over her, had not invented their coupling: these remained clear. What seemed slippery and opaque was the life he occupied without her. Lillian could only imagine it as a shell around blank air, the reasons for his absence spurious. And so, in the late weeks of winter, Lillian deliberately circled Abe's life, choosing the streetcar stop nearest his store, visiting his favorite bakery, buying from the pharmacy near his house. Twice she borrowed her brother's Packard and drove it up and down Abe's street. House lights on the first floor and often the second, occasional fluttery movements at the windows. Snowdrifts buttressed the side of the house. The front walk was cleanly shoveled. Ice shone on porch rails and shingles. The interior remained impenetrable, a kind of shadow into which she and Abe had disappeared.

She waited until March before visiting the jewelry store. The son, Irving, minded the counter. Beautiful boy, spitting image of his father but still soft, irresolute, except for that glimmer, the same pleasure lust she saw in Abe's private moments. In Irving the lust was more public but more diffuse. "Can I help you, Miss Schumacher?" A light purr in the voice.

No sound from the back room, where Abe set stones, though the door was ajar. She asked to see bracelets, and Irving opened up the case, pulled out a velvet card with four, let her hold them to the light and try them on. For her sister-in-law Bertha, she said. She'd have to confer with her brother, she'd send him over to look. And would Irving please give regards to his family, all best wishes for good health?

Two nights later, Abe returned to Lillian's flat, defeated and sad, his hands redolent of illness. Complied when she asked him, first, to bathe.

One thing Lillian knew: open the door to risk and the room will widen and stretch. The work of caution—automatic at first—becomes over time onerous and boring, another chore in a too-long list of chores. You can't manage it all, defer whatever seems inessential. And this was how she explained Abe's about-face: almost nightly, he visited. Seemed, in fact, oblivious to risk, foggy with exhaustion and despair. He wept when she touched him, wept when she did not. The weeping, she knew, was hidden from his family. Seeing Abe this way—shaken down to boy, neck-deep in bewilderment and sorrow—moved her. But she also preferred him care-less. He'd appear at her flat, late, and collapse on her bed, and after a time they'd make love without speaking. For an hour he might sleep. And though she knew better, some nights she'd meet him on Delaware, a few blocks from his house. Once, at two A.M. Lillian parked the Packard across the street from his house and he slipped out the back door and through the neighboring yard, crossing the snow-crusted lawns to the curb, her borrowed car.

They carried on this way until Rebecca died. During shiva, Lillian joined her brother and his wife when they paid their respects to the family. Red buds studded adjacent trees, crocuses bloomed in the Cohens' front yard, the bright greens of the new grass mixed with the winter browns. For the first time, Lillian entered the house on Lancaster. In the foyer the dark wood shone, wallpaper pattern of spray roses spilling down the hallway and into the parlor. There was a faint scent of cedar and baked sugar and tea, and in the parlor visiting relatives sat quietly with the daughters—the crazy one, the paper thief, Celia, perfectly still and paler than usual, Irving slumped beside her; the married daughter elegant in black, whispering to Abe, her husband standing guard beside them, adjusting his spectacles and surveying the room. The other daughters were ragged and red-eyed, Jo meeting Lillian's condolences with a scouring stare. The pattern of roses dropped behind the upright piano; sheet music lay open, a sonata. Lillian retreated to the hall which led in one direction to the fragrant kitchen, the other to the front staircase, with its fat maple banister and Persian runner, silent invitations to push farther into the house. She passed the formal dining room (more roses) before two synagogue women arrived, arms loaded with platters and casseroles, a jumble of piety and whispers, noo-dles and fish. Lillian stole outside to the empty front porch, away from the windows, and waited for Moshe and Bertha to finish with their sympathy.

Lillian would not have chosen that wallpaper: the clipped pink roses girl-ish, sentimental, falling in dainty lockstep. Still, the papered rooms felt like sugar bowls, and after she left that day the image of the spray roses returned to her. Davenport in dark wood, upholstery the color of biscuits and linen, Abe's reading chair a fine pale green. Upright piano, the scatter of black notes across the white pages of the open score. She pictured the parlor empty of visitors, the davenport clear of Celia and Irving, open, inviting, a place to let the day hush, to gaze up at roses, light patterned by budding trees, lazy piano softening the afternoon. That night, Lillian imagined her own bed as a davenport, lulled herself to sleep with the pretense of thick petals and buttery air and Abe's weight upon her.

That was the beginning of a more deliberate daydream, the trail of roses leading up and back to both glimpsed and unseen rooms: the wide white kitchen, the polished dining room table, and the tall glassed cabinets, company china and Passover dishes, thin-stemmed goblets, heavy brass candlesticks, silver Kiddush cup. And upstairs? The carpeted steps leading to an unlit pocket of space. And to pass through such space? Like passing through night, perhaps. Lillian knew about the windows, stout rectangles facing the street, a round moon of glass above them, smaller windows on the sides. She guessed at the floor plan: front and back stairways, the windows suggesting a division of rooms. In some of the rooms there would be beds, dressing tables, chairs. Cream walls? Some ought to be cream, a base that would hold the light but allow you to add color. And in the master bedroom, there ought to be violet and royal blue bedcovers and chairs, which would suit Abe. She imagined herself and Abe coupling in pale blue sheets, his broad back and thick arms wrapping her, intermittent dark freckles on the white skin, black eyelashes against the blue, and the steady rhythm and near ache of Abe moving inside her. Butterscotch and white for the front guest room, perhaps some fleur-de-lis.

She considered colors for other rooms, tending toward blues and greens, inventing a complete house the shape and size of Abe's house on Lancaster. Downstairs, the rose wallpaper stayed, the piano stayed, the parlor furniture stayed, and at moments the invented house and the real one seemed indistinguishable. In the fantasy house, Abe's children did not appear; presumably they had moved to another invented house, or, better, another city. That could happen, in the mind. The arrangement seemed beyond Lillian's will, as if Abe's house had chosen to occupy her and she could not refuse it. The invented house hummed, waiting to be manifest in the physical world.

You begin, of course, with where you are. Begin with the life you know, begin with sex. Try a simple request, and make the request late at night, after he has climaxed. A Thursday. Lillian and Abe were spooned together in her bed, Abe's hand still on her breast, when Lillian asked, "Shall we go to a restaurant next week?"

Simple and not simple, a meal in a restaurant. Or tea? Wasn't it what he had once proposed? A table, a waiter, a menu. Polite conversation. Nothing, compared to what they'd done. Tea but tea in public and now: a signal of earnest courtship or of scandal. He closed his eyes, sighed. She had seen him respond this way to Celia's incessant *could we will we can I* before he answered no. But to Lillian he said, "I don't know." To Lillian he said, "Perhaps in time."

A week later, she cooked a dinner at her flat. Abe arrived harried and distracted, and she poured him gin, set the table with a blue-bordered cloth, carried out plates. Roast beef and sweet potatoes, glazed carrots, salty bread. Tea and linzertorte. By dessert he was back to the Abe she wanted: alert gaze, body tipped in her direction, his cheeks slightly pink. "Does this feel like home?" she asked, and he answered yes. She stroked the back of his hand. "You don't invite me to your home."

"Oh but Lillian. You know why."

"Good reasons," she said. "Before."

"*This* is our place."

She hesitated. The blue-bordered tablecloth seemed part of a past life, and she thought of that other polished table, and the imagined linens and the glass bowls, a basket of pears. The invented house seemed wholly real and she did not know what this meant. "Not forever," she said. She loosened her fingers from his and rose, cleared the dinner plates and the empty serving platter and the used glassware. Then she offered him chocolate from the box he'd brought, square pieces decorated with waves of green.

"Tell me," Lillian said to her brother, "how a person buys a house."

Moshe had always been a big man, but here at his law office he seemed even larger than usual. An enormous, round-bellied suit, sighing at her. "Lilly, would you like a cigarette?"

She took one from him, allowed him to light it, noted the resemblance of his fingers to the cigar he lit for himself. "A little house?" he said. "Just for you?"

"Maybe that."

"Or maybe you're thinking a bigger house?"

"I think all sorts of things. Let's say any house."

"Are you asking can I buy you a house?"

"No. I want to know how a person buys a house."

"First," Moshe said, "a person needs to have money. Lilly, sweetheart, you do not."

"But if I did?"

Moshe squinted, as if he were adding numbers in his head. Pursed his lips, not unlike a fish. "A very large if. You understand that? You be careful, Lillian."

You cannot rush fate, Lillian told herself, no matter how sure you are of your path. For now, she was in God's hands; she imagined a light touch on the top of her head and refrained from talk of houses. Surprisingly, this seemed to work. In the spring of 1929, Rebecca Cohen's gravestone was unveiled, and two weeks later Abe again asked Lillian to tea. A Wednesday afternoon. They took a table in Jocelyn's tearoom, surrounded by middle-aged women. Abe bought tea and sweet cakes, inquired about her mother's health. Asked about the stationery business, where the paper was shipped from, if the shop owner traveled to New York, as Abe often did. Mentioned that her brother's law firm was growing admirably. Lillian watched his lips as he talked. This was a strange game, Lillian thought, but a pleasant one. She sipped her tea and folded her hands in her lap and spoke about her fondness for, of all things, gardens; she imagined kissing him in the tearoom. After an hour he asked if he might secure a taxicab for her.

Among the gossips there was murmuring the next day, there always would be murmuring about Lillian, despite the legitimacy of the tea with a widower. But Lillian's faith in God seemed justified. She felt a surge of hope: Why shouldn't she be happy? Why shouldn't Abe? On his next visit, he brought flowers to her apartment, and there seemed a new lightness to his mood. Now he wanted to make small but definite plans: tickets to the theater, an afternoon at the Falls. In May he suggested a restaurant dinner with Moshe and Bertha, followed by dessert and coffee at his house.

The evening they went to Little Paris, Lillian wore black silk and pearls, her hair cut that day in shoulder-length waves. Abe brought corsages for Lillian and Bertha. At Moshe's house, they drank illicit champagne, then drove to the restaurant, Bertha carrying Moshe's gin in her handbag. A waiter arrived with savory tarts, then with soup. Four courses. They drank the gin over ice. Through the dinner, Abe joked with Moshe and squeezed Lillian's hand and seemed purely happy; by midevening, Lillian was awash in grand hope. The soft night air seemed a confirmation, and on the drive to Abe's house, she leaned her head out the side window—the elms and maples in full leaf, the breeze pushing her hair from her face, Abe holding her hand, kissing her on the cheek and pulling her back into the car. And when they reached Abe's house it was quiet, the lilacs swaying in the light wind, perfuming the parlor, which was as Lillian envisioned: falling roses, empty davenport, pale green chairs. There was a bakery cake, chocolate, and Bertha brewed tea. In the china cabinet, Lillian found dessert plates: gilt edged, the inner pattern a ring of grapes on the vine, the fruit precise and dense and violet blue.

Would the evening have gone any differently if, instead, she'd taken down the everyday china, left the grapevines dutifully in place, stubborn tribute to the dead? Abe and Moshe lighted cigars and patted each other on the back, and Bertha—round and affectionate and drunk—concerned herself with cake, which she served in thick slices. Lillian sipped the milky tea, savored the chocolate. Abe sat beside her on the davenport, and it seemed that another life was beginning, that grief had fallen away and time had stopped, leaving them forever in this bright soft evening, this parlor, this house. Abe's fingers circled and circled Lillian's palm, sweet measured pressure he might later move to the rest of her body.

If the others sensed the presence of Abe's daughters in the house, they didn't think much of it. Why would they? Moshe and Bertha commonly entertained, their children and housekeeper discreetly migrating to the upper floors. Here on Lancaster, there had been little entertaining for years, but Abe—admittedly flushed with alcohol—seemed completely at ease, affectionate and unworried. It was after all Abe's own house, his parlor, his evening with Lillian and Moshe and Bertha. And the parlor seemed fully the parlor Lillian had imagined.

They were still eating cake when Lillian heard steps on the back stairway, an uneven thudding, the steps approaching from the kitchen through the long hall to the parlor. A muttering. And then in the parlor doorway stood Jo and Celia—Jo in another of her mud-colored dresses, Celia puffy-eyed, her thick hair disheveled. They stared at Lillian, Lillian and Abe, Lillian again. Celia swung her left arm back and forth.

Jo snorted. "You seem pleased," she said to Lillian.

From across the room, Moshe cleared his throat, and Jo registered his presence and placed her hand on Celia's swinging arm. Moshe smiled his expansive, warning smile and gestured at the cake, "Would you girls care for some dessert?"

"Mr. Schumacher," Jo said. "Thank you, no. Hello, Mrs. Schumacher. We'll go upstairs. Celia?"

"Hello." Celia relaxed her arm, then fixed her gaze on the dessert plates, and in that moment the evening tipped. "Those aren't yours."

"No," Lillian said.

"Celia," Abe said.

Bertha, drunk, traced the grape pattern with her index finger. "Beautiful," she said.

And Celia stepped into the parlor, her arm swinging again. "Not yours." She yanked Bertha's plate from her hand, then Lillian's from the table, bits of cake still on them.

Abe, white-faced, standing, lurched toward Celia. "Celia, leave the plates."

But Celia grabbed the other cake-stained plates, tucking them against her dress and retreating to the hall.

"Enough." Abe's voice was louder now and harsh, and Celia unblinking. "Not yours," she repeated, this time to her father.

Moshe licked his lips, a deliberately delicate gesture. Checked his watch, while Bertha glanced out at the swaying coned lilacs.

"You don't tell me," Abe said. "You do not tell me."

And now Celia turned back to Lillian. "You stay away from them."

"Celia, you will apologize," Abe said.

Celia backed up to the staircase, the plates crushed against her, chocolate crumbs falling over the parquet floor. "*You* apologize," she said.

"Jo, take your sister upstairs," Abe said.

Jo crossed her arms over her chest and dropped her voice, "If she wants to go."

Would knowledge have mattered? Lillian did not yet know that Celia only slept in her late mother's sickroom (a second-floor room which faced the street and the tall elms, and from which a familiar Packard could be remarked); that Jo had suffered insomnia since her mother's collapse; that Rebecca Cohen had not been an Isabel. These were things you tried not to know, truths that might starkly appear and pin you down anyway.

Neither Abe nor Jo nor Celia moved. There was the chugging of a car on Lancaster, and Moshe rose, smiling, stretching, as if nothing had transpired in the mood. "What about a nightspot?" he said. Ashed his cigar. "I think we should. Lillian? Bertha, love?" He set a hand on Abe's shoulder. "Abe?"

"What?" Abe said.

"Let's." Moshe ushered the Schumacher women to the front door, nodding to Jo and Celia, "Good evening, ladies." And then Lillian was out on the lawn, stranded it felt, her sister-in-law murmuring *That Celia's a nasty one* and strolling past her to the Packard. The upper reaches of the house were lightless, remote. Lillian's palms were damp with sweat, and the lilac-scented air seemed a strange trick. How does one forestall what has already passed? Lillian counted the windows. The ember of Moshe's cigar marked his progress down the front steps and the walkway, Abe and Celia and Jo now fragmented silhouettes through the open front door. *Lillian?* Moshe's hand a warm weight on her shoulder. *Lilly, come with me.* Cake still sweet in her mouth, thin breeze nosing a sycamore, the Packard sputtering awake. Then the puzzle of silhouettes shifted, lush grass spilling over Lancaster Avenue, her fingers not exactly her own, her body close to dissolving in the fragrant air, and the night sky unspeaking.

Caitlin Macy

Christie

from *The New Yorker*

W HEN YOU met Christie for the first time, it took only minutes to
learn that she was from Greenwich, Connecticut, but months
could go by before you got another solid fact out of her. After a couple of
years in New York, she realized that she had to give people a little more
information to stop them wondering, so once she'd mentioned Greenwich
she would quickly add that she'd gone to "the high school," meaning the
public one. The first time she said this, you'd find her forthrightness
refreshing—disarming, even, in the midst of so many pretenders. You'd be
prompted, perhaps, to admit something about yourself—the fact that you
were doing Jenny Craig, for instance, and had to sneak the packaged food
into your office microwave when no one was paying attention. But then
you'd overhear Christie making the same confession to someone else, and
it would lose its charm. It was just Fact No. 2, which, added to Fact No.
1—her childhood in Greenwich—represented the sum total of what could
be stated about Christie Thorn's background, about her entire life before
college and New York.

Plus, you couldn't help being suspicious of her motives in revealing Fact
No. 2. If, at a party, a group of people were standing around, sharing a corner
of the room, and someone made an opening bid—mentioning Hotchkiss
or St. George's, say—Christie would always pointedly interject, "Oh, I
wouldn't know. I went to public school. Greenwich High. That's right—I

was a good old suburban kid." Of course, Christie and the person who had mentioned boarding school were doing the same thing—preemptively defending themselves against attack—and yet you were tempted to give the Hotchkiss guy a free pass. With him, you could figure that his parents had divorced badly, or his mother was an alcoholic, or his brother had committed suicide (or perhaps it really had been an accidental overdose), or that in keeping with the family tradition Dad had gone crazy and now spent his days in slippers and a robe shooting intricate, archaic forms of pool. On account of one or more of these family problems, the young man felt insecure about himself as an individual, and so, in situations of social challenge, he mentioned boarding school a little too early, and a little unnaturally, to shore up his resolve. Still, whatever his problem, whatever the big bad family secret, it was just the slightly burned edge on a cake that everyone still wanted to eat. How bad could those family problems really be, you'd asked yourself more than once, if, at the same time, you had a house on the Vineyard? How bad—if you had the gray shingles, the weathered shutters, the slanting attic roof, the iron bedstead, the needle-point pillows proclaiming, "A woman's place is on the tennis court!," the *batterie de cuisine* of lobster pots and potato mashers from the forties, and the octagonal kitchen window, through which you could glimpse the dunes and smell the salt air—could anything really be?

Meanwhile, you'd assume that Christie had more to protect, that her history was more embarrassing, somehow: a chronological downsizing of suburban homes (all of them, albeit, technically still in Greenwich), a cheapness in things like bedding and glassware, or four people sharing one bathroom with a stand-up shower. And you wouldn't be wrong. The real story was simple, of course, simple and unnecessarily sad. Christie's father had gone into business for himself and had cash-flow problems. That was all. No one had murdered anyone; there wasn't a whiff of incest or abuse, embezzlement or even tax fraud. Mr. Thorn had owed money his whole life, but he paid his bills more or less on time, and, when he died, his life-insurance policy would pay off the mortgage on the house. He was an honest man with a clean conscience.

Yet Christie's conscience was not clean, and seemed never to have been. In a typical scenario from her adolescence, her father would plan a nice vacation for the family, then wouldn't have enough cash to cover it, Christie would throw a tantrum, and her mother, who spoiled her, would somehow find the money to appease her. Christie would go on the vacation, but she would go alone, with a similarly spoiled friend. She and the friend would go helling around Key West, say, or Miami Beach, feeling worse and worse and worse and laughing harder and harder. And then, and this was the kicker, Christie's mother would pick them up at LaGuardia (the friend's mother could never be bothered) and would want to know— would have been anxious about, primordially concerned about—whether they'd had a good time.

On the way back from one of these vacations when she was sixteen or seventeen, Christie and her friend checked in late and were bumped up to first class. They were separated, and Christie was seated next to a distinguished-looking older man. He drank Scotches and read a golf magazine, and, when the flight was delayed, the two became partners in peevish complaint, the man turning to Christie to include her in his "Can you believe this?" glare. Eventually, he asked her where she was from, and when she said, "Greenwich," he looked at her with a kind of absolute approval that she couldn't recall ever having inspired before. After that, whenever a flight of hers was delayed she'd shake her head and say, "Time to spare, go by air," as the Scotch-drinking man had, and when she met people she liked to make sure that they knew where she was from.

After college, after a prolonged phase of running around New York while drifting through a series of support jobs at big firms, and after she had slept with, I think, either fifty-five or sixty-five men, Christie found someone to marry. We spent a lot of time speculating as to who would be invited to the wedding (only a strange, angry girl named Mary McLean, who had made some Faustian bargain with Christie long before any of us met her, considered herself one of Christie's *real* friends), but in the end everyone was invited—and to the Pierre, no less. Throughout the evening, Christie wore a look of incurable dissatisfaction. Her face was gaudily made up, as if for a school play or an ice-skating competition. At the reception, her parents seemed frightened. It was as if they had been instructed to keep their mouths shut at all costs. A guest would shake Mrs. Thorn's hand in the receiving line and say, "Hi, I'm Jen Ryan. Christie and I were roommates at Trinity?" and Mrs. Thorn would nod, grim-faced, and say—literally—nothing. The groom's name was Thomas Bruewald, and he was gawky and tall, with an oversize head and a unibrow. His parents were never identified. Apparently they were foreign. He had grown up half over here and half over there—in Bavaria, was it? Or Croatia? At any rate, it wasn't Umbria or Aix or anywhere worth trying to lock in an invitation for. Bruewald had gone to one of those Euro institutes with the word "polytechnical" in the name. The champagne at the reception was a little too good, and some people had more than their fill and, by the end of the night, were making rude remarks. One guy said that Christie's parents must have taken out a second mortgage to pay for the wedding. "Didn't know you could get a second mortgage on a trailer," somebody else said. And then, of course, you got "Hey, wait a minute! There are no trailers"—the crowd in unison—"in Greenwich, Connecticut!" But nobody said that the groom was funny-looking. You could pick on Christie for trying too hard, you could note the moment when Mr. Thorn took off his tuxedo jacket and started doing body shots with the bridesmaids, but you didn't pick on the groom's looks. You just didn't go there.

Christie herself was quite pretty. She had large, unflawed features and blond hair that was only a shade or two lighter than her natural color. She was also thin. And, in an age when Manhattan had been overrun by the kind of chain stores you'd find at a suburban mall, these attributes had kept her in dates for a decade and the word "beautiful" had been lobbed over her head with surprising—to some of us, disturbing—frequency.

The groom had some kind of science-related job—engineering or drug research—that required a reverse commute to New Jersey. And, once the wedding was over, once the gifts had been ordered (they had registered for everything but the kitchen sink, in anticipation, evidently, of dinners for sixteen at which oysters would be served and finger bowls required), once the thank-you note from Christie—Christie Bruewald now—had arrived, it seemed that only the sparsest smattering of social interactions was indicated, coffee or a drink twice a year. There was even some thought that the newlyweds would move out of the city. Christie had always talked nonstop about children (little trophies, one presumed, to fill up that bottomless pit of dissatisfaction), and the suburbs had been mentioned more than once.

Christie's new thing, at our biannual meetings, was to brag about her visits to Thomas's family in Europe. It was mystifying—one would not have thought an "in" in the former East Germany particularly brag-worthy, and, in any case, everyone at the wedding had seen how cowed the guy was, how classic the trade they had made. Did she think we didn't see her boasts for what they were? She started to slip into conversation the fact that Thomas's uncle had a title, or had had one—she was vague on the details—and she mentioned that there was a castle in the family. Her Christmas card (sent yearly to all of us, even though we had not sent one to her in years) introduced the Bruewald family crest. It was all so ludicrous and pathetic, really, when they were living in a studio in a high-rise on York Avenue.

"So why do you even see her?" my husband would ask. (I was married now, too.) "If she's so awful, why don't you dump her? Just don't call back." Like most men, he had no patience with these pseudo-friendships between women that drag on for years. The question bothered me, and in my head I came up with three reasons that I continued to see Christie Bruewald, née Thorn, at six-month intervals. First, I enjoyed taking note of her pretensions. I enjoyed seeing how far she would go. In a way, I had exulted in the family-crest Christmas card. I had put it up on the refrigerator and shown it to everyone who came over. I was dying, now, to see what would follow. When I met her for coffee, I went prepared with a mental tape recorder to catch her appalling lapses in taste—not so much for myself as to pass on to everyone else. Second, there were, I have to admit, sparks of humanity in Christie's pretensions, and in her desires, that I felt were missing in the rest of my life. She had coveted *a huge diamond ring*. She had hoped *to land a guy with money*. She had wanted her wedding to be an extravaganza, *a day she'd remember for the rest of her life*. She wasn't "over it." She wasn't over anything. She knew what she wanted, and she wanted the kinds of things that the marketers of luxury goods describe as "the best"—Jacuzzis, chandeliers, access to the tropics in the middle of winter. Third, and finally, what got me, I suppose, were the indications of humanity in Christie's life that had nothing to do with her pretensions. The family crest on the Christmas card had been embossed onto a picture of the Bruewalds and their new baby in matching red-and-green velvet outfits. The little girl looked exactly like Thomas—an odd-featured brown-haired old man. She wouldn't have the advantage of Christie's looks, and, for someone as entranced by the superficial as Christie was, that must have been hard to take. You could say that I felt sorry for her.

Still, despite my three reasons, a year or so after my own wedding I went through a period when I felt it was important to burn the fat from my life.

Christie had begun to represent all that was wrong with New York—which, as usual, meant what I was tired of in myself. I wrote "Seeing people like Christie Thorn" on a list of things that were a waste of time, and when she called and left a message to start the back-and-forth that would culminate in our having lunch a few weeks later, I didn't call back.

Perhaps I ended it then simply because the interesting part appeared to be over. Though my own life still seemed to me a fount of infinite promise, hers felt blandly curtailed. I realized that there was a part of me that had almost wanted her to make it, on her own terms, whatever they might be. The sad thing about Christie's wedding was that it hadn't been outrageous at all; it had been just another overpriced New York wedding spearheaded by a bride with too much makeup on. I found it all too easy to imagine how her story would continue, how, inevitably, it would end. I lived with that story, kept the thread going in my mind, and added to it from time to time, when some event in my own life recalled Christie's unhappy mixture of envy and drive, of self-promotion and apology.

My version (wholly fictional) went something like this: Having married for money, Christie quickly discovers that she hasn't married for enough. Realizing her mistake only deepens the dissatisfaction she feels with her life, and, in order to convince herself that things can still change, she has an innocuous little affair in the first six months of her marriage. The second affair, a year later, is not so innocuous. Thomas is doing as well as he ever has, but this is New York, and after their second child the Bruewalds are unable to afford a big enough apartment in the city and they make the move to the suburbs. (For Christie, Brooklyn, or a bohemian setup with the baby in the living room, has never been an option.) They buy a starter house in one of the less well-known towns of Westchester. They socialize a lot and their favorite friends are people like themselves, but who make a little less than they do, and are jealous of them for some other reason as well—Christie's having lost the weight after her pregnancies, say. The kids are the usual product of a marriage like the Bruewalds'. They suffer from Christie's frustrated ambition and their father's subservience to it, and they end up angry and self-hating beneath a surface of entitlement. But the European influence helps to normalize them somewhat, and at least they know how to ski. When the children are grown and out of the house, Christie starts spending most of her time down at the time-share in Cancún, befriending other "party people," whose spouses turn a blind eye. But she and Thomas never divorce because she's afraid to be alone.

That would be about the size of it. It would end in a sorry, grasping old age, marked by an incivility to service people (flight attendants, doctors' secretaries) and a dye job that wasn't what it used to be.

It was what she deserved, wasn't it? There is order in things, and people who spend a hundred grand on a wedding they can't afford simply not to lose face should pay in some way. Who was she kidding?

It will be clear from my iteration of Christie's excesses that, as a couple, my husband and I have always prided ourselves on living within our means. When the time comes for us to move into a bigger apartment, we understand that staying in the city will mean living at the back of a building, in interior rooms that open onto shaftways. So it's only for kicks, just to see what we're missing, that we ask our broker to show us something fancy. We go prepared to look, to smile wistfully, and to depart, understanding that by any reasonable standards we have more than enough, and by any other standards we simply don't measure ourselves. When, high up in Carnegie Hill, on our way into one of those hushed old buildings that face the Park, our two-year-old daughter falls in love with the doorman, we take it, laughing, with endless hope for the future, as a sign that the girl knows quality when she sees it. "You can see him on the way out," we promise. "He'll still be there." Yet, when we fall in love with the apartment itself, we cannot take it as a sign of anything at all. It is smaller by a room than the others we've looked at; and costs more by . . . oh, about a hundred grand. Where are our wistful smiles now? Where is our comfort in reasonable standards? It is clear that we—and only we—are capable of fully appreciating the charm of this place. Who but we would actually enjoy the fact that the stove and the refrigerator appear, like the building, to be prewar? Who but we would keep the sixties-style wallpaper in the maid's room? (The ghost of Christie Thorn shakes her head in annoyance at the broker: "Total gut job in the kitchen!" "No closet space!" "No wet bar!") And then there is our daughter and the doorman, who is pretending to play hide-and-seek with her, while we stand wordless in the marble lobby, looking out at the green of the Park, doing sums in our head, reconsidering decisions of the past, decisions that might have netted us this apartment, pure and simple.

Because now nothing else will do.

The apartment is at the breaking point of our price range, and though on paper we can swing it, our broker calls that night with bad news: he's shopped us to the board, and they are reluctant to consider anyone whose liquid assets are as low as ours. That fast, it's over. We have been slotted into position. We know—and can laugh bitterly at the notion that this knowledge, in other circumstances, is supposed to be comforting—exactly where we are.

A week after the bad news, I walk by the building, daughterless this time. A man emerges, then two schoolgirls in uniform. I put my sunglasses on to hide the fact that I am staring in an ugly, covetous way. How tortured and unpleasant I must look compared with the woman my age who comes out next, well dressed, well coiffed, followed by two children, a girl and a boy, who are followed in turn by two nannies. For an incredible moment, I mistake the woman for an older, more sophisticated Christie Thorn. Out of habit I am pretending not to see even this twin of hers (the way you ignore a man in a bar who resembles your ex-boyfriend), when the doorman's greeting rings out—yes, as if in a dream—"Mrs. Brue-wald." "Hi, Lester." He asks how long she will be, and the woman says, "Oh, an hour or two. We're just going to go to the Park and do some shopping before Daddy gets home."

In a vile moment of Darwinian survival, I paste a smile on my face, and I call out, "Christie?"

We went to an Italian restaurant on Madison. Kids and nannies were dispatched to the Park. It was an off hour, three or four o'clock, and I remember I almost hated to dirty one of the white linen tablecloths, which were already set for dinner. We started with cappuccinos, then moved on to glasses of the house white. Later, when we got hungry, the waiter brought antipasto and some bread, and to wash it down I had another glass of white wine and Christie switched to red. I was longing for a cigarette, and eventually I asked her, "Do you still smoke?" "My God, I'm dying for one," she said, and took a pack out of her purse. We each smoked two.

I should explain that it was one of those surreally springlike days at the tail end of winter, the kind of afternoon when you flirt with the mailman, the coffee-cart man, and the busboy, when you long for a new pair of open-toed sandals and a good excuse to sit in a café all afternoon, ignoring your responsibilities and getting drunk. Well, we had one. There was catching up to be done—husbands, children, careers, in a nutshell.

From the beginning, I was drinking rather fast. All the information sharing, I realized, was making me uneasy. I, who used to rattle off insouciantly all the good things that had happened to me, was guarded now. I had something to protect, it seemed. I held back, forming half-truths for every potential question Christie might pose—asking myself, "Will I tell her about that or not? Will I act as if everything's fine or will I level with her?"—while she grew expansive with me, as she now could. The family crest was not a joke; it was not a sham. In some little town in the former East Germany, the Bruewalds were evidently a big deal. "All the money was tied up in this castle in Saxony—this huge, horrible, dark, awful house—and, the minute Onkel Guenther died, Thomas and I looked at each other and we were like, 'We're selling!' It was like, before he died we couldn't mention it, and the minute we got the news we never looked back. It was a done deal." They had sold the *Schloss*, auctioned the furniture, and inherited the lot, except, of course, for what was in trust for Hildie and Axel. (It had occurred to me that although Hildie still resembled her father, her appearance would be seen, later in life, as distinguishing; people would seek ownership of those peculiar looks, the way they would those of a rock star's eccentric-looking daughter. Only outsiders would make the obvious comments; insiders would know better.) In addition to the apartment on Fifth Avenue, the Bruewalds now owned a ski lodge in the Arlberg, a country house in New Jersey, and a mansion in Solln, which Christie described as "the Greenwich of Munich."

The sheer weight of the information had made me dizzy, but when she mentioned Greenwich I sat up and did her the one courtesy I could. I fed her the line. "That must be nice," I said. "It must feel like home." She drained her glass of wine, though she had already drained it once, and then she put it down and unexpectedly met my eye. She said, "You know, when we got the money I went out and got myself a two-hundred-and-fifty-dollar-an-hour shrink. I used to think I was a horrible person." She wasn't a horrible person, the shrink had told her; in fact, there was nothing wrong with her at all.

We split a third glass of wine and then a fourth, making the waiter laugh. During the fourth, I told her why I had been loitering outside her building—not hoping to get something out of it, just wanting to ante up with something real of my own. Christie laughed, the way you laugh at something you don't quite believe, and at first I interpreted her incredulity as an attack—that's how defensive I felt. "Oh, for Christ's sake!" she said. "You've got to be kidding!" I stared stonily at the table, the way I do when I'm both drunk and mortally offended. "No, no—listen. Thomas is on the board, and they owe him a big favor. This is no problem, no problem at all. Don't believe what they say about the liquid assets. It's just a way of keeping people out. Anyway," she said, "I'll tell them about your *Mayflower* ancestor."

"I told you about our *Mayflower* ancestor?" I said.

"Of course you did!" She smiled. "The first time we met."

There was nothing I could do but turn red and finish the wine. Christie went to the bathroom, and I sat there flipping a matchbook over and over in my hand. I had an anticipatory feeling, as if I were waiting for a date to return, as if we might be planning to go back to her deluxe pad and make out on her and Thomas's king-size bed. People had always said that Christie had a great body, and that's the kind of body it was—firm, relentlessly fit, and offered up as a commodity for others to comment on. In the early nineties, she had been an aerobics queen, logging two, three hours a day at the gym; now, of course, she was into yoga and Pilates, but, "to tell you the truth," she'd confessed earlier in the afternoon, "I kind of miss the screaming and the jumping up and down."

We had moved to the city at the same time—ten years ago now—and sitting there, playing with the matchbook, I tried to get a handle on what those ten years had amounted to. We had been single. Now we were *married* women with *children*. But, despite the italics in my head, I couldn't seem to take it any further than that. My thoughts drifted to the apartment, trying again, I suppose, to notch the progress we had each made. If my husband and I got the place, we'd be cash-poor for a few years. With both of us working, we could bring in x amount per year, put y aside, and contribute z to our 401(k)s. But, even considering promotions and raises, there was a limit to x. X was fixed, and there was only t—time—to increase it. But time ate up your life. You could say, "In ten years," "In twenty years." But the problem was that then whatever it was would be *in* ten years, or *in* twenty years. A decade, two decades of your life would have gone by before you attained it. The fixity of x was the most bittersweet thing I had thought of in ages. Of course, it was comparing myself with Christie that had brought on all these thoughts. When she came out of the ladies' room, looking as happy and drunk as I had felt a minute before, her innocence struck me like a storm. And I realized that what separated us, and perhaps had always separated us, was the understanding that I had only just reached: in life you can only get so far.

I walked home with the good news for my husband and daughter. It seemed that Christie and I were going to be friends again, or friends after all, I should say. My husband would be dubious, to say the least. "The same Christie Thorn you told me you would never have coffee with again?" Nor would he like the idea of her getting us past the board; it would take a week to make him understand what had changed in the course of an afternoon and why it wasn't the case that we were simply using her. Then again, I deserved a dose of his skepticism. I had carried on about her—had laughed in my best moments, but from time to time had been derisive, too, and even indignant. I asked myself, now, how I truly felt about all her pretensions. I went through them one by one—the wedding, the Christmas card, then little things, little remarks from her single days, her obsession with the "it" handbag every year, for instance. I came to the conclusion that none of it was worth getting worked up about. None of it was profound. As the shrink had evidently made clear, none of it had anything to do with Christie herself. On the contrary, I told myself, it was *your* problem.

Ruth Prawer Jhabvala

Refuge in London

from *Zoetrope*

A<small>LL THE</small> people—the lodgers—in my aunt's boardinghouse had a
history I had missed out on. I had been brought to England when I
was two—"our little Englander," they called me. I knew no other place,
and I felt that this made me, in comparison with them, rather blank. Of
course I liked speaking English as naturally as the girls at my school, and
in other ways too being much the same. But I wasn't, ever, quite like them,
having grown up in this house of European émigrés, all of them so different from the parents of my schoolfellows and carrying a past, a country or
countries—a continent—distinct from the one in which they now found
themselves.

They were not always the same lodgers. There was a quick turnover, for
some of them prospered and moved, others had to make different arrangements when they could no longer come up with the rent. My aunt, with
whom I lived in the basement, was a kind landlady, but beyond a certain
point she could not afford to be generous. Also—for my sake, she said—
she had to be more strictly moral than it was maybe in her nature to be.
The circumstances of émigrés are not so much bound by conventional
morality as by the emotional refuge they manage to find with each other.
There is always some looseness in these arrangements, odd marital and
extramarital situations: for instance, Dr. Levicus, who had started off in
one of the rooms with his wife to whom he had been married for thirty

years, replaced her with a young lady of twenty, also a refugee but nowhere near his level of refinement. My aunt was prepared to wink at such behavior; she knew how difficult life could be. But she did give notice to Miss Wundt, who, having taken her room as a single lady, had different men coming out of it in the mornings and could often be heard screaming insults after them as they made their shamefaced way down the stairs.

But the Kohls were tolerated year after year, though they were not at all regular with the rent, or in their morals. They were not expected to be; they were artists. Kohl was a painter, and in pre-Hitler Germany he had been famous. His wife, Marta, said she had been an actress, also a dancer, though not famous in either capacity. They rented the two top rooms but lived in them more or less separately. One room was his, his studio; she also referred to hers as a studio, though she didn't do anything artistic in there. She was much younger than he was and very attractive, a tiny redhead. It was unlikely that, if he had not been famous, she would ever have married someone so much older and so undistinguished in appearance. He was short and plump, also bald except for a fringe of hair at the back; he had an unattractive mustache that she called his toilet brush. He didn't seem to care that lovers came to visit her in her room; when that happened, he shut the door of his and went on painting. He painted all the time, though I don't think he sold anything during those years. I'm not sure what they lived on, probably on an allowance from some relief organization. For a time she had a job in the German section of the BBC, but she soon lost it. There were too many others far more competent and also more reliable than she, who found it impossible ever to be on time for anything.

Mann was another of our lodgers. His first name was Gustav, but no one ever called him anything except Mann. I disliked him. He was loud and boastful and took up more time in the second-floor bathroom we all had to share than anyone except Marta. Another reason I disliked him was that he was one of the men who spent time with Marta in her room, making Kohl shut the door of his. I had no such negative feelings about her other male visitors, but was as indifferent to them as Kohl seemed to be. He too was not indifferent to Mann. Whenever they met on the stairs, he said something insulting to him, which Mann received with good humor. "Okay, okay, my friend, take it easy," he said, and even soothingly tapped his shoulder. Then Kohl cried, "Don't touch me!" and jerked away from him. Once he stumbled and rolled down several steps, and Mann laughed. Mann also used to laugh whenever he passed me. I was sixteen at the time and not attractive, and he made me feel even less so by pretending that I was. "Charming," he said, fingering the navy school tunic I wore and hated. It was my last two years at school—I felt I was too old for it, I wanted to get out, longing for what I thought of as a real world.

Those particular years are probably difficult for most girls, and it didn't help that they happened to be the postwar ones in England, with drab food, drab climate, and clothes not only rationed but made of a thick standard material called "utility." But that didn't really matter; I wasn't so much responsive to what was going on outside as to what was going on inside me. My surroundings were only a chrysalis for me to burst out of and become something else. Only what? I didn't feel that I could ever be butterfly material, and whenever Mann looked at me and said his tongue-in-cheek "Charming," it was obvious that this was also his opinion.

It was different with Kohl. I often sat for him while he drew me. Unable to afford a model, he had already drawn most of the people in the house, including my aunt. She had looked at her portrait with round eyes and her hand before her mouth in only partly amused distress: "No—really?" she said. But it really was she, not perhaps as she was meant to be—as, in more hopeful years, she had expected to be—but how she had become, after the war, after survival, after hard domestic work she was not born to, and the habitual shortage of money that was also unexpected. It was my aunt who had brought me to England, more or less tearing me out of my mother's arms, promising her that she would soon be reunited with me. This never happened: after the age of two, I never again saw my mother, nor my father, nor any other relative. Only my aunt—her name was Elsa, but I called her La Plume (from my French lesson—"La Plume de ma Tante"). She was nearly fifty at the time; some nights I saw her asleep on her bed in a kitchen alcove—her heavy red swollen face, her graying hair bedraggled on a pillow, her mouth open and emitting the groans she must have suppressed during the day. It was this person whom she did not recognize in Kohl's drawing of her.

I was always ready to sit for my portrait. Once I was home from school, I had nowhere else to go. I didn't share many of the interests of my classmates, nor was I involved in their intense relationships, which were mostly with each other. When I was invited to their homes, I found them smaller than mine, more cramped in every way. They lived in semidetached or row houses, with rectangular stretches of gardens at the backs where their fathers dug and grew vegetables on their days off from their jobs as postmen or bus conductors. Only one family lived in each house, whereas ours swarmed with people, each one carrying a distinct history, usually the load of a ruined past. The unruly lives of our lodgers were reflected in the state of our back garden. It was wildly overgrown, for no one knew how to mow the grass, even if we had had anything to mow it with; buried within its rough tangle lay the pieces of a broken statue, which had been there ever since we moved in. Ours was one of the few tall old houses left that had not been pulled down in the reconstruction of the neighborhood in the thirties, or bombed during the war. Its pinnacle was Kohl's studio on the top floor, and when I sat for him, I felt myself to be detached from and floating above the tiled roofs of the little English villas among which our boardinghouse had come to anchor.

Kohl worked through the night, painting huge canvases in oil that one saw only in glimpses, for he either covered them with cloth or turned them to face the walls. These paintings were not interesting to me—in fact, I thought they were awful: great slashing wounds of color, completely meaningless, like someone else's nightmare or the deepest depths of a subconscious mind. But when he drew me, it was always in the day. He perched close to me, knee to knee, holding a pad on his lap and drawing on it in pencil or charcoal. While he was working, Kohl was always happy, almost ecstatic. He and his hand were effortlessly united in one fluid action over the paper onto which he was transferring me. He smiled, he hummed, he whispered a little to himself, blissfully, and when his eyes darted toward me, that blissful smile remained. "Ah, *sweet*," he breathed, now at his drawing, now at me. I too felt blissful; no one had ever looked at me or murmured over me in such a way; and although I had of course no sentiment for him—this small, paunchy, middle-aged man—at such moments I did feel a bond with him, not so much as between two persons but as something coming alive between us. There was always movement in the house, noise: doors, voices, footsteps, so many people were living in it. But we there at the top felt entirely alone and bound to each other in his art.

The one person who ever disturbed us was his wife, Marta—and she was not only a disturbance but a disruption into our silence, or an eruption into it. Although they were living separately in their separate rooms, she entered his as of right, its rightful mistress. Without a glance at me, she went straight to look over his shoulder at the drawing: she stood there, taking it in. I felt the instrument in his hand stumble in its effortless motion. There was a change of mood in everything except Marta, who kept standing behind him, looking, judging. She had one little hand on her hip, which was slightly thrust forward in a challenging way. Her glinting green eyes darted from the drawing to me and took me in, not as the subject of his drawing but as an object of her appraisal. After quite a long pause, she returned to the drawing and extended her finger to point out something. "Don't touch," he hissed, but that only made her bring her finger closer to show him what she judged to be wrong. He pushed her hand aside roughly, which made her laugh. "You never could stand criticism," she said, and walked away from him, sauntering around the room; if she found something tasty left on a plate, she ate it. He pretended to go on working, but I could feel his attention was more on her, and so was mine. She took her time before leaving, and even when she was half out of the door, she turned again and told me, "Don't let him keep you sitting too long: once he starts, he doesn't know when to stop." It took a long time for him to get back into his concentration, and sometimes he couldn't manage it at all and we had to stop for the day.

Once, when this happened, he asked me to go for a walk with him. I had noticed that he always took an afternoon walk and usually to the same place. This was a little park we had in the neighborhood—a very artificial little park, with small trees and a small wooden bridge built over a small stream rippling over some white stones. The place seemed dull to me—I was reading the Romantic poets for my Higher Secondary, and my taste was for wild landscapes and numinous presences. Now I saw that this park, which I despised, represented something very delightful to him. It was a spring day that first time I accompanied him, and I had never seen anyone so relish the smell of the first violets and their touch—he bent down to feel them—and the sound of starlings that had joyfully survived the winter. He made me take his arm, a gallant gesture that embarrassed me, and we paraded up and down the winding paths and under the trees that were not big enough to hide the sky. He said he loved everything that was young and fresh—here he pressed my arm a bit, tucked under his; when a blossom floated down and landed in my hair, he picked it out and said, "Ah, *sweet*," the way he did when he was drawing. We sat together on a bench, romantically placed beside the rippling stream, and he recited poetry to me: far from being anything young and fresh, it was something quite decadent, about a poet's black mistress or a rotting corpse. He explained that this had been a favorite poet of his in his younger days, when he had lived in Paris and sat in the same cafés as Braque and Derain.

After that first walk, he often asked me to go with him, but I usually refused. It embarrassed me to be seen arm in arm with him, a man who would be older than my father or my uncle, if I had had either one. He never tried to change my mind, but when I saw him walking by himself, he looked sad and lonely, so I went with him more often than I wanted to. It was a strange and entirely new sensation for me to see another person happy in my company when I myself had no such feeling at all. He was undoubtedly happy in that pathetic little park, listening to birds and smelling flowers, walking up and down with me, a sixteen-year-old, on his arm. But when we sat on the bench by the stream and he recited Baudelaire in French, I became wistful. I realized that the situation was, or should have been, romantic—if only *he* had been more so instead of the way he was, with an old homburg hat and his ugly mustache.

He began to invite me on other outings, such as his Sunday afternoon visits to galleries and museums. I went with him a few times but did not enjoy it, starting from the long tube ride where we sat side by side and I wanted people to think we were not together. Looking back now, all these years later, I see that it should have been regarded as a great privilege for me to see great paintings with an artist such as Kohl, who had once been famous (and would become so again). He kept me close beside him, standing in front of the paintings he had come to view, usually only two or three. He made no attempt to explain anything to me, only pointed at certain details that I wouldn't have thought extraordinary—light falling on an apple, or a virgin's knee—and saying, "Ah, ah, ah," with the same ecstasy as when he was working. Afterward he treated me to a cup of coffee. There were, at the time, only certain standard eating places in London that he could afford: dingy rooms with unfriendly elderly waitresses, especially depressing if it was raining outside, as it often was, and we had to remain uncomfortable in our wet coats and shoes. But he seemed to enjoy these occasions, even the bad coffee, and continued to sit there after the waitress had slapped down the bill in front of him. At last I had to tell him that my aunt would be worried if I came home too late. Then he regretfully got up; and it was only at that last moment, when he was picking up the bill, that his hand brushed against mine very delicately, very shyly, and he smiled at me in the same way, delicate and shy.

The only times I really liked to be with him were in his studio when he was drawing me. All I saw out of his window was a patch of sky with some chimneys rearing up into it. When it got dark and he turned on the light, even that view disappeared. Then there was only the room itself, which had an iron bed, often unmade, and a wooden table full of drawings, and the pictures that he painted at night, showing the backs of the canvases, piled one against another on every available space of wall. The floor was bare and had paint splashed all over it. He had a one-burner gas ring, on which I don't think he ever cooked; all I saw him eat was a herring or a fried egg sandwich bought at a corner shop. He seemed to be always at work, deeply immersed in it and immersing me with him. This was what I responded to—it was the first time I was in the presence of an artist prac- ticing his art, and later, when I began to be a writer, I often thought of it, and it inspired me.

Our occupation with each other was entirely innocent, but it went on too long and perhaps too often, so that others began to take notice. My aunt, La Plume, would call up, "Don't you have any homework?" or make excuses to send me on errands she didn't need. When I came down, she would look at me in a shrewd way. Once she said, "You know, artists are not like the rest of us." When I didn't understand, or pretended not to, she said, "They don't have the same morals." To illustrate, she had some anec- dote about herself and my mother, who had both been crazy about the opera and hung about the stage door in the hope of meeting the artists. Here she began to smile and forget about artists in general to tell me about a particular tenor. He had taken a liking to my mother, who looked more forward than she was, with her shingled hair and very short skirt showing a lot of silk stocking. He had invited the two girls to his flat. "His wife was there, and another woman we thought may have been another wife for him, you know, a mistress." Her smile became a laugh, more pleasure than outrage, as she remembered the atmosphere, which was so different from their own home that they had an unspoken pact never to tell about their visits to the tenor's flat. In the end, they stopped going; there were too many unexplained relationships and too many quarrels, and what had seemed exciting to them at first was now unsettling. Shortly afterward both of them became engaged to their respective suitors—a bookkeeper and a teacher (my father). When she had finished this story, she said, "So you see," but I didn't see anything, especially not what it might have to do with me, who anyway had no suitor to fall back on.

Marta began to come in frequently and to stay longer than she used to. She perched on a stool just behind him, so that he could not see but could certainly feel her. And hear her—she talked all the time, criticizing his drawing, the state of his cheerless room, the cold that he seemed never to notice, except that in the worst weather he wore gloves with the fingers cut off. In the end he gave up—his concentration was long gone—and he threw his pencil aside and said, "But what do you want?"

She stretched her green eyes wide open at him: "Want? What could I possibly want from you, my poor Kohl?"

But once she answered, "I want to invite you to my birthday party."

He cursed her birthday and her party and that made her open her eyes even wider, greener: "But don't you remember? You used to *love* my birthday! Each year a new poem for me. . . . He wrote poetry," she told me. "Real poetry, with flowers, birds, and a moon in it. And I was all three: flowers, birds, and moon. Now he pretends to have forgotten."

Birthdays were always made a fuss over, even for those lodgers whom no one liked much. I suppose that, in celebrating a day of birth as something special, everyone was trying to take the place of a lost family for everyone else. Usually these parties were held in our basement kitchen, which was the only room large enough—the rest of the house was cut up into individual small units for renting out. My aunt was known as a good sort and was the only one everyone could get on with; she was always willing for people to come down to her kitchen and tell her their troubles as though she had none of her own. For birthday parties she covered the grease stains and knife cuts on our big table with a cloth and made the bed she slept on look as much as possible like a sofa for guests to sit on. She arranged sausage slices on bread and baked a cake with margarine and eggs someone had got on the black market. Those who wanted liquor brought their own bottles, though she didn't encourage too much drinking; it seemed to make people melancholy or quarrelsome and spoiled the general mood of celebration.

Marta's party was held not in our kitchen but in her room at the top of the house. Since this was too small to accommodate many people, she had persuaded Kohl to open his studio across the landing for additional space. Although the two rooms were identical in size, their appearances were very different. While his was strictly a workplace, with nothing homelike in it, hers was all home, all coziness. There were colorful rugs, curtains, heaps of cushions, lampshades with tassels, and most of the year she kept her gas fire going day and night, careless of the shillings that it swallowed. There were no drawings or paintings—Kohl never gave her any—but a lot of photographs, mostly of herself having fun with friends, when she was much younger but also just as pretty.

On that afternoon, her birthday, she was very excited. She rushed to meet each new arrival and, snatching her present, began at once to unwrap it, shrieking. Apart from my aunt and myself, the guests were all men. She hadn't invited any of our female lodgers, such as Miss Wundt (who was anyway under notice to move out), and these must have been skulking down in their rooms with the party stamping on top of them. Not all the men lived in our house. Some I didn't know, though I might have seen them on the stairs on their visits to Marta, often carrying flowers. There was one very refined person, with long hair like an artist's rolling over his collar. He wasn't an artist but had been a lawyer and now worked in a solicitor's office, not having a license to practice in England. Another, introduced as a Russian nobleman, bowed from the waist in a stately way but was soon very drunk, so that his bows became as stiff as those of a mechanical figure. The reason he could become so drunk was that there was a great deal of liquor brought by the more affluent guests who were not our lodgers: for instance, there was one man who, although also a refugee, had done very well in the wholesale garment business.

Trying to keep up with the rest of the party, I too drank more than I should have. When my aunt saw me refilling my glass, she shook her head and her finger at me. I pretended not to see this warning, but Mann drew attention to it: "Let the little one learn how the big people live!" he shouted. And to me he said, "You like it? Good, ah? Better than school! Just grow up and you'll see how we eat and drink and do our etceteras!"

"Tcha, keep your big mouth shut," La Plume told him, and he bent down to hug her, which she pretended not to like. He was obviously enjoying himself, making the most of the unaccustomed supply of liquor by drinking a lot of it. But he was not in the least drunk—I suppose his big size allowed him to absorb it more easily than others. Of course he was loud as usual, with a lot of bad jokes, but that was his style. He appeared to dominate the party as though he were its host; and Marta treated him like one, sending him here and there to fill vases and open bottles. If he didn't do it well or fast enough, she called him a donkey.

The guests overflowed to the landing and through the open door into Kohl's studio. Some of them were looking at his paintings, making quite free with them. They even turned around those facing the wall, the big canvases he painted at night and never showed anyone. The lawyer with the long hair waved his delicate white fingers at them and interpreted their psychological significance. But where was Kohl? No one seemed to have noticed that he was missing. I became aware of his absence only when I saw the lawyer draw attention to a drawing of myself: "Here we see delight not in a particular person but in Youth with a capital *Y*."

It was Marta who shouted, "What rubbish are you spouting there? . . . And where's Kohl, the idiot, leaving the place open for every donkey to come and give his opinion. . . . Where is he? Why isn't he at my party? Go and find him," she ordered Mann, as though Kohl's absence were his fault.

Mann turned to me: "Do you know where he is?"

"How would she know?" Marta said.

"Of course she knows. She's Youth with a capital *Y*. She inspires him."

If I had been just a little bit younger, I would have kicked his shins; anyway, I almost did. But Marta laughed: "Sneaking away from my party, isn't that just like him. Go and find him if you know where he is," she now ordered me. "Oh yes, and tell him where the hell is my present?"

I was glad to leave the party. It was irritating to see people go into Kohl's studio and freely comment on his paintings. The lawyer's explanation of my drawing had been like a violation, not of myself but of Kohl's work and of my share in it, however passive. And it was not Youth, it was I—I myself!—whom no one had ever cared to observe as Kohl did. . . . I ran down the stairs furiously and then down the street and around the corner to the little park.

He was sitting on the bench beside the stream. He was holding a flat packet wrapped in some paper with designs on it that he must have drawn himself: an elephant holding a sprig of lilac, a hippo in a bathtub. When I asked him if it was for Marta, he nodded gloomily. I said, "She was asking for her present." He got angry, his face and ears swelled red, so I said quickly, "It was a joke."

"No. No joke. This is her character: to take and take, if she could she would suck the marrow from a man's soul. From *my* soul . . . Who's there with her? All of them? That one with the long hair and lisping like a woman? He thinks he knows about art but all he knows is how to lick her feet."

It was a lovely summer night, as light as if it were still dusk. How wonderful it was to have these long days after our gloomy winter: to sit outdoors, to enjoy a breeze even though it was still a little cool. It sent a slight shiver over the stream and flickered the remnant of light reflected in the water. During the day two swans glided there, placed by the municipality, but now they must have been asleep and instead there were two stars on the surface of the sky, still pale, though later they would come into their own and become shining jewels, diamonds. There was fragrance from a lilac bush. I would have liked to have a lover sitting beside me instead of Kohl, so angry from thinking of Marta.

I said, "Is it true you used to write a poem for her on her birthday?"

"She remembers, ha?" His anger seemed to fade, maybe he was smiling a bit under that ugly mustache brush. "Yes, I wrote poems, not one, not only on her birthday, but a flood. A flood of poems. . . . It's the only way, you see, to relieve the pressure. On the heart; the pressure on the heart."

I recognized what he said, having felt that pressure, though in an unspecified form. So far I didn't quite know what it was about, or even whether it was painful or extremely pleasant.

"Is he there—that Mann? What a beast. When he's on the stairs, there is a smell, like a beast in rut. *Musth* they call it. You don't know what that means." I knew very well but didn't say so, for he was wiping his mouth, as though it had been dirtied by these words or by his having spoken them.

"Here, *you* give it to her." He thrust his packet at me. "She'll get no more presents from me and no more poems and no more nothing. All that was for a different person . . . I'll show you."

He snatched the packet back, his hands trembled in undoing the knot; but he handled it carefully to avoid tearing the paper, which he—and so far he alone—knew to be valuable. Then he folded it back, revealing the contents. It was a drawing of Marta. He looked from it to me, almost teasing: "You don't even recognize her." He held it out to me, not letting me touch it.

The lampposts in the park were designed to resemble toadstools, and the light they shed was not strong enough to overcome what was still left of the day. So it was by a mixture of electric and early evening light that I first saw this drawing of Marta. It was dated 1931, that is, she must have been fifteen years younger when he painted it. Still, I certainly would have recognized her.

"Look at her," he said, though holding it up for himself rather than for me. "Look at her eyes: not the same person at all."

But they *were* the same eyes. It was a pencil drawing, but you could tell their color was green. Green, and glinting—with daring, hunger, even greed, or passion as greed. At that time I couldn't formulate any of that, but I did recognize that green glint as typically Marta. And her small cheeky nose; and her hair—even in the drawing one could tell it was red. He had drawn a few loose strands of it flitting against her cheek, the way he always did mine. Just the edges of her small, pointed teeth were showing and a tip of tongue between them: roguish, eager, challenging, the way she still was. But her cheeks were more rounded than they were now, and also her mouth had a less knowing expression, as if at that time it hadn't yet tasted as much as it had in the intervening years.

He covered the drawing again, taking care of it and of its wrapping. He was sunk in thoughts that did not seem to include me; and when he had finished tying the string, he failed to give the packet back to me but kept holding it in his lap. I reminded him that we had to leave, since they would soon be locking up the park for the night.

When we got to the gate, it *had* been locked. It was not difficult for me to find a foothold and to vault over, avoiding the row of spikes on top. He remained hesitating on the other side, clutching his drawing. I showed him where the foothold was and asked him to pass the drawing to me through the bars. He didn't want to do either but had no choice. With me helping him, he managed to get over, but at the last moment the back of his pants got caught on one of the spikes. The first thing he did when we were reunited was to relieve me of the drawing; the second was to stretch backward to see the rip in his pants. I lied that it was hardly visible; anyway, it was dark by now, and if we met people on the road, they would hardly bother about his torn seat. Nevertheless, he made me walk behind to shield him; every time we passed a lamppost he looked back at me anxiously: "Does it show?"

Near our house, we could see that the party was still in progress. Lights and voices streamed out into the street, and the shadows of people were moving against the windows. But inside we found that my aunt had left the party and was banging about in the basement kitchen, grumbling to herself: "Why don't they go home instead of turning my house into God know what."

It was impossible for Kohl with his torn pants to return to his studio, which was full of people he didn't like. "Take them off," La Plume said, "I'll sew them for you. . . . Go on, you think I haven't seen anything like what you hide in there?" But when he stepped out of them, she shook her head: "What does she do all day that she can't wash her husband's underpants?"

I fetched a blanket that he could wrap around his legs, which were very white, unsunned. They trembled slightly, not used to being naked, and ashamed of it. Looking back now, I'm glad I got the blanket and do not have to remember that great artist the way he was at that moment, trouserless in our kitchen.

When footsteps sounded on the basement stairs, he sat down quickly with his legs under the table where La Plume was sewing his pants. It was Mann who entered, to borrow more glasses for the party. "Cups will do," he said, and began to collect the few we had from our shelves. "And I'm not even asking for saucers."

"Thank you very much," La Plume said, "so in the morning we can drink our coffee from the saucer like cats and dogs."

"Be a sport, Mummy," he said.

"Who's your mummy! And where do you get that 'sport' business, as if you'd been to Eton and Oxford."

"Better than Eton and Oxford, I've attended the School of Life," he retorted—they were always on good teasing terms.

"Yes, in the gutters of Cologne," Kohl put in—not in a teasing way.

It was only then that Mann became aware of him: "So there you are. Everyone is asking for you: Where is the husband, the famous artist?" Next moment his attention shifted to the packet lying on the table: "Ah, her present that she's been asking for all day. I'll take it to her—I'll tell her you're busy down here, flirting with two ladies."

Kohl had instantly placed his hand on the packet, and wild-eyed, cornered, he glared up at Mann. Mann—a very big man but a coward—retreated quickly with our cups held against his chest.

"Take care you bring them back washed, you lazy devil!" La Plume shouted after him. But when he had gone, she said, "He's not a bad sort, though he gets on everyone's nerves. They say he was a very great idealist and gave wonderful speeches to the workers at their rallies."

"We've heard about the wonderful speeches—from him. From no one else," Kohl sneered. "And when the police came, he ran faster than anyone. It's only here he plays the big hero."

"Ah, well," sighed La Plume, "everyone lives as best they can." This was her motto. "Here," she said, handing him his trousers. "I wouldn't get very high marks for sewing, but they'll do." He got up to step into them—just in time, for while he was still buttoning them, Marta was heard calling from the stairs.

I had noticed that, whenever Marta came into a room, the air shifted somewhat. I don't know if this was due to other people's reactions to her, or to something emanating from her, of which she herself was unaware. I might mention here that she had a peculiar, very sweet smell—not of perfume, more of a fruit, ripe and juicy, not quite fresh.

"So where's my present? Mann says you have my present!" Her eager eyes were already fixed on it, but Kohl held on to it. "Give," she wheedled, "it's mine."

He shook his head in refusal, while secretly smiling a bit. But when she began to tug at it—"Give, give"—he shouted, "Be careful!" and let go, so that she captured it.

She untied it, the tip of her tongue slightly protruding. The paper came off and the drawing was revealed. She held it between her two hands and looked at it: looked at herself looking out of it. He watched her; the expression on his face became anxious, like one waiting for a verdict.

At last she said, "Not bad."

"Not bad!" he echoed indignantly.

"I mean me, not you." Her eyes darted to him with the same expression as in the drawing. She held it at another angle for careful study: "Yes," was her verdict, "no wonder you fell madly in love with me."

"I with you! Who was it who chased me all over town, from café to café, from studio to studio, like a madwoman, and everyone laughing at us both?"

"Me running after him?" She turned to La Plume: "Me in love with him? Have you ever heard anything so ridiculous in all your life?"

"No, not with me. With my fame."

He spoke with dignity and pride, and then she too became proud. She said, "Oh yes, he was famous all right, and I wasn't the only one to run after him. Naturally: a famous artist." She returned to the drawing, to his gift to her, and now she appeared to be studying not herself, as before, but his work.

"So?" he asked, valuing her opinion and awaiting her compliment.

This compliment seemed to be hovering on her lips—when Mann came storming into our kitchen, followed by some other guests. As with one gesture, Kohl and Marta seized the wrapping paper to conceal the drawing, but Mann had already seen it: "So that's the present he's been hiding!"

"Don't touch!" Marta ordered, but she held it out, not only for him but high enough for others to see. They crowded forward; there were admiring cries, and Mann whistled. It was a gratifying moment for both Kohl and Marta. La Plume glowed too, and so did I; we were really proud to have an artist in our house.

The lawyer spoiled it. He peered at the drawing through his rimless glasses; he thrust out his white fingers to point out beauties—the same way he had done with my portrait. He may even have said something similar about Youth with a capital Y, but Marta cut him short: "You really are a donkey," and at once she wrapped up the drawing.

"You know what, children?" said La Plume. "It's long past my bedtime, and if you don't clear out, I'm going to miss my beauty sleep."

Everyone clamored for Kohl to join them. Marta too said: "Come and drink champagne with us. *He* brought it, so he's good for something." She pointed briefly at the lawyer, who stopped looking crestfallen, but she had already returned to Kohl. She laid her hand on his shoulder in a familiar gesture we had never witnessed between them: "Come on—only don't give away any secrets. You're the only one who knows how old I am today."

"We all know," Mann said. "It's eighteen." No one heard him. Marta still had her hand on Kohl's shoulder; she said, "You used to like to drink. Often a bit too much, both of us . . . "

"Maybe," he said; he shook her hand off. "But next morning I was up at five, working, and you lay in bed till noon, sleeping it off."

"I never had a hangover."

"No, it's true—when you got up, you were fresh and fit and ready to start making my life a misery again." Marta may never have had a hangover, but there were days when she suffered a mysterious ailment about which she and La Plume whispered together. My aunt didn't want me to know about it, but when she wasn't there, Marta spoke to me as freely as she did to La Plume. It was something very private to do with her womb— I really would have preferred not to know; these were matters I wanted to keep buried in the depths of the unconscious where I could at least pretend they had nothing to do with me. Marta went into unwelcome detail, though she always warned me, "For God's sake, don't tell Kohl. He can't stand women being ill."

She did however confide in Mann and the lawyer and probably everyone else too. She even told all of us that her trouble was due to an abortion brought about by herself when she was married to Kohl. "I was nineteen years old, what did I know? With a knitting needle, can you believe it? As if I'd ever knitted a thing." When we asked if she had told Kohl—"Are you crazy? He'd have run off very fast on his fat little legs. We were bohemians, for heaven's sake, not *parents*."

Although she spoke this last sentence proudly, Mann stroked her hair with his big hand and said, "My poor little one."

She jerked her head away from him: "Don't be a sentimental idiot. I wasn't going to ruin my career. I was on my way—listen, I'd already been an extra three times, the casting director at UFA was taking a tremendous interest in me, his name was Rosenbaum and he'd promised me a real part in the next production. And then of course he was fired." She made the face—it was one of scorn and disdain—with which she looked back on that part of their past.

She was not the only one deprived of her future. The lawyer had had his own practice in Dresden; Mann, who was a trained engineer, had been a union leader and a delegate at an international labor conference. In England they were earning their livings in humbler ways, but Marta was never able to get anything going. She said it was because her English was not good enough, but Kohl said it was because she was a lazy lump who couldn't get out of bed in the mornings. It was true that she usually slept late and had her first cup of coffee at noon.

It may have been her waiflike quality that made one want to serve her, but there was also something imperious in her personality that blurred the line between wishes and commands. During the day, I was often the only person available, and as soon as she heard me come home from school, she called down for me. She said she was too sick to get out of bed, she was starving, and though she had called and called, no one had answered. She wasn't sulky, just pathetic, so that I was apologetic to have been at school and my aunt on a shopping trip a tube ride away where prices were cheaper. But there had been Kohl just across the landing—hadn't he heard her? She laughed at that: "Kohl! I could be screaming in my death agony, he'd stuff up his ears and not hear a thing." But again she was not reproachful, only amused.

He too was often waiting for me to come home from school: either he needed to finish a drawing of me or had an idea for a new one. Of course he never summoned me the way she did; he requested, suggested, timidly ready to withdraw. It was only when he saw that she had preempted me and was sending me about her business that his manner changed. Once he came into her room while I was washing her stockings in the basin and she was warming her hands before the gas fire. His face swelled red the way it did in anger: "What is she—a queen to be served and waited on? . . . You should have seen where she came from, before I pulled her out of the mire!"

She admitted it freely—that she came out of the mire—but as for his pulling her out: oh, there were plenty of others, bigger and better, to do that.

"Then why me? Why did I have to be made the fool who married her?"

"Because you wanted it more than anyone else. You said you'd die and kill yourself without me."

"And now I'm dying with you!"

It began to happen that on the days when I was sitting with him in his room, she would call for me from hers. Then he kicked his door shut with his foot; but I could still hear her voice calling, weak and plaintive, and it made me restless. I wanted to help her; and also, I have to admit, I wanted to be with her more than with him. I was bored with the long hours of sitting for him. And I was embarrassed by him, too young for his shy approaches, too unused to such respectful gallantry. I began to find excuses not to accompany him on his Sunday excursions, though I felt sorry when I saw him leave alone. Perhaps Marta felt sorry too: I heard her offer to go with him, and then his brusque, indignant refusal.

One day Kohl was waiting for me outside my school. He was standing beside someone's boyfriend, a tall youth with straw-colored hair and a big Adam's apple, this paunchy little old man who tucked his arm into mine and walked away with me. Next day I told everyone he was my uncle, and whenever he stood there again, it was announced to me that my uncle was waiting. I couldn't even tell him not to come—not for fear of hurting his feelings (though there was that too) but for not wanting anything significant to be read into his presence there. What could be significant? He was old, *old!* I wept into my pillow at night, ashamed and frustrated at some lack that it was ridiculous to think someone like him could fill.

On a Sunday when I had just told Kohl that I had too much homework to go with him, Marta called after me on the stairs to accompany her. I didn't dare accept there and then, with Kohl listening, but she knew how eager I was, and maybe he knew too: when we set out, I glanced up guiltily and there he was, standing at a window on the landing. It seemed she was as aware of him as I was: she put her arm around my shoulders and talked in the loud and lively way people do when they want to show others that they are having a good time.

After that first Sunday, I waited for her to invite me again, and sometimes she did. Outings with her were very different from those with Kohl. We were never alone, as I was with him, but there were Mann and the lawyer, and later others joined us, and they had conversations about art shows and films, and a lot to say about people they knew and seemed not to like. Although it hardly ever rained when I was with her— it inevitably did on Sundays with Kohl—they spent little time enjoying birds and sunshine. They gathered in cafés for afternoon coffee and cake, never in the sort of depressing eating holes that Kohl frequented but in large, lavish places; these were probably imitations of the luxury cafés they had once known. Their favorite was one called the Old Vienna, which was not too expensive but was smothered in atmosphere. There were chandeliers, carpets, red velvet banquettes, and richly looped creamy lace under the curtains that were also of red velvet. Here many languages were spoken by both clientele and waiters, and there were continental newspapers on poles for anyone who cared to read them. But few did—they were there to talk and laugh and pretend they were where and how they used to be. Some of the women were chic, with little hats and a lot of lipstick and costume jewelry. Yet Marta, not chic but bohemian with her red hair and long trailing skirt, drew more attention than anyone—maybe because she was enjoying herself so recklessly, surrounded by a group of friends, all male and all eager to supply and then light the cigarettes from which she flicked ash in all directions.

I was always excited after these excursions with Marta and her friends, and my aunt enjoyed hearing my descriptions of the café and its clientele, nodding in recognition of something she had once known. But Kohl frowned and told her, "You shouldn't let her go with them."

"But it's so nice for her! Poor child, what chance does she have to go anywhere?"

He said, "She's too young."

"Too young to go to a café?"

"Too young to go with people like that."

"Oh, people like that," La Plume repeated dismissively in her everyone-has-to-live intonation.

As so often with this mild little man, he became a red fighting cock: "You don't know anything! None of you knows—what she was like, how she carried on. Every day was carnival for her—and how old was she? Sixteen, seventeen, and I, who was forty, I, Kohl, became her clown. She made me her carnival clown."

"Yes, yes, sit down."

La Plume pressed him into a chair. She made tea for him, and he drank it with his hands wrapped gratefully around the cup. It calmed him, changed the mood of his thoughts though not their subject. "What could I do? For years and years I had been alone, and poor—*poor!* And now people were coming to my studio. When I went into a café there were whispers, 'It's Kohl, the artist Kohl.' So that was meat and drink for her, other people's whispers. . . . But she was always laughing at me, making a fool of me. Even her cap made a fool of me! This little striped monkey cap she wore riding on top of her hair. . . . Her hair was red."

"It's still red."

"Nothing like it was!" He gulped tea, gulped heat. "I painted her, I wrote poetry for her, I slept with her, I couldn't get enough of her. I tell you, she was a flame to set people on fire." He broke off, pleaded with me, "Come and sit for me. Come tomorrow? After school? I'll wait for you. I'll have everything ready."

That time I was glad to go. There was a stillness, a purity in his empty studio that I have never experienced in any other place; nor at any other time have I felt as serene as in the presence of this artist, drawing something out of me that I didn't know was there. But then Marta came in and stood behind him to comment on his drawing of me. Once he took off one of his slippers, which he always wore in the studio to save his feet, and he threw it in her direction. It hit the door, which she had already shut behind her. But as always with her intrusion, our peace was shattered.

All this was in my last two years at school: 1946, 1947. After that, things began to change, and some of our lodgers left us to resume their former lives or to begin new ones elsewhere. Mann, for instance, went back to Germany—to East Germany, where he was welcomed by the remnants of his party and returned to an active life of rallies and international conferences. The lawyer started a new practice of his own, taking up cases of reparation for his fellow refugees, which made him rich and took him all over Europe. Their rooms remained empty; there were no more émigrés of the kind my aunt was used to, and she did not care for the other applicants who spoke in languages none of us understood. Anyway, the landlord was keen to convert the house into flats and offered her a sum of money to quit. I was by this time living in Cambridge, having won a scholarship to the university, and stayed with her only during my vacations. She took a little flat over some shops in North West London and led a more restful, retired life, made possible by the monthly payments of refugee reparation the lawyer arranged for her.

He also offered to arrange such payments for Marta, but she was too disorganized to locate her birth certificate or any other of the required papers. She also seemed indifferent about it, as though other things mattered more to her. Before leaving, Mann had asked her to go with him, but first she laughed at him and then she said he was getting on her nerves and pushed him out. A few postcards arrived from him, upbeat in tone and with idyllic views of a cathedral and a river, which my aunt found in the wastepaper basket and put up in her kitchen.

The lawyer married a widow who had been at school with him and had survived the war in Holland. He moved into her flat in Amsterdam but was often in London on business. He began to bring people to Kohl's studio, and they brought other people—gallery owners, collectors, dealers— so it was often a busy scene. The visitors walked around the drawings on the walls, and Kohl turned over the large canvases for them to see; since he had only two chairs, Marta carried some in from her room, and then she stood leaning against the doorpost, smoking and watching. No one took any notice of her. They commented among themselves or turned respectfully to Kohl, who as usual had very little to say; but if Marta tried to explain something for him, he became irritated and told her to go away.

We all attended the opening of his first show at a gallery on Jermyn Street. It was packed with fashionable people, ladies with long English legs in the shiny nylons that had begun to arrive from America; the air was rich with an aroma of perfume and face powder, and of the cigars some of the men had been smoking before being asked to put them out. Marta wore an ankle-length, low-cut dress of emerald-green silk; it matched her eyes but had a stain in front that the dry cleaner had not been able to get out. She wandered around in a rather forlorn way, and no one seemed to know that she was the artist's wife. Many pictures were sold, discreet little dots appearing beside them. After this show, another was held in Paris, and after a while Kohl decided to move to Zurich. The pictures still left in the house were packed up under his supervision, and again Marta stood leaning in the open door to watch, and again if she tried to say anything, he became irritated.

When he was all packed up, he came into the kitchen with a present for me. As he walked down the stairs, Marta, who seemed to be aware of his every movement, leaned over the banister and gave a street-boy whistle to attract his attention. When he looked up, she called him vile names in several languages, so that by the time he reached us, his face and ears were suffused in red. Her voice penetrated right into the kitchen, where he, always shy of anything scatological, pretended that neither he nor we could hear it. Courtly and courteous, he presented me with one of the drawings of myself—but La Plume and I didn't even have time to thank him before Marta came whirling in. Instinctively, though not aware at that time of its value, I held my drawing close for protection.

She too was carrying a drawing; it was the one he had given her on her birthday. She held it under his nose: "Here, you ridiculous animal!" She tore it across—once, twice, three times—and threw the pieces on the floor. With a terrible cry, he crouched down to gather them up, while she tried to prevent him by stamping her high-heeled shoes on his fingers. He didn't seem to notice when he got up that there was blood on his hands. La Plume, clasping her cheeks between her hands, showed it to him, but he was concerned only that it should not stain the pieces of drawing that he was clutching in the same way I did mine. Marta was laughing now, as at a victory—was it over the blood? Or the torn drawing? My aunt said, "Children, children," in her usual way of trying to soothe tempers, but I did not feel that those two were children, or that there was anything child-like about their quarrel.

It was only when Marta had left us that he let go of the pieces of the drawing and laid them down on the table. "Let me see your hand," La Plume said, but he impatiently wiped the blood off on his sleeve and con-centrated on holding the drawing together. Although torn, it was still complete with nothing missing; he smiled down at it, first in relief, then in pure joy, and invited us to admire it with him—not Marta looking out of it with her insolent eyes but the work itself: *his*, his art.

He left the next day and I never met him again. I did see the drawing again: in spite of its damaged condition some collector had bought it, and it was often reproduced in books of twentieth-century art and also appeared in a book devoted to his work. Whatever we heard of Kohl himself was mostly through the lawyer, whom my aunt had engaged to recover some family property (she never got it). We learned that Kohl had rented a large studio in Zurich, in which he both lived and worked. He allowed his dealer to bring visitors, but hardly spoke to or seemed to notice them. He never attended any of his exhibitions, nor did he give interviews to the art magazines that published articles about his work. He was always working, his only recreation an evening walk in a nearby park. He had a maidser-vant to cook and clean for him, a village girl fifteen or sixteen years old whom he often drew. The lawyer thought he also slept with her. Other-wise there was only his work; during his few remaining years, he grudged every moment away from it. When he died, in 1955, his obituaries gave his age as sixty-four.

Marta stayed in the house till my aunt left, and after that she took a room elsewhere. She moved often, not always voluntarily. Once or twice she landed on La Plume's doorstep, having had to vacate her room in a hurry. She never said why, but my aunt guessed that it may have been for the same reason that she herself had had to give notice to Miss Wundt.

We don't know what she lived on. Her clothes looked thin and worn; there were buttons missing from her little jacket, and its fox-fur trimming was mangy. But she was always in a good mood and talked in her usual lively way. She heartily ate the food my aunt prepared for her—too heartily, like someone who really needed it—but she never tried to borrow money from us. Once she asked me to take her to the cinema, not for the feature film, only to see a newsreel she had been told about. When it came on, she nudged me—"Look, look, that's him! Mann!" It was a shot of an international banquet, with speeches in a language I couldn't identify under giant portraits of leaders also unidentifiable. It may have been Mann, but many of the other delegates could have been he, big and tall and cheering loudly as they raised and then drained their glasses in toasts to the speakers at the head table. She was convinced it was Mann—"The donkey," she laughed. "Can you imagine—he wanted to marry me. What a lucky escape," she congratulated herself. I had to leave, but since the ticket was paid for, she stayed on to see the feature film and to wait for the newsreel to come around again.

When Kohl died, it was reported in the newspapers that he had left the pictures remaining in his possession to a museum in New York and the rest of his estate to his maidservant. The lawyer told Marta that, if she could produce her marriage certificate, she would have a strong case for challenging the will. But she had no marriage certificate any more than she had a birth certificate, nor could she remember where the marriage had been registered, or when, in fact it seemed she couldn't remember if there had been any legal procedure at all. Whenever she spoke of Kohl, it was in the same way she did of Mann: congratulating herself on a lucky escape. She loved recalling the occasion when she had torn up his drawing—"Did you see his *face?*" she said, amused and pleased with herself. It turned out that this drawing was the only piece of work he had ever given her—just as the drawing he had given me was the only one of the many I sat for. I asked her, what about the poems that he had written to her? She tossed her hair, which was still red but now too red, a flag waved in defiance: "Who can remember every little scrap they once had? . . . Anyway, they were all a lot of rubbish. Other men have written much better poems to me." She admitted not having kept those either; she had had to move so often, everything had just disappeared.

And then she herself disappeared, and no one knew what had happened to her. We went to ask at the last address we had for her, but the mention of her name caused the landlady to shut the door against us. Years, decades have passed, and in all this time there has been no trace of Marta. I have stopped even speculating about her, though when my aunt was still alive we often did so, and there were conclusions that we did not like to mention to each other. Marta may have been run over or collapsed in the street and been taken to a hospital and died there, with no one knowing who she was, whom to contact. She may have—who knows?— drowned herself in the Thames on some dark night, maybe tossing the red flag of her hair, congratulating herself on having fooled everyone by never learning to swim.

I no longer live in London. Some years ago, I had some money trouble that finally led me to reluctantly sell Kohl's drawing. The sum I got for it was astonishing; it not only relieved me of my difficulties but gave me a sort of private income for a few years. I felt free to go where I liked, and since I had no one else close to me after La Plume, I was free in every way. I decided to go to New York. I had heard that there was a museum with one whole room dedicated to Kohl's work, and I went there the day after my arrival. Then I could not keep away.

All his drawings were on one wall, while the paintings took up the rest of the room. The drawings were mostly of Marta, some of me, and a few of other girls my age, one of them probably his maidservant. Although there was absolutely no resemblance between any of us, what we had in common was a particular and very evanescent stage of youth; and it must have been this that elicited his little gasps of joy, his murmurs of *"Sweet,"* and these marvelous portraits. But when I saw myself on the wall of the museum, I had the same feeling I had had while I was sitting for him: that I was not just a type or prototype for him, that it was not just any girl, some other girl, to whom he was responding but me, myself. *I* was the person at whom he had looked so deeply and with such delight, and in a way that no one ever had or, in fact, ever did again.

My decision to move to New York—where I have lived ever since— may have come partly and at first from a desire to remain close to the museum displaying his work. But although I can never get enough of studying the drawings, I can rarely bring myself to look at the paintings. They are no longer meaningless—everyone knows now how to interpret those savage, searing colors dripping off the canvas—but I still try to avoid them, even turning my back on them, unable to face what he faced, at night and in secret, through all the years we knew him. And I still wonder that, while he was possessed by these visions of our destruction, he was at the same time drawing—*"Sweet, sweet"*—what is now displayed on the other wall: girls in bloom, flowers in May.

Frances de Pontes Peebles

The Drowned Woman

from *Indiana Review*

I T WAS the summer of the year Juscelino Kubitschek was elected as president of the Republic, the summer when the drought in the farmlands got worse. The summer when someone mysteriously opened all of the birdcages at the Madalena Market, and for an entire Saturday morning canaries and parrots and sabiás flew free in the square as the vendors waved their hats and makeshift nets and tried to reclaim the birds. It was the summer when my grandmother's nurse washed ashore in front of our beach house. She wore a flowered dress and her shoes were missing. Her body was bloated and stiff, and one of her arms stood straight up in the air. No one knew what had happened to her.

We were finishing lunch when the body came ashore. Our cousin Dorany ran into our dining room.

"They just found a dead woman on the beach," he panted.

He was in his swim trunks and bare feet. I remember there was sand stuck to the hairs on his chest. My father would have never allowed Dorany into the dining room like that under normal circumstances. He put down his napkin and slid out from behind the table where he and my mother had just begun their meal. In our house, the children ate first and always at a separate table. Our meals were simple. Lunch was meat, beans, and rice. Dinners were always some kind of soup: black bean, or vegetable, or chicken, with a cup of cold milk. We were not allowed to have sugar.

Every once in a while my mother made us a plain yellow cake with a small swirl of chocolate in the center, which was a luxury. Looking back I realize we were well fed, even healthy.

My father's untouched serving of calf brains steamed on his plate. They were white and covered with tomato sauce, which looked to me like chunks of blood. My mother ate plain rice, steamed pumpkin, and black beans, all in separate piles on her plate.

My brothers and I stared at my father expectantly. He looked confused. I squirmed to the rim of my chair, making my skirt hike above my knees.

"Let's have a look, then," he said slowly.

With that we bolted from our chairs and ran from the house. My mother stayed behind. My father followed with Dorany at his side. He yelled at us to be careful crossing the road. It was a only a dirt path back then that separated our house from the beach, and the only car that passed was our own, but our father was concerned with decorum, not safety.

Our house was in Boa Viagem, near Piedade. We spent our summer breaks—from December until after Carnaval in February—at this house. All of the respectable Recife families did this. Our house was between our aunt Annali's and aunt Gilmara's houses. It was five doors down from the Heracles' house, and two doors down from the Brennand family's sprawling mansion that my father detested.

"What a waste!" he muttered each time we passed it in the car.

Back then, Boa Viagem was deserted except for those old homes. There were no high-rises, no Avenida, like today. We had to drive forty-five minutes just to find a bakery for fresh bread.

My brothers and I were the youngest of all of our cousins, and I was the only girl among this pack of boys. My brother Edgar was thirteen, I was twelve, Artur was ten, and João only seven. By February the beach's solitude began to wear on Edgar and me, especially during Carnaval. All we could do during those three days and four nights was chase each other with firecrackers, and light sparklers in the dark at the edge of the water. In later years, when we wouldn't go to the beach house anymore, we would finally spend Carnaval in the city. We would go to country-club parties and carry small vials of ether that my father bought for us. We would pour the ether into our handkerchiefs and sniff them throughout the night to make the room spin and the music play faster and faster.

A boy we knew died from sniffing too much ether. Geraldo Coelho was his name. He sniffed it until he fell unconscious on the dance floor and his cousins had to carry him to their car and take him to the hospital. I remember him because he was the only person, outside of my brothers, who ever asked me to dance. Strapless dresses were in style back then, and all of the other teenage girls were wearing them. I begged my mother and she got the seamstress to make me one with a matching jacket so I could leave the house without my father noticing I had a strapless on. I looked so silly in that dress. One of the boys at the country club joked, "Hey, Lúcia, you'd better be careful in that dress—if you raise your arms it'll fall right off!" Edgar punched him right in the face and Geraldo Coelho led me away from the brawl and onto the dance floor. He let me take a long sniff from his handkerchief and I couldn't stop laughing.

It was only when the ether wore off that I missed the silence of our old beach house Carnavals. But that summer, the summer when I was twelve, and it was February and I couldn't yet appreciate the quiet of the beach, a dead body was a big attraction.

A small crowd had already formed when we arrived on the sand. My aunt Annali stood sweating in her black dress and holding a rosary. Aunt Gilmara stood next to her, in an almost see-through linen robe, shaking her head. All of my older cousins, Annali's five sons, crowded at the edge of the water. The Brennand family and their servants huddled around the corpse. She lay on her side, with her bottom arm spread out on the sand. Her legs were bloated, and her skin was a pasty tan. Only the man who sold coconut water dared touch her, feeling for a pulse.

My uncle Paulo parted the crowd and directed the male servants to turn the woman over. We saw that it was my grandmother Dulce's nurse Rita. Her flowered dress was twisted. The side of her face was covered in sand. The arm that had been under her, and turned outwards when she rested on her side, now stood straight up, stiff in the air. The fingers of her outstretched hand were separated and it looked as if she was reaching up toward the sun, begging to be rescued from dry land. My uncle Paulo tried to force Rita's arm down but it would not go. My father had turned his back on Rita after she had been rolled over, until Artur and João laughed out loud at the sight of her uplifted arm. He turned around, slapped each of them across the face, and told them to go to the house.

My grandmother's wheelchair could not be pushed out onto the sand, so Aunt Gilmara's maid, a large woman who could lift three full buckets of milk at once, carried Grandmother Dulce out to the beach. My grandmother wore her best black dress and she looked like a doll bumping across the sand in the maid's arms, her tiny legs bobbing back and forth, making the embroidered beads of her dress swish and crunch against each other. Grandmother Dulce yelled over her shoulder at my mother, who held an umbrella over the old woman to protect her from the sun. When they reached the body my grandmother gasped, then covered her face with her hands and nodded, confirming that it was Rita.

"Emília!" Grandmother Dulce barked at my mother, who was staring back at the house, "my rosary." My grandmother proceeded to recite three Hail Marys while the maid who held her shifted in the sand. Everyone bowed their heads and mumbled the prayer, or pretended to. My uncle Paulo only moved his lips. My father looked down at the body, then shook his head impatiently. Only my grandmother's voice rose above the sound of the waves.

"Edgar," she cried when she finished, "call the civil police." My father nodded gravely and accompanied my grandmother and her entourage back to the house without giving Rita a second look.

The men dragged Rita's body farther up the beach so that the tide, which was steadily rising, would not wash it away. The crowd thinned out slowly, knowing that it would take the police hours to arrive. Aunt Annali and Aunt Gilmara went back to their respective houses. The coconut man went back to his stand at the top of the beach. My cousins and my brother Edgar slowly scattered, only after daring each other to touch the corpse. The Brennand ladies went back to sunbathing and their servants went back to work. Soon it was only me and Rita under the hot sun.

My grandmother Dulce was my father's mother. I always believed she was part Indian, because of her dark skin and her silence. When she did speak, her language betrayed her origins—she used perfect, precise, old-fashioned Portuguese. She gulped her vowels up into her nose and the back of her throat, and her sentences had a musical rhythm. On rare occasions she would suddenly seize my arm in her bird-of-prey grip and tell me random things.

"Lúcia," she would hiss from her wooden wheelchair, "when I came from Por-tu-gal we stayed in the first-class cabins," or "you must learn to speak cor-rect-ly, girl," and she often went on to say that she had not been tainted like the rest of us, that her language had been kept pure.

My grandfather Chico had left her everything—the deeds to the houses, the furniture, the cars, even the title to his import business. Grandmother Dulce was the one who placed Uncle Paulo at the head of the business. Grandmother Dulce was the one who pressured my father, who was still a bachelor at forty, to get married and start a proper family or else she would cut him off. And she was the one who, in the months after Rita died, insisted I be sent away to a Catholic boarding school because, she said, I was an animal and had to learn manners.

By the end of that summer at the beach house, I had punched a Brennand girl and knocked out her front tooth because she had called Rita a tramp. I had convinced Artur to help me steal our father's car and take it for a ride into the city, where we could find Rita's grave and put flowers on it. I controlled the steering wheel and the gearshift but could not reach the pedals. Artur sat curled on the floor and pressed the clutch and the gas when I told him to. We only made it a mile down the road before my father caught up with us.

The summer ended and I turned thirteen and was sent away to a school run by Belgian nuns. The nuns wore tiny habits that framed their faces and made them look pinched and small. In those days, you had to take everything with you to boarding school. My mother had to make a mini dowry for me—towels, sheets, blankets, and pillows. The nuns only gave us the bed and the mattress and we had to provide everything else.

Breakfast was bread and coffee. You could have one egg but you had to pay for it—it came out of your parents' pocket. Lunch was always some awful kind of stew. Dinner was bread and coffee again, with a mashed green banana. We had etiquette lessons on which fork to use, which knife, which spoon. During meals, if you did not eat with the right utensil, or if you talked to the girl next to you, they took away your food. I went through a lot of hungry days at that school. We were not allowed to talk—not during meals, not in the hallways, not in classes, not even in the showers. There was a nun who stood on a stepladder and looked over the tiled wall of the community shower to monitor us. She wore a metal whistle around her neck and would blow into it to warn us when the water was about to shut off. We had six minutes. It was hard to take a bath in such a short time because we were required to wear cotton camisoles that buttoned at our necks and our arms and went all the way down to our ankles. The camisole would get very heavy with soap and water, but we were never allowed to lift it up. We had to preserve our modesty.

That's why my father chose that particular school for me—because of its concern with modesty. They even made us change under our bedsheets each morning so as not to reveal ourselves to each other. It was silly really, because I could still see the other girls' bodies under their camisoles, and they could see mine. The water made the cotton fabric cling and everyone could see the outlines of everyone else. The water hit the camisoles of my classmates and over the years, it revealed breasts and hips and dark patches of hair. I mentioned this to my mother once, when I was home for vacation, and when I went back to school for my next term, I suddenly had a private shower at the end of the hallway with no monitor, and with hot water. My father had given the school extra money each month for this luxury. Even in my private shower I still wore the camisole, I was so used to it. After my grandmother passed away my parents took me out of the boarding school and placed me in Agnes Erickson, a modern Presbyterian girls' school near our home, and even then it took me a long time to get used to taking a bath in the nude.

I was her only female grandchild, so Grandmother Dulce had no choice but to leave me every feminine thing she owned—old silk fans, beaded dresses, a pearl necklace, and a collection of ornate brooches that I would never wear. The only thing she left me that I've kept is a picture of her as a girl in Porto, standing primly beside a boat on the Rio Douro. Written in faded ink on the back of the photograph is, *Dulce, 17 years old*, but when I look at the photo my grandmother looks no more than fourteen. I like to look at her face in this photo—her deceptively young face—because I see her more clearly than I did when I was a child and she was an old woman. The photo was taken before she came to Brazil, which she always referred to as *a country of savages*. It was taken before her husband died and she was left with a business she did not care to understand and a group of children who did not understand her. The photo was taken before all of that, and in it she looks innocent and almost kind.

That summer, in the days before Rita died, Grandmother Dulce seemed deceptively frail and required constant attention. It was Rita who dressed her each morning and put her in the sun. It was Rita who rubbed lotion onto my grandmother's hands and wrapped her long, thin piece of white hair into the smallest of buns. And it was Rita who held the wooden tablet with pegs in it steady while Grandmother Dulce made lace doilies, hooking strands of silk through one peg after another for hours on end.

I stood staring at Rita's body on the beach. Her dress was beginning to dry off and white salt caked over the fabric's small purple flowers. Her eyes were shut and her mouth slightly open. She looked trapped, frozen in the position in which she had washed ashore, like a starfish or a coral that becomes petrified when taken from the sea. I remembered how that morning Rita had not come back from her daily walk. My mother had had to dress and bathe Grandmother Dulce, and leave her on the porch with Artur. During their breakfast I heard my mother complain to my father about Rita's absence.

"Fire her, Edgar. Now you will have to fire her."

I stood under the burning sun until I couldn't bear looking at Rita's body any longer. I felt dizzy and hot, my throat stung, and my eyes watered from the reflection of the sun off of the bright sand. I ran to Aunt Annali's house and into her kitchen.

My aunt had a skinny cook named Doralice. Doralice was the darkest woman I had ever seen. I liked to watch her, because when she sweated her skin would shine and it looked like she was made of stone. She got mad when I stared at her so I had to watch her secretly, through the hole in the screen door, or from the open window. If she caught me she ran after me with a wooden spoon and swore she was going to beat me if I looked at her again. Doralice made desserts—fabulous creations that made me salivate every afternoon. She made chocolate cakes that oozed warm fudge from the inside and were covered with a white cream sauce on top, made of condensed milk. Once I had begged my mother for condensed milk. I begged for days, until she went to the store, bought seven cans of it, and made me sit and eat each one until I got so sick I couldn't leave the bathroom for a whole day.

That day, I did not hide from Doralice when I came in from the beach. I walked right into the kitchen and sat down on a stool by the butcher block. She was making my favorite dessert—a guava pudding, the color of bubble gum and decorated with blue-black prunes. Doralice arranged the prunes without acknowledging me.

"Rita's dead," I told her, my voice breaking, even though I tried my best to sound flippant about the whole thing.

"I know," Doralice said mechanically, arranging the prunes.

She and Rita used to smoke cigarettes together in the afternoons, on their breaks. Rita rolled the cigarettes and licked them. Doralice yelled at her not to get her red lipstick on them. They laughed and giggled a lot. Doralice was having an affair with the coconut vendor's son—a muscular young man who met her by the shed behind Aunt Annali's house once a week. I watched them once—I saw them kiss. I saw their pink tongues move in and out of each other's dark mouths. I saw his hand go under her skirt and her long leg wrap around his waist. I left when I saw that. I backed away from my hiding spot and ran, more afraid of seeing what they were going to do next than of getting caught.

During their breaks, Rita would tease Doralice and she would tease Rita right back. "He might not be rich, but at least he's mine and mine alone," she would say, growing serious. "You had better be careful, Rita. That's all I'm going to say. You're a grown woman, you can do what you want. You don't have to listen to me—but you have to know your place." Rita would puff on their cigarette and change the subject, asking Doralice what she was going to cook for dinner that night. Then Rita would smile and nod, and listen, just listen, until it was time for them to go back to work again.

"I said Rita's dead. Don't you care?" I yelped, hitting my fist against the wooden table. Doralice looked up, her eyes narrowed on me.

"What business of yours is it if I care?" she barked. "How do you know if I care or not? How does a spoiled little girl like you know anything at all? You didn't even know Rita."

She went for a spoon, but I jumped from the stool and yelled at her, "I knew Rita. I knew her better than anybody!" I ran from the kitchen out onto the porch.

My cousins, Uncle Paulo, and Aunt Annali ate lunch in their dining room and I watched them from the porch windows, wiping my nose on my shirt collar. They ate as a family, together at the same table. They did not have to keep their napkins in their laps or chew twenty-five times before swallowing. They got to drink real bottled Brahma Guaraná soda. My father only bought powdered Guaraná for us. Our maid Raimunda stirred the powder into a huge pitcher of water every day. It was chalky, not fizzy like the bottled soda my cousins got. It made me so mad.

. . .

Rita was a dark woman too. She had thick legs and tan skin—caramel-colored skin like Grandmother Dulce's, like my own. Every day she wore bright red lipstick, which she would reapply after lunch. She was ten years older than my mother and had small spider veins on her calves. Despite this, Rita liked to wear knee-length dresses and black high-heeled sandals with little flowers embroidered on the straps. Once, my grandmother's wheelchair ran over her foot and broke her middle toe. Rita limped into my father's study, where he was teaching me to play chess. "Edgar," she'd called him, "Edgar, I've hurt myself." And then I watched from the doorway as she sat in a chair across from my father, her foot in his lap, his hands shaking as he made her a splint from a Popsicle stick and gauze.

Rita would not help in the kitchen. She would not do any cooking or cleaning. She was educated, she said, trained as a nurse and would not do a maid's work. This infuriated my mother. Rita always smiled when she passed me in the hallways, or when she caught me watching her with my grandmother. In the afternoons, when Rita sat with Grandmother Dulce on the terrace, I liked to sneak into her room at the back of the house. It was at the end of a long hallway behind the laundry area, five doors down from Raimunda's room. Rita had a patchwork quilt on her bed and her pillows smelled like her perfume, a baby cologne that sat in a huge glass bottle on her dresser. She had celebrity magazines stacked in a corner and a thin book about Rio de Janeiro on her dresser. When I looked in her dresser drawers, I saw large brassieres and cotton underpants that were like my own, except her initials were not sewn into the corners.

One afternoon, as I sat cross-legged on the sandy wooden floor and looked through her things, I found in her bottom drawer, hidden under an old sweater, two gold boxes tied with pink ribbons. I opened the one box and there was nothing in it except for ten empty tinfoil cups. The other box had three chocolates left in it: one with a pink swirl, another in the shape of a heart, and a white one with a stamp of a coin in the middle. My mouth watered. Where had Rita gotten these chocolates? They were expensive and fresh, not covered in a white dust like the old chocolates I had once found in our pantry and tried to eat but could not. These were smooth and rich and as dark as Doralice's skin.

On another afternoon, while Rita cared for my grandmother, I snuck back to Rita's room and I caught my mother coming out of it. We were both flustered—trapped in a dead-end hallway with no excuses to make.

"What are you doing back here?" my mother asked, her face flushing.

"I . . . I . . . was looking for you." This was a lie and she knew it. I only looked for my mother when my father would tell me to get her. He was in Recife on business that day.

"What do you want?" she asked.

"I'm hungry." It was the only excuse I could think of. It was four o'clock and Raimunda had strict instructions not to let us into the pantry after lunch. My mother knew this. She looked relieved—it was a chance for both of us to escape. We went back to the kitchen and my mother cut open a mango for us.

"Lúcia," she said as she sliced the fruit with her knife, "there's a slip of paper in my skirt pocket. I don't want to touch it because my hands have juice on them. Take it out for me and tell me what it says."

My mother could not read or write very well. She tried to write grocery lists by herself, but always gave up and handed me the pen and paper. I would cross out her shaky writing and begin the list again as she stood in the pantry and called out the items we needed to buy. She was raised on a sugar plantation in Paraíba, and as the oldest girl among eight children, she had to quit school early to help her mother. She used to tell me that as a teenager she had gone into the city and had seen a car for the first time in her life. "After that," she'd said, "I told myself that one day I would ride in one of those machines. That one day I would have one of my own." So, when my father came into town in his white suit and convertible to sell imported machines to the local sugar mill, she saw her opportunity. She never phrased it that crudely, though.

This is her story of how they met: She was standing under an orange tree near the road and he saw her. He pulled his car alongside the tree and asked if he could have an orange. "One?" my mother said. "You can have the whole tree if you want it." She was seventeen. He was forty-one. They were married one year later, and a year after that, Edgar was born, and a year after that, I was born.

"What does it say?" my mother asked. I unfolded the paper, which looked as though it had been ripped out of a book.

"It's a poem," I said, recognizing the shape of the typed lines. Some of the words were too big for me to understand, but the ebb and flow of the rhymes made me recall the kiss between Doralice and her coconut boy, their tongues swirling in and out of each other, their hands and mouths and bodies moving in a perfect rhythm.

"What is it about?" my mother asked, placing the mango slices on a plate for us.

"Nothing," I mumbled, folding the paper up, and putting it back in her pocket. "It's about the ocean, that's all."

I always believed my father's family liked my mother—why wouldn't they? My mother had dark hair, an hourglass figure, and perfect skin except for the mosquito bites on her legs. My mother smelled like soap and talcum powder, and she carried a handkerchief in the belt of her dress to wipe her brow and neck on hot days. My mother taught Aunt Annali how to knit, and she used to rub aloe vera on Aunt Gilmara's back to relieve sunburns. But when my aunts had afternoon luncheons at their homes in the city, my mother never attended, even though she was always invited. She said she had too much to do at home, that she was too busy with the children. Once, when I pressed her on why she didn't accept an offer to go to lunch, she snapped at me and said, "The invitation is just a formality, Lúcia." Sometimes my mother would laugh with our maids, but would immediately catch herself and then leave the room to let them finish their work. When I was a girl, I believed she was just a shy and silent person. Many times she tried to teach me how to sew, how to make jam. But I was never interested. I wanted to read, to play chess, to hide and observe everyone except her.

The mango was the sweetest thing we had in the house that day, and my mother and I sat in the kitchen for a long time peeling back its red skin and sucking on its insides, without saying a word.

I wiped my eyes and left my aunt Annali's porch after they had finished eating dessert. I went back to the beach to check on Rita's body. My older cousins were playing football at the top of the beach, showing off for the sunbathing Brennand girls who had turned to watch them. My brothers were in the surf, starting a game we all liked to play in the afternoons, as the tide got higher. We liked to build forts by the edge of the water. We would dig moats in the sand and build barricades out of palm fronds, coconuts, and driftwood. Anything that was natural could be used; those were the rules. The waves would pound the forts when high tide would come and whoever's structure was left standing would win. We would scramble to keep our forts up the longest. Sometimes we stayed on the beach so long my mother had to send Raimunda to bring us in.

The tide was rising that afternoon. The water lapped up to Rita's toes whenever a wave hit. Her raised arm made a shadow across her body. My brothers argued. Artur yelled at Edgar that yes, a corpse was natural and that he could use it to barricade his fort. Edgar disagreed. João was already digging up sand around Rita

"Stop!" I yelled. "Don't touch her! Get away from her!" I walked up to Artur and pushed him hard. "No one can use her for their fort," I screamed, "Go play somewhere else."

Edgar smirked. João obeyed.

Artur narrowed his eyes. "I can do whatever I want."

I pushed him a second time and he fell to the sand. Edgar laughed and clapped me on the back. Artur started to run for the house to tell our mother, but Edgar grabbed his shoulder.

"Don't be a baby, Artur. She's right. I told you you can't use the body. It's not fair for the rest of us. Come on, let's build down the beach over there."

Artur considered this, then walked down the beach without looking at me. Soon, the three of them were laughing and yelling, scampering in the sand, fighting for pieces of wood and tackling each other for tufts of seaweed while I sat next to Rita. Her red lipstick had come off and her lips were pink and dry. Sand had crept into the corners of her mouth. I pictured Rita underwater, her body loose and free, her dress fluttering like a fin. I could picture the salt water going into and out of her, a sea creature taking up residence in her open mouth, small fish hiding in her hair. It was a shame she had been washed ashore. I thought of the rocks and shells I liked to pick up off the beach. They were so brilliant and colorful in the tide, but always dried off when I brought them home and became dull without the shine of the water. Like Rita, they were more beautiful in the sea. I took a handkerchief from my pocket—a small square of fabric that my grandmother had embroidered for me, decorating it with flowers and butterflies and my initials, LCR. I began to slowly wipe the sand from Rita's face.

· · ·

Two days before we found Rita's body on the beach, I had gone to her room and was surprised to find her there. Grandmother Dulce had taken an unexpected nap, complaining that she had not slept well the night before. Rita stood over her dresser, admiring a new gold box of chocolates and deciding which one she would have first. She saw me, looked surprised, then smiled and invited me in.

"Come here, Lúcia," she said.

She brushed back hairs from my face. Her nails felt so good on my scalp I almost closed my eyes.

"Do you want one?" She motioned to the box.

I looked at her, unsure.

"I promise I won't tell anyone. Our secret."

I nodded.

"Which one do you want?"

I pointed to the dark one, the one with a pink swirl. She took it from its wrapper and handed it to me.

"Try it."

I did. It was filled with a caramel crème that dripped on my chin. I smiled. So did Rita. She wiped my chin with her thumb. She took a nutty one out of the box and popped it in her mouth all at once. I heard it crunch. She gave me another, then another.

"It's a shame," she said, smiling, "that your mother doesn't let you eat these things. She shouldn't deprive her child. But she's a child herself, your mother." Rita took a chocolate between her fingers and stared at it. "She's too young up here," she pointed to her head, "to appreciate these things, but you aren't, are you? No, you aren't."

I felt Rita was trying to say that she and I were alike, and I felt flattered by this. Rita seemed different than the other hired help—more elegant somehow, more ambitious. As a girl I was fascinated by her ambition because I could not see the viciousness in it, or how useless and sad it was for a person in her position to even harbor it.

By the end of the afternoon we had finished the whole box of candies. Rita lay on her bed while I sat beside her, one leg up on the mattress, the other dangling above the floor. We made an appointment to go for a walk the next morning, together, during low tide. We would leave early so no one would even know we were gone. Rita liked to take walks along the beach in the mornings when the rocks and tide pools were exposed. I knew she took these walks because I had often spied her leaving in the mornings, silently closing the screen door and heading out to the beach without shoes on.

We took our secret walk the day before Rita died. She and I came back to the house giggling and whispering. The sun was out by then and we heard sounds in the kitchen. We had planned on separating; Rita would go in through the back door as usual and I would sneak in through the front. But just as we were about to part, we heard the back door open and my mother came out of the kitchen. She held a dishrag in her hand. Raimunda stared from the doorway with a concerned look on her face. My mother did not say a word. I thought she was going to slap me, but instead she hit Rita square across the face, then dragged me by the arm up to my room. I looked back and saw Rita holding her cheek in her hands.

I was confined to my room all day. I did not know what I had done wrong. I could only hear the murmurs of my parents' yells from my room. I was not allowed to have lunch. I felt feverish. I wept until I fell asleep. I woke up again and it was dark outside. I crept downstairs to try to sneak into the kitchen for some food, and saw that the lights were on in my father's study.

He was sitting at his desk and looking out the window, and I could not tell if he was staring out at the darkness on the other side of the glass, or at his own reflection. Then he saw me in the doorway.

"Tough day, wasn't it Lúcia?" he asked, smiling slightly. He looked tired and old.

"Yes," I replied.

He invited me in. Then he did something he had never done before—he searched his bookshelf and handed me a copy of *Robinson Crusoe*. We were never allowed to touch my father's books. Their different-colored leather bindings and illegible writing—most were written in German—fascinated me. My father had studied electrical engineering in Germany before the war, and had even worked in America, in New York City, until he was called back when Grandfather Chico died. I've always wondered what it must have been like for him—to have seen so many exotic places and then to come back here, to Recife, at a time when even simple electricity was a novelty to everyone but him.

He spoke very little about those sorts of things. It was only when he was older, in his late seventies, that he spoke about his time in Germany. I was the only one in my family who still visited him at that time, so I got to hear his stories. He had left my mother, had moved out of our family home and began living with a young black manicurist in a rough part of town. She was my age at the time, in her thirties, and I remember she liked to kiss him on the top of his bald head and this bothered me.

"You should read this, Lúcia," my father said that night in his study as he kneeled next to me. The chair I sat in was made of mahogany and was so tall my twelve-year-old legs could not touch the ground. "It's very good," he said. "It's about a man who is all by himself in the world," and he went on to tell me the entire story as I turned the book around in my hands.

I went to bed with the book under my arm and did not wake up until morning, when the first light started to peek through my windows and I heard the screen door slam and knew it was Rita.

Rita's body was almost dried off, but the water was lapping over her ankles. A smell, like bad breath, came from her. I stared at Rita's clean face. I had woken up that morning, my father's book in my arms, and had heard Rita leaving for her walk. A cluster of seaweed washed up near my feet. It was bright green with little seed balls that were the size of pearls. I popped these pearls between my thumb and forefinger, then looked at Rita's outstretched arm. I took the strand of seaweed and made a bracelet for Rita, tying it loosely to her stiff wrist. I searched for another strand and made her a necklace. Then I combed her hair with my fingers and made her a crown.

As I arranged her hair I heard a siren and knew that the Recife Civil Police had finally arrived. They pulled onto the sand in a green jeep accompanied by an old station wagon ambulance whose lights and siren were broken. Everyone remembered the body then, and came out of their homes. My cousins stopped their football game, my brothers forgot their forts. My uncle Paulo and my father spoke with the officers—two short men in green military uniforms—while two paramedics told me to move aside as they checked Rita for any signs of life. My father explained that we had found her that way, already stiff, brought in by the tide. The men in green were silent. Then I saw my uncle slip both of them fifty cruzeiros, "to avoid any confusion." The men in green nodded and said it was awful, how many accidental drownings there were this time of year on the beaches.

The paramedics brought over a stretcher. They lifted Rita by her shoulders and feet and plopped her on it. One medic laughed and mockingly shook Rita's outstretched hand.

"This happens every time," they said to my uncle. "After a while the bodies get stiff. You wouldn't believe the positions we find some of them in! We'll have to break her arm to get it down."

"Be careful not to cut your feet!" Rita had said during our secret walk.

We picked up starfish and Rita explained how they could lose an arm and grow it back. She giggled when she almost slipped on a rock covered with moss. We crouched over a tide pool and she pointed out the pink sea anemones, their tentacles swaying in the water. We saw black-spiked sea urchins and small fish flutter and hide under bands of seaweed. Then, Rita told me to be very still and we closed our eyes and listened to the ocean gurgle as it trickled into and out of the tide pools.

"You're growing up, Lúcia," she said softly, looking into the water.

I nodded.

"Things will happen to you soon . . . changes . . . do you know what I mean?"

I did. I knew because I had seen my aunt Gilmara, who liked to lie nude in her hammock on hot afternoons with only a small sheet covering her. Some afternoons the sheet shifted and I caught glimpses of her grown woman's body.

I knew why my mother got sick once a month and stayed in bed all day with the door locked. The doctor who treated her had seen me once, listening outside of her door, and he told me the story of Eve and the Serpent and said that one day I too would get sick each month, and one day I too would feel the pain of bearing a child.

"It is part of growing up," he had said, "and with it comes responsibility."

I knew all of these things awaited me, but I told Rita that I didn't. I let her talk, let her hold my hand and tell me, as we sat by the tide pool, how I would grow and change.

Rita did not know that her body would wash up on the beach the next day, bloated and foul-smelling. She did not know that at the end of the summer I would be sent away to boarding school. And she would never know that I would not develop . . . not get a period or breasts or pubic hair . . . until I was eighteen years old because, the doctors said, of a hormonal abnormality. Rita would never know that I only learned my retarded development was a serious problem through the whispers and hushed conversations of my aunts, and that my mother had to smuggle me in to see a women's doctor because my father had strictly forbidden it. Rita would never see me grow up lanky and quiet, stuck in my little girl's body without knowing why. And she would never know that in the years after her death we stayed at the beach house less and less, until we stopped going there altogether.

But I didn't know most of these things either, that summer, when they took my friend away on a stretcher, her seaweed bracelet bobbing on her stiff arm, making her look as if she were waving good-bye.

Tessa Hadley

The Card Trick

from *The New Yorker*

I T WAS 1974: not a good year, clothes-wise, if you were an eighteen-year-old girl, tall and overweight, with thick, curling hair and glasses. Gina liked best to wear a duffel coat, underneath which she imagined she hid herself. But this was summer, and she was on holiday, and she'd had reluctantly to leave the duffel coat at home. The fashion was for smocks and long skirts with deep frills and cotton prints, so she mostly wore a Laura Ashley dress in a blue sprigged cotton that was meant to look as if it had been faded by long-ago haymaking in meadows of wildflowers; its buttons gaped open across her bust and it was tight around her hips and its effect on her, she was quite sure, was not rustic but hulking and vaguely penitentiary. Sometimes as she walked, bitter tears stung her eyes at the idea of the sheer affront of her ugliness forcing itself upon the successive layers of the air. At other times, she was more hopeful.

Today, at least, the sun was not shining. When it shone—and it had shone every day since she arrived—it made things worse; it seemed such an insult to nature and beauty not to want to peel off all one's clothes and run around on the beach, not to be happy. But now the sky was a consoling soft gray, which dissolved from time to time into warm rain, and everybody was more or less muffled under raincoats and umbrellas. Because it was raining, Mamie had driven inland with Gina from the house on the coast, to visit Wing Lodge.

Mamie was her mother's friend, and Gina was staying with her and her family for a fortnight; although to call her a friend did not quite explain the relationship, since Mamie was also a client, for whom Gina's mother made clothes. Mamie was small and very pretty, with sloping shoulders and ash-blond hair and a face that was always screwing up with laughter. Her tan was the kind you can get only in the South of France. (She had a house there, too.) Her clothes seemed effortless—today, for example, a Liberty print blouse under a cream linen pinafore—but Gina had seen some of these things in the making and knew how much effort actually went into them: the serious scrutiny of pinned-up hemlines in front of the mirror, Mamie bringing things back ruefully, apologetically, after a week or two, with a nagging suspicion that a sleeve had been set in too high, or an inspiration that the seams would look wonderful with two rows of overstitching.

She was being very kind—very encouraging—to Gina. She had not made any mention of the Laura Ashley dress or of the barrette that had seemed an appealing idea when Gina brushed her hair that morning but was now bobbing against her cheek in a way that suggested it had slid to an altogether wrong and ridiculous place.

They stopped off on their way to Wing Lodge at a tearoom by the side of the country road; they were the only customers in a small room crowded with unbalanced little chairs and glass-topped wicker tables, smelling of damp and cake.

It'll probably be instant coffee, Mamie whispered with conspiratorial amusement. (Gina only ever had instant at home.) But I don't care. Do you? Or we could always risk the tea. And you've got to have a Danish pastry or something, to keep you going.

Complicatedly, Mamie was making reference to the fact that Gina clearly oughtn't to be eating pastries of any kind; but her diet, which was perpetual during this period of her life, alternating drearily between punishing obedience and frantic transgression, had been thrown into such chaos since she'd been staying at Mamie's—on the one hand, she was too shy to refuse the food that was pressed upon her; on the other, she didn't dare to raid the fridge or the cupboards in between meals—that she didn't even know whether she was being good or not. She took advantage of the lack of clarity to agree to the pastry.

Gina had just had her A-level results—three A's—and she was preparing for her Cambridge entrance examinations in November. Mamie professed an exaggerated awe of her cleverness.

You really make me so ashamed, she said, when she had finished charming the gray-haired waitress and giving very exact instructions as to how she liked her tea ("pathetically weak, no milk, just pour it the very instant the water's on the leaves, I'm so sorry to be such a frightful nuisance"). We're such duffers in my family. We've hardly got an O level between us—and that's after spending an absolute fortune on the children's education. Josh simply refused to go back to Bedales to do retakes. Becky left the day she was sixteen. She never even sat any exams. How I'd love for one of them to have your brains.

I'm not that special, Gina lied, her voice muffled through damp pastry flakes.

Somewhere in the deepest recesses of herself, Gina pitied Mamie and her children, precisely along the lines that Mamie suggested. The children—three older boys and a girl Gina's age—certainly weren't clever in the way she was. She'd never seen them reading a book; they hadn't known the other day at breakfast who Walter Gropius was; and she was sure that they were sublimely ignorant about all the things that seemed to her ultimately to matter in the world: literature and painting and the history of ideas. But that arrogant intellectual reflex felt so remotely subterranean as to be almost inconsequential, compared with her willingness to acknowledge every advantage that Becky and Josh and Tom and Gabriel had on the surface in the here and now, in honor and envy of which she was horribly ready to abase herself. And Mamie was surely disingenuous in her praise of Gina's brains. She was just being kind. She wouldn't have exchanged brains, really, for the easy personable charm that all her children had, not if it meant that they'd have awkward bodies and thick glasses.

And, even if they weren't clever, Mamie's children didn't actually say stupid things, as Gina did, tongue-tied with bookish awkwardness. On the contrary, they were funny and chatty and informed about practical matters. They confessed to being indifferent to politics but were sincerely charming and generous with the woman who came to clean and cook and iron for them every day, whereas Gina didn't know how to talk to her. And then they were masters of arts that Gina knew she would never be competent in, no matter how hard she tried: tennis, for example, and motorcycling, and snorkeling. She couldn't even ride a push-bike.

Gabriel, the oldest, had a darkroom and developed his own photographs; Becky posed for him, unembarrassedly arranging her face to look its best whenever called upon. If Gabriel turned the camera on Gina, she swiveled away, protesting and sulking, so he soon stopped trying. The house was filled with vivid black-and-white pictures, in which the lives of this family seemed poignant and enchanting, even beyond what you could grasp in ordinary everyday contact with them. Gina studied the photographs with the same yearning she felt over the fashion pictures in magazines: trying to understand how one might possess oneself with such certainty, and know so confidently how to live.

They were all beautiful. Gabriel and Becky looked like Mamie, small with pretty faces, turned-up noses, and huge eyes. The others looked like their father, who was in the South of France with friends. (A separation that seemed to Gina, whose parents did everything together, both strange and significant: her mother had hinted, out of confidences accorded while she was crawling around a hemline with her mouth full of pins, that all was not well in Mamie's marriage. Still, Dickie's absence was a great relief. Gina had seen him only once or twice, when he came to pick up Mamie after a fitting, but it had been enough to know that he was terrifying, tall and tanned and savagely impatient.) Tom and Josh—Josh was the nearest boy to Gina in age—were tall, with slim long bodies, fine skin taut over light strong bones, sensitive-knuckled hands and feet. She had got used to their near-nakedness on the beach in swimming trunks, or bare-chested in cutoff jeans. It was 1974: they wore their sun-bleached hair long, and they walked barefoot everywhere.

The spare bedroom Gina was staying in was on the ground floor of the house, and it opened onto the hall, whose dark parquet was always dusted with a layer of fine sand blown in from the beach. She spent a lot of time in her room—"working," she told them—and sometimes, when she peeped out of her door to see if the coast was clear to visit the bathroom, she saw the prints of the boys' bare feet in the sand, crossing the hall to the kitchen or the stairs. For some reason, this moved her, and her heart clenched in an excitement more breathlessly sexual than if she'd seen the boys themselves.

The visit to Wing Lodge had been part of the pretext for Gina's coming to visit Mamie in the first place. It was the house where John Morrison, her favorite novelist, had lived, and she had desperately wanted to make a pilgrimage there; but she was beginning to wish that she could have come on her own. She was burdened by her sense of Mamie's kindness: Mamie had clearly never read any of Morrison's books, and she could have no good reason, surely, to want to see his house. Gina worried over the things that Mamie would probably rather have done, and in more congenial company.

But when they arrived in the little town and found the house on one of its oldest streets, behind the church, a more complex unease began to dawn on Gina. Wing Lodge stood back behind a walled front garden, which even in the rain was very lovely: pale roses bowed and dripping with water, a crumbling sundial, a path of old paving stones set into the grass, leading to a bench under a gnarled apple tree.

Isn't it just charming? Mamie exclaimed, pausing on the porch to shake off the umbrella she had gallantly insisted on sharing with Gina, so that they were now both rather wet. This is such a treat. Thank you so much for bringing me here. I can't imagine why we've never been before.

Gina had thought that at last, at Wing Lodge, she would be on home ground. She knew so much about John Morrison, a friend of Conrad and Ford, given a complimentary mention by Henry James in "The New Novel." She had written the long essay for her English A level on his use of complex time schemes. She loved the spare texture of his difficult, sad books, and felt that she was exceptionally equipped to understand them. Faced with his most obscure passages (he wasn't elaborate like James but compressed and allusive), she trusted herself to intuit his meaning, even if she couldn't quite disentangle it.

But as she followed Mamie through the front door into the low-ceilinged hall she realized that she had miscalculated. She was not entering one of Morrison's books, where she could feel confident; she was entering his house, where she might not. Two middle-aged women sat at a table on which leaflets and a cash box were arranged; wood paneling polished to a glow as deep and savory as horse chestnuts reflected the yellow light from a couple of table lamps; tall vases of flowers stood against the wall on the uneven flagstone floor. Gina stepped flinchingly around a Persian rug that opened like a well of color at her feet.

This is Gina, Mamie told the women as she got out her purse to pay. She's the daughter of a very gifted and creative friend of mine. We're here today because she loves John Morrison's books so much and has written her A-level essay about him. She's very, very bright.

The women's smiles were coldly unenthusiastic. They advised the visitors to start in the room on the right and make their way around to the study, which was arranged as it had been in the writer's lifetime. If they went upstairs at the end of the tour, they would find an exhibition of editions of the works. Which might interest you, one of them suggested skeptically.

The house was furnished—sparely, exquisitely—with a mixture of antiques and curiosities and modern things: a venerably worn Indian tapestry thrown across an old chaise longue, an elm Art Deco rocking chair, drawings by Wyndham Lewis and Gaudier-Brzeska. It was dark everywhere, and the lamps were on in the middle of the day: the low, deeply recessed casement windows were running with rain and plastered with wet leaves. Mamie moved through it all with a kind of hushed rapture, absorbing the aura of the great man, despite the fact that she had no idea what he was great for.

So sweet! she whispered emphatically. What a darling place. What treasures.

Gina thought perplexedly of the letters Morrison had written from Wing Lodge: full of damp walls and leaking roofs and smoking chimneys and penetrating cold, as well as self-deprecating confessions of untidiness and neglect. She hadn't imagined that his house would be like this. How could he have afforded all these possessions? The rooms were like Mamie's: glossy with value and distinction, a kind of patina of initiated good taste.

Do they live here? she asked. Those ladies?

Oh, I should think so, wouldn't you? It feels very much like a home, not a museum. The widow stayed on here, apparently, until a few years ago. So I suppose they've just kept a few of the rooms as she left them. It's only open a couple of afternoons a week.

There was a photograph of Anne, the American wife and widow, on the plain writing table in the study: young, with a Katherine Mansfield fringe and bobbed hair and a necklace of beads the size of cherries. Morrison had been a world wanderer, with a Scottish father and a Norwegian mother. (You could feel the influence of a certain Scandinavian neurasthenia in his novels.) He had settled down at last, here in the South of England, written his best books here, and died here, in his fifties, in 1942.

Can't you just imagine being able to write at this desk? Mamie said encouragingly.

Gina looked at her dumbly across the charming room, with its waxed floor slanting quaintly to the window, unable to say how unlikely it seemed to her at this moment that anyone could ever have written anything worth reading in a house like this. She thought of art as a sort of concealed ferocity, like the fox hidden under the Spartan boy's shirt. It seemed to her that any authentic utterance would be stifled by the loveliness, the serene self-completeness of this room. What could one do here but self-congratulate: write cookery books, perhaps, or nostalgic reminiscences?

At the same time, she was filled with doubt, in case she was deluded, in case it turned out that art was a closed club after all, one that she would never be able to enter, she who had never owned one thing as beautiful as the least object here.

Sometimes Gina emerged victorious from her struggle with Mamie's pressing hospitalities, and succeeded in staying at home while everyone else went to the beach. (The sea was only a few minutes' walk across the dunes from the front door, but the beach they liked best for swimming and surfing was a short drive away.) She heard and winced at the little crack of impatience in Mamie's voice—"I suppose it's awfully impressive, to want to have your head buried in a book all day"—but that was worth incurring in exchange for the delicious freedom of having the house to herself for hours on end.

She didn't really spend all that time studying. She drifted from her books to the windows to the kitchen cupboards, eating whatever Mamie had left for her almost at once, and then spooning things out of expensive jars from the delicatessen (only enough so that no one could ever tell) and ferreting out the forgotten ends of packets of cakes and biscuits and nuts. She made herself comfortable with her bare legs up over the back of the collapsed chintz sofa, hanging her head down to the floor to read Becky's copies of *Honey* and *19*. In fact, she took possession of the lovely weather-washed old house with a lordly offhandedness that she never felt when the others were around. She ran herself copious baths perfumed with borrowed Badedas in the old claw-foot tub with its thundering taps. She tried on Mamie's lipstick and Becky's clothes. She browsed through the boys' bedrooms with their drawn curtains and heaps of sandy beach gear and frowsy smells of socks; she experimented with their cigarettes and once, for a dizzying hour, lost herself over a magazine of stunningly explicit sexual photographs she found stuffed down between one bed and the wall. (She didn't know whose bed it was, and the next time she felt for the magazine it was gone.) She sat in a deck chair on the sagging picturesque veranda whose wood had been rainwashed to a silvered gray, drinking Campari in a cocktail glass with a cherry from a jar and a dusty paper umbrella she'd found in a drawer; afterward, she cleaned her teeth frantically and chewed what she hoped were herbs from the garden so that no one would smell alcohol on her breath.

Once, after about an hour of this kind of desultory occupation, she happened to glance up through the open French windows from her dangling position on the sofa and was smitten with horror: she had been sure that they had all gone to the beach, but there was Tom, stripped to the waist, cutting the meadow of long grass behind the house with a scythe, working absorbedly and steadily with his back to her. Tom was particularly frightening: moody like his father, skeptical of the family charm, dissenting and difficult. Actually, he was the one whom Gina chose most often for her fantasies, precisely because he was difficult; she imagined herself distracting, astonishing, taming him.

Appalled to think what he might have seen of her rake's progress around his mother's house, she scuttled to her bedroom, where she spent the rest of the long day in what amounted to a state of agonized siege, not knowing whether he knew she was there, paralyzed with self-consciousness, avoiding crossing in front of her own window, unable to bring herself to venture out of her room even when she was starving or desperate to use the loo. Tom came inside—perhaps for lunch, or perhaps because he'd finished scything—and played his Derek and the Dominoes album loudly, as though he believed he had the house to himself. Gina lay curled in a fetal position on the bed, worrying that he might open the door and find her, but worrying, too, that if he didn't find her, and then learned that they had shared the house for the whole afternoon without her even once appearing, he might think her—whom he barely noticed most of the time— insane, grotesque.

She wept silently into her pillow, wishing he'd leave, and at the same time mourning this opportunity slipping away, this afternoon alone in the house with him, which was, after all, the very stuff of her indefatigable invention. They might have conversed intelligently over coffee on the veranda; she might have accepted one of his cigarettes and smoked it with offhand sophistication; he, surprised at her thoughtfulness and quiet insight, might have held out his hand on impulse and led her off on a walk down among the dunes. And so on, and so on, until the crashing, inevitable, too-much-imagined end.

When Gina was at her unhappiest during that long fortnight, she wanted to blame her mother, and for short passionate private sessions she allowed herself to do so. Her mother had been so keen on her accepting Mamie's invitation, ostensibly because she was worried that Gina was studying too hard but really because of a surreptitious hope, which had never been put into words, though Gina was perfectly well aware of it, that Gina might get on with Mamie's boys. "Get on with": it wouldn't have been, not for her mother, any more focused than that, a vague but picturesque idea of friendly comradeship, the boys coming, through daily unbuttoned summertime contact, to appreciate Gina's "character," as her mother optimistically conceived of it. Boys, her mother obviously thought, would be good for Gina. Apart from anything else, they might help to make her happy. But it would be disingenuous to make her mother solely responsible: when the holiday had been suggested, Gina had not refused. And this could only have been because she, too, had held out hopes, less innocent ones even, which appeared, in the event—as she should have known they would—to have been grotesquely, insanely, and characteristically misplaced.

There came another day of rain. At the end of a long afternoon of Monopoly and a fry-up supper, Mamie was suddenly visibly afflicted with panic like a trapped bird, shut up alone with her charm and a brood of disconsolate young ones, in the after-aroma of sausages and chips. When she proposed a surprise visit to friends who had a place twenty miles along the coast, she hardly paused to press Gina to join her, or Josh, either, who was building card houses on the table and said he didn't want to go. She and Becky and Tom and Gabriel set off with a couple of bottles of wine, some dripping flowers from the garden, and a palpable air of escape in their voices as they called back instructions and cautions, Tom shaking the car keys out of his mother's laughing reach, refusing to allow that she could manage his old car, which needed double declutching.

Gina was going home the next day. Mamie would run her into town to catch the train. Probably that was the explanation for the comfortable flatness she felt now; it didn't even occur to her to mind that Josh had stayed. She knew with a lack of fuss that it had nothing to do with her; he had stayed because he didn't feel sociable and because he had become idly fixated on a difficulty he was having with the card houses. The sound of the car driving away dissolved into the soft rustle of the rain, beneath which, if she pushed her hair back behind her ears to listen, she could also hear the waves, undoing and repairing the gravel of the beach. When Gina finished putting away the dishes, she sat down opposite Josh, watching him prop cards together with concentrating fingers; she was careful not to knock the table or even to breathe too hard. They talked, speculating seriously about why it was that he couldn't make a tower with a six-point base; he had built one right up to its peak from a three- and a four- and a five-point base, but for hours he had been trying and failing to do a six. Josh had a curtain of hair and a loose, full lower lip that made his grin shy and somehow qualified. There was silky fair beard growth on his chin. He was gentler than his brothers, and had a slight lisp.

There was a second pack of cards on the table, rejected for building towers because the corners were too soft. Gina picked it up and fiddled with it on her lap without Josh's noticing. The six-base tower came down with a shout of frustration, and Josh washed his hands in the mess of cards.

D'you want me to show you a card trick? Gina asked.

O.K., he said. Anything. Just don't let me begin another one of these.

Actually, I'm not going to do it, she said. You are. Put those cards out of the way. We'll use this older pack. It feels more sympathetic.

He was amiable, obliging, clearing the table, his eyes on her now, watching to see what she could do.

I'm going to give you power, she said. I'm going to make you able to feel what the cards are, without looking at them. You're going to sort them into red and black. It's not even something I can do myself. Look.

She pretended to guess, frowning and hesitating, dealing the top few cards facedown into two piles. I don't know. Black, red; black, black, black; red, red. Something like that. Only I don't have this magic. I'll turn them over. See? All wrong. But you're going to have this power. I'm going to give it to you. Give me your hands.

He put his two long brown hands palm down on the table. She covered them with her own and closed her eyes, squeezing slightly against his bony knuckles, feeling under the ball of her thumb a hangnail loose against the cuticle of his. Really, something seemed to transfer between them.

There, she said briskly, Now you've got the power. Now you're going to sort these cards into black and red, facedown, without looking. Black in this pile, red in this. Take your time. Try to truly feel it. Concentrate.

Obediently, he began to deal the cards into two piles, doing it with hesitating, wincing puzzlement, like someone led blindfolded and expecting obstacles, laughing doubtingly and checking with her.

I have no idea what I'm doing here.

No, you have. You really have. Trust it.

He gained confidence, shrugged, went faster: black, red, black, black, red, black, red, red, red. . . . Halfway through, she asked him to change it around: red cards on the right pile now, and black cards on the left. Readjust. Don't lose it. It's really just to keep you concentrating.

Then, when he'd put down his last card and looked at her expectantly, she swept up the two piles and turned one over in front of his eyes. So you see, if it's worked, this one should run from red to black. . . . Look, there you are!

She spread the second pile, reversing it so that it seemed to run the other way. And, this one here, from black to red . . .

Oh, no. No! That's just too weird. That's really weird, man. How did you do that? Jesus! He laughed in delighted bafflement, looking from the cards up to her face and back again.

She was laughing, too, hugging her secret. Do you want me to do it again, see if you can guess? Only, hang on a sec, I need the loo.

He didn't notice that she took the second pack of cards with her to the bathroom to prepare them. ("Shall we use these newer ones, see if it works with them?") Gina couldn't quite believe that he didn't see what she was doing. She had worked it out for herself the first time the trick was done on her.

It's just spooky, he said in awe, shaking his head. It doesn't make sense. There's just no way I could be getting these right. You must be making me deal them right, somehow.

No, it's you, it's you, she insisted. I can't do it. It's only you.

He wouldn't let her tell him how it was done, although she was longing to explain. He was right: it was better to hold off the climactic revelation with its aftermath of gray; the power of the mystery he couldn't break was a warm pleasure, satisfying and sensual between them. They ran their eyes over each other's face in intimate connection, smiling. He brimmed with puzzlement, and she was replete with knowledge.

As they leaned toward each other across the table, she could smell his sweat and the nut-oil odor of his skin, which had been soaking up the sun all summer. She could suddenly imagine with vivid realism, as she hadn't been able to do in all her daydreams, what it would be like to be pressed up against him, existing in the orbit of that hot decent embrace. She could imagine how the male taste and smell of him could become known to her and comfortable, as familiar as her own. In fact, leapfrogging audaciously over all the things that hadn't happened between her and Josh, she found she was actually even imagining herself bored and constrained in his arms, hunting around for something more, pushing away from him. She was shocked at this intimation that the impossible dream of bliss might conceivably turn out, in some later phase of existence, not to be enough for her.

The moment slipped away. After the third time, they gave up the trick and played Mastermind and battleships, exchanging talk in low, lax, friendly voices. The others returned, crashing through the garden, tipsily exalted, looking around at their home, surprised that it seemed not to have changed in their absence. When Gina climbed between the sheets in her pajamas, she found the pleasure of the evening persisting, a soft surprising parcel under her lungs. She examined it, and thought that it was probably happiness, a small preparatory portion of the great ecstasies she supposed life must have in store for her.

It was twenty-five years before she visited Wing Lodge again.

This time she was alone. She remembered that she had been there before, with Mamie, although she couldn't quite imagine why she had been staying with her; there had never been any real intimacy between their families. Dickie and Mamie had divorced not long afterward, and Mamie had died recently. One of the boys had drowned, years ago—she couldn't remember which. The visit now was uncharacteristic of Gina. She never went to stately homes or birthplaces; in fact, she gave ironic lectures at her university on the enthusiasm of the masses for traipsing humbly and dotingly around the houses where they would most likely—as recently as sixty years ago—have been exploited as estate hands or scullery maids. But then this was an unsettled time in her life, and she was doing uncharacteristic things. She had been divorced for five years, and now her new lover wanted to move in with her. On impulse, leaving her son with friends for the weekend, she had booked herself into a hotel and come down to this little town to be alone, to think.

She hadn't imagined that she would actually go inside Wing Lodge, although she had been aware, of course, that the town she had chosen to think in was the one where John Morrison, who remained her passion, had spent his last years. She had had a quixotic idea, perhaps, that by moving around in the streets he must have moved around in she might attain something of his clarity; needless to say, the streets remained just streets, full of cars and tourists, and, for someone used to London, there were disconcertingly few of them to explore. She had, with determined austerity, not brought any books away with her, imagining that not being able to read would concentrate her mind. But the habit of years was too strong to break overnight, and so, over drawn-out coffees in the wood-paneled tearoom, where the waitresses still wore white frilled aprons, she found herself reading the menu over and over, and then the ancient injunction against asking for credit in red calligraphy above the till, and then the discarded sports pages of a newspaper, rather than dwelling at last and with a new penetration on the purpose and shape of her life.

So it was in flight from herself, almost, and also because there simply wasn't that much else to do, that she eventually joined the little party of visitors being taken around Wing Lodge. She was a middle-aged woman now, tall and statuesque in a tan linen skirt and jacket, with a mass of thick dark curls in which new gray hairs were sprouting with a coarse energy that made her suspect that age was going to impose itself differently than she had envisioned: less entropy, more vigorous takeover. There were copies of her book about Morrison's novels in the little bookshop upstairs, but she wasn't going to own up to that; she followed the guide obediently about and listened with amusement to the way the wonderful works abounding in disruptive energy became, in the retelling, so much sad sawdust, so much argument, as Pound put it, for old lavender.

She wondered, too, whether the place was really arranged as it had been in Morrison's time. He and his wife had never had much money, even in the years of his critical success; and the couple was reported to have been indifferent to creature comforts. Friends had complained that although the conversation was excellent you never got a decent meal or a good night's sleep at Wing Lodge. Gina recognized one or two drawings that she knew Morrison had possessed, and a few things that he might have brought back from the East. But the rest must have come after he died, when his wife had inherited money from her family in America; it was then, perhaps, that she had turned Wing Lodge into this tasteful little nest. No doubt the frail, ladylike guide and her frail, ladylike, possibly lesbian companion, who presumably lived here quietly together on the days when they were not intruded upon by a curious public, had also added their bit of polish to the deep old charm.

In the study, where Morrison's writing table was set out with pens and notebooks, as if he had just this minute stepped out for a walk in the fields in search of inspiration, there was also a shallow locked glass case in which were displayed first editions of the novels and some of Morrison's longhand drafts, as well as the copies that his wife had typed up on her Olivetti, and on which Morrison had scribbled furiously in his dark soft pencil. Gina had handled his notebooks and manuscripts and was familiar with his process of composition.

When the others had moved on, she peered closely into the case at one of the notebooks. These longhand drafts were not difficult to read, although Morrison's handwriting was odd, with large capitals and crunched-up lowercase. She recognized the text immediately. It was the scene in "Winter's Day" when the middle-aged daughter declares her love for the doctor, in the house where her father is dying. They have left her father with the nurse for an hour, and the doctor is trying to persuade Edith to get some rest. A lamp is burning, although it is already light outside; they are surrounded by the overflow of chaos from the sickroom—basins and medicines and laundry. Edith tells the doctor, who is married, that she can't bear the idea that when her father is dead he will no longer come to visit. "Because we shan't have our talks—you could have no idea, because you're a man and you have work to do, of what these mean to me. My life has been so stupidly empty." She presses her face, wet with tears, against the woolen sleeve of his jacket. The doctor is shocked and offended that Edith's mind is not on her father. Also, he is not attracted to her: he pities her, and her plain looks, haggard with exhaustion, and bad teeth.

There were few corrections to this passage in the notebook. It was a kind of climax, an eruption of drama in a novel whose texture was mostly very still. But Morrison must have cut part of this scene in a later version. In the published book, all Edith said when she broke down was "Because we shan't have our talks . . . I will miss them." Gina's eyes swam with tears as she bent over the case, reading the original words. She was astonished. She never cried, she never got colds, so she didn't even have a tissue in her bag. Luckily, she was alone. She wiped her face on the back of her hand and decided not to follow the rest of the tour group upstairs to the bookshop. Instead, she made her way out into the exquisitely blooming back garden, and found a seat under a bower overgrown with Nelly Moser clematis and some tiny white roses with a sweet perfume.

Why did it move her so much, this scene of a woman relinquishing power over herself? It ought to disgust her, or fill her with rage—or relief, that a whole repertoire of gestures of female abasement was now, after so many centuries, culturally obsolete. No one would dream of using a scene like that in a novel these days. That wet face, though, against the rough woolen sleeve, sent Gina slipping, careering down the path of self-abandonment. (Was the sleeve still there in the published version? She couldn't at the moment remember for sure.) She could almost smell the wool and imagine its hairy texture against her mouth, although none of the men she had loved ever wore that kind of tweedy jacket, except her father, perhaps, when she was a little girl. It was sexual, of course, and masochistic: female nakedness rubbing up against coarse male fiber. There was the threat of abrasion, of an irritated reaction on the finer, more sensitized, wet female surface.

You could see how it all worked. You could rationally resist it, and you could even—and here was the answer, perhaps, to the question that had brought her down to Wing Lodge in the first place—feel sure that you would never be able to surrender yourself like that ever again. And yet the passage had moved her to unexpected tears. There was something formally beautiful and powerful and satisfying in it: that scene of a woman putting her happiness into a man's hands. Next to it, all the other, better kinds of power that women had nowadays seemed, just for one floundering moment, second best.

Gina sat for a long time. A bee, or some beelike insect, fell out of the flowers onto her skirt, and she was aware of the lady guide looking at her agitatedly from the French windows, probably wanting to close up the house. And there came to her, in a flood of regret for her youth, the memory of a card trick, the one where you secretly sorted the pack into black and red in advance so that your victim wouldn't be able to put a card down wrong.

Sherman Alexie

What You Pawn I Will Redeem

from *The New Yorker*

NOON

ONE DAY you have a home and the next you don't, but I'm not going to tell you my particular reasons for being homeless, because it's my secret story, and Indians have to work hard to keep secrets from hungry white folks.

I'm a Spokane Indian boy, an Interior Salish, and my people have lived within a hundred-mile radius of Spokane, Washington, for at least ten thousand years. I grew up in Spokane, moved to Seattle twenty-three years ago for college, flunked out after two semesters, worked various blue- and bluer-collar jobs, married two or three times, fathered two or three kids, and then went crazy. Of course, crazy is not the official definition of my mental problem, but I don't think asocial disorder fits it, either, because that makes me sound like I'm a serial killer or something. I've never hurt another human being, or, at least, not physically. I've broken a few hearts in my time, but we've all done that, so I'm nothing special in that regard. I'm a boring heartbreaker, too. I never dated or married more than one woman at a time. I didn't break hearts into pieces overnight. I broke them slowly and carefully. And I didn't set any land-speed records running out the door. Piece by piece, I disappeared. I've been disappearing ever since.

I've been homeless for six years now. If there's such a thing as an effec-

tive homeless man, then I suppose I'm effective. Being homeless is probably the only thing I've ever been good at. I know where to get the best free
food. I've made friends with restaurant and convenience-store managers
who let me use their bathrooms. And I don't mean the public bathrooms,
either. I mean the employees' bathrooms, the clean ones hidden behind
the kitchen or the pantry or the cooler. I know it sounds strange to be
proud of this, but it means a lot to me, being trustworthy enough to piss
in somebody else's clean bathroom. Maybe you don't understand the value
of a clean bathroom, but I do.

Probably none of this interests you. Homeless Indians are everywhere
in Seattle. We're common and boring, and you walk right on by us, with
maybe a look of anger or disgust or even sadness at the terrible fate of the
noble savage. But we have dreams and families. I'm friends with a homeless Plains Indian man whose son is the editor of a big-time newspaper
back East. Of course, that's his story, but we Indians are great storytellers
and liars and mythmakers, so maybe that Plains Indian hobo is just a plain
old everyday Indian. I'm kind of suspicious of him, because he identifies
himself only as Plains Indian, a generic term, and not by a specific tribe.
When I asked him why he wouldn't tell me exactly what he is, he said,
"Do any of us know exactly what we are?" Yeah, great, a philosophizing
Indian. "Hey," I said, "you got to have a home to be that homely." He just
laughed and flipped me the eagle and walked away.

I wander the streets with a regular crew—my teammates, my defend-
ers, my posse. It's Rose of Sharon, Junior, and me. We matter to each other
if we don't matter to anybody else. Rose of Sharon is a big woman, about
seven feet tall if you're measuring over-all effect and about five feet tall
if you're only talking about the physical. She's a Yakama Indian of the
Wishram variety. Junior is a Colville, but there are about a hundred and
ninety-nine tribes that make up the Colville, so he could be anything. He's
good-looking, though, like he just stepped out of some "Don't Litter the
Earth" public-service advertisement. He's got those great big cheekbones
that are like planets, you know, with little moons orbiting them. He gets
me jealous, jealous, and jealous. If you put Junior and me next to each
other, he's the Before Columbus Arrived Indian and I'm the After Columbus Arrived Indian. I am living proof of the horrible damage that colonial-
ism has done to us Skins. But I'm not going to let you know how scared I

sometimes get of history and its ways. I'm a strong man, and I know that silence is the best method of dealing with white folks.

This whole story really started at lunchtime, when Rose of Sharon, Junior, and I were panning the handle down at Pike Place Market. After about two hours of negotiating, we earned five dollars—good enough for a bottle of fortified courage from the most beautiful 7-Eleven in the world. So we headed over that way, feeling like warrior drunks, and we walked past this pawnshop I'd never noticed before. And that was strange, because we Indians have built-in pawnshop radar. But the strangest thing of all was the old powwow-dance regalia I saw hanging in the window.

"That's my grandmother's regalia," I said to Rose of Sharon and Junior.

"How you know for sure?" Junior asked.

I didn't know for sure, because I hadn't seen that regalia in person ever. I'd only seen photographs of my grandmother dancing in it. And those were taken before somebody stole it from her, fifty years ago. But it sure looked like my memory of it, and it had all the same color feathers and beads that my family sewed into our powwow regalia.

"There's only one way to know for sure," I said.

So Rose of Sharon, Junior, and I walked into the pawnshop and greeted the old white man working behind the counter.

"How can I help you?" he asked.

"That's my grandmother's powwow regalia in your window," I said. "Somebody stole it from her fifty years ago, and my family has been searching for it ever since."

The pawnbroker looked at me like I was a liar. I understood. Pawnshops are filled with liars.

"I'm not lying," I said. "Ask my friends here. They'll tell you."

"He's the most honest Indian I know," Rose of Sharon said.

"All right, honest Indian," the pawnbroker said. "I'll give you the benefit of the doubt. Can you prove it's your grandmother's regalia?"

Because they don't want to be perfect, because only God is perfect, Indian people sew flaws into their powwow regalia. My family always sewed one yellow bead somewhere on our regalia. But we always hid it so that you had to search really hard to find it.

"If it really is my grandmother's," I said, "there will be one yellow bead hidden somewhere on it."

"All right, then," the pawnbroker said. "Let's take a look."

He pulled the regalia out of the window, laid it down on the glass counter, and we searched for that yellow bead and found it hidden beneath the armpit.

"There it is," the pawnbroker said. He didn't sound surprised. "You were right. This is your grandmother's regalia."

"It's been missing for fifty years," Junior said.

"Hey, Junior," I said. "It's my family's story. Let me tell it."

"All right," he said. "I apologize. You go ahead."

"It's been missing for fifty years," I said.

"That's his family's sad story," Rose of Sharon said. "Are you going to give it back to him?"

"That would be the right thing to do," the pawnbroker said. "But I can't afford to do the right thing. I paid a thousand dollars for this. I can't just give away a thousand dollars."

"We could go to the cops and tell them it was stolen," Rose of Sharon said.

"Hey," I said to her. "Don't go threatening people."

The pawnbroker sighed. He was thinking about the possibilities.

"Well, I suppose you could go to the cops," he said. "But I don't think they'd believe a word you said."

He sounded sad about that. As if he was sorry for taking advantage of our disadvantages.

"What's your name?" the pawnbroker asked me.

"Jackson," I said.

"Is that first or last?"

"Both," I said.

"Are you serious?"

"Yes, it's true. My mother and father named me Jackson Jackson. My family nickname is Jackson Squared. My family is funny."

"All right, Jackson Jackson," the pawnbroker said. "You wouldn't happen to have a thousand dollars, would you?"

"We've got five dollars total," I said.

"That's too bad," he said, and thought hard about the possibilities. "I'd sell it to you for a thousand dollars if you had it. Heck, to make it fair, I'd sell it to you for nine hundred and ninety-nine dollars. I'd lose a dollar.

That would be the moral thing to do in this case. To lose a dollar would be the right thing."

"We've got five dollars total," I said again.

"That's too bad," he said once more, and thought harder about the possibilities. "How about this? I'll give you twenty-four hours to come up with nine hundred and ninety-nine dollars. You come back here at lunchtime tomorrow with the money and I'll sell it back to you. How does that sound?"

"It sounds all right," I said.

"All right, then," he said. "We have a deal. And I'll get you started. Here's twenty bucks."

He opened up his wallet and pulled out a crisp twenty-dollar bill and gave it to me. And Rose of Sharon, Junior, and I walked out into the daylight to search for nine hundred and seventy-four more dollars.

1 P.M.

Rose of Sharon, Junior, and I carried our twenty-dollar bill and our five dollars in loose change over to the 7-Eleven and bought three bottles of imagination. We needed to figure out how to raise all that money in only one day. Thinking hard, we huddled in an alley beneath the Alaska Way Viaduct and finished off those bottles—one, two, and three.

2 P.M.

Rose of Sharon was gone when I woke up. I heard later that she had hitchhiked back to Toppenish and was living with her sister on the reservation.

Junior had passed out beside me and was covered in his own vomit, or maybe somebody else's vomit, and my head hurt from thinking, so I left him alone and walked down to the water. I love the smell of ocean water. Salt always smells like memory.

When I got to the wharf, I ran into three Aleut cousins, who sat on a wooden bench and stared out at the bay and cried. Most of the homeless Indians in Seattle come from Alaska. One by one, each of them hopped a big working boat in Anchorage or Barrow or Juneau, fished his way south to Seattle, jumped off the boat with a pocketful of cash to party hard at one of the highly sacred and traditional Indian bars, went broke and broker, and has been trying to find his way back to the boat and the frozen North ever since.

These Aleuts smelled like salmon, I thought, and they told me they were going to sit on that wooden bench until their boat came back.

"How long has your boat been gone?" I asked.

"Eleven years," the elder Aleut said.

I cried with them for a while.

"Hey," I said. "Do you guys have any money I can borrow?"

They didn't.

3 P.M.

I walked back to Junior. He was still out cold. I put my face down near his mouth to make sure he was breathing. He was alive, so I dug around in his blue-jeans pockets and found half a cigarette. I smoked it all the way down and thought about my grandmother.

Her name was Agnes, and she died of breast cancer when I was fourteen. My father always thought Agnes caught her tumors from the uranium mine on the reservation. But my mother said the disease started when Agnes was walking back from a powwow one night and got run over by a motorcycle. She broke three ribs, and my mother always said those ribs never healed right, and tumors take over when you don't heal right.

Sitting beside Junior, smelling the smoke and the salt and the vomit, I wondered if my grandmother's cancer started when somebody stole her powwow regalia. Maybe the cancer started in her broken heart and then leaked out into her breasts. I know it's crazy, but I wondered whether I could bring my grandmother back to life if I bought back her regalia.

I needed money, big money, so I left Junior and walked over to the Real Change office.

4 P.M.

Real Change is a multifaceted organization that publishes a newspaper, supports cultural projects that empower the poor and the homeless, and mobilizes the public around poverty issues. Real Change's mission is to organize, educate, and build alliances to create solutions to homelessness and poverty. It exists to provide a voice for poor people in our community.

I memorized Real Change's mission statement because I sometimes sell the newspaper on the streets. But you have to stay sober to sell it, and I'm not always good at staying sober. Anybody can sell the paper. You buy each copy for thirty cents and sell it for a dollar, and you keep the profit.

"I need one thousand four hundred and thirty papers," I said to the Big Boss.

"That's a strange number," he said. "And that's a lot of papers."

"I need them."

The Big Boss pulled out his calculator and did the math.

"It will cost you four hundred and twenty-nine dollars for that many," he said.

"If I had that kind of money, I wouldn't need to sell the papers."

"What's going on, Jackson-to-the-Second-Power?" he asked. He is the only person who calls me that. He's a funny and kind man.

I told him about my grandmother's powwow regalia and how much money I needed in order to buy it back.

"We should call the police," he said.

"I don't want to do that," I said. "It's a quest now. I need to win it back by myself."

"I understand," he said. "And, to be honest, I'd give you the papers to sell if I thought it would work. But the record for the most papers sold in one day by one vendor is only three hundred and two."

"That would net me about two hundred bucks," I said.

The Big Boss used his calculator. "Two hundred and eleven dollars and forty cents," he said.

"That's not enough," I said.

"And the most money anybody has made in one day is five hundred and twenty-five. And that's because somebody gave Old Blue five hundred-dollar bills for some dang reason. The average daily net is about thirty dollars."

"This isn't going to work."

"No."

"Can you lend me some money?"

"I can't do that," he said. "If I lend you money, I have to lend money to everybody."

"What can you do?"

"I'll give you fifty papers for free. But don't tell anybody I did it."

"O.K.," I said.

He gathered up the newspapers and handed them to me. I held them to my chest. He hugged me. I carried the newspapers back toward the water.

5 P.M.

Back on the wharf, I stood near the Bainbridge Island Terminal and tried to sell papers to business commuters boarding the ferry.

I sold five in one hour, dumped the other forty-five in a garbage can, and walked into McDonald's, ordered four cheeseburgers for a dollar each, and slowly ate them.

After eating, I walked outside and vomited on the sidewalk. I hated to lose my food so soon after eating it. As an alcoholic Indian with a busted stomach, I always hope I can keep enough food in me to stay alive.

6 P.M.

With one dollar in my pocket, I walked back to Junior. He was still passed out, and I put my ear to his chest and listened for his heartbeat. He was alive, so I took off his shoes and socks and found one dollar in his left sock and fifty cents in his right sock.

With two dollars and fifty cents in my hand, I sat beside Junior and thought about my grandmother and her stories.

When I was thirteen, my grandmother told me a story about the Second World War. She was a nurse at a military hospital in Sydney, Australia. For two years, she healed and comforted American and Australian soldiers.

One day she tended to a wounded Maori soldier, who had lost his legs to an artillery attack. He was very dark-skinned. His hair was black and curly and his eyes were black and warm. His face was covered with bright tattoos.

"Are you Maori?" he asked my grandmother.

"No," she said. "I'm Spokane Indian. From the United States."

"Ah, yes," he said. "I have heard of your tribes. But you are the first American Indian I have ever met."

"There's a lot of Indian soldiers fighting for the United States," she said. "I have a brother fighting in Germany, and I lost another brother on Okinawa."

"I am sorry," he said. "I was on Okinawa as well. It was terrible."

"I am sorry about your legs," my grandmother said.

"It's funny, isn't it?" he said.

"What's funny?"

"How we brown people are killing other brown people so white people will remain free."

"I hadn't thought of it that way."

"Well, sometimes I think of it that way. And other times I think of it the way they want me to think of it. I get confused."

She fed him morphine.

"Do you believe in Heaven?" he asked.

"Which Heaven?" she asked.

"I'm talking about the Heaven where my legs are waiting for me."

They laughed.

"Of course," he said, "my legs will probably run away from me when I get to Heaven. And how will I ever catch them?"

"You have to get your arms strong," my grandmother said. "So you can run on your hands."

They laughed again.

Sitting beside Junior, I laughed at the memory of my grandmother's story. I put my hand close to Junior's mouth to make sure he was still breathing. Yes, Junior was alive, so I took my two dollars and fifty cents and walked to the Korean grocery store in Pioneer Square.

7 P.M.

At the Korean grocery store, I bought a fifty-cent cigar and two scratch lottery tickets for a dollar each. The maximum cash prize was five hundred dollars a ticket. If I won both, I would have enough money to buy back the regalia.

I loved Mary, the young Korean woman who worked the register. She was the daughter of the owners, and she sang all day.

"I love you," I said when I handed her the money.

"You always say you love me," she said.

"That's because I will always love you."

"You are a sentimental fool."

"I'm a romantic old man."

"Too old for me."

"I know I'm too old for you, but I can dream."

"O.K.," she said. "I agree to be a part of your dreams, but I will only hold your hand in your dreams. No kissing and no sex. Not even in your dreams."

"O.K.," I said. "No sex. Just romance."

"Good-bye, Jackson Jackson, my love. I will see you soon."

I left the store, walked over to Occidental Park, sat on a bench, and smoked my cigar all the way down.

Ten minutes after I finished the cigar, I scratched my first lottery ticket and won nothing. I could only win five hundred dollars now, and that would only be half of what I needed.

Ten minutes after I lost, I scratched the other ticket and won a free ticket—a small consolation and one more chance to win some money.

I walked back to Mary.

"Jackson Jackson," she said. "Have you come back to claim my heart?"

"I won a free ticket," I said.

"Just like a man," she said. "You love money and power more than you love me."

"It's true," I said. "And I'm sorry it's true."

She gave me another scratch ticket, and I took it outside. I like to scratch my tickets in private. Hopeful and sad, I scratched that third ticket and won real money. I carried it back inside to Mary.

"I won a hundred dollars," I said.

She examined the ticket and laughed.

"That's a fortune," she said, and counted out five twenties. Our fingertips touched as she handed me the money. I felt electric and constant.

"Thank you," I said, and gave her one of the bills.

"I can't take that," she said. "It's your money."

"No, it's tribal. It's an Indian thing. When you win, you're supposed to share with your family."

"I'm not your family."

"Yes, you are."

She smiled. She kept the money. With eighty dollars in my pocket, I said good-bye to my dear Mary and walked out into the cold night air.

8 P.M.

I wanted to share the good news with Junior. I walked back to him, but he was gone. I heard later that he had hitchhiked down to Portland, Oregon, and died of exposure in an alley behind the Hilton Hotel.

9 P.M.

Lonesome for Indians, I carried my eighty dollars over to Big Heart's in South Downtown. Big Heart's is an all-Indian bar. Nobody knows how or why Indians migrate to one bar and turn it into an official Indian bar. But Big Heart's has been an Indian bar for twenty-three years. It used to be way up on Aurora Avenue, but a crazy Lummi Indian burned that one down, and the owners moved to the new location, a few blocks south of Safeco Field.

I walked into Big Heart's and counted fifteen Indians—eight men and seven women. I didn't know any of them, but Indians like to belong, so we all pretended to be cousins.

"How much for whiskey shots?" I asked the bartender, a fat white guy.

"You want the bad stuff or the badder stuff?"

"As bad as you got."

"One dollar a shot."

I laid my eighty dollars on the bar top.

"All right," I said. "Me and all my cousins here are going to be drinking eighty shots. How many is that apiece?"

"Counting you," a woman shouted from behind me, "that's five shots for everybody."

I turned to look at her. She was a chubby and pale Indian woman, sitting with a tall and skinny Indian man.

"All right, math genius," I said to her, and then shouted for the whole bar to hear. "Five drinks for everybody!"

All the other Indians rushed the bar, but I sat with the mathematician and her skinny friend. We took our time with our whiskey shots.

"What's your tribe?" I asked.

"I'm Duwamish," she said. "And he's Crow."

"You're a long way from Montana," I said to him.

"I'm Crow," he said. "I flew here."

"What's your name?" I asked them.

"I'm Irene Muse," she said. "And this is Honey Boy."

She shook my hand hard, but he offered his hand as if I was supposed to kiss it. So I did. He giggled and blushed, as much as a dark-skinned Crow can blush.

"You're one of them two-spirits, aren't you?" I asked him.

"I love women," he said. "And I love men."

"Sometimes both at the same time," Irene said.

We laughed.

"Man," I said to Honey Boy. "So you must have about eight or nine spirits going on inside you, enit?"

"Sweetie," he said. "I'll be whatever you want me to be."

"Oh, no," Irene said. "Honey Boy is falling in love."

"It has nothing to do with love," he said.

We laughed.

"Wow," I said. "I'm flattered, Honey Boy, but I don't play on your team."

"Never say never," he said.

"You better be careful," Irene said. "Honey Boy knows all sorts of magic."

"Honey Boy," I said, "you can try to seduce me, but my heart belongs to a woman named Mary."

"Is your Mary a virgin?" Honey Boy asked.

We laughed.

And we drank our whiskey shots until they were gone. But the other Indians bought me more whiskey shots, because I'd been so generous with my money. And Honey Boy pulled out his credit card, and I drank and sailed on that plastic boat.

After a dozen shots, I asked Irene to dance. She refused. But Honey Boy shuffled over to the jukebox, dropped in a quarter, and selected Willie Nelson's "Help Me Make It Through the Night." As Irene and I sat at the table and laughed and drank more whiskey, Honey Boy danced a slow circle around us and sang along with Willie.

"Are you serenading me?" I asked him.

He kept singing and dancing.

"Are you serenading me?" I asked him again.

"He's going to put a spell on you," Irene said.

I leaned over the table, spilling a few drinks, and kissed Irene hard. She kissed me back.

10 P.M.

Irene pushed me into the women's bathroom, into a stall, shut the door behind us, and shoved her hand down my pants. She was short, so I had to lean over to kiss her. I grabbed and squeezed her everywhere I could reach, and she was wonderfully fat, and every part of her body felt like a large, warm, soft breast.

MIDNIGHT

Nearly blind with alcohol, I stood alone at the bar and swore I had been standing in the bathroom with Irene only a minute ago.

"One more shot!" I yelled at the bartender.

"You've got no more money!" he yelled back.

"Somebody buy me a drink!" I shouted.

"They've got no more money!"

"Where are Irene and Honey Boy?"

"Long gone!"

2 A.M.

"Closing time!" the bartender shouted at the three or four Indians who were still drinking hard after a long, hard day of drinking. Indian alcoholics are either sprinters or marathoners.

"Where are Irene and Honey Boy?" I asked.

"They've been gone for hours," the bartender said.

"Where'd they go?"

"I told you a hundred times, I don't know."

"What am I supposed to do?"

"It's closing time. I don't care where you go, but you're not staying here."

"You are an ungrateful bastard. I've been good to you."

"You don't leave right now, I'm going to kick your ass."

"Come on, I know how to fight."

He came at me. I don't remember what happened after that.

4 A.M.

I emerged from the blackness and discovered myself walking behind a big warehouse. I didn't know where I was. My face hurt. I felt my nose and decided that it might be broken. Exhausted and cold, I pulled a plastic tarp from a truck bed, wrapped it around me like a faithful lover, and fell asleep in the dirt.

6 A.M.

Somebody kicked me in the ribs. I opened my eyes and looked up at a white cop.

"Jackson," the cop said. "Is that you?"

"Officer Williams," I said. He was a good cop with a sweet tooth. He'd given me hundreds of candy bars over the years. I wonder if he knew I was diabetic.

"What the hell are you doing here?" he asked.

"I was cold and sleepy," I said. "So I lay down."

"You dumb-ass, you passed out on the railroad tracks."

I sat up and looked around. I was lying on the railroad tracks. Dock-workers stared at me. I should have been a railroad-track pizza, a double Indian pepperoni with extra cheese. Sick and scared, I leaned over and puked whiskey.

"What the hell's wrong with you?" Officer Williams asked. "You've never been this stupid."

"It's my grandmother," I said. "She died."

"I'm sorry, man. When did she die?"

"Nineteen seventy-two."

"And you're killing yourself now?"

"I've been killing myself ever since she died."

He shook his head. He was sad for me. Like I said, he was a good cop.

"And somebody beat the hell out of you," he said. "You remember who?"

"Mr. Grief and I went a few rounds."

"It looks like Mr. Grief knocked you out."

"Mr. Grief always wins."

"Come on," he said. "Let's get you out of here."

He helped me up and led me over to his squad car. He put me in the back. "You throw up in there and you're cleaning it up," he said.

"That's fair."

He walked around the car and sat in the driver's seat. "I'm taking you over to detox," he said.

"No, man, that place is awful," I said. "It's full of drunk Indians."

We laughed. He drove away from the docks.

"I don't know how you guys do it," he said.

"What guys?" I asked.

"You Indians. How the hell do you laugh so much? I just picked your ass off the railroad tracks, and you're making jokes. Why the hell do you do that?"

"The two funniest tribes I've ever been around are Indians and Jews, so I guess that says something about the inherent humor of genocide."

We laughed.

"Listen to you, Jackson. You're so smart. Why the hell are you on the street?"

"Give me a thousand dollars and I'll tell you."

"You bet I'd give you a thousand dollars if I knew you'd straighten up your life."

He meant it. He was the second-best cop I'd ever known.

"You're a good cop," I said.

"Come on, Jackson," he said. "Don't blow smoke up my ass."

"No, really, you remind me of my grandfather."

"Yeah, that's what you Indians always tell me."

"No, man, my grandfather was a tribal cop. He was a good cop. He never arrested people. He took care of them. Just like you."

"I've arrested hundreds of scumbags, Jackson. And I've shot a couple in the ass."

"It don't matter. You're not a killer."

"I didn't kill them. I killed their asses. I'm an ass-killer."

We drove through downtown. The missions and shelters had already released their overnighters. Sleepy homeless men and women stood on street corners and stared up at a gray sky. It was the morning after the night of the living dead.

"Do you ever get scared?" I asked Officer Williams.

"What do you mean?"

"I mean, being a cop, is it scary?"

He thought about that for a while. He contemplated it. I liked that about him.

"I guess I try not to think too much about being afraid," he said. "If you think about fear, then you'll be afraid. The job is boring most of the time. Just driving and looking into dark corners, you know, and seeing nothing. But then things get heavy. You're chasing somebody, or fighting them or walking around a dark house, and you just know some crazy guy is hiding around a corner, and hell, yes, it's scary."

"My grandfather was killed in the line of duty," I said.

"I'm sorry. How'd it happen?"

I knew he'd listen closely to my story.

"He worked on the reservation. Everybody knew everybody. It was safe. We aren't like those crazy Sioux or Apache or any of those other warrior tribes. There've only been three murders on my reservation in the last hundred years."

"That is safe."

"Yeah, we Spokane, we're passive, you know. We're mean with words. And we'll cuss out anybody. But we don't shoot people. Or stab them. Not much, anyway."

"So what happened to your grandfather?"

"This man and his girlfriend were fighting down by Little Falls."

"Domestic dispute. Those are the worst."

"Yeah, but this guy was my grandfather's brother. My great-uncle."

"Oh, no."

"Yeah, it was awful. My grandfather just strolled into the house. He'd been there a thousand times. And his brother and his girlfriend were drunk and beating on each other. And my grandfather stepped between them, just as he'd done a hundred times before. And the girlfriend tripped or something. She fell down and hit her head and started crying. And my grandfather kneeled down beside her to make sure she was all right. And for some reason my great-uncle reached down, pulled my grandfather's pistol out of the holster, and shot him in the head."

"That's terrible. I'm sorry."

"Yeah, my great-uncle could never figure out why he did it. He went to prison forever, you know, and he always wrote these long letters. Like fifty pages of tiny little handwriting. And he was always trying to figure out why he did it. He'd write and write and write and try to figure it out. He never did. It's a great big mystery."

"Do you remember your grandfather?"

"A little bit. I remember the funeral. My grandmother wouldn't let them bury him. My father had to drag her away from the grave."

"I don't know what to say."

"I don't, either."

We stopped in front of the detox center.

"We're here," Officer Williams said.

"I can't go in there," I said.

"You have to."

"Please, no. They'll keep me for twenty-four hours. And then it will be too late."

"Too late for what?"

I told him about my grandmother's regalia and the deadline for buying it back.

"If it was stolen, you need to file a report," he said. "I'll investigate it myself. If that thing is really your grandmother's, I'll get it back for you. Legally."

"No," I said. "That's not fair. The pawnbroker didn't know it was stolen. And, besides, I'm on a mission here. I want to be a hero, you know? I want to win it back, like a knight."

"That's romantic crap."

"That may be. But I care about it. It's been a long time since I really cared about something."

Officer Williams turned around in his seat and stared at me. He studied me.

"I'll give you some money," he said. "I don't have much. Only thirty bucks. I'm short until payday. And it's not enough to get back the regalia. But it's something."

"I'll take it," I said.

"I'm giving it to you because I believe in what you believe. I'm hoping, and I don't know why I'm hoping it, but I hope you can turn thirty bucks into a thousand somehow."

"I believe in magic."

"I believe you'll take my money and get drunk on it."

"Then why are you giving it to me?"

"There ain't no such thing as an atheist cop."

"Sure, there is."

"Yeah, well, I'm not an atheist cop."

He let me out of the car, handed me two fivers and a twenty, and shook my hand.

"Take care of yourself, Jackson," he said. "Stay off the railroad tracks."

"I'll try," I said.

He drove away. Carrying my money, I headed back toward the water.

8 A.M.

On the wharf, those three Aleuts still waited on the wooden bench.

"Have you seen your ship?" I asked.

"Seen a lot of ships," the elder Aleut said. "But not our ship."

I sat on the bench with them. We sat in silence for a long time. I wondered if we would fossilize if we sat there long enough.

I thought about my grandmother. I'd never seen her dance in her regalia. And, more than anything, I wished I'd seen her dance at a powwow.

"Do you guys know any songs?" I asked the Aleuts.

"I know all of Hank Williams," the elder Aleut said.

"How about Indian songs?"

"Hank Williams is Indian."

"How about sacred songs?"

"Hank Williams is sacred."

"I'm talking about ceremonial songs. You know, religious ones. The songs you sing back home when you're wishing and hoping."

"What are you wishing and hoping for?"

"I'm wishing my grandmother was still alive."

"Every song I know is about that."

"Well, sing me as many as you can."

The Aleuts sang their strange and beautiful songs. I listened. They sang about my grandmother and about their grandmothers. They were lonesome for the cold and the snow. I was lonesome for everything.

10 A.M.

After the Aleuts finished their last song, we sat in silence for a while. Indians are good at silence.

"Was that the last song?" I asked.

"We sang all the ones we could," the elder Aleut said. "The others are just for our people."

I understood. We Indians have to keep our secrets. And these Aleuts were so secretive they didn't refer to themselves as Indians.

"Are you guys hungry?" I asked.

They looked at one another and communicated without talking.

"We could eat," the elder Aleut said.

11 A.M.

The Aleuts and I walked over to the Big Kitchen, a greasy diner in the International District. I knew they served homeless Indians who'd lucked into money.

"Four for breakfast?" the waitress asked when we stepped inside.

"Yes, we're very hungry," the elder Aleut said.

She took us to a booth near the kitchen. I could smell the food cooking. My stomach growled.

"You guys want separate checks?" the waitress asked.

"No, I'm paying," I said.

"Aren't you the generous one," she said.

"Don't do that," I said.

"Do what?" she asked.

"Don't ask me rhetorical questions. They scare me."

She looked puzzled, and then she laughed.

"O.K., Professor," she said. "I'll only ask you real questions from now on."

"Thank you."

"What do you guys want to eat?"

"That's the best question anybody can ask anybody," I said. "What have you got?"

"How much money you got?" she asked.

"Another good question," I said. "I've got twenty-five dollars I can spend. Bring us all the breakfast you can, plus your tip."

She knew the math.

"All right, that's four specials and four coffees and fifteen percent for me."

The Aleuts and I waited in silence. Soon enough, the waitress returned and poured us four coffees, and we sipped at them until she returned again, with four plates of food. Eggs, bacon, toast, hash-brown potatoes. It's amazing how much food you can buy for so little money.

Grateful, we feasted.

NOON

I said farewell to the Aleuts and walked toward the pawnshop. I heard later that the Aleuts had waded into the salt water near Dock 47 and disappeared. Some Indians swore they had walked on the water and headed north. Other Indians saw the Aleuts drown. I don't know what happened to them.

I looked for the pawnshop and couldn't find it. I swear it wasn't in the place where it had been before. I walked twenty or thirty blocks looking for the pawnshop, turned corners and bisected intersections, and looked up its name in the phone books and asked people walking past me if they'd ever heard of it. But that pawnshop seemed to have sailed away like a ghost ship. I wanted to cry. And just when I'd given up, when I turned one last corner and thought I might die if I didn't find that pawnshop, there it was, in a space I swear it hadn't occupied a few minutes ago.

I walked inside and greeted the pawnbroker, who looked a little younger than he had before.

"It's you," he said.

"Yes, it's me," I said.

"Jackson Jackson."

"That is my name."

"Where are your friends?"

"They went traveling. But it's O.K. Indians are everywhere."

"Do you have the money?"

"How much do you need again?" I asked, and hoped the price had changed.

"Nine hundred and ninety-nine dollars."

It was still the same price. Of course, it was the same price. Why would it change?

"I don't have that," I said.

"What do you have?"

"Five dollars."

I set the crumpled Lincoln on the countertop. The pawnbroker studied it.

"Is that the same five dollars from yesterday?"

"No, it's different."

He thought about the possibilities.

"Did you work hard for this money?" he asked.

"Yes," I said.

He closed his eyes and thought harder about the possibilities. Then he stepped into the back room and returned with my grandmother's regalia.

"Take it," he said, and held it out to me.

"I don't have the money."

"I don't want your money."

"But I wanted to win it."

"You did win it. Now take it before I change my mind."

Do you know how many good men live in this world? Too many to count!

I took my grandmother's regalia and walked outside. I knew that solitary yellow bead was part of me. I knew I was that yellow bead in part. Outside, I wrapped myself in my grandmother's regalia and breathed her in. I stepped off the sidewalk and into the intersection. Pedestrians stopped. Cars stopped. The city stopped. They all watched me dance with my grandmother. I was my grandmother, dancing.

Reading *The O. Henry Prize Stories 2005*
The Jurors on Their Favorites

Each juror read all twenty stories without knowing who wrote them or where they were published.

Cristina García on "Refuge in London" by Ruth Prawer Jhabvala

It is a paradox that sometimes nothing seems as distant from us as the recent past, what has only just disappeared. What "Refuge in London" by Ruth Prawer Jhabvala so beautifully evokes is the last days of a lost world, a world of a mere half century ago but one originating in a sensibility centuries older. In a shabby, postwar London boardinghouse crowded with a motley assortment of refugees (a lawyer, a businessman, and upstairs, an artist famous in prewar Germany and his wife), a sixteen-year-old girl recalls the parade of these characters and their influence on her formation. Through her finely drawn awareness, we see not only the disappearance of the old cultural order smashed by the forces of global war, but also the timeliness of the artistic struggle whatever the period, whatever the circumstances.

"Refuge in London" has several themes: the ruinous effect of time on youthful promise, the way genius attracts its own public attention, and perhaps, most of all, the demands and responsibility of an artist's life; all emerge in clean, well-crafted prose whose nuance and shading match the characters' complex and, at least for now, unfathomable lives. The nature of refuge is often awkwardly managed (or outright bungled) in fiction, where the tendency can be to indulge in the drama of personal upheaval. Instead of hearing the noise of displacement, the reader experiences the routine of living that plays out afterward—and then after that—as the refugees struggle to reclaim their material and psychic footing. It is a smaller, more difficult story to tell, but it is also what makes "Refuge in London" all the more poignant and rewarding.

Cristina García is the author of the novels *Dreaming in Cuban*, *The Aguero Sisters*, and *Monkey Hunting*. She edited *Cubanísimo: The Vintage Book of Contemporary Cuban Literature*. García lives in California.

Ann Patchett on "What You Pawn I Will Redeem" by Sherman Alexie

I read too much and I read too critically. Both things are occupational hazards for writers. We have a lot of books to get through. Writers reading are like magicians going to catch a show at a magic club. You sit in the audience thinking, Oh, I can see how he's sawing her apart. We long to be amazed again, since it was that sense of amazement brought on by words that led us to this job in the first place, but once you know how to pull the strings and work the levers yourself it's never quite the same.

When I read, one of three things happens: 1) I think something is bad, and I immediately break it down technically so that I can say why it is bad; 2) I think something is good, and I immediately break it down technically so that I can say why it is good; 3) I simply step into the story. I do not see how it is working. I do not care. I am in that world, walking around with those people. For the number of pages I am given to read, they are my life.

The third option is rare, breathtaking, and akin to falling in love. Sherman Alexie's story, "What You Pawn I Will Redeem," is exactly such an experience. I want to stuff it in every mailbox I know. As a writer he is nowhere to be found on the page. He does not preen or try to impress. He has nothing to prove to his reader, only something to tell them. Like me, Sherman Alexie is in love with his homeless Spokane Indian narrator and so he simply steps aside to let his character have every inch of the stage. From the very first sentence the voice takes over and you know you will no longer be thinking about the art and craft of fiction because you will be too busy listening. Alexie follows this man through his world not as a character but as a human being. Every turn in his day is unexpected and true. As I read I was moved by sorrow, compassion, and joy. I felt all three things deeply and separately in the course of twenty pages. We are lucky when we get that much from life—we should be nothing short of rapturous when we get it from short fiction.

Ann Patchett is the author of the novels *Taft*, *The Magician's Assistant*, *Patron Saint of Liars*, and *Bel Canto*, as well as the memoir *Truth and Beauty: A Friendship*. She lives in Tennessee.

Richard Russo on "Mudlavia" by Elizabeth Stuckey-French

As usual, this year's *O. Henry* anthology is full of fine stories, but the one that burrowed deepest under my skin was by Elizabeth Stuckey-French. I loved everything about "Mudlavia"—the deceptive simplicity of its storytelling; the way its private and public stories play off each other; its fond, gentle humor; the heartbreaking, hard-won wisdom of its narrator, who comes to understand that "life eventually takes away everything it gives."

Which stories burrow under our skin, of course, has a lot to do with who we are and how as readers we allow ourselves to be approached. I admit that I've always been a sucker for a good coming-of-age story, especially if it involves, as such tales so often do, the loss of innocence. What makes "Mudlavia" work so wonderfully within its appealing genre is that its private story of a boy coming to terms with difficult truths—that the pain in his knee is no rheumatism to be cured by mud baths, that his doting mother is tragically unhappy in her marriage to his controlling father, that magical Mudlavia may be a con game—dovetails so perfectly with its public story of America's own impending loss of innocence. In "the last summer of peace" before the beginning of the first world war, the narrator and his mother fully believe that "as a nation . . . we were getting bigger, better, and more stylish." The story slyly asks whether America, with its unbridled, energetic optimism, is itself a kind of con game (in the literal sense of the term, where "confidence" is itself the dubious guarantor of the future). Are we a nation that first underestimates, then misdiagnoses its own ills, bullishly promising, like Mudlavia, more than it can hope to deliver by way of a cure? It's this public story that signals "Mudlavia"'s considerable ambition, that tips us off to the fact that Stuckey-French is hunting bigger game than at first we might suppose.

No doubt the other reason that the story particularly appealed to me

356 / *Reading* The O. Henry Prize Stories 2005

was that its true subject is the power of the literary imagination, or, if you prefer, of narrative itself. It's not just the boy protagonist who comes of age in "Mudlavia," but also his mother, and it's the act of storytelling that allows for their transformation from innocence to experience. The lies the narrator tells "Harry Jones" as the two are sheathed each morning in soothing mud are not just untruths, but narrative inventions that draw equally upon his youthful imagination and his growing knowledge of the real world, his first adolescent attempts to acknowledge the frightening complexities of his family, his world, even his own body. But the story's finest and most unexpected turn occurs when his mother takes up his narrative, embracing it as her own and thereby allowing her son to understand that she shares his need for another reality, as well as his joy in invention.

For me, though, it's the story's flash-forward ending that seals the deal. By the end the boy has become a man who, with every reason to be bitter and disillusioned, has made a separate peace, preferring the "good" life he's lived to the "happy" one promised by Mudlavia. The pursuit of happiness may be our constitutional right as Americans, but, he seems to imply, it's always been the most childish aspect of our collective American dream. Elizabeth Stuckey-French has given us a story with the emotional and intellectual weight of a longer fictional work. Only the very best short fiction manages that.

Richard Russo is the author of *Mohawk*, *The Risk Pool*, *Nobody's Fool*, *Straight Man*, and *Empire Falls*, as well as *The Whore's Child and Other Stories*. Russo lives in Maine with his family.

Writing *The O. Henry Prize Stories 2005*
The Authors on Their Work

Sherman Alexie, "What You Pawn I Will Redeem"
"What You Pawn I Will Redeem" started out simply as a writing exercise. I thought, "Hey, I'll take highly stereotypical urban characters (homeless Indian, Korean grocery store owner, white cop, white pawnshop owner) and see if I can write a story that humanizes all of them. I'll make them decent and loving." I wrote the first draft very quickly, in a few hours really, and thought it was cute and sentimental, so I set it aside. A year or so later, as I was gathering stories for my latest collection, *Ten Little Indians,* I came across the story again, reread it, and was surprised by its quiet power. I don't think I've published anything that's ever received as much fan mail. Heck, I got fan mail from writers who haven't liked anything else I've ever done. This story's journey still feels magical to me.

Sherman Alexie is a Spokane/Coeur d'Alene Indian from Wellpinit, Washington, a town on the Spokane Indian reservation. He is the author of *Ten Little Indians, The Toughest Indian in the West*, and *The Lone Ranger and Tonto Fistfight in Heaven*, among other books. Alexie lives in Seattle with his wife and two sons.

Wendell Berry, "The Hurt Man"
I am always pleased when I know that a story I have imagined has grown from a real story. This is pleasing to me because I always need assurance of

the connection between imagination and reality. "The Hurt Man" grew out of a family story about my great-grandmother. That story came to me a long time ago in only a few sentences, and so what I have imagined surely bears little resemblance to what actually happened. The old story grew into imagination, so to speak, over many years. It became writable finally when I began to see it as an episode in the early life of Mat Feltner, a character I began writing about in 1960.

Wendell Berry has farmed a hillside in his native Henry County, Kentucky, for over thirty years. He is the author of more than forty books of fiction, poetry, and essays, including *Jayber Crow, Citizenship Papers*, and, most recently, his collected stories, *That Distant Land*. A former professor of English at the University of Kentucky, he has received numerous awards for his work, including the T. S. Eliot Award, the Aitken Taylor Award for Poetry, and the John Hay Award of the Orion Society. Berry lives and works in Kentucky with his wife, Tanya Berry, and their children and grandchildren, who live and farm nearby.

Kevin Brockmeier, "The Brief History of the Dead"

I wrote "The Brief History of the Dead" in November of 2002. Whenever I'm beginning the sort of narrative that I hope might turn into a novel, I try to approach the first chapter as though it were an independent short story, as a way of easing myself into the water. That was what happened with "The Brief History of the Dead," and the story has indeed become the first chapter of a novel-in-progress. William Maxwell, whose "The Thistles in Sweden" is one of my all-time favorite stories, talks about using an image or a metaphor as a way of developing the structure of his books: he would envision a tree with its center cut out, for instance, or a walk across flat ground toward distant mountains, and he would adopt that image as a sort of imaginative compass while he was writing. The image I had in mind as I wrote "The Brief History of the Dead" was that of one thing spreading open inside another—doors opening within doors opening within doors. Most of the doors never close, and my hope was that this would give the city and its inhabitants a sense of ongoing existence in the mind of the reader. I tried to fit as much of the life of the city into the story as I could—as much of the landscape, as many of the people, and as many of their dreams and expectations and notions about the place where they found themselves—while I elaborated on my central premise, that of a world of the dead-but-still-remembered undergoing its own quiet apocalypse.

Kevin Brockmeier is the author of the novel *The Truth About Celia*, the story collection *Things That Fall from the Sky*, and two children's novels, *City of Names* and the forthcoming *Grooves; or, the True-Life Outbreak of Weirdness*. His stories have appeared in *The New Yorker, Best American Short Stories*, and *The Year's Best Fantasy and Horror*, among other publications, and have been included twice before in *The O. Henry Prize Stories*. He lives in Little Rock, Arkansas.

Timothy Crouse, "Sphinxes"
To my mind, one mark of a true human being is the desire to know, and to share knowledge, once acquired. What motivates me to write my stories is the need to come to grips with an actual situation, and, having understood its deepest meanings, express its multiplicity of levels. Since this story, which still remains alive in me, required much elaboration, I have to admit, paraphrasing Paul Valéry, that I prefer one reader who reads it several times to many who read it once.

When beginning the story, I made this note: "Being—God?—leaves us free within a prison." Not for nothing do we have the concepts of the *no*, the *yes*, the *perhaps*. How wonderful when the *yes* or the *no* presents itself as a clear choice; but this world is the kingdom of the *perhaps*. In my perception, the Great Teacher is a bystanding witness to this same problem of the *no*, the *yes*, and the regrettable *perhaps*. What a collection of sphinxes play on the keyboard of this planet.

Timothy Crouse has been a contributing editor for *Rolling Stone* and the *Village Voice*, and the Washington columnist for *Esquire*, writing numerous articles for these and other publications, including *The New Yorker*. His 1974 book, *The Boys on the Bus*, was reissued in 2003. He translated, with Luc Brébion, the Nobel laureate Roger Martin du Gard's *Lieutenant-Colonel de Maumort*. The new version of *Anything Goes* that he coauthored with John Weidman was staged at the Royal National Theatre, London. He is writing a book of short stories, collaborating on a screenplay, and cotranslating works by the Chilean poet David Rosenmann-Taub. Crouse lives in Chapel Hill, North Carolina.

Charles D'Ambrosio, "The High Divide"

I just checked the folder in my computer where I've kept the various versions of "The High Divide" and there are, no kidding, 116—plus there's a sheaf of papers in my old Steelcase file cabinet that includes typewritten scenes and scribbled notes and a handful of rejections from people who, I would love to imagine, had some ideas that this story was destined to knock around, alone and unloved, stupid and blind, until it found its present shape and home. Of course, going forward the floundering hardly felt that way. Despite writing lots of versions over the course of twelve years, there was very little agony involved in making the story—it just seemed that every two or three years I'd haul it out and write a bunch of drafts and forget about it until the next time. It was like owning a pet that didn't need to be fed very frequently. Big and little things changed along the way. At one point the crazy father was on the loose and the narrator lost the tip of his tongue when a basketball fell on his head. The dead mother was alive and the whole family lived in a bungalow in West Seattle with blackberry vines scrabbling up through the floor. Somewhere in all this the story ballooned to about twelve thousand words. In order to reduce the word count, I had to lock the nutty father away in a mental institution. Committing the father also softened the narrator's anger, which in turn cut down the number of personal cruelties in the story. The pain spread out beyond the petty question of personal fairness, widening into sympathy. All the quotes were removed from the dialogue—which is how I'd had it originally—and that fixed a tonal problem, since all the dialogue was written to sound reported rather than realistic. Thus my first vague impulse was integrated back into the narrator's voice. The sentences felt healthy and true again. The engine driving the story had always been anger, but in the last stages of rewriting a new note of love crept in. If anger is endless and the deepest urge of love is toward completion, then love, I'd have to say, did the trick—however unliterary that insight may seem.

Charles D'Ambrosio is the author of *The Point and Other Stories* and *The Dead Fish Museum*. His fiction appeared in *The New Yorker*, *The Paris Review*, and various anthologies, including *The Pushcart Prize* and *Best American Short Stories*. His nonfiction appears regularly in *Nest Magazine* and *The Organ Review of Arts*. D'Ambrosio lives in Portland, Oregon.

Ben Fountain, "Fantasy for Eleven Fingers"

I was sitting at my daughter's piano recital watching all those kids ripping the keyboard in that extraordinary way which we tend to take for granted, the fingers hitting the keys *bam-bam-bam-bam* as if each separate finger had its own brain, and two things occurred to me more or less simultaneously. One, that artistic skill and achievement of this sort are an everyday miracle that ought to blow our minds, and, two, how would throwing an extra finger into the mix change things? I walked around with those notions for a couple of days, pretty sure that I wanted to write a story about a piano prodigy, a young girl, with eleven fingers, and after a few more days I realized that I'd begun thinking about her in the context of that lost, hyperattenuated world of the Jewish intelligentsia of fin de siècle Vienna. Which felt right to me; after that it was just a question of doing the work.

Ben Fountain grew up in the tobacco country of eastern North Carolina, graduated from the University of North Carolina and Duke University Law School, and practiced law in Dallas before quitting to write fiction. His stories have appeared in *Harper's*, *Threepenny Review*, *Zoetrope*, and *The Pushcart Prize*, and in 2002 he won the Texas Institute of Letters Short Story Award. He is working on a novel set in Dallas, where he lives with his wife and their two children.

Paula Fox, "Grace"

My family and I took in a small stray dog many years ago. She was rather like Grace, both timid and stubborn. The title refers not only to the dog in the story, but also to John Hillman's implied evolution to a state of grace.

Paula Fox was born in 1923, and in the 1960s began to publish both novels and books for young people. Since her first novel, *Poor George*, and first book for children, *Maurice's Room*, she's published another twenty-eight books, the most recent a memoir, *Borrowed Finery*. Fox lives in New York City.

Nell Freudenberger, "The Tutor"

I started writing this story during a two-month stay in Bombay. I knew I was writing a book that would take place mostly in India, but I didn't like the idea of "looking for" stories. At the same time I made choices that seem, in retrospect, suspiciously scavengerish: I rented a room in a family-owned boardinghouse that doubled as a maternity hospital; I pestered a Parsi friend to take me walking around the Towers of Silence, the sacred compound where Zoroastrians expose their dead; I spent an inordinate amount of time convincing the staff of the historic David Sassoon library to give me reading privileges. Some of my happiest (but least "exotic") days in Bombay were spent with a friend of a friend from home, who had set up a business tutoring high school students for college entrance exams. One afternoon he mentioned that the teenage girls he taught were bored by poetry, with the exception of Marvell's "To His Coy Mistress." The idea that sixteen-year-old girls in Bombay were responding to Marvell fascinated me; according to my friend, they immediately understood the poem as a seduction strategy. That got me started, and I finished the story after I came home to New York. I hope that my feeling for Bombay is in "The Tutor," but I also know that the core of the story is something native to me: my own response to certain poems as a teenager. I worried that being away from home would either keep me from writing stories, or help so much that I would depend on it; I like the idea that my friend's anecdote, for which I'm grateful, is one I could have heard at home. Maybe stories aren't such delicate things that a trip over the ocean can make or break them.

Nell Freudenberger's stories have been published in *The New Yorker*, *The Paris Review*, and *Granta*. *Lucky Girls*, her first book, won the PEN/Faulkner Malamud Award for Fiction. She has taught English in Bangkok and New Delhi. Freudenberger lives in New York City.

Tessa Hadley, "The Card Trick"

For me, the oddest thing about this story, "The Card Trick," is that inside it I have made up the whole career of an imaginary celebrated novelist, John Morrison; and even some of his work. This is not something I've ever done elsewhere. It was surprisingly easy to supply the biography, and an impression of the novels; much easier than making up one's own work. I just imagined a whole oeuvre, absolutely of its period, intense and melancholy, austere. I thought of a writer I'd love to discover, and read. Well, of course, I didn't actually have to write John Morrison's novel, only imagine how it ought to be, if it was really good: which is the easy bit. In retrospect, I'm struck by my cheek in inventing him. He's almost too much— too big—to be used only in one story; I am playing with the idea of bring- ing him into something else, to do him justice, make his influence on the history of the novel more strongly felt and pervasive. The idea of bringing Literature into literature, so to speak, really interests me. All my own liv- ing has been so saturated with my reading, it seems a kind of lie to leave books out of books.

But the germ of the story began with the card trick itself: the only even moderately good one I know. I did try to write enough into the story so that anyone who cared to follow it could see how it was done. I remember learning this trick as a child, from a boy, in fact (reversing what happens in the story), son of a family friend. I had been too shy to talk to him, until we came together over this trick. I remember the wonderful sense of power it gave me, dissolving awkwardness and incapacity, giving me a way of performing with a mastery that otherwise I didn't seem to have. The twist, that the trick *seems* to hand over mastery from the performer to the subject who unknowingly deals out, is an adult irony overlaid onto the child's excitement. I have made it have something to do with sex, with the way women have sometimes made themselves abject in order to keep con- trol. Gina—unknowingly, of course—may be up to something like this, in her teenage helplessness.

Tessa Hadley was born in Bristol, England. She has published two novels, *Accidents in the Home* and *Everything Will Be All Right*, and her stories have appeared in *The New Yorker*, *Granta*, and *The Big Issue*, among others. She is the author of *Henry James and the Imagination of Pleasure*, and teaches English and creative writing at Bath Spa University College. Hadley has lived in Cardiff, Wales, for more than twenty years.

Ruth Prawer Jhabvala, "Refuge in London"

In earlier years I wrote mostly about India—or rather, my experience of India—but later I more often turned back to my European background. Although of course the characters and setting of "Refuge in London" are the usual lies and fusions that the fictional memory performs, I did grow up as a refugee in London during the war years. And I did sit for a once- famous artist, who was also a refugee and couldn't afford another model; and he did read Beaudelaire to me from a little book he must have acquired in Paris during his youthful years there. Later, when he returned to Germany (where he again became successful), he gave me that book and I took it with me to India. I still have it there. He had drawn a book-plate for me and pasted it inside, and that is the only drawing of his I possess.

Ruth Prawer Jhabvala was born in Germany in 1927 and escaped to England with her parents in 1939. She went to school and college in London, where she met and married the Indian architect C. S. H. Jhabvala. They lived in India from 1951 to 1975. She published her first novel in 1955, and since then has published twelve novels, including *Heat and Dust* and *A Backward Place*, and six collections of short stories. She has written most of the screenplays for the films of Merchant Ivory, with whom she has been associated since 1962. Jhabvala lives in New York, with frequent return visits to India.

Edward P. Jones, "A Rich Man"

In *Lost in the City*, there is a story, "A New Man," which has a teenager, Elaine Cunningham, who runs away from home and is never found. "A Rich Man" takes place several years later. I may well have had a need to say something about what happened to Elaine. So I created "A Rich Man." Elaine is not the primary focus of the new story, but we have some idea of where she is headed.

Edward P. Jones is the author of *The Known World*, a novel that won the Pulitzer Prize and the National Book Critics Circle Award for fiction, and *Lost in the City*, winner of the PEN/Hemingway Award in 1992. He is the recipient of a fellowship and award from the Lannan Foundation. Jones lives in Washington, D.C.

Gail Jones, "Desolation"

This is a deliberately wordy story about unspeakable shame and the silent metaphysics of dislocated experience. In every large city there are diasporic lost souls, and in cities, too, there are pleasure seekers and wanderers. I wanted—with as much concision as possible—to forge a meeting that tips from community, even possible romance, into sudden desolation. The Death in Vegas concert supplies a kind of aesthetic analogy to the structure of the story in its alienated form, its repetitions, and its decontextual-ized images. For all this, "Desolation" is a kind of love story.

Gail Jones is the author of two collections of short stories, *The House of Breathing* and *Fetish Lives*, and two novels, *Black Mirror* and *Sixty Lights*. She teaches in the Department of English, Communication, and Cultural Studies at the University of Western Australia and lives "in the most remote city in the world," Perth.

Caitlin Macy, "Christie"

In his introduction to the red book—his *Collected Stories*—John Cheever wrote, "My favorite stories are those that were written in less than a week and were often composed aloud." After I finished my novel it took me a long time to get my short-story legs back. Then one day when I was toiling and sweating to get out some other story, "Christie" came to me almost whole. "Christie came from Greenwich, Connecticut," I thought, "and that was all anyone knew of her background." This original first line of the story was later edited for clarity but much of the opening passage remains intact, exactly the same as when I first heard it—"heard" because this was a rare instance for me of the composing aloud that Cheever describes. Because I had a lot of fun writing the story, it amused me that readers' reactions were largely of the "chilling," "incredibly depressing," "disturbing," "sad," "scary" ilk—a clear instance of one's story having a life of its own, and one that its author could not have predicted. As for the subject matter, I have always been fascinated by girls like Christie Brue-wald née Thorn who move to New York, dye their hair blond, eat frozen yogurt for dinner, snag a man. I hope my soft spot for the Christie type comes through even the angst-y, bitter, teeth-gnashing voice of the narrator.

   I am fond of the story for another reason: it proved to me that the daily forced march over the blank page is not necessarily in vain because inspiration may be more likely to come out of it—out of one's daily work—rather than out of a passive, here-I-am-waiting-to-be-inspired stance, something that I had never clarified for myself.

Caitlin Macy is the author of the novel *The Fundamentals of Play*. She is at work on a collection of short stories, tentatively titled *Spoiled*. Macy lives in New York City with her husband and daughter.

Michael Parker, "The Golden Era of Heartbreak"

This story arose out of the usual straddle: one leg in experience and the other, more weight-bearing leg in a calculated exploitation and exaggeration of same. As always I started with music—the rhythm of the narrator's desire—and landscape—the flat, bleakly beautiful Sound country of northeastern North Carolina. Two other things helped this story along: a Whiskeytown song called "Excuse Me While I Break My Own Heart Tonight," and the fact that, while writing it, I was training for an Ironman triathlon, and had self-inflicted suffering on the brain.

Michael Parker is the author of four books of fiction, including the novel *Virginia Lovers*. His short fiction has appeared in *Five Points*, *Shenandoah*, *The Oxford American*, *The Black Warrior Review*, *New Stories from the South: The Year's Best 2002*, and *The Pushcart Prize Anthology*. He teaches in the MFA writing program at the University of North Carolina at Greensboro, and has received fellowships in fiction from the North Carolina Arts Council and the National Endowment for the Arts. Parker lives in Greensboro, North Carolina.

Dale Peck, "Dues"

This is a funny story. I wrote a preliminary version while housesitting in upstate New York for a friend of a friend. I was in the middle of the country with no one around, and I fell into a pattern of sleeping for two or three hours and being awake for four or five hours, so that I'd find myself waking up at three in the morning and reading and writing until eight and then going back to bed—a staccato rhythm echoed in all the starts and stops in the story. I was also reading a lot of Coetzee at the time (*Boyhood*, *Life & Times of Michael K*, *Waiting for the Barbarians*) and so much of his terseness crept into the story that it ended up stymieing me. I put the manuscript away until July 2002, when, through a tangential impulse, I was inspired to pull it out and rewrite it as a September 11 story. My inspiration was the mining accident in Quecreek, Pennsylvania. Nine miners were trapped for three days after an underground stream flooded the shaft they were working in; by the time rescue workers managed to drill into the shaft it was assumed the miners would all be dead, but they all made it. I think the experience reawakened the sense of helplessness many Americans had felt about not being able to rescue anyone from the World Trade Center, and rechanneled it into the herculean efforts that led to the miners' rescue, and it's this idea—of looking for someone who's dead but finding someone who's alive—that became central to "Dues." There's actually a second half of the story planned (or a second story with the same character) which takes place at the site of the mining accident, but that's still in note form, and will probably decide to get written, like "Dues," when I least expect it.

Dale Peck is the author of three novels, *Martin and John*, *The Law of Enclosures*, and *Now It's Time to Say Goodbye*; a memoir, *What We Lost*; and a collection of essays, *Hatchet Jobs*. He teaches in the Graduate Writing Program of New School University. Peck lives in New York City.

Frances de Pontes Peebles, "The Drowned Woman"

The idea for "The Drowned Woman" came to me during a plane ride with my mother four years ago. It was a nine-hour flight from Recife to the United States, and neither of us could sleep. The cabin was dark. A movie played. A few restless people padded up and down the aisle in their socks. I don't know what triggered her memory, but my mother turned to me and said that once, as a little girl, she and her friends saw an unknown woman washed up on the beach with her arm petrified from rigor mortis. I asked questions, and all my mother said was, "I don't know. I don't know." Then she fell asleep.

Sitting in that dark plane, I was amazed by the drowned woman, by the stiff arm. But later, I was more amazed by my mother, by the fact that, as a child, she had seen a corpse, washed up and rigid, and had never mentioned it. I started writing about the drowned woman, creating a name and a story for her. After several drafts, the story became less about the woman and more about the little girl.

Frances de Pontes Peebles is a recipient of a Sacatar Artist's Fellowship and a J. William Fulbright Fellowship. Her stories have appeared in *Indiana Review* and *Missouri Review*. Peebles lives in Pernambuco, Brazil, with her dogs Oscar, Lorenço, Negão, and Xuxa.

Ron Rash, "Speckle Trout"

When I was a child, I loved to fish the small creek on my grandparents' farm. Brook trout was the technical name for the fish I caught, but in the

North Carolina mountains they were called speckle trout. My grandparents loved to eat them, and I was expected to bring back what I caught for supper. They were beautiful creatures—red and olive spots on their flanks, orange fins—and I always felt some sadness as I slipped them onto my stringer. I was especially haunted by how quickly their bright colors faded. These trout were also rare, found only in small, isolated creeks. As I got older I searched for them in places sometimes a mile or two away from any road, places where a rattlesnake bite or broken leg could have life-threatening consequences. I also ignored a few No Trespassing signs. Unlike the young man in my story, I was never caught, but that fear was always present.

Ron Rash's family has lived in the southern Appalachian mountains since the mid-1700s. He grew up in Boiling Springs, North Carolina, and holds the John Parris Chair in Appalachian Studies at Western Carolina University. His poetry and fiction have appeared in many magazines, including *Sewanee Review*, *Yale Review*, *Georgia Review*, *New England Review*, and *Poetry*. He is the author of two story collections, *The Night the New Jesus Fell to Earth* and *Casualties*; three volumes of poetry, *Eureka Mill* and *Among the Believers Raising the Dead*; and two novels, *One Foot in Eden* and *Saints at the River*. Rash lives in Clemson, South Carolina.

Nancy Reisman, "Tea"

I'm interested in the way that longing can shape one's perceptions of reality and in the delicate balance between hope and self-delusion. One reason I'm drawn to Lillian's character is that I think of her as a realist, a highly pragmatic woman, yet her relationship with Abe moves her into wishful, unsteady territory. It's an emotionally fraught mix, but I think this combination of pragmatism and wild hope is what has enabled her to survive and to sustain an unconventional life in a tradition-bound community.

Nancy Reisman is the author of a novel, *The First Desire*, and *House Fires*, which won an Iowa Short Fiction Award. She teaches at the University of Michigan. Her work has been anthologized in *Best American Short Stories* and *Bestial Noise: The Tin House Fiction Reader*, and has also appeared in *Five Points*, *Tin House*, *New England Review*, *Michigan Quarterly Review*, and *Glimmer Train*, among others. Reisman lives in Ann Arbor, Michigan.

Elizabeth Stuckey-French, "Mudlavia"

I began "Mudlavia" years ago. It started with a conversation I had with Harold Watts, a family friend and colleague of my father's in the Purdue University English Department. Harold's mother took him to the Mudlavia Hotel and Resort in 1916, when he was ten years old, hoping to heal his aching knee with mud baths. Harold generously told me all about his visit there, giving me many intriguing details, including a description of the character I call Harry Jones, the cushion man, whom Harold and his mother thought was a gangster.

I wrote an early draft of this story in which I didn't stray much from the facts Harold told me, but it wasn't very dramatic and I had to put it aside. From the start, however, I tapped into a voice that I found mesmerizing, and it was the voice that drew me back into the story when I picked it up again over a decade later. When I reread it a plot suggested itself right away, but it took me a number of rewrites until I allowed the inevitable to happen at the end. After finishing this story I didn't want to leave Mudlavia, so I am in the midst of writing a novel set there.

The real Mudlavia Hotel burned down in 1920. I often wish I could go there. If I could, I know I'd be a much better person.

Elizabeth Stuckey-French is the author of a novel, *Mermaids on the Moon*, and a collection of short stories, *The First Paper Girl in Red Oak, Iowa*. She teaches at Florida State University. Her stories have appeared in *The Atlantic Monthly*, *Gettysburg Review*, *Southern Review*, and *Five Points*, among others. Stuckey-French lives in Tallahassee, Florida.

Liza Ward, "Snowbound"

I wrote this story during a bout of loneliness at the end of one very hot summer in Missoula, Montana. The hills had turned brown. Fish struggled in the shallow water of the Clark Fork River, and dark plumes of smoke crowded the horizon. It felt like the end of something. There seemed to be no one anywhere to verify my existence, and I slipped into a strange internal world, dragging this character, Susan, along with me. After a while it was hard to tell who was leading whom. I fantasized about winter, a frozen place white as the moon where new truths emerged, where everything was subjective. I remembered how our garden in Brooklyn looked to me as a girl, buried in snow, our pint-sized terrier hopping through the magic blue light as a confused rabbit might, and the way it felt like the city was yawning. Anything could happen on a snowy day, and I had the feeling that anything could happen in this story. I had no idea where it was going, only that my character was writing her own version of history, assuaging her fear of abandonment with a fictional world where people found each other. She knew she didn't want to spend her life alone the way her father was going to now that her mother had left. I guess her dream, her invented story, gave her hope.

Liza Ward was born in 1975, and grew up in New York City. Her first novel is *Outside Valentine*, and her stories have appeared in *The Atlantic Monthly*, *Antioch Review*, *Agni Review*, *Georgia Review*, and *Best New American Voices*. Ward lives in Massachusetts.

Recommended Stories

Ann Darby, "Pity My Simplicity," *Prairie Schooner*
Andrea Dezso, "The Numbers," *McSweeney's*
Tamas Dobozy, "The Inert Landscapes of György Ferenc," *Colorado Review*
E. L. Doctorow, "Walter John Harmon," *The New Yorker*
Stephanie Koven, "The Events Leading up to the Accident," *Antioch Review*
Barbara Klein Moss, "Little Edens," *Southwest Review*
Alice Munro, "Runaway," *The New Yorker*
Paul Murray, "Anubis," *Granta*
Julie Orringer, "The Smoothest Way Is Full of Stones," *Zoetrope*
Michael Redhill, "Long Division," *Zoetrope*
Annette Sanford, "One Summer," *New Orleans Review*
Shauna Seliy, "Blackdamp," *Alaska Quarterly Review*
Katherine Shonk, "The Wooden Village of Kizhi," *Georgia Review*
Scott Snyder, "About Face," *Epoch*
Jay Teitel, "Luck," *Toronto Life*

Publications Submitted

As of this collection, *The O. Henry Prize Stories* will be published in January rather than in October. The change in schedule has led to a change in title. There was always a difference between the year in which stories were published in magazines and the year in which *The O. Henry Prize Stories* was published. Although it may appear that we are skipping 2004, in fact, *The O. Henry Prize Stories 2006*, our next collection, will be based on stories originally written in English and published in Canada and the United States in 2004.

Because of production deadlines for the collection, it is essential that stories reach the series editor by November 8 of the year in which they are published. If a finished magazine is unavailable before the deadline, magazine editors may submit scheduled stories in proof or in manuscript. Stories may not be submitted or nominated by agents or writers. Please see our Web site http://www.ohenryprizestories.com for more information about submission to *The O. Henry Prize Stories*.

The address for submission is:

> Professor Laura Furman, The O. Henry Prize Stories
> English Department
> University of Texas at Austin
> One University Station, B5000
> Austin, TX 78712-5100

The information listed below was up-to-date as *The O. Henry Prize Stories 2005* went to press. Inclusion in the listings does not constitute endorsement or recommendation.

580 Split
P.O. Box 9982
Oakland, CA 94613-0982
Julia Bloch, Danielle Unis,
    Managing Editors
five80split@yahoo.com
www.mills.edu/580Split
Annual

96 Inc
P.O. Box 15559
Boston, MA 02215
Julie Anderson, Vera Gold, Nancy
    Mehegan, Editors
mail@96inc.com
www.96inc.com
Annual

African American Review
English Department
Indiana State University
Terre Haute, IN 47809
Joe Weixlmann, Editor
http://aar.slu.edu
Quarterly

Agni
236 Bay State Road
Boston, MA 02215
Sven Birkerts, Editor
agni@bu.edu
www.bu.edu/agni/
Biannual

Alaska Quarterly Review
University of Alaska Anchorage
3211 Providence Drive

Anchorage, AK 99508
Ronald Spatz, Editor
ayaqr@uaa.alaska.edu
www.uaa.alaska.edu/aqr
Biannual

Alligator Juniper
Prescott College
220 Grove Avenue
Prescott, Arizona 86301
Miles Waggener, Managing Editor
aj@prescott.edu
www.prescott.edu/highlights/
    alligator_juniper.html
Annual

American Literary Review
University of North Texas
P.O. Box 13827
Denton, TX 76203-1307
Lee Martin, Editor
americanliteraryreview@yahoo.com
www.engl.unt.edu/alr/
Biannual

Another Chicago Magazine
3709 North Kenmore
Chicago, IL 60613
Barry Silesky, Editor and Publisher
editors@anotherchicagomag.com
www.anotherchicagomag.com
Biannual

Antietam Review
41 S. Potomac Street
Hagerstown, MD 21740
Philip Bufithis, Editor

www.washingtoncountyarts.com
Annual

The Antioch Review
P.O. Box 148
Yellow Springs, OH 45387
Robert S. Fogarty, Editor
www.antioch.edu/review/
home.html
Quarterly

Appalachee Review
P.O. Box 10469
Tallahassee, Florida 32302
Laura Newton, Mary Jane Ryals,
Michael Trammel, Editors
Biannual

Arkansas Review
Department of English and
Philosophy
Box 1890
Arkansas State University
State University, AR 72467
William M. Clements, General
Editor
delta@toltec.astate.edu
www.clt.astate.edu/arkreview
Triannual

Ascent
English Department
Concordia College
901 8th Street South
Moorhead, MN 56562
W. Scott Olsen, Editor
ascent@cord.edu
www.cord.edu/dept/english/ascent
Triannual

At Length
P.O. Box 594
New York, NY 10185
Jonathan Farmer, Editor
info@atlengthmag.com
www.atlengthmag.com
Quarterly

Atlanta Review
P.O. Box 8248
Atlanta, GA 31106
Daniel Veach, Editor and Publisher
www.atlantareview.com
Biannual

The Atlantic Monthly
77 North Washington Street
Boston, MA 02114
Benjamin Schwarz, Literary Editor,
and C. Michael Curtis, Senior
Editor (Fiction)
Letters@theatlantic.com
www.theatlantic.com
Monthly

The Baltimore Review
P.O. Box 410
Riderwood, Maryland 21139
Barbara Westwood Diehl, Managing
Editor
www.baltimorewriters.org
Biannual

Bellevue Literary Review
Department of Medicine
NYU School of Medicine
550 First Avenue, OBV-612
New York, NY 10016
Danielle Ofri, Editor-in-Chief
www.BLReview.org
Biannual

Beloit Fiction Journal
Box 11
Beloit College
700 College Street
Beloit, WI 53511
Clint McCown, Editor-in-Chief
www.beloit.edu/~english/
 bfjournal.htm
Annual

BIGnews
302 E. 45th Street
4th Floor
New York, NY 10017
Ron Grumberg, Editor
MainchanceNY@aol.com
www.Mainchance.org/BIGnews
Monthly

Black Warrior Review
Box 862936
Tuscaloosa, Alabama 35486
David Mitchell Goldberg, Editor
bwr@ua.edu
www.webdelsol.com/bwr
Semiannual

Bomb
594 Broadway, 9th Floor
New York, NY 10012
Betsy Sussler, Editor-in-Chief
bomb@echonyc.com
www.bombsite.com/firstproof.html
Quarterly

Book
252 West 37th Street
5th Floor
New York, NY 10018
Jerome V. Kramer, Editor-in-Chief

www.bookmagazine.com
Bimonthly

Border Crossings
500-70 Arthur Street
Winnipeg, Manitoba R3B 1G7
 Canada
Meeka Walsh, Editor
bordercr@escape.ca
www.bordercrossingsmag.com
Quarterly

The Boston Book Review
30 Brattle Street, 4th Floor
Cambridge, MA 02138
Kiril Stefan Alexandrov, Editor
BBR-Info@BostonBookReview.com
Monthly

Boston Review
E53-407, MIT
Cambridge, MA 02139
Deborah Chasman, Joshua Cohen,
 Editors
bostonreview@mit.edu
www.bostonreview.net
Published six times per year

Boulevard
PMB 325
6614 Clayton Road
Richmond Heights, MO 63117
Richard Burgin, Editor
www.richardburgin.com
Triannual

The Briar Cliff Review
3303 Rebecca Street
P.O. Box 2100
Sioux City, IA 51104-2100

Tricia Currans-Sheehen, Editor
www.briarcliff.edu/bcreview
Annual

Callaloo
English Department
322 Bryan Hall
University of Virginia
Charlottesville, VA 22903
Charles Henry Rowell, Editor
www.press.jhu.edu/journals/
  callaloo
Quarterly

Calyx
P.O. Box B
Corvalis, OR 97339-0539
Ron Duncan, Senior Editor
calyx@proaxis.com
www.proaxis.com/~calyx
Biannual

Canadian Fiction
P.O. Box 1061
Kingston, Ontario K7L 4Y5 Canada
Geoff Hancock, Rob Payne, Editors
Biannual

The Carolina Quarterly
Greenlaw Hall CB# 3520
University of North Carolina
Chapel Hill, NC 27599-3520
Tara Powell, Editor
www.unc.edu/depts/cqonline
Triannual

The Chariton Review
Truman State University
Kirksville, MO 63501
Jim Barnes, Editor
Biannual

The Chattahoochee Review
2101 Womack Road
Dunwoody, GA 30338-4497
Lawrence Hetrick, Editor
www.chattahoochee-review.org
Quarterly

Chelsea
P.O. Box 773
Cooper Station
New York, NY 10276-0773
Alfredo de Palchi, Editor
Biannual

Chicago Review
5801 South Kenwood Avenue
Chicago, IL 60637
Eirik Steinhoff, Editor
chicago-review@uchicago.edu
http://humanities.uchicago.edu/
  orgs/review/
Quarterly

Cimarron Review
205 Morrill Hall
Oklahoma State University
Stillwater, OK 74078-0135
E. P. Walkiewicz, Editor
http://cimarronreview.okstate.edu
Quarterly

Colorado Review
Department of English
Colorado State University
Fort Collins, Colorado 80523
David Milofsky, Editor
creview@colostate.edu
www.coloradoreview.com
Triannual

Commentary
165 East 56th Street
New York, NY 10022
Neal Kozodoy, Editor
editorial@commentarymagazine.com
www.commentarymagazine.com
Monthly

Concho River Review
P.O. Box 1894
Angelo State University
San Angelo, TX 76909
James A. Moore, General Editor
www.angelo.edu/dept/english/
    concho_river_review.htm
Biannual

Confrontation
English Department
C. W. Post Campus of Long Island
    University
Brookville, NY 11548-1300
Martin Tucker, Editor-in-Chief

Conjunctions
21 East 10th Street
New York, NY 10003
Bradford Morrow, Editor
conjunctions@bard.edu
www.conjunctions.com
Biannual

Crab Orchard Review
Southern Illinois University
    Carbondale
Carbondale, IL 62901-4503
Richard Peterson, Founding Editor
www.siu.edu/~crborchd
Biannual

Crazyhorse
English Department
University of Arkansas at Little Rock
Little Rock, AR 72204
Ralph Burns, Lisa Lewis, Editors
www.ualr.edu/~english/chorse.htm
Biannual

The Cream City Review
University of Wisconsin-Milwaukee
P.O. Box 413
Milwaukee, WI 53201
www.uwm.edu/Dept/English/ccr/
Biannual

Cut Bank
English Department
University of Montana
Missoula, MT 59812
cutbank@selway.umt.edu
www.umt.edu/cutbank
Biannual

Daedalus
Norton's Woods
136 Irving Street
Cambridge, MA 02138
James Miller, Editor
daedalus@amacad.org
Quarterly

Denver Quarterly
University of Denver
Denver, CO 80208
Bin Ramke, Editor
www.denverquarterly.com
Quarterly

DoubleTake
55 Davis Square

Somerville, MA 02144
Robert Coles, Founding Editor
bklm@doubletakemagazine.org
www.doubletakemagazine.org
Quarterly

Epoch
251 Goldwin Smith Hall
Cornell University
Ithaca, NY 14853-3201
Michael Koch, Editor
www.arts.cornell.edu/english/
    epoch.html
Triannual

Esquire
1790 Broadway
New York, NY 10019
David Granger, Editor-in-Chief, and
    Adrienne Miller, Literary Editor
www.esquire.com
Monthly

Faultline
English and Comparative Literature
    Department
University of California-Irvine
Irvine, CA 92697-2650
faultline@uci.edu
www.humanities.uci.edu/faultline
Annual

Fence
303 East Eighth Street, #B1
New York, NY 10009
Caroline Crumpacker, Matthew
    Rohrer, Editors
fence@angel.net
www.fencemag.com
Biannual

Fiction
English Department
City College of New York
New York, NY 10031
Mark Jay Mirsky, Editor
www.fictioninc.com
Biannual

The Fiddlehead
The University of New Brunswick
P.O. Box 4400
Fredericton, NB E3B 5A3 Canada
Ross Leckie, Editor
www.lib.unb.ca/Texts/Fiddlehead
Quarterly

First Intensity
P.O. Box 665
Lawrence, KS 66044
Lee Chapman
leechapman@aol.com
http://homepage.mac.com/
    firstintensity/
Biannual

The First Line
P.O. Box 250382
Plano, TX 75025-0382
David LaBounty, Jeff Adams, Editors
info@thefirstline.com
www.thefirstline.com
Quarterly

Five Points
English Department
Georgia State University
University Plaza
Athens, GA 30303-3083
David Bottoms and Pam Durban,
    Editors

www.webdelsol.com/Five_Points/
Triquarterly

The Florida Review
Department of English
University of Central Florida
Orlando, FL 32816
Pat Rushin, Editor
www.flreview.com
Biannual

Fourteen Hills
The Creative Writing Department
San Francisco State University
1600 Holloway Avenue
San Francisco, CA 94132
Jody Brown, Editor-in-Chief
hills@sfsu.edu
http://mercury.sfsu.edu/~hills
Biannual

Fugue
Department of English
Brink Hall 200
University of Idaho
Moscow, Idaho 83844-1102
Scott McEachern,
    Managing Editor
Biannual

Gargoyle
P.O. Box 6216
Arlington, VA 22206-0216
Lucinda Ebarsole, Richard Peabody,
    Editors
atticus@atticusbooks.com
Annual

The Georgia Review
University of Georgia

Athens, GA 30602-9009
T. R. Hummer, Editor
garev@uga.edu
www.uga.edu/garev
Quarterly

The Gettysburg Review
Gettysburg College
Gettysburg, PA 17325
Peter Stitt, Editor
pstitt@gettysburg.edu
www.gettysburg.edu/academics/
    gettysburg_review
Quarterly

Glimmer Train Stories
710 SW Madison Street
Suite 504
Portland, OR 97205-2900
Linda Burmeister-Davies, Susan
    Burmeister-Brown, Editors
www.glimmertrain.com
Quarterly

Good Housekeeping
959 Eighth Avenue
New York, NY 10019
Ellen Levine, Editor-in-Chief, and
    Laura Matthews, Literary Editor
www.goodhousekeeping.com
Monthly

Grain Magazine
Box 67
Saskatoon, Saskatchewan S7K 3KI
    Canada
Elizabeth Philips
grainmag@sasktel.net
www.grainmagazine.ca
Quarterly

Grand Street
214 Sullivan Street
Suite 6C
New York, NY 10012
Jean Stein, Editor
info@grandstreet.com
www.grandstreet.com
Quarterly

GRANTA
1755 Broadway
5th Floor
New York, NY 10019-3780
Ian Jack, Editor
www.granta.com
Quarterly

The Green Hills Literary Lantern
P.O. Box 375
Trenton, MO 64683
Joe Benevento and Jack Smith,
    Editors
http://ll.truman.edu/ghllweb
Annual

The Greensboro Review
English Department
134 McIver Building, UNC-
    Greensboro
P.O. Box 26170
Greensboro, NC 27402-6170
Jim Clark, Editor
jlclark@uncg.edu
www.uncg.edu/eng/mfa
Biannual

Gulf Coast
Department of English
University of Houston
Houston, Texas 77204-3013

Mark Doty, Executive Editor
www.gulfcoastmag.org
Biannual

Gulf Stream
English Department
FIU Biscayne Bay Campus
3000 NE 151 Street
North Miami, FL 33181-3000
Lynn Barrett, Editor
Biannual

Hampton Shorts
Box # 3001
Bridgehampton, NY 11932
Barbara Stone, Editor-in-Chief
hamptonshorts@hamptons.com
Annual

Happy
240 East 35th Street
Suite 11A
New York, NY 10016
Editor
Quarterly

Harper's Magazine
666 Broadway
New York, NY 10012
Lewis H. Lapham, Editor
www.harpers.org
Monthly

Harpur Palate
Department of English
Binghamton University
P.O. Box 6000
Binghamton, NY 13902-6000
Toiya Kristen Finley, Managing
    Editor

http://harpurpalate.binghamton.edu
Biannual

**Harrington Gay Men's Fiction
   Quarterly**
Thomas Nelson Community
   College
99 Thomas Nelson Drive
Hampton, VA 23666
Thomas L. Long, Editor-in-Chief
www.tncc.vccs.edu/faculty/longt/
   HGMFQ
Quarterly

Harvard Review
Lamont Library
Harvard University
Cambridge, MA 02138
Christina Thompson, Editor
harvreview@fas.harvard.edu
www.hcl.harvard.edu/houghton/
   departments/harvardreview/
   HRhome.html
Biannual

Hawaii Pacific Review
Hawaii Pacific University
1060 Bishop Street
Honolulu, HI 96813
hpreview@hpu.edu
Annual

Hayden's Ferry Review
Box 871502
Arizona State University
Tempe, AZ 85287-1502
Salima Keegan, Managing Editor
hfr@asu.edu
www.haydensferryreview.org
Semiannual

Hemispheres
1301 Carolina Street
Greensboro, NC 27401
Randy Johnson, Editor
www.hemispheresmagazine.com
Monthly

High Plains Literary Review
180 Adams Street
Suite 250
Denver, CO 80206
Robert O. Greer, Jr., Editor-in-Chief
Triannual

The Hudson Review
684 Park Avenue
New York, NY 10021
Paula Deitz, Editor
www.hudsonreview.com
Quarterly

The Idaho Review
Boise State University
English Department
1910 University Drive
Boise, ID 83725
Mitch Wieland, Editor-in-Chief
http://english.boisestate.edu/
   idahoreview/
Annual

Image
3307 Third Avenue West
Seattle, WA 98119
Gregory Wolfe, Editor
image@imagejournal.org
www.imagejournal.org
Quarterly

Indiana Review
Indiana University
Ballantine Hall 465

1020 E. Kirkwood Avenue
Bloomington, IN 47405-7103
Danit Brown, Editor
www.indiana.edu/~inreview
Biannual

Inkwell
Manhattanville College
2900 Purchase Street
Purchase, NY 10577
Jeremy Church, Editor
inkwell@mville.edu
Annual

The Iowa Review
308 English/Philosophy Building
University of Iowa
Iowa City, IA 52242-1492
David Hamilton, Editor
www.uiowa.edu/~iareview
Triannual

Italian Americana
University of Rhode Island
Feinstein College of Continuing
    Education
80 Washington Street
Providence, RI 02903-1803
Carol Bonomo Albright, Editor
Biannual

The Journal
Ohio State University
Department of English
164 W. 17th Avenue
Columbus, OH 43210
Kathy Fagan, Michelle Herman,
    Editors
http://english.osu.edu/journals/
    the_journal/default.htm
Biannual

**Kalliope, A Journal of Women's
    Literature & Art**
Florida Community College at
    Jacksonville
11901 Beach Boulevard
Jacksonville, FL 32246
Mary Sue Koeppel, Editor
SKoeppel@fccj.org
http://www.fccj.org/kalliope/
    kalliope.htm
Biannual

Karamu
English Department
Eastern Illinois University
Charleston, IL 61920
Annual

The Kenyon Review
Kenyon College
Gambier, OH 43022
David H. Lynn, Editor
kenyonreview@kenyon.edu
www.kenyonreview.com
Triannual

Kiosk
State University of New York at
    Buffalo
English Department
306 Clemens Hall
Buffalo, NY 14260
eng-kiosk@acsu.buffalo.edu
http://wings.buffalo.edu/epc/mags/
    kiosk.htm
Annual

Knight Literary Journal
P.O. Box 449
Spout Spring, VA 24593
Charles Cutter, Editor

editor@knightjournal.com
www.knightjournal.com
Annual

The Land-Grant College Review
P.O. Box 1164
New York, NY 10159
Dave Koch, Josh Melrod, Editors-in-
Chief
editors@land-grantcollegereview.com
www.lgcr.org
Biannual

The Laurel Review
Department of English
Northwest Missouri State University
Maryville, MO 64468
William Trowbridge, David Slater,
Beth Richards, Editors
m500025@mail.nwmissouri.edu
Biannual

Literal Latté
61 East 8th Street
Suite 240
New York, NY 10003
Jenine Gordon Bockman, Editor
Litlatte@aol.com
www.literal-latte.com
Bimonthly

The Literary Review
285 Madison Avenue
Madison, NJ 07940
René Steinke, Editor-in-Chief
tlr@fdu.edu
www.theliteraryreview.org
Quarterly

The Long Story
18 Eaton Street

Lawrence, MA 01843
R. P. Burnham, Editor
TLS@aol.com
www.litline.org/ls/longstory.html
Annual

Louisiana Literature
SLU-10792
Southeastern Louisiana University
Hammond, LA 70402
Jack B. Bedell, Editor
lalit@selu.edu
http://louisianaliterature.org/
Biannual

The Malahat Review
University of Victoria
Box 1700
STN CSC
Victoria, British Columbia V8W 2Y2
Canada
Marlene Cookshaw, Editor
malahat@uvic.ca
www.malahatreview.ca
Quarterly

Manoa
English Department
University of Hawaii
Honolulu, HI 96822
Frank Stewart, Editor
www.manoajournal.hawaii.edu
Biannual

The Massachusetts Review
South College
University of Massachusetts
Amherst, MA 01003-7140
Mary Heath, Paul Jenkins, David
Lenson, Editors

massrev@external.umass.edu
www.massreview.org
Quarterly

McSweeney's
826 Valencia Street
San Francisco, CA 94110
Dave Eggers, Editor
mcsweeneys@earthlink.net
www.mcsweeneys.net
Quarterly

Michigan Quarterly Review
University of Michigan
3032 Rackham Building
915 E. Washington Street
Ann Arbor, MI 48109
Laurence Goldstein, Editor
MQR@umich.edu
www.umich.edu/~mqr
Quarterly

Mid-American Review
Department of English
Bowling Green State University
Bowling Green, OH 43403
www.bgsu.edu/studentlife/
    organizations/midamericanreview/
    index2.html
Biannual

Midstream
633 Third Avenue, 21st Floor
New York, NY 10017-6706
Joel Carmichael, Editor
info@midstream.org
Nine issues yearly

The Minnesota Review
Department of English
Carnegie Mellon University

Baker Hall 259
5000 Forbes Avenue
Pittsburgh, PA 15213-3890
Jeffrey J. Williams, Editor
editors@theminnesotareview.org
www.theminnesotareview.org
Biannual

Mississippi Review
Center for Writers
The University of Southern Mississippi
Box 5144
Hattiesburg, MS 39406-5144
Frederick Barthelme, Editor
www.mississippireview.com
Biannual

The Missouri Review
1507 Hillcrest Hall
University of Missouri-Columbia
Columbia, Missouri 65211
Speer Morgan, Editor
tmr@missourireview.com
www.missourireview.com
Triannual

Ms.
P.O. Box 97313
Washington, D.C. 20077-7049
Elaine Lafferty, Editor
info@msmagazine.com
www.msmagazine.com
Quarterly

Nassau Review
English Department
Nassau Community College
1 Education Drive
Garden City, NY 11530-6793
Paul A. Doyle, Editor
Annual

Natural Bridge
Department of English
University of Missouri-St. Louis
8001 Natural Bridge Road
St. Louis, MO 63121
Ryan Stone, Editor
natural@admiral.umsl.edu
www.umsl.edu/~natural
Biannual

The Nebraska Review
Writer's Workshop
Fine Arts Building 212
University of Nebraska at Omaha
Omaha, NE 68182-0324
James Reed, Fiction and Managing
  Editor
Biannual

Neotrope
P.O. Box 172
Lawrence, KS 66044
Adam Powell and Paul Silvia, Editors
apowell10@hotmail.com
www.brokenboulder.com/
  neotrope.htm
Annual

Nerve
520 Broadway, 6th Floor
New York, NY 10012
Susan Dominus, Editor-in-Chief
info@nerve.com
www.nerve.com
Six issues yearly

New Delta Review
English Department
Louisiana State University
Baton Rouge, LA 70803-5001

new-delta@lsu.edu
http://www.english.lsu.edu/journals/
  ndr
Biannual

New England Review
Middlebury College
Middlebury, VT 05753
Stephen Donadio, Editor
NEReview@middlebury.edu
www.middlebury.edu/~nereview
Quarterly

New Letters
University of Missouri-Kansas City
5101 Rockhill Road
Kansas City, MO 64110
Robert Stewart, Editor
www.newletters.org
Quarterly

New Millennium Writings
P.O. Box 2463
Knoxville, TN 37901
Don Williams, Editor
www.mach2.com
Annual

New Orleans Review
Box 195
Loyola University
New Orleans, LA 70118
Christopher Chambers, Editor
www.loyno.edu/~noreview
Biannual

New York Stories
La Guardia Community College/
  CUNY

31-10 Thomson Avenue
Long Island City, NY 11101
Daniel Caplice Lynch, Editor-in-Chief
Triannual

The New Yorker
4 Times Square
New York, NY 10036
Deborah Treisman, Fiction Editor
www.newyorker.com
Weekly

News from the Republic of Letters
120 Cushing Avenue
Boston, MA 02125
Keith Botsford, Editor
rangoni@bu.edu
www.bu.edu/trl
Biannual

Night Rally
P.O. Box 1707
Philadelphia, PA 19105
Amber Dorko Stopper, Editor-in-
    Chief
NightRallyMag@aol.com
www.nightrally.org
Triquarterly

Night Train
85 Orchard Street
Somerville, MA 02144
Rod Siino and Rusty Barnes, Editors
www.nighttrainmagazine.com
Biannual

Nimrod
The University of Tulsa
600 S. College
Tulsa, OK 74104

Francine Ringold, Editor-in-Chief
nimrod@utulsa.edu
www.utulsa.edu/nimrod
Biannual

Noon
1369 Madison Avenue
PMB 298
New York, NY 10128
Diane Williams, Editor
noonannual@yahoo.com
Annual

The North American Review
University of Northern Iowa
1222 West 27th Street
Cedar Falls, IA 50614-0156
Vince Gotera, Editor
nar@uni.edu
www.webdelsol.com/
    NorthAmReview/NAR
Five issues yearly

**North Carolina Literary
    Review**
Department of English
2201 Bate Building
East Carolina University
Greenville, NC 27858-4353
Margaret D. Bauer, Editor
www.ecu.edu/nclr
Annual

North Dakota Quarterly
The University of North Dakota
Grand Forks, ND 58202-7209
Robert Lewis, Editor
ndq@sage.und.nodak.edu
www.und.nodak.edu/org/ndq
Quarterly

Northwest Review
369 PLC
University of Oregon
Eugene, Oregon 97403
John Witte, Editor
Triannual

Notre Dame Review
The Creative Writing Program
Department of English
University of Notre Dame
Notre Dame, IN 46556
John Matthias, William O'Rourke,
    Editors
English.ndreview.1@nd.edu
www.nd.edu/~ndr/review.htm
Semiannual

Now & Then
Center for Appalachian Studies and
    Services
Box 70556
East Tennessee State University
Johnson City, TN 37614-0556
Jane H. Woodside, Editor
cass@etsu.edu
http://cass.etsu.edu/n&t
Triquarterly

Nylon
394 West Broadway, 2nd Floor
New York, NY 10012
Gloria M. Wong, Senior Editor
nylonmag@aol.com
www.nylonmag.com
Monthly

Oasis
P.O. Box 626
Largo, FL 34649-0626

Neal Storrs, Editor
oasislit@aol.com
Quarterly

The Ohio Review
344 Scott Quad
Ohio University
Athens, OH 45701-2979
Wayne Dodd, Editor
www.ohio.edu/TheOhioReview
Biannual

One Story
P.O. Box 1326
New York, NY 10156
Hannah Tinti, Editor
questions@one-story.com
www.one-story.com
About every three weeks

Ontario Review
9 Honey Brook Drive
Princeton, NJ 08540
Raymond J. Smith, Editor
www.ontarioreviewpress.com
Biannual

Open City
270 Lafayette Street, Suite 1412
New York, NY 10012-3327
Joanna Yas
editors@opencity.org
www.opencity.org
Annual

Orchid
3096 Williamsburg
Ann Arbor, MI 48108-2026
Maureen Aitken, Keith Hood, Cathy
    Mellett, Editors
editors@orchidlit.org

www.orchidlit.org
Semiannual

Other Voices
English Department (MC 162)
University of Illinois at Chicago
601 South Morgan Street
Chicago, IL 60607-7120
Lois Hauselman, Executive Editor
othervoices@listserv.uic.edu
Biannual

Owen Wister Review
University of Wyoming
Student Publications
Box 3625
Laramie, WY 82071
Annual

The Oxford American
201 Donaghey Avenue
Main 107
Conway, AR 72035
Marc Smirnoff, Editor
www.oxfordamericanmag.com
Quarterly

Oxford Magazine
English Department
356 Bachelor Hall
Miami University
Oxford, OH 45056
Oxmag@geocities.com

Oyster Boy Review
P.O. Box 77842
San Francisco, CA 94107-0842
Damon Sauve, Publisher
staff@oysterboyreview
www.oysterboyreview.com
Quarterly

The Paris Review
541 East 72nd Street
New York, NY 10012
Brigid Hughes, Editor
www.parisreview.com
Quarterly

Parting Gifts
3413 Wilshire Drive
Greensboro, NC 27408
Robert Bixby, Editor
rbixby@aol.com
www.marchstreetpress.com
Biannual

Partisan Review
236 Bay State Road
Boston, MA 02215
partisan@bu.edu
http://www.bu.edu./partisanreview/
Quarterly

Phoebe
George Mason University
4400 University Drive
Fairfax, VA 22030-4444
Emily Harrison, Editor
phoebe@gmu.edu
www.gmu.edu/pubs/phoebe
Biannual

Playboy Magazine
680 North Lake Shore Drive
Chicago, IL 60611
Jonathan Black, Managing Editor
www.playboy.com
Monthly

Pleiades
Department of English and
  Philosophy

Central Missouri State University
Warrensburg, Missouri 64093
Kevin Prufer, General Editor
kdp8106@cmsu2.cmsu.edu
www.cmsu.edu/englphil/pleiades
Semiannual

Ploughshares
Emerson College
120 Boylston Street
Boston, MA 02116-4624
Don Lee, Editor
www.pshares.org
Triannual

Post Road
853 Broadway
Suite 1516
Box 85
New York, NY 10003
Catherine Parnell, Managing Editor,
 or Jaime Clarke, David Ryan,
 Founding Editors
www.postroadmag.com
Biannual

Potomac Review
P.O. Box 354
Port Tobacco, MD 20677
Eli Flam, Editor and Publisher
potomacreview@mc.cc.md.us
http://www.montgomerycollege.edu/
 potomacreview
Quarterly

Pottersfield Portfolio
P.O. Box 40, Station A
Sydney, Nova Scotia B1P 6G9 Canada
Douglas Arthur Brown, Managing
 Editor
pportfolio@seascape.ns.ca

www.pportfolio.com
Triannual

Prairie Fire
423-100 Arthur Street
Winnipeg, Manitoba R3B 1H3
 Canada
Andris Raskans, Editor
www.prairiefire.mb.ca
Quarterly

Prairie Schooner
201 Andrews Hall
University of Nebraska
Lincoln, NE 68588-0334
Hilda Raz, Editor-in-Chief
www.unl.edu/schooner/
 psmain.htm
Quarterly

Prism International
University of British Columbia
Buchanan E-462
1866 Main Mall
Vancouver, BC V6T1Z1 Canada
Billeh Nickerson, Editor
prism@interchange.ubc.ca
www.prism.arts.ubc.ca
Quarterly

Provincetown Arts
650 Commercial Street
Provincetown, MA 02657
Christopher Busa, Editor
cbusa@attbi.com
www.provincetownarts.org
Annual

Puerto del Sol
MSC3E

New Mexico State University
P.O. Box 30001
Las Cruces, NM 88003-8001
Kevin McIlvoy, Editor-in-Chief
Puerto@nmsu.edu
www.nmsu.edu/~puerto/
  welcome.html
Semiannual

Quarry Magazine
P.O. Box 74
Kingston, Ontario K7L 4V6 Canada
Andrew Griffin, Editor-in-Chief
quarrymagazine@hotmail.com
Quarterly

Quarterly West
200 S. Central Campus Drive
University of Utah
Salt Lake City, UT 84112-9109
David Hawkins, Editor
www.utah.edu/quarterlywest
Biannual

Raritan
Rutgers University
31 Mine Street
New Brunswick, NJ 08903
Richard Poirier, Editor-in-Chief
Quarterly

Rattapallax
523 LaGuardia Place
New York, NY 10012
Martin Mitchell, Editor-in-Chief
rattapallax@hotmail.com
www.rattapallax.com
Biannual

Red Rock Review
Department of English J2A

Community College of Southern
  Nevada
3200 East Cheyenne Avenue
North Las Vegas, NV 89030
Richard Logsdon, Senior Editor
richard_logsdon@ccsn.nevada.edu
Biannual

River City
Department of English
University of Memphis
Memphis, TN 38152
Mary Leader, Editor-in-Chief
rivercity@memphis.edu
http://www.people.memphis.edu/
  ~rivercity/
Biannual

River Styx
634 North Grand Boulevard,
12th Floor
St. Louis, MO 63103-1002
Richard Newman, Editor
www.riverstyx.org
Triannual

Rosebud
P.O. Box 459
Cambridge, WI 53523
Roderick Clark, Editor
jrodclark@rsbd.net
www.rsbd.net
Quarterly

The Saint Ann's Review
129 Pierrepont Street
Brooklyn, New York 11201
Beth Bosworth, Editor
sareview@saintanns.k12.ny.us
Biannual

Salamander
48 Ackers Avenue
Brookline, MA 02445-4160
Jennifer Barber, Editor
Biannual

Salmagundi
Skidmore College
Saratoga Springs, NY 12866
Robert Boyers, Editor-in-Chief
pboyers@skidmore.edu
Quarterly

Salt Hill
Syracuse University
English Department
Syracuse, NY 13244
Ellen Litman, Editor
salthill@cas.syr.edu
http://students.syr.edu/salthill/
Biannual

Santa Monica Review
Santa Monica College
1900 Pico Boulevard
Santa Monica, CA 90405
Andrew Tonkovich, Editor
www.smc.edu/sm_review
Biannual

The Seattle Review
Padelford Hall
Box 354330
University of Washington
Seattle, WA 98195
Colleen J. McElroy, Editor
Biannual

Seven Days
P.O. Box 1164
255 South Champlain Street

Burlington, VT 05042-1164
Pamela Polston, Paula Routly,
 Coeditors
sevenday@together.net
www.sevendaysvt.com
Weekly

The Sewanee Review
University of the South
735 University Avenue
Sewanee, TN 37383-1000
George Core, Editor
rjones@sewanee.edu
www.sewanee.edu/sreview/home.html
Quarterly

Shenandoah
Troubador Theater, 2nd Floor, Box W
Washington and Lee University
Lexington, VA 24450-0303
R. T. Smith, Editor
http://shenandoah.wlu.edu
Quarterly

Sonora Review
English Department
University of Arizona
Tucson, AZ 85721
sonora@u.arizona.edu
www.coh.arizona.edu/sonora
Biannual

The South Carolina Review
Center for Electronic and Digital
 Publishing
Clemson University
Strode Tower, Room 611, Box 340522
Clemson, SC 29634-0523
Wayne Chapman, Editor
cwayne@Clemson.edu

www.clemson.edu/caah/cedp/
   scrintro.htm
Biannual

South Dakota Review
Box 111
University Exchange
Vermillion, SD 57069
Brian Bedard, Editor
sdreview@usd.edu
www.usd.edu/sdreview/
Quarterly

Southern Humanities Review
9088 Haley Center
Auburn University
Auburn, AL 36849
Dan R. Latimer, Virginia M.
   Kouidis, Editors
www.auburn.edu/english/shr/
   home.htm
Quarterly

The Southern Review
43 Allen Hall
Louisiana State University
Baton Rouge, LA 70803-5005
James Olney, Editor
jolney@lsu.edu
Quarterly

Southwest Review
Southern Methodist University
307 Fondren Library West
Dallas, Texas 75275
Willard Spiegalman, Editor-in-Chief
swr@mail.smu.edu
www.southwestreview.org
Quarterly

St. Anthony Messenger
1615 Republic Street
Cincinnati, OH 45210-1298
Pat McCloskey, O.F.M., Editor
StAnthony@AmericanCatholic.org
www.americancatholic.org
Monthly

StoryQuarterly
431 Sheridan Road
Kenilworth, IL 60043
M. M. M. Hayes, Editor
storyquarterly@hotmail.com
www.storyquarterly.com
Annual

StringTown
93011 Ivy Station Road
Astoria, OR 97103
Polly Buckingham, Editor
Stringtown@aol.com
Annual

The Sun
107 North Roberson Street
Chapel Hill, NC 27516
Sy Safransky, Editor
TheSunMagazine@pcspublink.com
www.thesunmagazine.org
Monthly

Sundog
English Department
Florida State University
Tallahassee, FL 32311
www.sundog@english.fsu.edu
www.english.fsu.edu/sundog
Biannual

Sycamore Review
English Department

1356 Heavilon Hall
Purdue University
West Lafayette, IN 47907
sycamore@expert.cc.purdue.edu
www.sla.purdue.edu/academic/engl/
sycamore/
Biannual

Talking River Review
Division of Literature and Languages
Lewis-Clark State College
500 8th Avenue
Lewiston, ID 83501
Biannual

Tameme
199 First Street
Los Altos, CA 94022
C. M. Mayo, Editor
editor@tameme.org
www.tameme.org
Annual

Tampa Review
The University of Tampa
401 West Kennedy Boulevard
Tampa, Florida 33606-1490
Richard Matthews, Editor
http://tampareview.ut.edu
Biannual

The Texas Review
English Department
Sam Houston State University
Huntsville, TX 77341
Paul Ruffin, Editor
eng.pdr@shsu.edu
Biannual

Third Coast
English Department

Western Michigan University
Kalamazoo, MI 49008-5092
Shanda Hansma Blue, Editor
Shanda_Blue@hotmail.com
www.wmich.edu/thirdcoast
Biannual

The Threepenny Review
P.O. Box 9131
Berkeley, CA 94709
Wendy Lesser, Editor
www.threepennyreview.com
Quarterly

Tikkun
60 West 87th Street
New York, NY 10024
Thane Rosenbaum, Literary Editor
magazine@tikkun.org
www.tikkun.org
Bimonthly

Timber Creek Review
8969 UNCG Station
Greensboro, NC 27413
John M. Freiermuth, Editor
Quarterly

Tin House Magazine
P.O. Box 10500
Portland, OR 97296-0500
Rob Spillman, Editor, and Win
McCormack, Editor-in-Chief
tinhouse@pcspublink.com
www.tinhouse.com
Quarterly

Toronto Life
59 Front Street E.
Toronto, Ontario M5E 1B3 Canada
John Macfarlane, Editor

www.torontolife.com
Monthly

Transition Magazine
W. E. B. DuBois Institute
Harvard University
69 Dunster Street
Cambridge, MA 02138
Henry Louis Gates, Jr., and Kwame
    Anthony Appiah, Editors
transition@fas.harvard.edu
www.transitionmagazine.com
Quarterly

Triquarterly
Northwestern University
2020 Ridge Avenue
Evanston, IL 60208
Susan Firestone Hahn, Editor
www.triquarterly.org
Triannual

Two Rivers Review
P.O. Box 158
Clinton, NY 13323
Phil Memmer, Editor
tworiversreview@juno.com
Biannual

The Virginia Quarterly Review
One West Range
P.O. Box 400223
Charlottesville, VA 22904-4223
Staige D. Blackford, Editor
vqreview@virginia.edu
www.virginia.edu/vqr
Quarterly

War, Literature & the Arts
English and Fine Arts Department
United States Air Force Academy

Colorado Springs, CO 80840-6242
Donald Anderson, Editor
donald.anderson@usafa.af.mil
www.wlajournal.com
Biannual

Wascana Review
English Department
University of Regina
Regina, Saskatchewan S4S 0A2
    Canada
Michael Tussler, Editor
Michael.tussler@uregina.ca
www.uregina.ca/arts/
    english/wascana/wrhome.htm
Biannual

Washington Review
P.O. Box 50132
Washington, DC 20091-0132
Clarissa K. Wittenberg, Editor
www.washingtonreview.org
Bimonthly

Washington Square
Creative Writing Program
New York University
19 University Place, Room 219
New York, NY 10003-4556
Sarah Kain, Editor-in-Chief
www.nyu.edu/gsas/program/cwp/
    wsr.htm
Biannual

Watchword
3288 21st Street #248
San Francisco, CA 94110
Amanda L. Green, Danielle Jatlow,
    Liz Lisle, Editors

danielle@watchwordpress.org
www.watchwordpress.org
Biannual

Weber Studies
Weber State University
1214 University Circle
Ogden, UT 84408-1214
Brad Roghaar, Editor
weberstudies@weber.edu
http://weberstudies.weber.edu
Triquarterly

West Branch
Bucknell Hall
Bucknell University
Lewisburg, PA 17837
Paula Closson Buck, Editor
www.bucknell.edu/westbranch
Biannual

West Coast Line
2027 East Academic Annex
Simon Fraser University
Burnaby, British Columbia V5A 1S6
    Canada
Roy Miki, Editor
wcl@sfu.ca
www.sfu.ca/west-coast-line
Triannual

Western Humanities Review
University of Utah
English Department
255 South Central Campus Drive,
    Room 3500
Salt Lake City, UT 84112-0494
Barry Weller, Editor
whr@mail.hum.utah.edu
http://vegeta.hum.utah.edu/whr
Biannual

Whetstone
Barrington Area Arts Council
P.O. Box 1266
Barrington, IL 60011-1266
Sandra Berris, Marsha Portnoy, Jean
    Tolle, Editors
Annual

Whistling Shade, the Twin Cities
    Literary Journal
P.O. Box 7084
Saint Paul, MN 55107
Anthony Telschow, Rhoda Niola,
    Editors
editor@whistlingshade.com
www.whistlingshade.com
Quarterly

Wind
P.O. Box 24548
Lexington, KY 40524
Charlie Hughes, Leatha Kendrick,
    Editors
books@windpub.org
Biannual

Windsor Review
English Department
University of Windsor
Windsor, Ontario N9B 3P4
    Canada
Katherine Quinsey, General Editor
uwrevu@uwindsor.ca
Biannual

Witness
Oakland Community College
Orchard Ridge Campus
27055 Orchard Lake Road
Farmington Hills, MI 48334
Peter Stine, Editor

witness@webdelsol.com
www.occ.cc.mi.us/witness
Biannual

Worcester Review
6 Chatham Street
Worcester, MA 01609
Rodger Martin, Managing Editor
www.geocities.com/Paris/LeftBank/
    6433
Annual

Wordplay
P.O. Box 2248
South Portland, ME 04116-2248
Helen Peppe, Editor-in-Chief
wordplay@maine.rr.edu
Quarterly

Writers' Forum
University of Colorado
P.O. Box 7150
Colorado Springs, CO 80933
C. Kenneth Pellow, Editor-in-Chief
kpellow@mail.uccs.edu
Annual

Xavier Review
Xavier University
Box 110C
New Orleans, LA 70125
Thomas Bonner, Jr., and Richard
    Collins, Editors
rcollins@xula.edu
Biannual

**Xconnect: Writers of the
    Information Age**
P.O. Box 2317
Philadelphia, PA 19103

D. Edward Deifer, Editor-in-Chief
xconnect@ccat.sas.upenn.edu
http://ccat.sas.upenn.edu/xconnect
Annual

The Yale Review
Yale University
P.O. Box 208243
New Haven, CT 06250-8243
J. D. McClatchy, Editor
yalerev@yale.edu
Quarterly

The Yalobusha Review
P.O. Box 186
University, MS 38677-0186
yalobush@sunset.backbone
    .olemiss.edu
www.olemiss.edu/depts/english/
    pubs/yalobusha_review.html
Annual

Zoetrope: All-Story
916 Kearny Street
San Francisco, CA 94133
Tamara Straus, Editor-in-Chief
www.zoetrope-stories.com
Quarterly

ZYZZYVA
P.O. Box 590069
San Francisco, CA 94159-0069
Howard Junker, Editor
editor@zyzzyva.org
www.zyzzyva.org
Triannual